Regicide

Storm Cloud

by

Eric Heicher

DORRANCE
PUBLISHING CO
EST. 1920
PITTSBURGH, PENNSYLVANIA 15238

Dorrance Publishing Co
585 Alpha Drive
Suite 103
Pittsburgh, PA 15238
Visit our website at *www.dorrancebookstore.com*

ISBN: 978-1-6376-4098-2
eISBN: 978-1-6376-4940-4

PROLOGUE
A Dark Omen

An orange burst of light illuminates the night sky of a sleepy little town in the middle of nowhere. Most of its denizens have already retired to bed, but those still stirring look up in dismay at a sight they hoped never to see. The brazier is lit. The town is under attack! Who would want to come all the way out to this little backwater, and for what purpose? Those questions are on everyone's mind as the small contingent of volunteer guards runs through the street. There was some commotion at the old shrine at the edge of town.

The guards arrive at the entrance to see a lone sentry lying dead in a pool of blood. The other must have lit the brazier. A shadowy blur is spotted quickly making its way north out of town. Whoever it is, they're fast. The guards can barely keep up. There's worry they will lose track of the fiend as he disappears over a hill, but as they reach the crest, the guards stop in their tracks in surprise. A hooded figure is standing before them, backlit by the moon. The guards spread out and cautiously approach. "Why did you attack our town?" one demands.

A smile can just barely be made out from under the strange man's hood. He remains silent, staring coldly at the townspeople. The guard continues to interrogate, "Who are you? Why did you come here?" The hooded man stands unwavering, almost mocking with his wry smile. The guards begin to close in until one notices something strange. A small patch is sky is pitch black, completely devoid of stars. He screams for everybody to get back as he realizes the terrible truth. With a wave

1

of a hand, the hooded figure sends a giant ball of Dark magic screaming downward at the men. There is no time to get clear.

The town's citizens' gaze turns toward the north as a horrific boom like divine thunder followed by fiery blast that makes the blaze of the brazier dim by comparison. A few are brave enough to venture toward the source with torches in hand while a small child stares from his window gripped tightly by a feeling of immense dread. The searchers' worst fears are realized as they approach the ebon, smoldering remains of the clearing. They quickly scramble to see if there are any survivors. Most of the bodies are charred beyond recognition. It looks like no one survived. Wait!

There's a faint groan, and one of the bodies struggles to crawl. Someone runs over to the poor soul. His wounds are dire. His would-be rescuer instantly knows he only has a few moments of life left. The victim looks up and utters a single word, a name before the life fades from his eyes. The man stands in stunned silence struggling to grasp what he was told. ♛

CHAPTER 1
A Butterfly's Wings

The sun rises once again for the tiny village of Hanover. It has been ten years since that terrible night. The pain of loss has faded, but the memory is stained eternally. A spiky, blond-haired, blue-eyed young man, Shine, slowly stirs from his bed as mother calls from downstairs. He takes much longer than normal to rise out of bed and get dressed, and that's saying something. That is because today is no ordinary day. He dons his favorite sky blue tunic and throws on a pair of green cotton pants. With equal parts fear and determination, Shine makes his way downstairs. His mother hears him and rises off the couch.

As Shine enters the living room she smiles and greets, "I thought you would never get out of bed. You must be nervous."

"Very," Shine openly replies.

"I don't suppose there's any way I can talk you out of this."

Shine is adamant, "You know there isn't. I made up my mind on this a long time ago."

Mother sighs and shakes her head. "This is insane. The best case is you end up in prison for the rest of your life, and the worst is it's a suicide mission. You're still so young. Why do you insist on such a dangerous, reckless path for yourself?"

Shine responds with steel resolve, "Because he has to be stopped. This reign of terror has gone on for far too long."

"I understand, but it's not like you can just waltz into the palace and cut the king's head off."

Shine chuckles and admits, "Actually, that's more or less exactly what I plan on doing."

His mother's warm smile returns. "Smartass." It quickly fades. She hesitates before asking, "Just tell me this much, are you really doing this for the good of the people, or are you just trying to avenge your father?" Shine remains silent. "I thought as much. King Pious needs to be stopped nonetheless, so I suppose the ends justify the means. You should speak to the mayor before you go. He wanted to give you some parting advice."

"Thanks. I will."

"Oh, and there is one other thing." She walks over to the chest in the corner and kneels down to open it. Shine assumes she is going to do the typical mom thing and give him a blanket to keep warm on the journey. His mother removes the sheets and blankets from the chest along with a long wood panel. A false bottom? Now Shine is curious. His eyes widen as he watches his mother lift a sword from the box and walk back over.

He can barely speak, "I-Is that...?"

"That's right. This was your father's sword, Rashida."

"I thought you said you buried it with dad."

"I was at first, but I had this strange feeling. It was almost like your father was telling me from beyond the grave to hold onto it for you."

"Is what he said about it true?"

"That it can destroy evil itself? I have no idea, but your father believed that. He often referred to it as Evil's Bane. I don't know about all that, but you'll need protection out there, and this way your father will always be with you in spirit. If you ever find yourself faltering, all you need to do is gaze upon it."

Shine can barely hold back his tears. What a strange sensation. The wounds from ten years ago were just ripped wide open, yet he couldn't feel happier nor prouder. He barely chokes out a thank you as he takes hold of Rashida. His mother gives him an old bronze sheath, and he fastens it to his belt before sheathing his father's sword. His eyes fill with determination.

"This sword," he starts. "This sword will be the blade that cuts down Pious. Thank you, Mother." Tears stream down her face as she hugs him tight. Her baby is about to leave, and he may never come back. Her tears are almost enough to make Shine stay, but he knows in his heart what he must do. He stops and says a final goodbye before exiting the house. As the door closes behind, his mother utters a prayer under her breath.

"Richard, please watch over him."

Shine heeds Mom's advice and heads over to the mayor's residence. It just a short walk over to the largest house in Hanover. All the homes are pretty small, so that's not saying much. Everything is made of wood. Hanover is too small a town too far away from any quarries for stone to be a feasible building material. The only structure that is stone is the shrine at the edge of town. It is the sole remnant of an ancient village that once stood not far away. The village was nearly completely destroyed by some unknown calamity making identifying the people and their culture impossible. The only clues are within the shrine, but even those are suspiciously non-descript.

The mayor's house is open to the public during daylight hours, so there's no need to knock before entering. He set up a large office in one of the rooms for official business. Shine heads in and finds Mayor Harper waiting for him in the study. "Ah! Shine, my boy!" he cheerfully exclaims. "I'm glad you stopped by."

"Mom said you wanted to talk to me."

"Yes, that's right! You're about to embark on one helluva of a journey. I just wanted to give you a little advice before you headed out."

"Okay. What's up?"

The mayor scratches his mostly bald head. "What you're about to attempt is damn near impossible. It's probably totally impossible all on your own."

"Gee, thanks for the vote of confidence," Shine replies sarcastically.

The mayor shrugs and continues, "Hey, the truth hurts sometimes." He pauses to gaze at the weapon fastened to Shine's belt. "Good. You already have a blade. Now, you're going to need allies if you wanna take down Pious. Lucky for you, we're in the middle of nowhere. His gaze doesn't often fall upon this backwater, which makes it a perfect place to start a rebellion."

"Really?" Shine says flatly. "The people here aren't exactly lining up to come with me."

"Not here, no, but Bristol is twice our size and, in recent years, has become a hiding place for outlaws, mercenaries, and anyone else seeking relief from Pious's iron grip. If you ask around, you may find some willing companions."

Shine is skeptical. "You sure? The taxmen sure have no trouble finding us."

"They only care about gathering coin. I doubt anyone would be dumb enough to give them reason to do anything more. People have adjusted to not being able to openly protest or even speak ill of the king or the military. They still do, believe me. Gain just a little bit of a person's trust, and you'll be surprised what they're willing to share."

"That's helpful. I'll be sure to ask around."

"I'd try the pub first. Alcohol has a way of loosening lips. Oh, and don't draw too much attention. With the influx of... err... people of ill-repute, Bristol has shored up its guards, and they don't take any bullshit."

Shine facetiously stands in attention. "I shall be on my best behavior."

"See that you are. It's going to be really embarrassing if you end up in jail on the very first day of your journey. One last thing." Mayor Harper pulls a map from his inner coat pocket. "Here. Elysia is a big place. You'll need a good map."

"Thanks. This will be a huge help. I've never been past Verde's Woods."

"Elysia is a beautiful place. Try to appreciate the sights every once in a while when you're out there."

"I will. Anything else?"

"Nope. That 'bout covers it. Good luck, Shine."

With that, Shine makes his exit and heads north towards the gate. Hanover now is surrounded by wooden walls dotted with a few guard towers. It was kind of a kneejerk reaction to the attack, but it's a thing now and mainly for show at this point. Only a couple people bother to keep sentry nowadays. Nothing ever happens, so it's a boring but cushy job. A few of the other villagers gawk at the wannabe hero. Shine tried to recruit his fellow Hanoverites. That venture was a spectacular failure. Most people thought he was joking, followed by insane, when they realized he was serious, making him the topic of many rumors and juicy gossip.

As he approaches the gate, a voice rings down from one of the towers, "Yo, Shine!" Shine looks up to see the familiar grin of Ray. He is one of the few townspeople who still works sentry duty, and the only one that enjoys it. He's also one of the few people to take Shine seriously albeit not enough to take up arms. "Come up here. I wanna talk to you before you go," he says while motioning for Shine to climb up. After a short ascent up the ladder, Shine meets Ray in the tower.

"What's up?"

"So, the day has finally come, eh? The day when you go stick it to King Pious. You must be nervous."

"Yeah, it feels like an impossibly large task, but I'm going to take it one step at a time and work my way through."

"Glad to hear it. I see you're already armed." Ray pauses and takes a long look at the hilt of the sword. "Hmm… That hilt looks awful familiar… Is…is that your father's sword?"

"Yep. Rashida. My mother saved it for me."

"Well, don't that just beat all! Haha! I thought she buried it with him."

"You and me both."

"I'm sure it will serve you well. Be careful out there, Shine. These are dangerous times. Even the wildlife seems to be on edge. People have been saying even docile creatures are actin' more aggressive lately."

"That's weird. Any idea why?"

Ray places a hand behind his head. "Nope. No idea. Anyway, I just wanted to wish you luck on your quest. Avenge our town and end that tyrant's reign." He casts his eyes to his feet before sorrowfully adding, "I'll never forget that night."

"You were watching the shrine, right?"

"Yeah, we've had a few bandits try and sneak in here or there looking for loot, so we started keepin' watch. Nothing could have prepared us for that night, though."

"I'm glad you escaped," Shine says thankfully. A look of sadness replaces Ray's cheerful demeanor. Shine has never seen him look so sullen before. "Are you all right, Ray?"

There is a long silence before Ray sighs deeply and explains, "I wasn't at my post that night. The day before, a few friends and I were partying, and I got tanked worse than I've ever been in my entire life. I was so hungover, my headache didn't go away until sundown the next day. I was on my way to the shrine feeling like shit and decided to go to sleep under a tree instead. I was so out of it even all the commotion afterwards couldn't wake me up. If I was at my post like I should have been maybe—"

"You'd be dead, too," Shine interjects. "There was nothing you could have done to stop someone like that. He could have wiped out the entire town singlehandedly if he wanted."

"I know that, yet part of me feels responsible. Survivor's guilt, I suppose. That's why I keep watch here. I won't let anyone hurt our town ever again."

"There's one thing I don't understand about what happened. I heard all Pious stole was a gem. Why all the bloodshed for something so trivial?"

"That gem wasn't some ordinary stone. It's called the Obsidian Gem. When Hanover was first founded, the settlers stumbled across the shrine. Most of it was buried in the hillside, but they dug it out, and upon exploring it, they found the gem sitting on a pedestal in something that looked like an altar. It was the talk of Elysia for a bit. Researchers, scientists, mages, all sorts of people came to our fledgling village to examine the shrine and the gem."

"What did they find out?"

"Not much, I'm afraid. The shrine seems to have been built to honor some pagan god, but no one is quite sure what people built it, let alone what gods they worshipped. The Obsidian Gem is an entirely different ball of wax. It is pitch black and seems to absorb the light around it. Scientists were unable to figure out what it is made of, and those poor mages…" Shine feels a sense of nostalgia wash over him. When he was younger, Ray was always telling him stories and legends. This is the first time he has heard this story despite it taking place right in town. He is more curious than ever.

"What happened to the mages?" he asks with childlike wonder.

"The gem had a pretty intense magical aura around it. No one could quite place it, but it felt… Dark. Three mages headed into the shrine and plied their craft in order to get some sort of reaction from the stone, and boy, did they ever. They tried to use an unbinding spell to let out some of the gem's power. They were cautious, only using the bare minimum amount of energy, but it didn't matter. The gem reacted violently. The story goes, there was a bright flash of light that the entire town could see. When people went into the shrine to see what happened, there was no sign of the mages. They searched the room, and all they could find were three charred outlines on the walls. The mages were vaporized. After that happened, no one dared to enter the shrine, let alone touch the gem, again."

Shine is floored. It takes him a few moments to process everything before reacting. "Wow, that's quite a story. So, that's why no one is allowed in there. How come I've never heard of this until now?"

"The town was afraid someone may try to use the gem's power again but were too scared to try to destroy it, so they said the shrine was 'structurally unstable' and deemed it off limits. No one was supposed to talk about what happened ever again, *buuut* my family has a history of loose lips. My great-great-great-grandfather told his son who told his kids and so on."

Shine clenches his fists in anger. "That bastard. That's why Pious stole it, isn't it? As if he didn't have enough power already. How much will be enough for him?"

"It's never enough. Not for men like him. They just want more power."

Shine feels more determined than ever now. King Pious must be stopped at all costs. He thanks Ray for the advice and the story and climbs down from the guard tower. It is just a few miles northwest to reach the bridge, and a few more miles south from there to reach Bristol. ♛

CHAPTER 2
Strange Bedfellows

It is pleasant spring day. The weather is clear with the exception of a few clouds scattered across the azure sky. There is a gentle breeze. Shine couldn't have asked for a nicer day to begin his journey. As he walks past an old oak tree he used to love climbing, a tiny field mouse scurries from the tall grass onto the path in front of him. It sniffs the air and looks up at Shine. *Confidant little critter*, he thinks to himself. Unexpectedly, the mouse lets out a hiss and begins moving aggressively toward Shine who cautiously tries to circle past it. The mouse beelines toward him, prompting a kick. There is a slight rustle as it lands in the grass. It pops up and shakes its head before scurrying away.

Ray wasn't kidding about the animals being more aggressive. Since when do mice attack humans like that? Turning to walk back onto the path, there's a much louder hiss. He spins around to see a patch of tall grass shivering. A large mouse the size of a poodle bursts out and stares dead at Shine with its beady red eyes. It hisses again, and Shine has seen enough. "The hell with this!" he yells aloud before taking off running.

The mouse gives chase for a bit but eventually gives up and retreats. Shine bends down with hands on knees to catch his breath. Not the ideal start, but at least the bridge is a lot nearer from all that running. Rushing water from Elysia River is within earshot. The river isn't particularly wide here, but the current is quick due to the fact that two rivers converge into one a little way north. Shine crosses the bridge and, before long, finds himself just outside Bristol.

A couple guards are keeping watch. That's a new sight. There never used to be sentries before. They're wearing bulky, red-tinted platemail and are holding iron spears. They pay Shine little mind as he heads into town. They're not concerned with some scrawny kid. Shine decides to take the mayor's advice and seek out the pub. On the way he sees several posters urging citizens to fulfill their civic duty by joining the military. Shine scoffs. As if.

The pub isn't hard to find. Shine spots it on the corner where the two main roads leading out of town intersect. Once he is close enough, he reads the sign and immediately chuckles. Lucy's Alehouse. Sounds like the perfect place to find people with loose lips. He's a bit thirsty, too, so this will be the perfect place to start. Once inside, he pops up onto a stool at the bar and orders a root beer while keeping a sharp ear for any anti-Pious sentiments. Unfortunately, there aren't too many patrons in the establishment at the moment, and the ones who are talking are doing so too quietly to eavesdrop. Shine digs a few coins out of his pocket as the female bartender, presumably Lucy, serves the root beer. Sipping from the mug, he takes a slow look around the pub. No one really jumps out as being an eager dissident. What does a dissident even look like? This may be tougher than he thought.

One patron does manage to catch his eye. An old man with a pointy gray hat, long gray beard, and longer gray wool robes is sitting by himself at a table in the middle of the pub drinking tea. Not the ideal comrade, but he looks like he's seen a thing or two in his day. Perhaps he'll be able to point Shine in the right direction. Shine finishes his root beer, hops off the stool, and heads over to the old man. "Excuse me? Sir?"

The old man looks up with his faded blue, almost gray eyes but doesn't respond. "May I join you?" Shine asks politely.

The old man shrugs and says, "Suit yourself."

Shine takes a seat across from him. Here goes nothing. "I'm new in town, and I'm looking for some information."

"Oh?" the old man replies unenthusiastically. He takes a sip of tea.

Shine leans in so no one else can hear. "I guess I'll get right to it," he says softly. "I want to start a rebellion."

"A rebellion!" the old man exclaims. "Oh, ho ho! That is rich!"

In a panic, Shine quickly looks around the room expecting a confrontation. Nobody even so much as glances over. It seems there is no need to be clandestine after all. Shine leans back in his chair and continues, "I'm serious. Pious is a bloodthirsty tyrant who needs to be stopped at all costs. I'm looking for comrades to aid me in taking him down. You look like you've been around the block a few times. I was hoping you would know of anyone in town that may be willing to help."

The old man's curiosity has been piqued. He raises an eyebrow and studies the young man in front of him. "That is some serious talk, young man. What does a boy like you know about the goings on in the world? What makes you think such drastic action must be taken?"

"That bastard kil—" Shine nearly blurts. A quest for vengeance isn't a great selling point, so he takes a moment to gather his thoughts for a better pitch. "The longer Pious is in power, the more people will suffer. Look at everything that has happened since he took the throne. Taxes have been raised again and again to the point to where many cannot afford to live. He is stripping our rights one by one. People get thrown in jail or worse simply for speaking their minds. Now there's even talk of war going around. Where will it end? Things will keep getting worse unless he is taken out of power."

The old man gazes at Shine for a long time. He can see the fire in his eyes. "Hmm… You do make a strong point. Things have gotten worse, more than someone as young as you can truly know. Pious used to be a kind, noble king. Then, around twenty years ago, he changed seemingly overnight. He came reclusive, shuttering himself inside Leed's Castle. Everything went downhill quickly from that point on. People are afraid and on edge. You can feel the apprehension in the air wherever you go. I don't know what can be done to stop him, but we must try. You have convinced me, lad. I will accompany you on your journey."

Shine is shocked. He just wanted information not some old geezer following him around. This guy looks like he can barely walk let alone fight. He tries to let the old man down easy, "Hold on, now. I was just asking you for information. I mean, no offense, old man, but it looks like your adventuring days are long over. You would just slow me down."

The old man's eyes widen in anger. "Me slow *you* down?" he states emphatically. "Ha! Kids these days. They can't even see power when it's literally sitting across from them."

Shine scoffs, "Power? What power is that? The stench of death?"

"If I were so inclined, I could melt your head from your shoulders in an instant," the old man replies boldly.

"Wait a sec. Are you saying you're a—?"

"Yes, you dolt. I am a mage. A fairly adept one at that, if I do say so."

Now Shine is excited. He's never seen a mage before. The magical arts are something he had always found fascinating but had zero aptitude for. They say magic comes from one's blood. In other words, you have to be born a mage. "I'm sorry, I didn't realize you were a mage. That changes everything. I'm sure your abilities will be a great help."

"I have always preferred wizard myself. It used to be a prestigious title, but it has faded into obscurity in recent years. My name is Marduk. It is a pleasure to meet you."

"Shine. I am honored. I have never met a mage... err... wizard before."

"Really? They're everywhere nowadays. Where are you from?"

"Hanover."

"Ah, that explains it. A small town that doesn't practice magic. There are many sights to behold out there. I believe seeing the world is the true path to enlightenment."

"I'm sure we'll see all sorts of amazing things. Before we get to that, I was hoping to have more than just one ally before heading out. Do you know of anyone else in town that may want to join our cause?"

"Hmmm..." Marduk strokes his beard. "There is a dojo in town. I don't know if anyone there will be the rebellious type, but we should be able to find a strong, able-bodied fighter or two. If you speak to them with the same passion as you did me, perhaps we can gain some allies."

"All right then. Lead the way, Marduk."

Shine heads out of Lucy's Alehouse with a new companion. Things are off to a good start. As they begin to walk down the road, a couple of Bristol's guards run past. Marduk leads the way. It is only a few blocks to the dojo. As they head around the corner, another pair of guards run by. Someone must be up to some mischief.

As they continue down the street, a diminutive man hops out from the bushes and hurries down an alley. The pair pay him no mind and continue on their way. As they approach the alley, Shine can't help but to look down it. There he sees the man doing what appears to be picking a lock on the last building down. The door opens slowly, and the man sneaks inside. "Well, would you look at that?" Shine remarks.

"What is it?"

"That man just snuck into that building. Pretty bold considering how many guards there are now."

"Aye. That it is." Marduk smiles and looks at Shine. "Are you thinking what I am thinking?"

"Oh yeah. A brave thief may come in handy, and they're usually anti-authority. Let's see what he is up to."

Shine and Marduk hurry to the door and enter. It's a warehouse. There's a maze of various-sized barrels and crates filling the room. It didn't seem so large from the outside. Finding their target may be a little tricky. Shine instructs Marduk to wait by the door in case he misses the thief before cautiously venturing forward. After a couple turns through hallways made of wooden crates and shelves, he hears what sounds like a wooden crate being pried open. Shine slowly peers around the corner and spots the tiny man crouched down over a box. It's a dead end and a narrow enough space that Shine can easily block the way simply by standing in the middle. This is too perfect. "What are you doing in here?" Shine boldly inquires.

The thief slowly stands up and begins to turn around, arms raised above his head. "I can explain, officer. I was just uh—Wait. You're not one of the guards." Shine is now able to get a good look at the diminutive vagrant. His cleanshaven face looks a little aged. He must be in his thirties. The little man has small, beady brown eyes and short, black, messy hair. He's wearing a simple V-neck green tunic and brown cotton pants. His shoes look like they're made of soft leather, most likely to muffle his footsteps while sneaking. There's a dirt smudge on his left cheek, and he has an unpleasant odor of booze and BO.

"Stealing from the warehouse?" Shine crossly accuses.

The thief puts an innocent expression on his face. "Me? Stealin'? Of course not. Stealing is immoral and illegal. You"—he points at Shine— "you were about to steal sumthin', weren't ya?"

"Yep," Shine sarcastically replies. "You caught me. Man, you're good."

The thief puffs his chest out. "Yep. I sure am. A novice like you could never get past a master thief like—Crap! You tricked me!"

"I wasn't even trying to. You kinda walked into that one all by yourself. What's a 'master thief' doing stealing from a warehouse anyway?"

"Food."

Shine gives a couple sarcastic claps. "Legendary. I guess even master thieves gotta eat sometime."

"It's not for me. It's... Never mind. So, what now? Are ya gonna call the guards?

"Nah. I don't care that you're stealing food. I could actually use someone sneaky like you. I'm looking for people to join me on an adventure."

The thief perks up at the word 'adventure.' "Hmm... What kinda adventure?"

"I'm heading north to King Pious's castle. To kill him."

Shine gives a speech akin to the one he gave Marduk and asks, "You in?"

"Maybe. He has it comin' for sure. So many people are sufferin' 'cause of him. However, as a master thief, I can't just join up with anyone. Ya have ta prove yerself."

"What do you have in mind?"

"A simple test. Some of King Pious's guards are garrisoned in town. Steal sumthin' from 'em and get back here without bein' seen, and I'll join ya."

Shine smiles. "Sounds like fun. All right, I'll be back." He heads back to Marduk, who notices the thief isn't in tow.

"I take it things did not go as planned?"

"Actually, they went pretty well. He is interested but wants me to complete a task for him. He said some of Pious's men are garrisoned here, and he wants me to steal something and bring it back here."

"Oh? And you trust this man will still be here when you come back? He is a thief after all."

"I believe so. He seemed genuinely interested in our cause. Any idea where we should look?" Marduk ponders for a bit and recalls seeing some soldiers around a warehouse on the south side of town. They had turned the depot into a makeshift base. There are only a handful, so this mission shouldn't be too difficult to complete.

The sun is just beginning to set as they head to the south side of town. On the way, Shine notices that several buildings have fallen into disrepair. It seems Bristol is going through some tough times. Undoubtedly, King Pious and his high taxes are to blame. Soon they approach the warehouse. Two soldiers clad in military-issue black steel plate armor are standing guard at the door. "Maybe there's another door or an open window," Shine ventures. "Or maybe we could cause a distraction."

"I am way ahead of you, my boy," Marduk calmly replies. He tells Shine to wait and walks down the sidewalk. The guards are on edge. Even seeing an old man walking down the street is enough for them reach for blades. They eye Marduk warily as he continues his approach.

One of them barks, "You there! Stop!" The wizard takes a couple more steps forward before doubling over, pretending to be in pain. He clutches at his heart and collapses face down. The soldiers rush over to help. One of them rolls Marduk onto his back while the other is asking if he can hear him. The sly old man's eyes pop open and with a wave of a hand casts a sleep spell on the guards, who immediately pass out. One of the guards has a keyring with a couple keys on him. Marduk snags it. Impressed, Shine gleefully joins the wizard and uses the keys to head inside the warehouse.

They crouch down and cautiously move about while keeping their eyes peeled for anything to steal. Sneaking past a couple guards playing cards and turning down a hallway made of shelving, they find a wide-open area. There are three soldiers lounging around. At the north end of the building there is a desk against the wall with a lit candle. One of the guards is standing there and appears to be reading something. Another is sitting propped up against a wall, and the last one is standing on the south side of the room. Shine points above that guard's head as he spots a few barrels lying in some rope netting above. If they can take out the net, the barrels will knock out the guard and hopefully draw all the others over to him. They hide behind a large crate. From here they can quickly get to the desk and back through the hall without being seen. Now there is just the matter of that net.

Marduk points a finger at it. Shine's eyes widen as he sees a faint green light glow from the mage's fingertip. The wizard takes careful aim and looses a razor-sharp gust of wind at his target. The wind's power fades quickly but manages to strike the net. Only a small tear. Darn. Marduk prepares another shot but doesn't have to. Just enough ropes were severed to destroy the net's integrity. It slowly sags down from the weight of the barrels before tearing wide open.

The barrels crash down upon the unsuspecting soldier. The other two jump up from the sudden sound and see their comrade unconscious amongst wood and apples. One of them yells for help, and the soldiers playing doormen rush over, too. Shine stays low and quickly makes his way towards the desk. He spots a letter and grabs it. The sneaky bandits quickly exit. Once they're around the block and a safe distance away, Shine bursts with laughter. "That was a blast!" he excitedly exclaims. "What a rush! That was some impressive magic you used back there."

"Oh, that was nothing," Marduk replies humbly. "Those were mere parlor tricks."

"If you say so, man. C'mon let's head back to our thief."

Back at the first warehouse, the thief is waiting right where they found him. Shine causally says, "Here ya go," as he hands him the letter.

The thief unrolls it and takes a gander. "Let's see here… A letter containin' the soldiers' orders. Very nice. Okay! Ya just earned yerselves a master thief! Ed's the name." Shine and Marduk introduce themselves, and Shine inquires to what the orders are. They are pretty straightforward. It would seem Bristol is now on King Pious's radar, and he wanted some men here to keep eyes and ears out for any potential dissenters. The party probably shouldn't stay too long if that's the case. Shine lets Ed know there's one more stop, the dojo. Ed responds, "Sounds good to me, but if it's all the same ta y'all, there's somewhere I wanna go first."

"Where's that?" asks Marduk.

"I have to deliver this food I was stealin'. It's not far on the west side of town."

"Okay," agrees Shine. "It's getting late. After we deliver the food, we should get a room at the inn and hit up the dojo in the morning."

Marduk replies, "You can stay at the inn if you like. I shall retire home. I need to gather my staff, and I have a few supplies to bring. I was also thinking we should stock up on necessities. We may already have enough weaponry. I see Shine already has a sword. What about you, Ed?"

Ed grins and pulls out a concealed dagger. "I'm good." He then reveals a pouch sitting in his inner coat pocket. It makes a metallic cling as he slaps it with his hand. "I'm stayin' at the inn as it is if ya wanna join me, Shine. These donations should cover the room and supplies."

"And where did you get all those coins?" Shine wryly inquires. "Hard labor?"

"I'm a pretty good pickpocket, and for some reason, the guards like to keep their coins on 'em."

The three men head to the west side of town. They are greeted by a dismal neighborhood filled with houses in disrepair. Many of them have holes in the rooves; others have broken windows or other damaged areas. It is a depressing sight. Bristol was always a fairly wealthy town.

"What happened to this place?" Shine dejectedly asks.

Ed answers, "This town used to do great trade supplyin' the rest of Elysia with lumber from Verde's Woods. However, the town don't own it. A merchant named Verde does."

"One man owns all of Verde's Woods?" Shine gasps in amazement.

"Yup," Ed continues, "Lorde Verde. They say he's da richest man in Elysia, maybe all of Terra. Long story short, the fairies that live in the woods have started attackin' people, so Verde closed the road goin' through it to keep people safe. Problem is that road is the only viable route from 'ere to the rest o' Elysia, so Bristol is completely cut off from trade. Pile high taxes on top o' that and ya got a town that's sufferin' terribly."

"I'll say," Shine agrees. "You would think the king would want to give aid, but instead he just taxes the Hades out of them and doesn't lift a finger to help. He has a huge army, but he'd rather send soldiers to search for dissenters than escort trade caravans. Disgusting."

"That's why I'm joinin' ya," Ed replies. "But first things first. We're here." The group finds themselves in front of a small hovel. This one is in particularly bad shape. There are multiple holes in the roof, and the rest of it looks like it will collapse at any moment. All three wooden steps leading to the front door are broken, and the door has a large crack in it, too. Ed gently knocks at the door. A woman slowly opens it. Her eyes are sunken, and she looks like she hasn't slept in a week. She warily eyes Shine and Marduk. "It's okay," Ed says warmly. "They're with me. I got somethin' for ya."

The woman lets the trio inside. A couple rats dart across the floor. Even they look malnourished. There are two children, a boy and a girl both wearing dirty clothing sitting on the floor. Their eyes light up when they see Ed. He smiles and says, "It's not much, but it should last you a couple days." He opens his satchel and takes out several loaves of bread and half a dozen apples. The woman graciously thanks him, and after an elbow nudge, so do her children.

As they exit the home, Shine can barely contain his anger and sadness. He just witnessed firsthand the suffering his nation is going through. He's happy to have met Ed. Seeing that impoverished, starving family confirmed what he already knew and strengthened his resolve. It is clear as the night sky above this is the right path. The party finds their way to the inn to stay the night.

The following morning, Marduk, with staff in hand, meets the others in front of the dojo. Ed's hair is still a mess, but at least he bathed. There's no telling if this venture will be successful, but hopefully there will be at least one person there willing to join the cause. It doesn't take long to find a prospect. Almost as soon they enter, a poor chap goes flying out of the ring situated in the middle of the dojo and spills hard onto the ground.

A woman stands alone in the ring. She is a curious sight, tall—at least six, two—with bronze skin and some impressive biceps, but her face looks young. She can't be more than eighteen. She has large, almond-colored eyes and dark brown hair tied in a ponytail extending just past her shoulders. She isn't dressed in what one would expect one to find in a place like this. No, this young lady is wearing a bronze cuirass, thick, leather boots, and a leather and bronze skirt. It's the type of thing one would expect to see on a battlefield, not in a dojo. She's obviously strong, seeing as she just flung some poor guy like a rag doll. She leans back on the turnbuckles perhaps awaiting the next challenger.

Shine decides to hop in and introduce himself. As he enters, the woman looks him up and down. She doesn't look impressed. "That was quite a throw," Shine says casually. "You must be pretty strong."

The woman doesn't even look at him as she responds, "Are you lost, kid? You must be lost. You don't look like a fighter."

Shine isn't used to being disrespected. Hanover is a tightknit community where everyone treats others kindly. He wants to snap at her but restrains. He forces a smile and replies, "No, not really, but I am looking for a fighter."

The woman's head turns slightly in his direction. She has one eye him. It's not much, but it's a start. She asks in a mocking tone, "What's wrong? Is some big, bad bully gonna beat you up?"

Shine matches her sarcastic demeanor, "The biggest bully. My friends and I are headed to Leed's Castle to beat him up."

The lady laughs and turns to face Shine. "You must be joking. What business does a runt like you have at the castle?"

"We're going to pay Pious a visit. We're going to kill him."

The woman howls with laughter. "You are just precious!" she mocks. "What did the mean ol' king do to you?" Shine begins his now typical "tyrant" speech, but the woman cuts him off before completing the first sentence. "Spare me the pitch. I can't stand that son of a bitch. I was thinkin' of heading there myself actually."

Shine is relieved. This was easier than he thought it would be. "So, you'll join us then?" he asks directly.

The woman scoffs, "As if, kid."

Okay, maybe this won't be so easy. "Why not? We have the same goal," Shine persists.

She glances over at his counterparts. "You and your little friends have no chance. Look at you." She eyes Shine up and down. "You're a shrimp traveling with an even shrimpier shrimp and an old geezer. What could you possibly do against someone like Pious?"

Shine stares into her eyes with fiery intent. "Whatever it takes. We're going to stop him with or without you."

"I'm not sure if that's confidence or stupidity, but you have some balls, that's for sure. But I'm not going to join up with a bunch of weaklings. Tell ya what, kid. If you can beat me in a sparring match, I'll join your little crew."

Shine smiles and obliges, "Deal." He puts on a brave face but has no idea what he's doing. He's gotten into a few scuffles with the other kids at home, but he's never been in a real fight before. Still, he has to find a way to beat her. He puts up his dukes in a basic boxing stance. The woman doubles over with laughter. He's getting real sick of being mocked but knows he must keep his cool.

Once she recovers, she asks, still laughing a bit, "Is that how you're gonna take Pious down? What are ya gonna do, give him a black eye? Hahaha!"

"What do you have in mind then?"

"That sword ya got there ain't just for show, is it? I vastly prefer weapons training anyway." She looks over at the corner of the dojo and whistles. One of the men perks up and picks up what is basically an oversized woodcutter's axe. He tries to hurry over to the ring but struggles with the weight. When he finally gets to the ring, the young woman reaches through the ropes and takes the giant axe with one hand. She walks into the center of the ring and effortlessly lays it over her shoulders. "The name's Julia, by the way."

"Shine." Somehow this feels like a better scenario. Shine has trained with Ray a few times with swords and picked up a couple moves. He's far from an expert, but he has more skill with a blade than bare fists. *Wish me luck, Dad*, he says to himself. He begins to reach for Rashida. Before unsheathing it, Ed makes his way over and hops up onto the apron.

"Umm… Shine?" he asks nervously. "Are ya sure about this?"

Shine turns his head back at Ed. "Yeah. Don't worry, I'll be fine."

"It's just… uh… that chick looks like she can tear yer arm off and beat you to death with it, and now she's got a ginormous axe. She's gonna cut your fucking head off."

Marduk makes his way to ringside to add, "Indeed. I think you should reconsider this course of action."

Shine turns to face his anxious new cohorts and emphatically states, "If I can't win a simple sparring match, then I have no business trying to take down Pious and should just go back home. I got this."

He hears Julia behind him, "Having second thoughts?"

Shine turns back to his opponent. "Not a chance. Let's go." He draws his sword and slowly approaches. Julia wastes no time making the first move. She swings her axe in horizontal fashion aiming at Shine's shoulders. Such a big weapon is going to have a slow swing. Blocking it should be simple. Shine holds Rashida tightly with both hands and braces. Blocking the blow was, in fact, easy; however, the force of impact sends him flying backwards on his ass, nearly tumbling through the ropes.

He hears more words of encouragement from Ed, "Oh yeah, he's dead." Shine maneuvers his torso back through the ropes and stands. Julia doesn't seem to be taking this seriously, which is good because she easily could have ended things with a follow up. That may not happen a second time. Blocking strikes is off the table. Her strength is too much to deal with directly, but those swings will be sluggish. The confined space of a ring isn't ideal, but there's enough room to maneuver.

Shine is going to have to use his quickness to dodge and get in close. He moves forward, just out of Julia's range. He feigns an advance to the left, then the right to see how his opponent reacts. She doesn't. Julia knows she has the reach advantage. She contemplates advancing and ending it, but she's curious to see what this shrimp will do.

She doesn't have to wait long as her opponent rushes head on. She takes a one-handed swing, but Shine ducks under and goes in for a strike. He must be careful not to actually connect with the slash and cause her serious harm. That uncertainty causes hesitation, and Julia smacks him away with her free hand. Before he can recover, his adversary is on the attack and swings the axe downward with both hands. Shine just barely manages to leap away and scrambles to the ropes. He uses them to pull himself up.

Julia charges again. Shine darts forward and dives under the swing, rolling through to remain on his feet. He uses one of the moves Ray taught. Before she can spin around, Shine kicks the back of Julia's knee as hard as he can. It buckles! She falls onto it. Wasting no time, Shine grabs the shoulder of her weapon arm and wraps his other around her neck. He places his blade at her throat. Julia looks at him with surprise and fear in her eyes. What is this little man going to do? Shine releases her and sheaths Rashida.

Julia lays her weapon on the ground and rises to face her opponent. "That was a nice move, kid. You've got some fight in you."

"As do you," Shine humbly replies.

"All right, a deal's a deal. I guess I'm joining you guys." She and Shine exit the ring where she is formally introduced to the geezer and shrimp.

Ed looks up at her and remarks, "Whew! Yer a tall glass o' water, girl. It's not every day ya see a chick with gorilla strength." Julia isn't sure if that was meant to a be an insult or compliment. She throws a punch in case it's the former. Ed nonchalantly hops back out of range. "Yer strong, but I'm quick," he jeers.

Shine glares at him. "Be nice, Ed. We're all on the same team." He pauses briefly before adding, "Besides, she'll rip you in half if she ever does get her hands on you."

Julia smiles and proudly affirms, "Damn right." An intimidating stare pierces Ed's eyes. "Watch yourself, little man."

Marduk is unamused. He impatiently asks, "If you two are finished flirting, can we please move on?" Ed and Julia both blush a bit at the idea they were being flirtatious.

Julia changes the subject by telling them a little about herself. She hails from a city called Cid. Though it's in the middle of Elysia, it is a sovereign city-state. They are a warrior race that practices ancient traditions steeped in martial and chi arts. They may not officially be part of Elysia, but they have always provided warriors as military aid in exchange for vital goods and protection dating back to the Great War. Until recently, Cid had always been on good terms with Elysia. King Pious's tyranny changed that, and Cid now refuses to give him warriors. There is much tension in Cid, for the people fear Pious may one day decide to annex them by force.

Julia always preferred weapons training over hand to hand. Her master was able to instill some basic fighting fundamentals but little else, so he advised she take her training on the road, traveling around Elysia seeking out warriors to train and spar with. Her new allies notice she didn't say anything about her family or friends, but no one decides to pry. It is clear why she has so much distain for King Pious. She'll fit right in.

The party exits the dojo with a new member. The foursome uses the guards' "donations" to buy a backpack plus some food, blankets, and other various items they may need. Shine carries the pack on his back, and the party heads out of town. Shine admires Marduk's staff as they walk. It is just a simple oak staff with a hunk of amber melted to the top, but to Shine, it is a new, exciting sight.

Marduk explains to him that even a basic staff can be quite useful for channeling and controlling magic. There are plenty of more finely crafted staves out there, but they get expensive quickly as the quality improves. The wizard speaks fondly of an ornate staff he once proudly held. It had a rare black pearl at the head and a gold-plated copper shaft. Unfortunately, a dragon chomped it in half. ♛

CHAPTER 3
Creepy Forest

The party soon crosses the bridge just north of Bristol. From here, the only way north to the bulk of Elysia is through Verde's Woods. The vast woodland is sprawled out in front of them. Shine's amazement is redoubled. How can one man own that much land? There is only one road leading into the woods. A lone sentry stands guard. He isn't dressed in the same armor as Bristol's guards nor Pious's men. His armor is dark green, like sage. Ed informs the group that the man is one of Lord Verde's personal guards. Apparently, he has a small army in his employ. The guard stands in attention as the party approaches. "Hold!" he sternly commands. "This road has been closed on the order of Lord Verde. Turn back now." They stop about ten feet from the sentry.

Marduk is the first to speak, "Yes, so we have heard. Is it true that the fairies have been attacking people who enter?"

"That is correct," the guard stoically replies. "It is too dangerous for travelers to enter, and therefore, the road has been closed."

Julia takes a bold step forward. "We're not some weaklings. We can take care of ourselves. Let us through."

The guard remains adamant. "Absolutely not. Turn back now."

"Or what?" Julia asks in a threatening tone. "There's four of us and one of you."

Shines quickly intervenes to ensure things don't escalate. "There's no need to resort to violence. He's just doing his job." Shine looks to the guard. "That being said, my aggressive friend is right. We all have weapons, and we have supplies. We can take care of ourselves. We have important business to the north and must get through the woods." He sees the guard beginning to waiver and adds, "We want to pass through peacefully, but we will go through you if we must."

The sentry sighs and shrugs. "Fine. Whatever. Just don't come cryin' to me if you wind up dead."

He steps aside and allows the heroes through. There are several paths that snake through Verde's Woods, but the main road is more or less a straight line. It is paved but seems to be in desperate need of maintenance. There are many cracks and potholes dotting the granite roadway. It doesn't take long for the group to find their path blocked by a large fallen tree. Climbing over would be cumbersome, and there is a dirt path that leads around.

Shine pulls out his map. Luckily, the path is marked. It's a roundabout but easier route through some marshland that will lead right back to the main road. Upon entering the marshes, Ed remembers some bandits once used this area of the woods as a hideout. They are long gone, but maybe some loot got left behind. The former hideout is just a little east off the beaten path and around a small, peat laden pond. There's a narrow strip of grass between the murky, water and the weeping willow trees leading to a natural downhill path. Carefully avoiding low branches and vines, the party makes their way down.

Before long there's a small, empty clearing. There's not much to see, but some evidence the area was previously occupied remains. Charred wood from fire and a torn shirt are all that's left. Or are they? Ed walks behind a large rock to take a leak when he notices a small, wooden shield on the ground. The metal rim has some rust, and there is a crack in the middle, but it's useable. Ed finishes his business and shows the others what he found. He and Marduk aren't interested in wielding a shield, and Julia's large weapon doesn't pair well with it, so Shine is one to equip it. Julia takes the backpack allowing Shine to fasten the shield to his back.

The party heads back onto the path. They are about halfway through the marshes when they come across a small grove of dead trees covered in spiderwebs. There isn't any good way around, so through the deadwood it is. After five steps in, three large spiders descend on silk strands in front of them. "Ewww. I hate spiders," Julia remarks. The arachnids are each about three feet long sporting long, spindly legs and some fierce looking mandibles. Friendly they are not. Once descended onto the dirt, they each let out a loud hiss and raise their front legs in an aggressive posture. So much for capturing prey in webs. These critters opt for a more direct approach.

Julia puts the backpack down, and the party draws their weapons. The foursome are apprehensive. This is their first fight. A few spiders should be no problem, but there's no telling if the party will have any chemistry in battle. Shine gets to test his new old buckler when one of the arachnids charges at him. It lunges but is easily pushed back by the shield. Shine tries to kill it with a sword thrust, but the spider hops backwards and rejoins the others. They hiss in unison before attacking. Marduk stays back a few steps as the other three take the spiders head on.

Julia effortlessly slices hers in half with a mighty axe swing. Shine thrusts as his lunges, skewering its midsection. Its legs flail for a short bit before curling. Shine grimaces in disgust as he pushes the spider off his blade with his shield. Green, sour smelling blood coats Rashida. Gross. Ed isn't able to take his target out in a single hit. He dodges to the side as the spider lunges and slices a couple of its legs off with his dagger.

The spider spins around to attack again. Before it can, it bursts into flames. Marduk launched a small fireball from the rear. It tries to move forward at Ed but dies after a couple steps. Ed thanks the wizard for the assist, and the party continues onward. They stop briefly at a pond to wash the blood off their weapons. As they're cleaning, faint giggling echoes all around. Ed's ears perk up. "Did y'all hear that?"

"Yes," Marduk replies. "Fairies, no doubt." Shine suggests they shouldn't stay too long.

Fairies may be small and slender but can be fierce when they want to be. Some have formidable skill with magic. Others flutter about and strike with wooden swords, and still others are skilled archers. The heroes make their way past the marshes and back onto the main road. Before long they are confronted by another fallen tree. More eerie giggling. Is this the fairies' doing? Best not stay to find out. They take another route around unencumbered.

The path rejoins the main road about a half mile south of the exit. Yet another fallen tree blocks the way. There is no path around this one, so it's time to climb. Ed may be shortest, but he is also the nimblest, so he volunteers to climb up first and help the others over. He sprints toward the tree and leaps as high as he can. He nearly gets to the top in a single bound and manages to secure a good grip on the bark. It's just inches further to reach the top. As his head rises over, a glint of light flashes in front of him. Ed leaps down off the fallen tree in surprise. He looks up to see an arrow pierced through top of the tree right where his head would have been. He gulps and turns toward his companions.

"Um... Guys?" Before he can finish his thought, two fairies gently flutter over the fallen tree and hover above the party. More giggles from behind. Two more fairies fly out from the woods. The party is surrounded! One fairy on each side is wielding a small, wooden sword. One in front has a bow and a quiver of arrows, and one behind has a small wooden staff.

All four titter in unison before one speaks, "Hee hee! Lookie here! More silly humans to play with."

Another flutters about on butterfly wings and adds, "You'd think they'd learn. Humans are so dumb." The party needs a strategy and quick. Shine hastily gives out some orders. His allies know there's no time for debate and just hope he knows what he's talking about. Shine and Julia will take the two in front. Shine's buckler can protect against the arrows, and Julia's brute force will make short work of their fragile foes if she can land a hit. Marduk will take on the mage, and Ed will take the warrior to the rear. The party splits up and faces their opponents.

Their enemies are coordinated in their strikes. The archer quickly fires a couple arrows at the pair in front of it while the warrior swoops down at Julia. The mage lets out a blinding burst of light from its staff while the other warrior dives at Ed. Shine easily blocks his arrow. Julia manages to dodge the other but cannot evade the sword. Her upper right arm gets sliced pretty good, but it's far from a serious wound. She shudders to imagine if that sword was made of metal. Shine charges the warrior and takes a swing. It laughs while easily fluttering away. Shine quickly raises his shield in defense as another arrow screeches at his head. The other fairy attacks. Shine manages to block with Rashida, and Julia takes a shot at the warrior, who flits away again. Hitting these little buggers is proving difficult.

Ed and Marduk seem to match up better against their foes. Though blinded, Ed is able to use his agility to evade the warrior's sword swing but cannot counter. Marduk directs a gust of wind at the mage. It's nothing harmful; however, it forces his adversary to brace, thus preventing any follow up attack. It also gives Marduk an idea. If he can stun one of them with a gust, Ed can use his quickness to strike. Before Marduk can act, the mage launches a fireball at him. He fires one of his own to cancel it out. Meanwhile, Ed and the warrior fairy are bouncing back at forth in a stalemate. Every strike is either met or evaded. They pause to size each other up after a fierce clash. Marduk's foe launches another fireball. This time Marduk tries to dodge. He winces as the flame grazes him. Sure, he could have easily used his magic to block, but he saw an opportunity he did not want to pass up. As he dodges, he fires a gust of wind at the warrior who is caught unaware. The swordsfairy is stunned momentarily. That's more than enough time for Ed to strike. He slices one of the fairy's butterfly wings off. It slowly sinks to the ground in pain, unable to fly. It lets out a shrill scream as Ed follows up with a finishing blow, piercing his foe's chest. One fairy down.

The mage is filled with anger at the sight of its slain brother. It flies back a safe distance from the humans. "You'll pay for that," it seethes as its body begins to glow red. It is gathering mana! There are several possibilities Ed and Marduk must consider. It isn't hurt; therefore, it's not trying to heal, and it most likely doesn't have the power or skill to revive its comrade. That means it's either using magic to augment its physical abilities or is preparing a powerful spell.

Either way, offense seems like the best defense right now. It is too far away to take it down the same way they did the other. Marduk tells Ed to flank him as he gathers mana. He knows a powerful spell, too: a flurry of five fireballs. Such an attack is better suited when dealing with multiple opponents. It's not ideal against a single target. There's a good chance the fairy will be able to dodge, and that's when it will be up to Ed to follow up.

The fairy mage ceases to glow. No attack comes. It must have buffed itself. It zips around from one side of the path to the other with blistering speed. Marduk knows he must aim well, spreading the fireballs across the breadth of the path to maximize the chances of a hit. He does just that, but the fairy dips and darts around the blazing balls before charging Marduk head on. Even a small, wooden staff will do a lot of damage at that speed, and Marduk's flourish left him exposed. Fortunately, despite his nonchalant attitude, Ed is vicious when his friends are in danger. He doesn't miss a beat and rushes to meet the mage's charge. He lunges and swipes at it with his dagger. The fairy is able to dodge but is spun in a one-eighty. Ed plants his foot in the ground and springs towards his enemy. He slices horizontally at its torso.

The fairy manages to fly backward just enough to escape with just a small cut. It prepares to square off against Ed. Before either can make a move, the fairy's eyes roll back in its head, and it crumbles to the ground. It made a grave error and forgot all about the other opponent and suffered a hard conk on the head by the wizard's staff. If it were against a human, the blow would be far from fatal, but fairies are much smaller and weaker boned. Blood pours from its head after the killing bash.

Ed and Marduk swiftly move to aid their allies. Not a moment too soon either. Shine and Julia are having a rough go of it. The warrior effortlessly evades another of Julia's swings after it attacked Shine. Shine was able to block with his shield, but his left leg is grazed by the archer's arrow. Both heroes are short of breath whilst their opponents look like they're just warming up. They smile as they see their companions rejoin them. Four on two will make things much easier.

The fairies know they will soon be overwhelmed and move to take out their opponents before the cavalry can get into position. The archer fires a couple arrows at Julia to keep her at bay while the warrior tries to strike Shine. This time Shine leaps to the side, allowing the warrior's inertia to carry it past him. It raises its sword in defense as Ed attacks. It blocks the dagger, but it cannot do anything to stop Shine from impaling it from behind. Only one fairy left. It frantically surveys the battlefield and determines discretion is the better part of valor. It cries while fluttering up and away, disappearing through the trees.

The party stops to catch their breath. They cannot help being jovial. Who knew fighting as a unit would be so exhilarating? There's an unmistakable chemistry, making the victory all the more meaningful. This synergy is a sign of great things to come. The more the heroes battle together, the more in sync they'll become. Julia is the most boisterous of the four. "Whooo!" she exclaims. "That was fucking amazing! We're quite the team!"

"King Pious ain't got no chance!" Ed grins.

Shine's response is more measured, "We fought well together, but let's not get ahead of ourselves. We still have a very long way to go."

Marduk nods in agreement. "Wise words, indeed. An overinflated ego has been the downfall of many men."

"Don't get cocky. Is that what you mean?" inquires Julia.

"Precisely," confirms Marduk. Shine agrees but can't help feeling a little cocky. This was their first real test, and they performed better than he could have hoped. As he revels in victory, he notices the warrior fairy he killed has a pouch on him. There's a pair of small earrings with sapphire studs inside. He shows them to his friends.

"Ooo… Pwetty." Ed remarks in a childlike tone. "I bet we can pawn these for a few coins in the next town."

Marduk has his own suggestion, "Better yet, I'm sure they'll fetch a higher price at a magic shop."

"Why's that?" asks Julia.

"Gems like these have intrinsic magical properties. Sapphires are thought to represent purity and wisdom. A skilled mage can enchant them to augment the wearer's magical abilities or ward off poison and disease."

Shine asks, "You can't enchant them yourself, Marduk?"

"Sadly, no. Enchantments are not my field of study. I suppose we could always have them enchanted and use them ourselves, but considering our lack of funds, selling them seems to be the wiser option."

"We'll hold on to them in either case," Shine decides. "Once we get to the next town, we can figure out what to do. By the way, what town is next?"

Ed laughs. "Wow, ya really haven't been anywhere outside of Hanover, huh? Salem is nearest town. It's a small, sleepy town, kinda like yours. It's about a day's walk from the woods past Verde's Ranch."

Shine's eyes widen. "He has a ranch, too? I guess I shouldn't be surprised. If you can afford to buy an entire forest, a ranch must be cheap in comparison. So, how far is it to Leed's Castle? I know it's pretty much smack in the middle of Elysia, but that's about it."

"Hmm…" Ed thinks. "From here, at least a week, week and a half if you go straight there only stoppin' to eat, sleep, and shit."

"That's closer than I imagined. I hope we're ready by the time we get there."

Julia shrugs. "What's the worst that can happen?"

"We all die a horrific, painful death," Ed replies flatly.

"Oh, don't be such a baby," Julia jeers. Shine changes the subject asking if everyone is ready to continue. They are, and the party makes their way over the fallen tree and, shortly after, out of the woods ☗

CHAPTER 4
Lifestyles of the Rich and Paranoid

The party is greeted by a vast meadow. Some hills and trees are speckled across the landscape. Trouble doesn't take long to come calling. Three men on the road ahead spot suspicious people exiting the woods and approach. They are dressed in the same armor as the bloke that was guarding the woods. More of Verde's men. The one in the middle has a plume of orange-dyed animal hair on the top of his helmet curving down the back like a ponytail. He's probably their leader. Verde's men stop a few feet in front of Shine and crew. The two underlings move to either side, surrounding the party. Back into the woods is the only unblocked path.

The leader speaks to his men, "Well, well, well, look at what we have here, boys. Looks like some trespassers." He stops to sneer down at their quarry. "Don'tcha know the woods are closed?"

Shine calmly explains, "We received permission from one of your men on the other side."

"Sure, ya did. Sure," the leader flippantly replies. "The guard just let you stroll on by. Do you think we're idiots?"

"Well…" Ed starts.

"Excuse me?" Shine asks defensively.

"We know what you're up to."

"Really? Enlighten us."

"You're headed o'er to Lord Verde's place, aren't you?"

"Lord Verde? We have no business with him. We are traveling north."

"Ha! A likely story. We know you were comin' to rob the lord. We caught your scout a couple days ago."

Shine looks at him quizzically. "Okay, you lost me."

Marduk tries to reason with the men, "Sirs, please. As my companion explained, we are simple travelers. We have no desire to rob Mr. Verde."

"That's *Lord* Verde!" the leader snaps. "You're not gonna talk your way outta this. Lord Verde ordered us to arrest any trespassers on sight."

"For the last time, we're not thieves!" Shine pleas.

"Explain it to Lord Verde." The men draw their swords.

Julia's blood boils. She really, *really* hates being threatened. "Like hell we're going with you! I'll—"

Marduk quickly intervenes. "Julia! Enough. They have us surrounded. We'd be cut down before we could draw our weapons. We have no choice but to go with these men. Hopefully, Lord Verde will be more understanding."

The leader is amused by that notion. "Hahaha! Good luck with that. Now, come on." His men collect the party's gear and roughly escort them to Lord Verde's manor.

The door of the cell makes a loud, metal clang as it slams shut. It is now nightfall. Moonlight beams in from thin, high, barred windows. "Sleep tight! Hahahaha!" the guard leader jovially exclaims as he locks a cell. He and his men head out of the cellar-turned-dungeon. There are six cells total, three on each side. The heroes were separated into four different ones. What kind of man has his own dungeon?

Shine sighs heavily and says, "Well, this sucks."

Marduk concurs from the neighboring cell, "This certainly isn't good."

"What's the next move, Shine?" asks Julia from caddy-corner.

Shine doesn't really have any idea. "I guess we just wait for Lord Verde and explain ourselves."

Marduk is skeptical about that course of action, "Do you think that's wise? The guards scoffed at that suggestion. Not a good sign."

Julia doesn't like Shine's idea either. "Well, we have to do something. I want my weapon back. I feel naked without it."

Even in their predicament, Ed, who is in the cell next to hers, cannot resist being a smartass, "No one wants ta see ya naked. It's scary enough down here."

"What did you say?" Julia angrily counters. "You're *sooo* lucky we're in separate cells."

Ed continues pushing buttons, "Why don't ya use yer gorilla-like strength to smash yer way out?"

"I'm warning you, runt."

"C'mon, barbarian woman. Get ta smashin'."

"You bastard! I'm going to kill you!"

"*Ooo...* I'm shakin'."

Shine's posture droops in exasperation. "I've allied with idiots..."

Marduk tries to focus the group, "As entertaining as you two are, I think it would be best if we made an escape plan."

"Oh, I got that figured out already," Ed nonchalantly replies.

Marduk strokes his beard. "Hmm...? Okay, let us hear it."

"I'm gonna pick the lock, and we're gonna sneak outta 'ere."

That's enough to satisfy Shine. "Simple yet effective. I like it."

From the darkness calls a faint, female voice, "Umm... Hello?" Everybody perks up in surprise.

"Who's there?" Shine questions.

The unknown person meekly continues, "M-Me. My name's Artemis. Pleased to meet you."

"You've been in here the whole time?" Shine grills. "Why didn't you say anything?"

"Well, I was sleeping before you all started yelling."

"Oops. Sorry about that," Shine sheepishly apologizes. "We didn't even notice you."

"Actually, I did," Julia informs.

"Same 'ere," adds Ed.

"I saw her as well," Marduk confirms.

Shine is slightly embarrassed he's the only one not to notice this person. Luckily for him, it's too dark for the others to see him blush. "Whatever. So, this Verde guy's guards got you, too."

"Yes," explains Artemis, "I was coming out of Verde's Woods. His men spotted me. They said I was trespassing, accused me of being a thief, and threw me in here."

Marduk replies, "The same thing happened to us. I recall the guards saying something about capturing a scout. I suppose they meant you."

"Um... Can I ask you something?" Artemis timidly asks.

"Sure," Shine answers warmly.

"I…Uh… I heard you talking about escaping. Could you let me out, please?"

As if she needed to ask. Shine assures her, "Sure. Of course, we will. Ed, pick the lock before the guards come back."

Ed hops into action. "On it. Stand back and watch a master thief work 'is magic." He removes a hairpin from inside his tunic and begins to manipulate the lock. After a minute, he pauses and gazes vacantly at it.

"Having trouble?" Julia jeers. Ed ignores her and keeps trying. He smiles as he hears that all too familiar metal click and opens the cell.

"Nice work!" congratulates Shine.

Ed replies smugly, "Piece o' cake."

Shine presses, "Get the rest of us outta here."

Within minutes, Ed releases his allies, and they move to rescue Artemis. She thanks them profusely as she is freed. Everybody now gets a good look at the girl. She is dressed in a white linen shirt with long, green sleeves, and a spider silk skirt dyed green to match. She has long, blond hair, and hazel eyes rest above a tiny, slender nose. Her fair skin almost seems to glow in the pale moonlight. Now that she can get a good gander at her rescuers, she can see they are fatigued. She speaks softly and kindly, "You guys look tired. I can help with that." She removes a small vial of cherry red liquid from her pocket.

"Is that a vitality potion?" Marduk asks.

"Yes. It isn't much to split four ways, but even a couple sips should perk you up a bit." She is correct. The heroes each drink some and instantly feel more energetic. They don't quite feel like they can take on the entire world, but the boost of energy will make escaping a little easier. Artemis smiles. "There, feel better?"

Shine smiles back. "Much better, thank you."

"You guys recover quickly. I still have one more of those plus a mana potion."

Marduk raises an eyebrow. "Are you able to use magic, Artemis?"

"Nope." She starts to blush and looks down at her feet. "It's… I made them. It's a hobby of mine."

Marduk is impressed. "That's quite the hobby. I'd love to know more, but we have more pressing matters at the moment."

"I'll say," Ed adds. "Let's get the fuck outta here."

The fivesome make their way to the other end of the dungeon. After passing through a short corridor, they find themselves in a fairly large room with a couple lit torches hanging on the walls. To the left is a steep stone staircase leading up out of the dungeon. To the right is a wooden door. A storage room perhaps. Ed moves to pick the lock, but Julia just kicks it in.

Inside they find their gear, Artemis's included. She has a curved wooden bow made from a willow tree. Its string is made of strengthened spider silk. There's plenty of spiders and wood in this region, so it's a pretty common bow. She also has a quiver, but only a few arrows remain, six with iron tips to be exact. Hopefully, they don't run into too much trouble while absconding. Before that, the group takes a minute to introduce themselves.

Shine, Julia, and Marduk all give short, general greeting. Ed, however, takes Artemis by the hand. He stares up into her hazel eyes. "Edward. Pleased to make the acquaintance of such a lovely young lady. Worry not, lass, I shall protect you from harm." Artemis isn't sure how to react. All she can muster is a few um's and ah's. Julia smacks Ed in the back of the head.

"Knock it off, Romeo. Don't worry, he's harmless. Annoying, but harmless."

"R-Right," Artemis replies tepidly before reintroducing herself. "I'm Artemis. Pleased to meet you all."

Shine takes the opportunity see if this girl would make a good ally. "You carry around a bow. Are you a warrior, Artemis?" he probes.

"Umm… No, not really. I use it to hunt. Everyone in my village says I'm the best archer they'd ever seen."

"Impressive." Shine nods. "I didn't take you for a hunter. You got that sweet, innocent thing going on."

"Food started becoming scarce. Our crops were withering. I don't like shooting animals, but it was that or starve to death."

"Reason enough. I'm actually looking for allies to join me on a quest. Surely, there will be a lot of fighting. If you think you can handle it, we could use someone skilled with a bow."

"I don't know… Maybe. What kind of quest?"

"I'll tell you all about it later. For now, let's concentrate on getting out of here."

"Right. Let's hurry."

The party reequips their weapons, Julia puts on the backpack, and they ascend the stone steps leading out. Everyone, including Artemis, were blindfolded when being brought in, so no one knows what will be waiting on the other side. They find themselves at the end of a long corridor with red-painted walls. Elaborate, lit candelabra line one side. Ed instantly realizes the locale.

It's Verde's manor. That means Lord Verde built a dungeon inside his own mansion. That's kind of creepy, but there's no time to dwell on it. The only concern right now is finding an exit. The corridor connects to another one in a T intersection. The party goes right. They come to another intersection where they can either head straight or turn right. There's a door on the left just ahead.

Before they can decide where to go, it opens, and a couple of Verde's green clad men come. They instantly spot the intruders. The corridor is just wide enough to move two by two. Not much room to maneuver, especially with two guards bearing down. Two quickly becomes one. Artemis fires an arrow into one's eye. He crumples dead on the floor. Julia steps forward. As the other guard tries to swing his sword, she thrusts the butt of her axe into his chest. He doubles over and falls to his knees. It's over for him. Julia ends it with a swift downward strike. Shine turns to congratulate Artemis for her perfect shot but stops when he sees she looks like she's about to cry. Her hands are trembling violently. "What's wrong?" he worriedly asks.

She casts her eyes to the floor, "I... I don't like killing people. I've hunted animals to survive, but killing people..."

Maybe she isn't cut out for combat. Oh well. Shine wonders if he'll have as hard a time when he needs to take a life. He tries his best to comfort her. "Hey, it's okay. Most people are the same as you. There's nothing wrong with that. You saw we were in danger and acted. That's all. Was that the first time you've killed someone?"

Artemis nods. "I've shot to wound bandits before, but I've never shot to kill, but...but those guards were rushing us with swords and I... I just..."

Ed empathizes, "Yeah, killin' ain't no small thing, but you showed keen survival skills. It gets easier after a bit. Trust me."

Julia has a far less gentle hand, "I hate to break it to you, girly, but these men have no problem killing us. You acted quickly this time. You'd better keep it up 'cause if you hesitate, even for a moment, you'll get yourself or one of us killed, and I'm going to be really pissed if I die because of some weakling."

Artemis nods in acknowledgment. She hates the situation but hates the thought of dying more. She just prays they can escape without any further confrontations. The party decides to try going through the door the guards came from. It's a storage room. An odd place to patrol. Maybe they were putting something away. Or maybe they were checking on that fancy chest against the wall. It looks to be made of steel and is painted bright red like the walls. For a guy named Verde, he sure seems to like the color red. The edges are plated with gold. The chest alone would fetch a high price. Too bad it's so heavy.

Shine tries to open it, but it's locked. Ed has an idea. He jams his dagger in the slit between the base and lid. He tries to force it open, to no avail. Julia pushes him aside and tries her luck. She manages to pry the chest open. A pair of steel daggers lay inside. The hilts are plated with gold, and each one is adorned with a tiny metal skull near the base of the blade.

"Holy crap," Ed amazes.

"I'll say," Shine adds. "I'd say our money issue is over."

"Screw that," Ed rejects. "I'm keepin' these. This ol' knife of mine is about finished. It's been a while since I had a good set o' daggers. You thought I was deadly before. Wait 'til ya see me start dancin' with these ladies." He tosses his old dagger in the chest and closes it. He twirls his new toys around before tucking them in his belt.

The party hides the slain guards in the storage room before continuing onward seeking an exit. They cautiously sneak past any guards they come across. Who knows how many men Verde has? Best not create a ruckus. Up a flight of stairs. When being taken to the dungeon, they were led down two stairwells. There should be a way outside on this floor. Down another hall, around the corner, there's a sentry standing about ten feet away watching a door. Snoring can be heard loud and clear from the other side. That must be Verde's bedroom. He is snoring so loudly, the guard can probably be taken out without him waking up, but the party decides not to risk it and doubles back around.

They enter a large kitchen, which leads to a dining room. There are several long, wooden tables. Several men are lounging. One has his helmet off and is enjoying a scrumptious-looking steak. This must be the guards' mess hall. Steak dinner. Lord Verde takes good care of his people. Taking out one guard will be easier than three, so the heroes decide to head back towards the bedroom. As they turn around, the blade of Julia's axe catches a soup ladle hanging from a shelf. It falls down into a metal sink with a loud clang. Crap! That got the guards' attention. Two of them immediately spring into action. Another comes around the corner to join the fun. The one who was eating stares longingly at his steak before grabbing his sword and helmet and joining his comrades.

Shine and friends have the numbers advantage, but as things get loud, that may change quickly. This needs to be ended quickly. Shine, Ed, and Julia advance into the dining room to meet their attackers while Marduk and Artemis hang back for support. The counters at the edge of the kitchen create a choke point. Only one soldier will be able to advance at a time if they break through the first line. One of the guards charges head on. He's targeting Ed.

That's something the thief is used to. He's been in more than a few scrapes, and the enemy always seems to pick on the small fry. Artemis tries to take out the charging guard with an arrow, but he knocks it away with his blade and continues. Ed easily rolls under the swing. It was a big mistake for the guard to charge in ahead of his comrades. Now our heroes have him flanked, and backup is too late. Shine takes a swing. It's blocked easily enough, but there's nothing stopping Ed from thrusting one of his fancy new daggers into a kidney. Verde gives his men decent quality armor but not enough to stop a powerful thrust from a razor-sharp blade. The guard cries in pain and crumbles to the ground. Ed is adept at hitting vital organs. Blood pours from the wound. If he receives aid soon, survival is possible, but in any case, the fight is over for him.

While Shine and Ed were dispatching the overzealous adversary, Julia stepped forward to cut off the other three. She is an intimidating sight with her giant axe, but the guards are unhindered. She takes a wide swing, attempting to take all three out at once. It takes two to stop the blow with swords. She is exposed, but the support crew is on it. When the free guard tries to flank, Artemis pierces his shoulder while Marduk casts Wind Burst. The wind isn't sharp enough to pierce the armor, but it pushes his target back. This grants Ed and Shine time to get into position.

Shine engages, which results in a sword duel. Ed tries to circle around to the other two enemies' rear and winds up in duel of his own as the middle guard manages to intercept the cunning thief. Julia takes another swing at the remaining opponent. It's aimed well enough, but the guard is in too close. He moves underneath and counters. Julia manages to turn her body enough to avoid the blade. There's a loud, metal scrape as it scratches her cuirass. She uses her bulk to push him away, but in the wrong direction. She acted on impulse, momentarily forgetting about the support behind her.

The guard sees his chance to attack the wizard and charges forward. Artemis hastily fires an arrow that's off the mark, nearly hitting Julia. Marduk angles his staff at the guard. The amber glows gently. The enemy slows from the sleep spell. Putting a charging enemy to sleep is far easier said than done. The guard presses forward but is abated to the point where Julia is able to get over. Holding her axe out horizontally with both hands, she lifts it up over the guard's head and guides the handle into his throat. She tries to choke him out while Marduk continues his spell. In seconds, their adversary succumbs to the combo.

Only two sentries remain. No, make that one as Ed slices his foe's throat with a spinning slash. Shine and his adversary's swords are locked, each trying to overpower the other. The guard is larger and stronger. He overpowers Shine, who ends up thrown to the side. He falls over body of the guard Ed just killed. Shine is exposed! If the enemy is quick, he can follow up with a strike before aid can come, or so he thinks. He makes it just one step forward before a fireball plows into his chest. Metal armor plus fire is a bad formula for the recipient. The metal quickly heats, searing the guard's body. He can't even scream as his body goes to shock, and he collapses.

It wasn't the cleanest battle, but the heroes managed to get through it unscathed. There's no time to revel in victory. The noise surely drew the attention of more guards. They quickly make their way across the dining room and out to a long hallway. They must be on the edge of the mansion because there's a wall immediately to the right of the door. Sounds of heavy footsteps and the glow of torches can be made out at the other end. More men are coming, and fast. The party heads through a door directly in front of them. From there, they quickly but quietly sneak through a series of large rooms filled with all sorts of elaborate décor. Five rooms in all, and there's a door leading to yet another. How huge is this place? This door slows them down a little as Ed has to pick the lock.

They head through and are now in an enormous library. The shelves are at least twelve feet high and completely encircle the room. There are several more evenly spaced throughout the middle. It feels like every book in Terra is there. The party begins to spread out to find the next door but stop suddenly as footsteps echo. They duck out of sight as a lone guard turns down an aisle and begins walking in their direction. The poor sap. He has no chance.

Ed cannot resist having some fun. He motions for Julia to circle around the other side of the shelf. He then proceeds to leap into plain view, waving his arms and making all sorts of weird noises. The odd appearance freezes the guard as his brain tries to process the strangeness that just appeared out of thin air. He quickly regains his composure and shouts, "What are ya doin' in here?" before moving towards the odd, little man. He freezes again as Julia knocks him out from behind with the butt of her axe. Even Marduk cannot help but to giggle in amusement.

Alright, enough fun and games. There's got to be an exit nearby. The library must be on the edge of the manor, as there are no doors leading in the same direction of the others. The party exits and find themselves in another hallway, or rather, the other end of the one they accessed from the dining room. They are at the opposite corner now as they continue forward. Before long there's a large set of ornately carved wooden doors. Assuming this means the front door is that way, they head through.

Now the heroes are in a foyer larger than most people's entire houses. Beautiful marble sculptures of knights and lions line the walls, glowing from the light of two parallel rows of candle stands. The stands line a long, red carpet. The candles aren't particularly bright, or maybe the room is just so massive it's dimly lit despite them all. Moonlight shines in as clouds part, making things brighter. Shine points forward as he just makes out another set of double doors on the other side of the room.

The group quickly makes their way to them. As they are about a third of the way across, a steely voice bellows from behind, bouncing off the marble walls, "Going somewhere?" They don't look back. Freedom is too close to deal with whoever is there. As they begin to run for the doors, a spear sails overhead and pierces the ground just in front. Eek! That could have easily impaled someone. No choice now, they have to turn and face this final foe.

Three guards are standing in the foyer. One has another spear in hand. As the men advance forward, the heroes recognize the orange plume on the helmet of the one holding the spear. The one opposite him seems to just be an average grunt. The one in the middle is who has the party's attention. It seems Orangey was a leader but not THE leader of the guards. How far does Verde's chain of command go? Anymore ranks and you'd have to call it an army.

The man in the middle is clad in heavy, red-colored armor. His helmet has a full guard not just a half like the rest, and the suit looks to be expertly crafted, embossed with beautiful curves and engravings. His helmet has a plume, too, only his is black. He is an impressive, intimidating sight with a voice to match. Stepping forward, flanked by his men, he repeats himself in a booming voice, "Going somewhere?"

Shine replies timorously, "Uh… Yeah, nice place 'n' all, but we really should be going."

"Aww… Really? You haven't even gotten the grand tour yet. First stop, the graveyard!"

Very few people can pull of making such a cheesy line sound so threatening. The three guards swiftly advance. The Grunt and Boss pull out their shortswords while Orangey leads with his long spear. The Boss hangs back a little and begins to glow. He seems to be casting a buff spell like the fairy in Verde's Woods. *This guy is a mage?* Shine thinks to himself. The other guards glow briefly, and the party feels a rush of energy emanate from the trio.

The Boss not only strengthened his own physical attributes but his comrades' as well. The heroes take defensive positions. Julia steps out in front flanked by Ed on the left and Shine on the right. Artemis and Marduk move back to their support positions. Artemis tosses the wizard a mana potion. It's too small a dose to fully rejuvenate him, but it should be enough to last through the battle. Artemis, on the other hand, is down to her last two arrows. She is going to have to make them count.

Julia slings the backpack behind her. The heroes face off against the guards. Orangey is the first to advance. He comes from the left using his reach advantage to create an opening for Grunt. He lunges the spear at Ed's chest. Picking on the little guy again, eh? The nimble thief effortlessly sidesteps the lunge as well the next two but cannot get close enough to counter. Grunt goes after Shine while Boss charges Julia.

Shine blocks with his shield, then he and Grunt clash swords, beginning a duel. Boss's sword crashes against Julia's axe. He is just as strong as her. No! He's stronger! Julia feels herself getting pushed back. Bossy significantly increased his crew's physical strength. Artemis and Marduk see she is in peril. The archer cannot get a good angle, but the wizard can. He scores a hit on Boss's shoulder with Wind Burst. It doesn't do much, but it's enough for Julia to be able to push her foe away.

Ed is forced to break rank, moving towards the left side of the room as he tries to find a good angle to advance on Orangey, but that damned spear is keeping him at bay. Luckily, he has a secret weapon. The thief pulls a smoke bomb from his pants pocket and whips it to the ground. No longer able to see his target, Orangey frantically thrusts his spear here and there into the dark cloud, but to no avail. His foe pops out in good striking position. He is in close, away from the point of the spear. From there, Ed rushes his foe. Orangey manages to pull the spear close, gripping it tightly in both hands now. He turns and blocks Ed's first strike. His increased strength pushes Ed away right as he sees a flash of light in his peripheral. Intuitively knowing an attack is coming, he tries to pivot to block but isn't fast enough.

Orangey is pelted by Marduk's Fireball. Normally just one is enough to fell an enemy wearing metal armor, but this is no ordinary fighter. Orangey is staggered by the blast yet still manages to block Ed's follow up and kick the thief away. Ed falls to one knee upon landing, wincing in pain. That strength buff is proving troublesome.

Meanwhile, it is three on two with Julia and Shine still squaring off against Boss and Grunt while Artemis gives support. The archer has been hesitant thus far not wanting to waste one her final two remaining shots. Boss is clearly the biggest threat. If they can swiftly take out the weaker grunt, it will be three on one, hopefully offsetting the power difference. Julia is holding her own, albeit barely. She and Boss are matching blows, but Boss's superior strength threatens to overwhelm. Each time their weapons collide, she is pushed back a little, which allows her opponent to attack continuously. It's only a matter of time before that sword finds its mark.

Shine and Grunt are at a stalemate. Shine is trying to keep a level head, but he cannot help feeling frustrated that a single low-ranking guard is giving him so much trouble. However, he does have his foe's full attention. Artemis can pick her spot and end it. She notches an arrow. As she draws the bowstring back, she whispers an incantation. Energy begins swirling around the arrowhead like a vortex. Closing one eye, she calmly locks on to her target and waits. The opportunity to strike soon comes.

Grunty pushes Shine away as their swords cross. Shine stumbles backwards. Seeing his chance, Grunt tries for a finishing blow. Shine manages to sidestep the downward slice but spills to the ground. As Grunt turns to follow up, he is facing Artemis almost square on. Without a moment's hesitation, she lets the arrow rip. A loud bang echoes throughout the room as if she'd fired a rifle.

The enchanted arrow blazes towards its mark. It doesn't just penetrate the armor, it shatters it like glass. The arrow lodges deep in the Grunt's chest. His ally's buff is the only reason he wasn't instantly killed. He even has enough strength to block Shine's next attack, but not the one after. He crumples onto the floor. Blood gushes from the wounds, and life quickly fades from his eyes.

That got Boss's attention. He couldn't care less about losing one lowly guard; however, he is keenly aware of the numbers disadvantage. He effortlessly kicks Julia away and slashes his sword at Shine. An arc of wind as sharp as his blade screeches towards the hero. Shine senses it coming at the last instant and dives out of the way. He screams out in pain as the wind slices deeply into his sword arm nearly causing him to drop Rashida. His shoulder slumps. It is going to be hard to continue this fight. Seeing her foe turned away, Artemis prepares her final arrow. Before she can take aim, Boss pivots toward her and sends another sharp gust flying. The archer dives out of the way. Julia attacks with a fierce downward strike. It catches her enemy off guard, and now she's the one able to continuously attack.

As Julia pushes Boss back, Artemis runs over to Shine who is still down on one knee. He is bleeding badly. It's not a fatal wound if treated quickly. It's serious enough where he may pass out from the loss of blood. Artemis takes his injured arm in her hands. "Let me help you." Her voice is so gentle yet so confidant. Shine instantly feels at ease. Her hands begin to glow softly as does the cut shortly after. Shine's eyes widen in amazement as the wound slowly heals. In a matter of seconds, it has closed completely. You couldn't even tell he had been sliced open. Artemis releases his arm and takes a step back. She is noticeably fatigued, struggling to catch her breath. Shines gets back to his feet and back into the fight.

As he hurries to aid Julia, Ed and Marduk still have their hands full with Orangey. The spearman has been holding his weapon close to the body allowing him to attack Ed and still be able to block the wizard's magic. Marduk shoots another Fireball. Orangey spins the spear with both hands at a frightening speed. The force generated stops the ball of flame in its tracks, blowing it out like a birthday candle. The wooden handle isn't even singed. Ed tries to flank but is caught right under the chin by the wooden end of the spear. It hurt like Hades, but the thief considers himself lucky. A spilt second sooner or later and it would have been the blade. The blow did generate some cobwebs, however. Seeing his enemy dazed, Orangey changes his stance, readying to thrust the spear into Ed's chest.

Marduk must act quickly. He uses his sleep magic to try and stop the attack. He succeeds! Orangey staggers a bit but remains upright. He desperately tries to shake off the spell. Marduk is running out of stamina fast and is forced to break the spell after a few moments. Those precious seconds were enough to allow Ed to go on the offensive. He springs into the air driving both daggers almost straight down at his foe. Orangey pulls his spear close and raises it to block. He is too slow. Both daggers find their mark on each shoulder. The strikes are perfect, piercing the slim, unprotected space between Orangey's neck and the edge of the armor. Blood spatters up from the wounds as he collapses onto both knees. From there it's elementary. Ed pulls his daggers from his foe and finishes things with a quick slice of the throat. A sickly gargle escapes Orangey as he falls dead to the floor.

Only one enemy remains! Shine and Julia manage to time their attacks well, keeping constant pressure on Boss. One of Shine's slashes even managed to contact their foe's chest plate, but the armor is too thick, leaving him unscathed. Artemis is locked on for her final Piercing Shot. Boss is staggered by one of Julia's strikes. She and Shine follow up in unison trying to deliver a fatal blow, but their opponent is just too powerful. He not only blocks both weapons with his, he shoves them both several feet back. His back is now completely turned to Artemis. She fires her final arrow.

Boss senses it is coming. In one fluid motion, he spins around, smacks the arrow out of the air like a gnat, continues spinning, and swings is blade low at Shine's legs thus countering Shine's counter. Out of pure instinct, Shine leaps into the air over the sweeping slash. Boss maintains momentum, twirling in another three sixty. Shine goes flying backwards as his enemy's spinning punch lands squarely in his chest whilst still in the air. The force of the hit sends him bouncing along the floor until finally rolling to a stop. His eyes roll back in his head as he lies crumpled on his side. All the wind has been knocked out of him. The only good news is he flew far enough to be well out of range of their foe's blade.

Regicide: Storm Cloud

Boss's incredible spinning move left him open. Julia approaches his rear and swings her axe downward as hard as she can. Boss moves forward just enough to keep the blade from hitting squarely. It contacts his shoulder. Against most people, it would have cut deeply, maybe even ended the battle, but Boss's armor takes the brunt. The attack barely draws blood. He pushes Julia away with his free arm and strikes with his blade. Julia tucks her stomach in, but she cannot completely avoid it. She winces in pain as it slices through her armor and into flesh. It's not too deep a cut, just a little bit deeper than the one she'd landed. Ed rushes over. He tries the same leaping strike that worked against Orangey. Boss is too quick and too strong. He effortlessly catches the thief midflight and tosses him like a ragdoll. Ed tumbles along the floor coming to a stop not far from Shine.

Things aren't looking good. Only one melee fighter is still standing. Artemis is out of arrows, and Marduk is low on mana. The one bright spot is Julia is strong enough to weather their enemy's fierce attacks. Even that won't last much longer. Someone is going to have to go something drastic to turn the tide, or it's all over. Marduk decides to pull out an old spell. He is gripped by anxiety. It has been a while since he's used it. This could easily fail or, worse, backfire.

He cautiously focuses his remaining mana into his staff. He'll only get one shot at this. Artemis makes her way over to Shine and Ed. Julia is taking Boss's attacks head on, but her strength is fading. She can only withstand a couple more attacks before her guard breaks, and her adversary knows it. Artemis only has enough energy left to heal one of her allies. Shine is already slowly getting back up, so she tends to Ed. The thief pops up to his feet. He sees Julia fading and charges in recklessly. There's no time for strategy. He just needs to draw the enemy's attention so Julia can recover. He thinks better of leaving his feet again and tries a combination of fluid strikes with dual blades. His foe blocks and counters; Ed rolls out of the way.

Marduk's spell is ready. The amber staff head sparks and crackles with electricity. With a mighty yell, the wizard thrusts his staff towards their enemy. A bolt of lightning zig zags through the air. Boss turns to face it, but there's nothing he can do except brace. A piercing buzz echoes throughout the room. The metal armor makes a perfect conduit, aiding the electricity in shocking Bossy. A combination of raw strength and sheer force of will is the only reason he can even still stand. Unfortunately for him, his muscles are paralyzed.

Shine rejoins the fight just in time to thrust his blade into their foe's back. The thick armor stops the blade from going too deep. Ed finds a soft spot and drives a dagger into one of the joints between plates. Finally, Julia lets out a bloodcurdling scream as she swings her axe upward at their foe's chest. The force of the swing sends Boss up into the air, and then crashing down hard onto his back. The thick armor provided enough protection to make the furious attack survivable, but he's barely conscious. This fight is over. Shine stands over him to make sure he doesn't get up again. Boss gasps, "But how...?" before passing out.

The heroes reconvene near the center of the room. They are battered and exhausted, but they survived. The others are all staring at Shine who can barely catch his breath from the pain and fatigue yet has a beaming smile on his face. "Yer awfully happy," Ed comments.

Still panting, Shine replies, "I can't help it. That was by far our toughest challenge, and we succeeded. I'd say things are looking up for us."

Marduk agrees, "Yes, yes. That was quite the skirmish. It felt good being in the flow of a heated battle once more. It has been a long while since I have been in combat. I can feel myself slowly regaining my magical prowess."

Shine nods. "That's good. It seems magic is a lot more common than I realized."

Marduk seems confused. "What do you mean?"

"Well, the guard leader used magic at the beginning of the fight, and Artemis used magic to heal me." He looks to Artemis and says, "I thought you said you couldn't use magic."

Marduk is the one to respond, "That was not magic they were using. It was chi."

Now Shine is the confused one. "Chi?"

Marduk laughs and says, "You really haven't seen much of the world have you, my boy? I'll explain it to you later. We shouldn't tarry here any longer."

The rest of the group agrees, and they head out of Verde's mansion. According to Artemis, Salem is the nearest town. It is to the north, and she knows the way. They should arrive by sunrise. On the way, Marduk explains to Shine the difference between magic and chi. Aesthetically, they look the same, but they come from hugely different sources.

Magic comes from the mind. It is mental energy manifested into physical form. Not everyone can use magic. One must be born a mage, and even then, it takes many years to hone and master. Magic has many different effects. It can take on elemental properties like Wind or Fire, be focused to increase magical or physical attributes, and even cause physical conditions, such as being poisoned or put to sleep. It is said the most powerful mages can revive someone from death or cause someone to die instantly, though Marduk has only heard tales of such feats.

Chi comes from potential energy stored in the body. Warriors can train to tap into this energy and use it at will. Because it uses one's own stored energy, anyone can use it. However, that doesn't make it easy to learn. It takes a high level of stamina and concentration to properly, effectively use chi. Overall, it isn't as powerful as magic, but it is more common. Like magic, it can take on elemental forms and buff physical attributes. It is most commonly used to increase the power of one's attacks like Artemis's Piercing Shot. A simple arrowshot suddenly becomes a devastating attack.

It can be difficult at first to tell whether someone is using magic or chi, but they have a distinctly different feel to them. Magic radiates outward and feels almost as if wind is blowing in every direction at once. It can feel anywhere from a gentle breeze to a gale. Chi feels heavy, like the gravity around the user increased. The stronger the chi, the larger the radius and more profound the effect. There are even legends that the strongest masters can crush their enemies to death with nothing more than the chi resonating from their bodies. As far as Marduk knows, these legends are just that, nothing but folk tales. It is a lot of information for Shine to take in. Learning it makes him all the more curious about the world. What other strange and wonderful things will he encounter? For a moment, he forgets all about his quest. ♛

CHAPTER 5
Witching Hour

Just as the sun begins to rise, the party reaches Salem. It is a small village about the same size of Hanover. It was built at the edge of the massive Crystal Lake, the largest lake in Elysia. The village has seen more than its share of misfortune over the last decade. The lake used to be pristine, filled with mineral water so pure it was said it could ward off disease. It was chock full of fish to boot. In the center of the lake, there is a small island with a cave.

The cave was filled with all sorts of various minerals, undoubtedly why the water contained them. With such a wonderous water source, crops flourished. The village is surrounded by woodlands providing lumber and game. Salem prospered from the trade these resources generated. The people were healthy and happy. No one knows how or why, but about ten years ago, Crystal Lake began to become stagnant. Now it is a dead swamp. Not even peat grows. All the fish have died, and the water is unpotable.

The minerals in the cave corroded in unnatural fashion, precipitating talk a curse has befallen the town. Crops withered. The number of wildlife slowly dwindled. The town was able to survive from a source of well water and by trading lumber for other resources. Even with the fresh well water, crops still would not grow. It is if the soil has been poisoned. The villagers concluded Salem must have been cursed. A divine punishment for their sins. When one enters Salem now, they feel a sense of dread and foreboding in the air.

Our heroes feel no differently while heading towards the inn. Something feels off about this place, but they are in desperate need of a hot meal and a long rest. If not for the faint light of the rising sun, it'd be pitch black outside. There are no streetlights. Not a single house has a lit candle. As the party turns and heads down a narrow path leading to the inn, a couple villagers rush past. One says to the other, "It's finally happening. Hurry." Despite being dead tired, the heroes have to see what's going on.

Those villagers looked scared. Something is amiss. They head back up the main road. Before long, they can see torchlights. People can be heard, but it's just muffled noise. It sounds panicked. Upon approach, they find themselves amongst a large crowd of people. It seems like the entire village is there. The gathering is surrounding a small shrine in the town center. The party pushes their way to the front. Whilst making their way through, one of the villagers snarls at Artemis, "Great, *you're* here, too."

Once at the front, they finally can see what all the fuss is about. A girl in a hooded black robe and long, matching hair is standing with her back against a statue of Theon, the god of the prominent religion, Theonism. She looks to be about the same age as Shine. A middle-aged, balding man with mostly grey hair is standing before her. She is terrified. As she eyes the outsiders, she desperately cries out, "Help! They're going to kill me!"

Shine frantically looks around the crowd. "What in Hades is going on here?"

A villager yells at the frightened girl, "What have you done with our children?"

Another points and accuses, "You killed them, didn't you?"

From the back, "I say burn her!"

Another chimes in, "Yeah! Let's get rid of her once and for all!"

Marduk looks to his friends. "This isn't good. They are really riled up. I think they may actually harm that girl."

Shine isn't about to let that happen. "Who's in charge here?" he demands.

The crowd ignores him. "Kill her!"

"Return our children, you monster!"

"You've caused us nothing but trouble!"

Ed looks around and realizes. "They're completely ignorin' us."

"I'll handle this," Julia responds. She takes a deep breath. "Ahem… ALL OF YOU, SHUT THE HELL UP!" The rabble stops. The villagers turn their focus to the outsiders.

"That got their attention," observes Shine. "Nice work, Julia." He addresses the mob, "Why are you all ganging up on this girl? Who's in charge here?"

The balding man standing opposite the girl turns around. He eyes the heroes through thick spectacles and answers, "I'm the mayor of this town. What are you people doing here?"

Julia fires back, "We could ask you the same thing. Who do you think you are attacking this girl?"

"That's none of your concern, outsiders," the mayor sternly replies. "This issue is between we villagers of Salem. Leave us to our business."

The mob's jeers pick up again, "You tell 'em, Mayor!"

"Yeah! Get the hell out of our town!"

Shine is fired up now. "Like Hades we will! No one's doing anything without explaining yourselves. If anyone makes a move on that girl, we won't hesitate to take them down." He turns to the mayor. "I suggest you calm your people down."

The mayor begrudgingly complies and explains the situation. He doesn't like outsiders nosing into Salem's matters but wants to prevent violence at all costs. Perhaps that can now be avoided. "Fine," he begins. "It's a bit of a long story. I've been the mayor of Salem for thirty or so years. We used to be a booming, prosperous settlement. A little over a decade ago, strange happenings befell our town. Our great Crystal Lake seemed to become poisoned by an unknown source. Almost all wildlife around the lake perished, and our pristine lake turned into a dead swamp in a decade's time. Our crops withered and died. On top of all that, healthy people began developing deformities. Then children were being born with them."

"Get to the point," Julia demands impatiently.

The mayor continues, "It would seem a dark curse has befallen our village. We've been desperately trying to figure out its source."

Shine raises an eyebrow in skepticism. "And you think this girl has something to do with that curse?"

Someone in the crowd shouts, "That's right! She's an evil witch!"

"Now she's stolen our children!"

"Give them back!"

The frightened girl pleads, "That's insane! I wasn't even a villager here when all this started! Why are you all so afraid of me?"

Shine needs to backtrack to ensure he understands. "Okay, slow down. One thing at a time. So, there's a curse and now missing children, and you think she is involved even though she wasn't even a villager here when everything started. Is that right?"

The mayor replies, "Correct. Wendy is an orphan. We found her alone in the woods, half-starved, seven years ago. The lake and crops were already beginning to die."

Ed scratches his head. "'Kay. I'm confused. Howdya come to the conclusion she's the cause?"

"Because of her abilities. You see, Wendy practices black magic."

The mob starts up again, "That's right! She's a witch!"

"A witch!"

Shine looks at the girl. "It's Wendy, is it? Is that true?"

She nods. "Yes, it's one of my hobbies. These people think my magic is evil, but it's really no different than any other magic. Even if I was skilled enough to cast curses, why would I curse my own home?"

Another wild accusation flies out from the mob, "Because you're evil! You were plotting against us before we ever found you, weren't you? You probably killed your parents so we'd take you in!"

Another villager piles on, "You were trying to infiltrate our village! Now you stole our children! How could you?"

Shine asks the mayor, "What's this about missing children?"

"Lately, several of our children went missing. We don't really know much more than that. However, there have been reports of a large bear roaming around the village. With everything that has happened, our people are on edge. I can't say for sure if Wendy is the cause of everything or not, but people are scared. They're ready to jump to any possible conclusion. I've tried my hardest to keep the peace, but now with our children going missing, I fear the villagers are at their breaking point."

"So, you're going to condemn this girl without a shred of evidence?" Shine counters.

"I'm saying I might not be able to stop everyone this time."

The mob is growing restless. "Enough talk!" someone yells. "Let's kill her and put an end to this!"

Artemis meekly tries to voice her opinion, "Um… Excuse me…?"

Another villager shouts, "Yeah! Burn the witch!"

Artemis tries again, "Hey… You guys…"

"Burn her!"

"HEEEEYYYYY!" Artemis screams at the top of her lungs. That quiets the crowd, at least for the moment.

"Who's that?" asks a villager.

Someone replies, "Is that Artemis?"

A snide voice from the back says, "Great... Now there's two freaks to deal with."

Shines turns to Artemis. "Artemis, you're from here?"

She begins to blush as she answers, "I am. I mean— Well... I was." She addresses the crowd, "Don't you people see? You all did the same thing to me. You drove me out of town, too. Nothing changed. You all have to stop pointing fingers at people and work together to find the real reason."

The party is shocked by this news. Shine is concerned. "Artemis... Why didn't you say something sooner?" He feels bad bringing her back into the town that shunned her.

Artemis casts her eyes downward. "I-I thought if you knew I was banished, you'd all abandon me, too. You all seemed so nice, I didn't... I just wanted to travel with you."

"You idiot," Shine softly assuages.

"Shine..."

"You fought alongside us to get out of Verde's manor. You could have run off afterwards, but you guided us here so we could rest. As far as I'm concerned, you're one of us now."

"That's right!" Ed encourages. Julia and Marduk reassure her, too.

Artemis wipes a tear from her eye before saying, "You guys... I don't know what to say."

"Ahem!" the mayor interjects. "I'd hate to break up this touching moment, but we have an important matter to get back to."

Shine replies, "These two problems seem to be one and the same. What reason did you have for exiling Artemis? Do you think she's a witch, too?"

"No. As I mentioned before, people were developing physical deformities. Many became hideously disfigured, turning into twisted husks of their former selves. With all that was happening, these poor souls who became known as Outcasts were not well received. I exiled them to the island at the center of the lake. It has a giant cavern so at least they have some shelter."

Shine cannot hide his distain. "What?! You didn't even try to help them?!"

"Please understand. The villagers wanted to burn them alive. I didn't want to exile them, but I had little choice. I doubt any other town would take them in. At least there's food and shelter in the cave."

Julia expresses her displeasure, "It sounds like these people aren't very good at handling a crisis."

The mayor continues, "After everything, mass hysteria is to be expected. So far, I've at least managed to stop any blood from being shed."

Ed has a question for Artemis, "Where's yer parents anyway? Didn't they try to help you?"

"Th-They died a few years ago. Of scarlet fever."

"I'm sorry to hear," Shine consoles. He turns his attention back to the mayor. "There's one thing I don't understand. It sounds like you're saying Artemis was exiled due to a deformity, but she looks pretty normal to me."

Artemis is the one to answer, "Oh, you didn't notice?" She pushes her hair back. "See my ears? They're pointy like a fairy."

Shine had in fact noticed this but didn't think anything of it. Anger wells up inside him. "Your ears? That's all? You people banished her for something so petty!?" The mayor tries to explain, but Shine cuts him off. "I don't give a damn! You people are so ignorant, you'll condemn someone over nothing rather than try and figure out the real cause of your problems! Nothing changed when you exiled Artemis, so now you turn and blame someone else. I've heard enough. No one is going to lay a finger on Wendy until we figure exactly what's going on here."

Someone in the crowd tries to argue, "This is none of your business, outsider. We sh—"

"Shut up! If anyone takes a single step towards us, I'll cut you down myself!"

The crowd murmurs. Eventually someone walks over to the mayor. "These people look serious. What's the call, Mayor?"

The mayor takes a few moments to assess things before replying, "I agree with the outsiders."

The villager steps back in shock. "What?!"

Another villager protests, "You're not serious, are you? For all we know, she summoned them here. This could just be more of her black magic!"

"Enough!" the mayor shouts adamantly. "I refuse to pass judgment on Wendy until we can prove she's to blame. We've done enough finger pointing."

Marduk is relieved the mayor chose peace. "Thank you, Mayor. I am happy to see you are more level-headed than your villagers. I have a proposal for you."

"I'm listening."

"The issue of the missing children seems to be the village's most immediate problem. What if we find them for you?"

"You would do that for us?"

"The villagers have lost their objectivity. You need a fresh set of eyes and ears in order to address this issue. Additionally, it will go a long way in proving Wendy's innocence. You said earlier a large bear had been seen near the village. Do you think it could be what took the children?"

"It's possible. The animals around here have been acting strangely for a while now. I wouldn't rule it out."

"Great," Shine replies. "We have a lead. How about it, Mayor? Will you let us help you?"

The mayor nods in agreement. "Yes, I think that's the best course of action."

"Good. I just have one condition."

"Name it."

"We take Wendy with us. It's obvious she's not safe here."

The mob groans and grunts. They don't like that suggestion. "Don't do it, Mayor! They'll let her escape!"

"She's probably a shapeshifter! I bet *she's* the bear!"

The mayor holds his ground, "I have made my decision. These outsiders will take Wendy with them and try to find what happened to our children. Everyone, return to your homes at once!"

Disapproving grumbles rumble from the crowd as they begrudgingly disperse. One of them sounds relieved, "Phew! I really thought things were going to get violent this time."

Someone else seethes, "You're making a big mistake, Mayor."

Wendy walks up to her saviors. "Thank you. I don't know what they would've done if you hadn't shown up."

Shine replies, "Don't mention it. I wasn't about to let them judge you without any proof. For now, you're with us. Do you have any idea where to find this bear?"

"I'm not sure, but there's a small cavern southwest of here. It'd be a good place to look."

Ed yawns and stretches. "So much fer gettin' some shut eye. No rest for the wicked."

Shine says to Wendy, "Sounds good." He looks directly into her eyes. "By the way, if you really are some evil witch, I'll kill you myself."

Wendy's eyes quiver. "Umm…"

Shine smiles and replies, "If you're innocent, you have nothing to worry about, right?"

"Yeah. I just wasn't expecting you to say something like that."

With the crowd fully dispersed, the mayor is ready to take his leave. "You seem to have everything under control here. If you find anything, I'll be at my house. It's the large stone one."

"Will do," Shine replies. He formally introduces himself to Wendy as does everybody else.

"Julia. It's nice to meet you."

"Edward. Master thief and protector of damsels in distress."

Wendy awkwardly responds, "Right…"

"Just ignore him," Julia advises.

Marduk and Artemis say hello, and Wendy introduces herself, "My name's Wendy. It's nice to meet all of you and thanks again."

Shine smiles and says, "Don't worry about it. Let's go! ♛

CHAPTER 6
Unforgiven

As the group exits Salem, Artemis spots a quiver propped up along the side of a house. She "borrows" a half dozen arrows in case this becomes a hunting trip. Wendy guides the heroes, heading southwest through the woods. It's about an hour and a half walk to the cave. During the journey, Julia is wanting to know something. "I'm curious, Wendy. You don't seem to have any parents either. Did the fever claim them as well?"

"No. As far as I know, they're still alive and kicking. We were passing through Salem on the way to Caddis. We were moving there. Shortly after we left Salem, I got this really nasty rash all over my body. With all the talk of people developing deformities, my parents thought I had as well. *Sooo*, they freaked out and abandoned me in the woods. Some villagers from Salem eventually found me. I was too ashamed to tell them I was abandoned, so I said wolves ate my parents."

"Damn," comments Julia. "They abandoned their own daughter? Hearing that makes me feel like they should have been mauled by wolves. Oops! I'm sorry."

"It's okay. I made my peace with it. I've been taking care of myself since then."

Shine gives his two cents, "That makes you an easy target to scapegoat. I think this is the most depressing place on Terra. Let's find these kids as quickly as possible. I don't want to stay here any longer than we have to."

The party eventually reaches the cave. There are fresh tracks leading inside, so it's time to go spelunking. The sun has completely risen, but it does little to light the cavern. Julia takes a torch out the backpack and lights it. The party ventures in. They hear a low grumble. It's a small cave, so it only takes them about a minute to find the source. Julia slowly lays the torch down as they see a very large bear near the cave wall. It is staring down a frightened boy. "That's one big ol' bear," Ed remarks.

Marduk advises caution. Something doesn't seem quite right about this beast. "Something seems off about it," he warns. "Its movements are strange, and its eyes are red. Be on guard." The party readies their weapons. Julia shouts at the bear to get its attention. It turns away from the boy, who scrambles behind a rock. The beast stops just a few feet before the heroes. Standing on its hind legs, it lets out a deafening roar. As it returns to all fours, four cubs emerge from a room behind it. They look normal enough, but instead of hiding behind Momma, they join her, two on each side. They growl threateningly. How strange. Shine is reminded of the mice he saw as he left Hanover. Salem's mayor is the second person to warn about the wildlife, and the is the second strange encounter with fauna. What is happening in Elysia?

There's no time to ponder. The heroes decide to attack first. Marduk prepares his flurry of fireballs. Five balls of flame, five targets. Wendy focuses magic into her staff as well. Artemis draws an arrow back. She whispers a different incantation. This time, the arrowhead turns an icy blue. Shine and Ed charge the cubs nearest Momma while Julia takes her head on. One of the other cubs swipes at Shine as he attacks its sibling. Artemis releases her arrow at its feet. As it pierces a front leg, ice explodes from the head encasing both the cub's front legs in ice. It struggles to break free to no avail. That should keep it a bay for a couple minutes. With the assist, Shine makes quick work of his target.

Ed lands a blow on his but has to fall back as he is double teamed. Julia just barely avoids Momma's obscenely long claws. The party hears Marduk shout to get down. They quickly oblige, and the wizard launches his attack. Two fireballs collide with the cubs Ed was dealing with. Another hits the one with frozen legs. The other two were on line to hit Momma, but she lets out another earth-shaking roar so powerful, it destroys them. It also sends the party flying backwards.

With the cubs dealt with, only Momma remains. Her body begins to glow. Shine feels the air growing heavy. Did she just use chi? Momma charges at him with exceptional speed. She swipes a huge paw at his head. Shine manages to block with Rashida but is sent flying back again. He ends up right between Artemis and Marduk. Momma charges the three of them. Artemis fires an arrow into one of her front legs, barely slowing her. Wendy fires a ball of black mana. It explodes against Momma's head, but she keeps right on coming. Marduk looses a flash of bright light from his staff. That stopped her!

As Momma growls and shakes her head in pain, Julia moves in from the rear. Before she can attack, she hears Ed behind her, "'Xcuse me!" He leaps onto her shoulders and springboards onto Momma's back. The beast bucks like a bronco as Ed drives his daggers deep. Julia nearly cleaves off a hind leg with her axe. Momma's legs buckle; her head drops. Shine thrusts Rashida into her skull to end things. It was a fairly easy battle, but an odd one.

Julia is the first to comment, "Damn, that thing was tough. You weren't kidding about it not being normal."

"It was a frightening creature indeed," confirms Marduk. "It almost seemed like it was possessed by something."

Wendy adds, "The animals around here have been acting strangely lately. Even deer are getting aggressive. Oh well, the important thing is it's dead, and that child is safe."

"Right," agrees Shine. "We should look around and see if any other children are here."

"Uh oh. That's not a good sign," Ed murmurs forebodingly.

"What is it?" Artemis worries.

Ed picks up something off the ground. "It's a hat. Looks pretty torn up."

Marduk strokes his beard. "That is most troubling. Wendy, how many children went missing?"

"Uh, four."

Shine eyes the boy warily peeking from behind the rock. "Hopefully, there's three more kids here. This poor guy is still shaking. We should comfort him."

Wendy beckons the boy. After much hesitation, he slowly walks over still shaking with fear. As soon as Wendy tries to talk to him, he bursts out crying.

Artemis frowns and frets, "Aww… The poor thing is terrified."

Wendy tries to console him. She speaks gently, nearly whispering, "Shhhh… It's okay. You're safe now. That monster can't hurt you anymore."

The boy sniffles and tries to speak, "I-I-I was so scared. I-I thought it was gonna eat me."

"We're just happy we got here in time. Can you tell us your name?"

"J-Jo-John."

"Nice to meet you, John. Are there any other kids in here?" John bursts into tears once more.

"That's not a good sign," Shine muses.

Julia feels the same. "I hope that doesn't mean what I think it does."

Wendy tries talking to John again, "I know this is difficult, but you have to tell us what happened. Are all the other kids safe?" John sniffles and shakes his head no. "That's good, John. You're doing great. Now, how many other kids are with you?"

"...Two."

"One short..." Artemis sadly concludes.

Wendy can't help but to hesitate before asking the most important question, "John...? Did something happen to one of the kids?" He nods his head. "Did the bear get one of them?" He nods again.

"Damnit," Ed grumbles with ire.

Julia's heart sinks. "We were too late..."

Wendy asks John, "Where are the other kids?" He turns and points. There's another chamber.

"Okay. Follow us, John. We're going to get the other kids and get out of here. Okay?"

Julia scoops up the torch, and the party heads inside. This chamber is smaller than the other. The torch provides enough light to fully illuminate it. They spot two kids, a boy and girl, sitting against the back wall. A grim visage is with them. Bloodstained bones lay in a corner. They're small, like a child's, and nearly picked clean, clothing and all. Artemis has to turn her head away.

The girl meekly asks, "Is the monster gone?" The boy is too scared to say anything. The heroes collect the children and head out of the cave. Ed gives the girl a piggyback ride all the way back to Salem. Upon returning, the kids immediately run home. The party walks to the mayor's house to deliver the bittersweet news. They find the mayor going over some documents in his study. He rises to greet them.

"Welcome back. Did you find the children?"

"We did," Wendy affirms. "It turns out a giant bear did take them."

"Is that so?" the mayor ponders. "How odd. Why would a bear kidnap children?"

Shine shrugs and says, "We're not sure. My best guess is that food is getting scarce for it, just like in town. It was probably stocking up."

The mayor isn't convinced. "An interesting theory. Still, bears simply don't behave that way. If anything, it would have killed its prey right in the village."

"It was certainly no ordinary bear," Marduk explains. "Its eyes were glowing red, and it was moving erratically. When we fought it, it was much stronger than an average bear. Frighteningly strong. It even used chi. It seems there may be more to this curse after all."

The mayor responds rejectingly, "Chi, you say? I highly doubt that. Anyway, you dealt with this bear, and Wendy was with you the entire time?"

Shine nods. "Yep. She fought alongside us."

"Are all of the children safe?"

There is a long, awkward silence before Wendy sullenly delivers the news, "We were too late. The bear got one of the children." She shows the mayor the tattered hat. "This is all that remained."

The mayor is clearly saddened. "That's Bill's favorite hat. No doubt about it. How unfortunate."

"Yeah…" Wendy empathizes. "I'm not looking forward to breaking the news to his family."

Shine asks the mayor, "Are you convinced that Wendy is innocent now?"

"In my eyes, she's absolved of all blame. I sincerely doubt a single person could have the power to cause everything that's happened, and there's no evidence at all. Unfortunately, I also doubt the villagers will blame her any less."

Wendy already knows this. There's no way the people of Salem will ever trust an interloper like her. She doesn't hate them for it. If anything, she pities them. She speaks to the mayor, "That's okay. I don't plan on sticking around here any longer. I think it's best if I leave."

"I hate to see you leave under these circumstances, but I agree it would be for the best."

"Where do you plan on going?" Shine inquires.

"Well, I don't really have a plan. I was hoping I could travel with you guys for a bit."

Shine smiles. "I have no issue with that. If there's no objections, welcome to our party." Everybody nods in agreement.

Wendy's eyes light up. "Thank you! I've been meaning to ask where you are traveling to. You aren't exactly run-of-the-mill travelers."

Shine decides it's best to fill her in after they've concluded their current business. "We're on an important quest, but that's a conversation for later."

That's good enough for Wendy, who gladly replies, "Sure. I'm just happy I have a place to go."

Ed sidles up to her and expresses, "And I'm happy I have another pretty girl to talk to."

Wendy isn't sure how to reply. "Aww…" She delays. "That's sweet, but I like my men… taller."

Shine busts out laughing, "You have no luck with women do you, Ed?"

The mayor gets things back on track, "I don't mean to be rude, but if you have no other business to discuss, I must ask you to take your leave."

"Oh, sure," Shine replies sheepishly. "We'll get out of your hair."

As the party turns to exit, Artemis speaks up, "Um… Actually, there was something I wanted to ask you." The group turns back toward the mayor, curious to what this could be about.

"Go ahead, child," the mayor answers with a hint of impatience.

"I've heard rumors that there is still some pure mineral water deep inside of Crystal Cave. Is that true?"

"I'm sorry, that rumor is just that, a rumor. It's far too dangerous to explore the lower levels, and the Outcasts aren't exactly fond of us." The rest of the party has no idea what in Hades is going on.

Julia queries, "Okay, I'm lost. What are you two talking about?"

Shine adds, "Yeah, why do you need mineral water?"

The mayor elucidates, "I don't know if you saw the island at the center of the lake. It used to house many beneficial minerals. So many that we made a great a deal of money mining and trading them. The minerals would also end up in the lake water, purifying it to the point where people claimed simply drinking it could cure illness and ward off evil itself. At the same time the lake began dying, the minerals seemed to disappear, too. At first, we just thought we mined them all, but every new area we tried had few, if any, minerals. We eventually gave up on mining altogether."

"That is very strange," Marduk distresses. "How could the minerals disappear?"

"Saying they disappeared isn't an apt description. It's more like they changed. They lost all their luster and are barely recognizable from the cavern itself. They lost all their properties as well."

Shine is beginning to understand why the people of Salem are the way they are. "Knowing all that's happened here, it's hard to blame the villagers for being so freaked out. A lot of stuff that shouldn't happen… happened."

"Poetically put," comments Ed.

"Shut up," Shine snipes before asking Artemis, "You still haven't explained why you want the mineral water."

"I need it to save King Vanajit." Shine has no idea who that is. Luckily for him, everything he needs to know is about to be explained.

Marduk is even more curious now. "Vanajit? The Fairy King?"

No one is prepared for what Artemis tells them. "When you guys found me, I was returning from trying to speak with him. The fairies have always been kind to me, so I thought maybe I could talk some sense into him, but the path to the palace was blocked off, and the fairies refused to help. They told me he didn't want to speak with me. They said he's sick and tired of people wandering through his woods. The fairies have always been mischievous, but they never attacked people until recently. It's like he's become cursed by something. It's said there's a spring hidden in the deepest part of Crystal Cave with water so pure, it can even lift curses."

As insane as that sounds, Shine believes her. "There seems to be a lot of talk about curses lately. Strange events are definitely taking place. Before I left my home, I would have said you were crazy, but now… I suppose it wouldn't hurt to try."

Artemis's eyes glow with excitement. "Really? You'll help me?"

Shine nods and warmly replies, "Of course. We're your friends. How about it, Mayor? Can we check out Crystal Cave?"

"No one calls it by that name anymore," replies the mayor. "Since we banished the Outcasts there, it took a much more solemn name, the Cave of Lost Souls. I see no reason to prevent you from exploring it. If the rumor is true, maybe it will give Salem some hope once again. Talk to the boatman, Hans. He'll give you a boat. Oh! I almost forgot. I wanted to give you something for your trouble."

The party politely declines, but the mayor insists. He walks into the next room and soon returns. He hands Shine a small pouch of coins. "I'd like to give you more, but our village simply cannot spare it. This is from my personal savings." Reward in hand, the party exits the mayor's house. Wendy wants to stop by her house before they continue. The party is exhausted. They decide to rest and relax at the inn for the rest of the day. They can go exploring tomorrow. Wendy heads home. She will meet them by the pier.

As they party enters the inn to get some much-needed rest, Shine pulls Artemis aside. He says to her, "I think it's about time I told you what our mission is. We're heading to King Pious's castle. To kill him."

Artemis takes a step back. She anxiously probes, "Kill him…? Why?" Shine does his "tyrant" spiel he is getting very comfortable reciting. This time there is a pressing question he must know the answer to. As he finishes his speech, Artemis is clearly uncomfortable. "I agree he needs to be removed from power, but killing him?"

"Does he strike you as the type that will change his ways if we just ask nicely?"

"…I suppose not."

"Look, I get that you're not comfortable taking lives. I'll understand if you want to part ways here. However, if you do stay, a situation may arise where you will have to deal the killing blow. If you're not capable of that, then you shouldn't come with us."

Artemis can barely muster a response, "I… I'm not sure…"

"That's understandable. We have plenty of time for you to decide before we reach Leed's Castle. For now, let's get some rest." They retire with the rest of the crew. ♛

CHAPTER 7
Meet the Outcasts

The next day our heroes set out for the Cave of Lost Souls. First, they stop to stock up on supplies. Julia's armor is sliced open, and Shine needs a new shield. The crack has widened across the entire width. The party could use some more food, too. The Cave of Lost Souls is a big place. It could take days to find this spring, assuming it even exists. The reward they received for saving the children covers their expenses.

The general store adds to the depressing ambience. Many shelves are bare. The heroes almost feel guilty purchasing rations the villagers may need more. They only take a couple days' worth of food. That with what they already have will have to last until they reach a more prosperous vista. Shine also purchases some new pants. Cotton is far from ideal combat attire. Now he is sporting more durable spider silk pants. Spider silk provides similar protection as leather but tends to resist magic a bit better.

Onto a shop that sells armaments. It isn't much better for the opposite reason. This store is well stocked because nobody has purchased anything in a good while. Many pieces are collecting dust. Shine purchases a bronze round shield and a bronze chainmail top. He immediately feels more secure with this flesh covered by metal. Chainmail is much lighter than platemail, too, so his movement won't be encumbered. Julia ditches her bronze cuirass for a leather set. The deciding factor was she really likes the leather boots it comes with. This new armor won't offer as much protection, but it's lighter. She noticed her moves have been a bit sluggish. This should remedy that. She was also concerned about magic. She saw what Marduk's spells did to their metal clad enemies, and she'd rather not get burned alive by a mage.

The rest of the party is satisfied with their current gear. Artemis purchases some more arrows. With such a hearty supply of wood, they are cheap here, plus she got a nice discount. It turns out that John's father owns the shop. She is now stocked with two dozen arrows. Gear upgraded, the group heads to the pier on the north side of town. Wendy is awaiting them.

There is a boathouse nearby and a small, out-of-the-way house near it. That must be where Hans lives. As the heroes approach, Hans is busy chopping wood. His daughter is sitting on the ground playing with dolls. Wait a sec! That's the girl from the cave. As Hans puts down his axe to greet the guests, his daughter tells him just who they are. With a beaming smile on his face, Hans strides over to the heroes. His daughter is not far behind. She shyly thanks them before running back to her dolls. Hans is more than happy to rent a boat to the rescuers without asking for a single coin in return. What they did for his family is something he could never repay, so it's the very least he can do. It will be tight quarters with six people on such a small boat, but it will suffice. Julia volunteers to row. After all, she is the strongest of the group.

The lake is huge. It will take a while to reach the island. Shine takes the opportunity to inform Wendy of their quest. She is curiously blasé about it. As Julia rows, Wendy tells them a bit about her magic. Everyone is interested to learn why the villagers are so afraid of her. Black magic sounds like something an evil warlock or a demon would use, not a sixteen-year-old girl. It isn't intrinsically evil despite its name. It is the counterpart of light or Holy magic. Holy magic is the power of creation. It is used primarily to heal people, but it can be manifested into a deadly force. For example, templars can focus Holy magic into their blades making them unnaturally sharp.

The black or Dark magic Wendy uses is destruction incarnate. It shatters the bonds of matter itself, making it extremely dangerous to wield. It can also be used to cast curses. It is hard to tell where fact ends and myth begins, but the stories go, Dark magic can be used to cause blight or serious illness, fatigue, and even death itself. Wendy can use it to poison people. It comes in handy if you want to debilitate someone. Her reputation forced her to learn to defend herself, and she's had to do it more than once. After a while, people learned not to mess with her and left the young witch in peace. Up until the children went missing, all she had to deal with is accusing stares and whispers of her alleged malfeasance.

Like with all mages, her staff aids to augment her magic, especially her Poison spell. It was crafted from a willow tree and adorned with a hunk of enchanted sapphire. When Dark mana is applied to a crystal or gem, its properties reverse. Instead of sapphire warding off illness, it helps to cause it. It's frightening traveling with someone with such abilities. Everyone is happy she is on their side.

As Wendy finishes scaring the hell out her new friends, the rowboat reaches the island shore. As they step onto solid ground, the surroundings seem innocuous. There's no evidence it's inhabited. A steep hill leads to the cavern's maw. The island isn't particularly large, but the caverns extend deep underground. The area above ground is merely the tip of the iceberg. The party lights a torch, but it is soon clear it isn't necessary. Torches line the cave walls of the long tunnel, plus there's a few lit stands scattered about the floor.

Julia extinguishes theirs and puts it back in the pack. Rail tracks mark the trail deeper into the system. Before long they find the inhabitants, the Outcasts, when the tunnel ends in a large, well-lit chamber. There are tents all along the walls and even a poorly crafted wooden cabin. A huge bonfire burns in the center. A large cauldron rests above it bubbling with some strange-smelling stew.

The denizens look strange. There must be at least thirty. Their clothing is ragged, skin all different shades of green. They peer curiously to see who ventured into their home but warily keep distance. Even from afar, the heroes can clearly see the deformities the mayor spoke of as they walk through the chamber. Many have pointed or otherwise misshapen ears. Some faces are twisted and contorted. One looks to be in constant joy, another in pain. Another has a hunchback, and quite a few have mismatched limbs in both length and muscle tone.

As the party approaches the other side, they spot a gate closing this chamber off from the rest of the cavern. The rail tracks lead that way, too. There's a minecart not far from the gate. The Outcasts probably use the carts to transport supplies. They head over to the gate. A single Outcast is standing guard. He's holding a spear with a warped wooden handle, and the metal tip has some rust on it. He was casually leaning against the wall but stands in attention as they approach. Shine says to him, "We need to get through here."

Without missing a beat, the guard deadpans, "Not happening."

Shine persists, "We have permission to explore the cave from the mayor of Salem."

"He has no jurisdiction here. He lost that right when he exiled us to this damned cave."

"We spoke to him about that. It seems like he didn't have any other options."

"You're barking up the wrong stalagmite, buddy. If you really want to enter the inner caverns, talk to our leader, Conway. Be warned, he doesn't like outsiders very much."

The party considers simply beating the guard up, but this is unfamiliar territory. Who knows what lies ahead? Diplomacy is the more appealing option. Conway isn't hard to find. He is sitting on a throne that looks like it was carved from the cave itself. He is an odd sight, which is saying something considering how the rest of the Outcasts look. Though he's sitting, it's obvious Conway is quite tall. Not six or even seven feet either, he's at least eight. His skin is dark green. His clothes are slightly less ragged than the rest. His body is slender. It doesn't look like he has an ounce of body fat.

Even stranger, a huge hammer even taller than him rests on its head alongside the stone throne. Its handle is thick and made of some type of dark wood. The head is solid iron. It must be incredibly heavy. That's this lanky dude's weapon? As the party approaches, the other Outcasts quietly make their way closer to see what unfolds. Conway wastes no time. "What are you outsiders doing here?" he crossly demands.

"We came to explore the cavern," answers Shine. "We're investigating a rumor."

Conway folds his lanky arms across his chest. "A rumor? You must be talking about the hidden spring."

"Exactly. Do you know anything about it?"

"Not really. Not like I'd tell you if I did. We don't like your kind pokin' around in here. Leave before I force you to do so."

Marduk tries to reason with him, "We heard what happened to your people. I'm truly sorry for your plight. I assure you we come in peace."

"I couldn't care less what your intentions are. The moment we were exiled was the moment we severed all ties to the outside world. We've adapted to life here. We're finally beginning to prosper. I'll be damned if I let some outsiders destroy what we've worked so hard to achieve."

"We mean you no harm," pleads Artemis. "I've heard the spring contains water that can dispel evil itself. I need it to save someone. If the stories are true, that water might be able to help everyone, including you."

Conway doesn't budge, "I already told you, we're content with our life here. Now please leave while I'm still in a good mood."

Shine sighs and surrenders, "It looks like there's no way he's going to let us explore. Sorry, Artemis. These people have been through enough. Let's leave them in peace." Conway's ears perk up at the sound of the name he just heard. Artemis disappointingly agrees with Shine.

As the party begins to take their leave, Conway stops them. "Hold on a sec. You, the blonde girl. He just called you Artemis, didn't he?"

"Yes, that's right."

Conway places his hand on his chin as he leans forward in his throne. "Your ears... They're pointy. I'd recognize those ears anywhere." After a brief pause, he begins to laugh. "Hahaha! You were pint sized the last time I saw you. Look at you now. It would seem you've been spared from our affliction."

Blushing, Artemis timidly replies, "Um... Thank you. I don't mean to be rude, but do I know you?"

"You were pretty young back then. My skin wasn't green back then either. It's natural that you wouldn't remember me. We were all banished here while you were still a child. Have you been living in Salem this whole time? How are your parents?"

Artemis still has no idea who this man is, but it's clear he knows her well. "...They died," she sadly answers. "Scarlet fever. I left shortly after. I would have been exiled, too, if I hadn't. That's why we're here. Strange things seem to be happening everywhere, not just in Salem. I'm trying to find the spring to try to help everyone."

"I see. So, even your cute, pointy ears were deemed unacceptable. Bastards! I truly don't care what happens to that town or the world. However, you were innocent. I don't know if it's your kind nature, or if you were simply too young to be jaded into judging people by their looks, but you were always kind to us Outcasts. Speaking of looks, you have quite an interesting entourage. How did you come to meet these people?"

"Umm... Well, let's see... I was returning from Verde's Woods. I was trying to get an audience with King Vanajit. He seems to be afflicted by some dark force. I decided to head back to Salem to try to find the spring so I could help him. Upon leaving, I was arrested by Verde's guards. Lord Verde had closed off the woods. They accused me of plotting to steal from the manor. They threw me in the dungeon. About a day later, these people were captured for the same reason. They helped me escape, and we've been traveling together ever since."

Conway takes a long gaze at the heroes before addressing them, "Is this true?"

Shine confirms, "Yes. It turns out this shy, innocent-looking girl is one hell of a fighter when need be."

Conway is appreciative. "I'm glad to know there's still some goodness left in the world. As far as exploring the caverns goes, you'll still need to prove yourselves."

Shine quizzically looks at Conway. "Prove ourselves? How?"

"There are many powerful, dangerous creatures in these caves. We fought tooth and nail just to secure this room. Shortly after, the creatures have left us alone for the most part. We're not sure if they got used to our presence, or we just don't taste very good, but they'll likely be highly aggressive towards you. If you're not strong enough, they'll tear you to shreds. That's why you must fight me. If you can defeat me, I'll let you pass." Conway stands up. His lanky frame towers over the party. He takes that massive hammer and effortlessly lifts it from the ground with one hand. He slings it over his shoulder and awaits their decision.

Shine asks, "Six on one, Conway? That doesn't seem fair."

"It's not," Conway smugly ripostes, "for you."

Wendy tries catch him off guard by quickly striking with her Dark Ball. Shine, Ed, and Julia charge in to follow up and overwhelm their opponent. Conway easily blocks the Dark magic with his hammer head. He maneuvers his body and twirls the hammer to swat Ed and Shine away. He sidesteps Julia using her own momentum against her, shoving her away. He arches his spine and head back and to the left as an arrow whizzes by. Marduk shoots his lightning bolt. Conway points the head of his hammer at the surge, and it harmlessly disperses as it collides with the iron. The wooden handle safely insulates the voltage. Conway sidesteps another Dark Ball while swinging his hammer wide to prevent the melee attackers from getting within striking distance.

The heroes pause to assess the situation. This Conway fella is no joke. He's swinging that massive weapon around like it's a pocketknife. How the hell can he do that with those scrawny arms? Artemis figures her Ice Arrow can slow him down enough for her friends to get a shot in. Ed sees her taking aim and draws Conway's attention. He zigzags towards the giant and manages to get past the hammer! Or so he thought. Conway drew him in on purpose. He greets the thief with a knee to the gut. The blow is much more powerful than it looks, and Ed goes flying backwards.

Conway looks down with slight irritation as a block of ice encases his feet and part of his lower legs. Shine and Julia charge in while the archer and mages prepare to strike in unison. Even with his legs frozen, Conway effortlessly knocks Shine away. He shatters the ice with nothing but pure strength as Julia swings her axe down at full force. Her eyes widen in disbelief as her opponent catches it with one hand. He flings the axe and, by extension, Julia away. Her allies launch their coordinated attack. Artemis's Piercing Shot zooms toward its target with balls of flame and darkness right behind. Conway's hammer glows as he focuses chi into it. He smashes the arrow midflight with a devastating swing. The shockwave generated destroys the mages' magic.

Conway is impressed with his opponents' skills, but he has seen enough. It is time to end it. Hammer still radiating with energy, Conway leaps several feet in the air, raising the mighty weapon above his head. Whatever he's about to do won't be good. The heroes brace themselves. All except for Julia. She foolishly charges Conway, attempting to intercept him. Even with her lighter armor, there's no way she can cover the distance. As Conway lands, he pummels the hammer into the earth as hard as he can. The cavern shakes so violently, there's fear it will collapse. Wide cracks splinter outwards from the epicenter.

Everyone is sent flying backwards at great velocity. They smash down on the ground, stunned by the quake. Because of her reckless charge, Julia is by far the closest one to Conway. She rolls onto her stomach and struggles to get to her feet. Conway wastes little time in walking over to her. Julia is still down on all fours when she raises her head to see that massive hammer pointed dead at her. She shuts her eyes tightly as her head drops back down. She waits in terror for her adversary to smash her head open like a watermelon. Her friends can only watch in horror, too far away to give aid. Conway slings his weapon back over his shoulder. He's made his point. Our heroes still have much to learn.

Conway simply says, "It's over," as he turns his back to Julia and walks back toward his throne. Everyone eventually gets to their feet. To the Outcasts, this is just a normal day. As impressive as Conway's fighting abilities are, they have grown accustomed to seeing them on full display against the many deadly creatures lurking within the caverns. For our heroes, it couldn't feel more opposite. This is the first time they have fought as a group and lost. Not only that, they didn't even stand a chance. It is a sobering reminder of just how much they still need to grow.

Julia took it the hardest. She is standing alone, fists clenched tight. She'd never admit it, but she's fighting back tears. "Stupid! Stupid! Stupid!" she shouts to herself. "How could you be so stupid?" She was the one Conway had dead to rights. She feels like she let her friends down. Pride has blinded her to the simple truth that there was no way they would ever had been victorious.

As Conway returns to his throne, he sternly addresses the party, "You all still have a long way to go. Now leave." Shine turns to Artemis and apologizes. She can only manage a nod of acknowledgement as tears well up in her eyes. Now she won't be able to help King Vanajit.

Dejected, Shine and crew slowly make their way out of the cave. The row back seems to take an eternity. No one utters a word. They go back to the inn to regroup. As devastating and disappointing that loss was, it was never part of the mission. Time to shake it off and refocus. Shine unrolls the map onto a table. Where to next? King Pious is to the east in Leed's Castle. Mountains and canyons cut off the western region of Elysia from the rest of the nation; however, there is a bridge that will lead them to their objective. It's about a three-day walk from Salem to Hasina Bridge. They are already prepared for the trip but decide to set out in the morning. Everyone could use some R&R to decompress.

The party go their separate ways and wander about town. Ed resorts to old habits, looking for easy marks to pickpocket or scam but decides against it. These people have suffered enough. Julia unsuccessfully looks for someone to spar with. Artemis winds up playing with the kids they rescued plus a couple of their friends. Shine just lounges in the inn reflecting on his journey thus far and the path ahead.

While wandering about town, Marduk spots Wendy reading something under a tree. Whatever it is, it's old. The pages have yellowed, and there's obvious signs of wear. Curiously, he inquires to what she's reading. To his surprise, it's a research document. The subject is chemistry. It would seem the young witch has more than one passion. She aspires to be great alchemist one day.

It is an incredibly difficult art to learn, let alone master. One must not only have intimate knowledge of how elements and chemicals bond and react to one another but also be able to precisely tune mana. A slight miscalculation when mixing chemicals or using the wrong amount of mana can end up in disaster. So far, she's only managed to create firecrackers and a flashbang. After their defeat, she is studying up on how to create items to use on the battlefield. Things like fire and shrapnel bombs are fairly easy to make. She just needs the materials. Marduk is impressed by her aspirations and encourages her to constantly challenge her mind. By the end of their conversation, all thoughts of doubt brought on by defeat have left them. ♛

CHAPTER 8
Light the Way

In the morning, the heroes venture out from Salem en route to Hasina Bridge. It is an uneventful three days for a change. No one tries to capture them; no critters want to kill or eat them. A fair amount of time is spent camping from dusk until morning. It presents ample opportunity for the group to get to know one another. Shine already told the rest everything there is to know about him with the exception of one great detail, how King Pious killed his father. There really isn't much else to tell. Hanover isn't exactly bustling. Most would describe it as a boring backwater. Much of the first evening is spent by telling stories around a roaring campfire.

Marduk has a plethora of tales from his adventures as a youth. He is well traveled having visited most places Terra has to offer. However, it has been decades since he retired to a peaceful life in Bristol. Most of his tales involve at least one of his compatriots meeting an unfortunate end, which was more than a little of the reason for his retirement. His skills have significantly dulled in turn. Ed has his share of misadventures, too, but they all revolve around drinking, gambling, womanizing, or thieving, usually several at once. He once even played poker with Lord Verde. Wendy and Julia don't have much to tell. The witch's new friends are already aware of her pariah status. Despite Marduk's prying, she hasn't said much about her passion for alchemy. Julia's exposition isn't anything noteworthy either. She's the only child of two loving parents living in a city-state with a strong traditions of combat and martial arts. Life is simple in Cid.

Artemis has an interesting narrative to tell. She elaborates more of her association with the fairies of Verde's Woods. After her parents died, she had to fend for herself. Nobody wanted to take her in on account of her pointy ears. Shortly after, she was cast out of Salem entirely. The hatred and fear she endured from those she thought were her friends was traumatizing. She was afraid to go to another town for fear she would be shunned. After a bit of milling around aimlessly living off the land, she found her way to Verde's Woods. She can't explain why, but upon entering, she felt a serene sensation she hadn't experienced in a long time. The woods are full of game and edible plants for those savvy at discerning them from the poisonous ones. It wasn't ideal but would suffice.

She spent nearly five years making Verde's Woods her home. Living in the wilderness is a tough life, as one could imagine. The fairies didn't make it any easier, at least not a first. For a while, Artemis was one of their favorite targets for their mischief. On three separate occasions, she fell victim to snare traps that pulled her high off the ground and left her hanging from tree limbs. They'd pilfer her arrows right from the quiver on her back or steal rabbits and squirrels she managed to capture. Their most cruel trick was using a little illusionary magic to make some poisonous berries look edible. That wasn't a fun night. The poor archer's insides felt like they were on fire for hours.

That was the night she decided to beat the fairies at their own game. Aside from snare traps, they also loved digging pits and covering them with spider silk meshing and concealing it with leaves. Artemis had fallen victim to these a couple times as well. Each time, a couple fairies would flutter over the pit to point and giggle at the stupid human girl. One day, while walking about, she recognized the trap just inches before walking over the pit. At first she was relieved just not fall and suffer more mockery. Then she had a clever notion.

She searched the area and found a good-sized stone. After chucking it onto the spider silk meshing, she let out a terrified yell like she'd fallen once again before hiding in some nearby bushes. Soon after, two fairies fluttered in already giggling. The snickering stopped once they saw the pit was empty. Someone whistled behind them. They turned to see Artemis standing there with a freshly crafted bow in hand. An arrow was nocked and ready to fire. Of course, she didn't kill them. She had made her point. The fairies frantically flew away crying. The fairies didn't mess with her very often after that day, and when they were bold enough to try, Artemis managed to outsmart them on most occasions.

Word around Vanajit's palace quickly spread. It is not often a human bests them in cleverness. It is even less often humans don't try to harm or kill them. Fairy wings fetch a high price on the black market due to their magnificent patterns and magical properties. Many have been killed or mutilated by poachers. King Vanajit had a narrow line to walk. He couldn't idly stand by and let the humans abuse them, but he also understands most humans are simply passing through the woods in peace. His subjects pleaded for him to outright declare war, but he knew such an act would be their undoing. Humans are simply too numerous and too savage to be defeated in open conflict. Then there's the matter of this young girl who decided to live in the woods. *Their* woods. This was considered an egregious affront to many. However, the story of how she had two of them dead to rights but did not fire was striking. Artemis was slowly gaining the fairies' respect.

Her friends are all on the edges of their seats, staring at the young archer as she tells her tale. Shine is in disbelief. He thought Ray's stories were regaling. Ray has nothing on this. Marduk asks Artemis, "Is this game of wits how you managed to befriend the fairies?"

"Well, not exactly," Artemis starts.

One night, some poachers managed to capture several fairies using net traps. Tripwires were hung along the treetops. When the wires are tripped, wire nets are sprung. This method of capture was particularly brutal because to ensure the fairies wouldn't escape, the poacher would simply kill them while trapped and then cut off their wings. That night Artemis heard the high-pitched cries. Knowing it meant distress and fearing the worst, Artemis ran towards the cries. Five fairies in total were captured.

She was too late to save them all. Two were already slain at the hands of a pair of poachers. One of them was just finishing removing its wings when he realized they weren't alone. Before he could react, an arrow was lodged deep in his leg. His comrade tried to rush Artemis. He received an arrow to the shoulder in exchange. She refused to kill them, though if anyone deserved to die, it was these cruel men. The poachers hobbled off, and Artemis freed the remaining fairies.

The grateful fairies insisted she accompany them to the palace. This confused the girl. In all her time in the woods, she never saw the slightest inkling someone built a castle. The path to the palace is a hidden one by ground. Brush and thick vines obscure the way. Upon arriving, the castle wasn't what she was expecting at all. That's because there wasn't one. The term 'palace' has a different meaning to fairies.

Artemis found herself at the edge of a massive open clearing. A beautiful stone fountain was situated in the center. Magnificent flower and herb gardens were planted everywhere, illuminated by moonlight. The only lodgings were small huts made of vines and leaves. They are only really used to for protection against the elements, sleep, or more intimate encounters. Mostly, the fairies flit about the massive clearing tending to the many gardens or training.

The three fairies Artemis rescued insisted she tell King Vanajit what had transpired. Her selfless act melted his heart. Clearly this isn't a typical human. Not only did she rush to help those in need, she refused to take a life. At that moment, the king gave his blessing for Artemis to live in the palace as one of them. From that night forward, she stayed, oft helping with the gardens. She also trained with their archers. It was there where she picked up an interest in herbalism and began learning how to use chi. She felt at peace. She'd finally found a new home.

That all changed just two short weeks ago. Vanajit had been growing increasingly uneasy of the humans traversing the woods, chopping down trees, and, most of all, poaching until he finally grew ireful and announced for his subjects to attack any humans seen in the woods. Artemis was in the palace at that moment. She desperately pleaded for Vanajit to reconsider, which fell on deaf ears. Vanajit cast a Wind spell upon her. Everything turned bright; all she could hear is the rush of wind. When the spell subsided, she found herself standing outside the woods. She tried to move on and live her life, but she couldn't bring herself to abandon the fairies. She sensed for a while that Vanajit was changing, becoming darker. She ventured back into the woods to try and speak with him again but was turned away. That's when Verde's guards captured her.

The rest of the party is in awe. Everyone is speechless for a good while. Finally, Wendy exudes, "You poor thing! First you were cast out by Salem and forced to live in the woods, then the fairies shunned you, too. If that wasn't bad enough, some paranoid rich guy's goons grabbed you after. Man, I thought my life was rough."

Marduk concurs, "Indeed, things have been most difficult for you."

Ed encourages, "But ya didn't let it keep ya down. That's our gal!"

"You look all sweet and innocent, but there's the heart of a warrior hiding underneath," Julia smiles.

Artemis's face is beet red. "Aww... You guys... Thanks."

Shine concludes, "Wow, you all have way more interesting lives than me. I never realized just how sheltered I was in Hanover."

"Ah, so that's it," Ed playfully goads.

Shine bites, "What's it?"

"This whole revolution thing. Yer just bored, ain'tcha?" Everyone bursts with laughter in unison.

Aside from exchanging stories, the party spends camp time honing their skills. Artemis tries to show Shine, Ed, and Julia how to use chi while Marduk and Wendy train to improve their magic. Harnessing and controlling chi comes easiest for Julia. It was part of her training, but she had always struggled with it before. Since she joined up with Shine, it's like a switch flipped inside of her. The loss to Conway gave her quite a motivational nudge, too. She starts with some basic chi involving channeling energy to further increase physical strength. She also begins to learn how to channel chi into her axe. Conway was able to use some incredible moves by doing so. Mastering that skill will be a great boon in combat. Ed's first goal is using it to heighten his senses to become even more adept at dodging and striking weak points and vital organs. Shine has the least combat experience and thus has the hardest time. When they reach the bridge, he still hasn't advanced to the point where he can use chi in battle. He knows he's going to need to vastly improve for them to have a chance, but right now, they have bigger problems.

The party looks on in dismay at the distressing sight in front of them. Hasina bridge has been completely destroyed. A deep canyon stretches below. A narrow river snakes along the bottom. There is no way across. The canyon is too wide. Climbing down and up the other side would be extremely treacherous, and they do not have any climbing gear. Marduk notices char on the wood where it is broken. Someone may have destroyed the bridge on purpose, but who and why remain mysteries for now. The party ponders heading through the mountains, but the range is quite wide. It'd be a long and dangerous venture. Wendy's eyes light up as she has a much better idea.

Tempora is directly to the south. It is a mining town tucked away in the foothills. It is home to a massive mining tunnel that leads all the way to the other side of Aker range to the desert. From there, it'd just be about five miles to the desert city, Giza. Following the road all the way back to Salem and making a horseshoe around to Tempora would take too long, so the party decides to make their way south through the foothills. They're disappointed by the delay, but the silver lining is they can use the additional time for more training.

It will take another three days to reach Tempora. This leg of the journey begins peacefully, too, much to Julia's chagrin. She's been itching for some action since they left Salem. She feels like she has something to prove and is dying to see the benefits of her recent training. At dusk of the second day, the opportunity presents itself. As the party seeks a good place to set up camp, a band of thieves spies from the hills. They try to sneak close to the heroes to launch an ambush. Luckily, Ed is there. He's used to looking over his shoulder and senses the incursion well before they are in position. He warns his crew, and Shine demands the bandits show themselves. There are six in total. Everybody should have a chance to see how they've improved.

The battle doesn't go down quite like that. Julia cannot contain her excitement. With a rebel yell she charges the thieves before her friends are ready. The bandits lick their chops at the easy mark advancing in the fading sunlight. Julia takes out five singlehandedly. Nobody can even touch her. By focusing chi into her axe, it becomes an extension of herself. She is able to swing it faster and with more control. She effortlessly spins, pivots, and evades the foes' strikes. Her party looks on in awe and terror as their friend goes berserk. It looks chaotic, but she is in full control. As she's taking number five down, the final bandit sees an opening. Before he can flank Julia's rear, an arrow pierces him between the eyes. Julia turns and sees the dead man. She scowls at Artemis. "I had him!" she insistently bellows. Artemis simply shrugs and says she's sorry. Her voice is too meek for Julia to hear.

Julia grumbles in frustration as she returns to the party. As they set up camp, Ed goes out to "examine" their would-be attackers. They have almost one hundred coins between them, undoubtably taken from some unsuspecting traveler. None of their weapons seem to be of any use or value, so he pockets the coins and returns to the fire just in time for dinner. More stories are exchanged. Julia regales everyone with the tale of how some blonde chick stole her kill. The heroes set out again in the morning. They make good time. It is midday when they reach Tempora.

Tempora Mine is on the other side of town. Technically, it isn't part of Tempora, but the only road to it goes through town. After stopping for lunch at a small diner, the heroes head directly to the mine. Soon after leaving town, they find themselves on a winding road leading north. On either side of the road, there are clay pits and quarries. Life in Tempora is simple. If you're a man, you probably work the quarry or mine. Some women tend to the inn and shops while the rest are housewives. It is large but close-knit town. People are happy there. It's also one of the few places not being taxed to death by King Pious. The coal, marble, and ore from Tempora not only provides building materials for the kingdom, the many metals keep his army well equipped. Pious may be cold, but he's not foolish enough to encumber his most important resource.

Before long, our heroes reach the mine. The entrance is half wooden building and half mountainside. The main area is where the miners keep their gear and have morning meetings. On one side there are hangers and shelves containing everything one would expect to find. Heavy boots and clothing caked with dirt, pickaxes, and a single hardhat. The hat has a light affixed. It must be dark down below, and electric lighting hasn't made its way here yet. Thus far, the only place with electricity in Elysia, nay, all of Terra, is the city it was first harnessed, Port New Haven.

A large elevator leads underground to the mines. A tall, broad-shouldered, muscular man with a stubbled beard is standing by it. He's a foreman. He remains stone-faced as the odd-looking troupe approaches. Before they can ask, he speaks to them, "I know, I know. The bridge is out, and you want to pass through here. I'm getting really sick of having this conversation. No civilians are to go down there. It's too dangerous."

It would seem some smooth talking will be necessary. Shine tries his hand, "We're not exactly your everyday civilians. We're aware it's dangerous down there. It's nothing we can't handle."

The foreman's expression doesn't change. "I can tell by looking that you can handle yourselves in combat, but that's not the issue. The tunnel goes under the mountains. It's pitch black down there. Normally, that wouldn't be an issue, but pockets of volatile gases come and go like phantoms. If you bring an open flame down there, you'll surely blow yourselves halfway to Hades. You'll also likely cause a cave-in and put my men in danger."

"So, you're saying if we had a contained flame, we could go down there?"

"No. That's just one more reason not to let you. Even if you had the right gear, there's no way in Hades I'd risk letting you down there. It's simply too dangerous for people to just go wandering through."

As the foreman finishes speaking, one of the miners shouts from across the room, "Hey, boss!"

"Thomas? Why aren't you in the mine?"

"I was coming back from lunch, and the damn light wouldn't come on. I've been trying to fix it, but the damn thing is busted. Did the new helmets come in yet?"

"Damnit. That's just what we need. No, they ain't here yet."

"Shit. What should I do? Do you want me to try and manage with this one?"

"No, with our luck you'd get lost, or a monster would get you. Just stay up here with me. I could use a hand with paperwork anyhow."

"Righto, Matthew! Err... I mean, boss."

Shine sees a chance to negotiate. "Who ships the helmets?"

The foreman answers, "An elderly couple usually delivers them, the Stubblebottoms. They're pretty old. I hope they didn't croak. They're kind of odd but make some damn good lanterns. They live in the lighthouse in Caddis."

"So," Shine wryly asks, "say if we made sure that shipment got here as soon as possible, would you let us into the mine?"

The foreman grumbles as he realizes he walked right into that proposition. After some musing, he answers, "Every light that breaks equals one less man working. The shipment is almost a week late already. I... I suppose if you helped get them here quickly, I could see letting you down there." A deal has been struck! The heroes must seek out the elderly light producers. Caddis is a port city on the northern coast. That is a bit annoying seeing as they must backtrack once again, but the reward is more than worth it. The party decides to stay in Tempora overnight. It will take about a week to get to Caddis. Heading off the road in a northwesterly direction will get them to the road at the edge of the woods around Salem. From there, Caddis is almost directly north. ♛

CHAPTER 9
Bounty

Five days later, our heroes are on the northbound road to Caddis. It will only be a couple more days from here. Another long, uneventful trip. That soon makes an unwelcome change. As the massive woodlands become a blur in the distance, a trio of horsemen are spotted riding through the hilly plains. They turn onto the road heading towards the party who in turn step off the thoroughfare to grant the riders space. The horsemen mirror the heroes and continue their approach. More bandits?

Shine and friends ready themselves. The men slow their advance once near. They aren't wearing military armor or even matching outfits. Judging from their gear, the one in the middle is a swordsman, and the other two are an archer and mage. The horses have slowed to a trot. They are just a few feet from the party when the one in the middle shouts, "Hold!" He must be the one in charge. All three of the men freeze. They stare down at the heroes from atop their mounts.

The leader greets in a friendly tone. The party isn't sure if he's being genuine or condescending when he chirps, "Hello there, travelers." He pauses as he eyes Shine at the front of the group with a hand on Rashida's hilt. "You wouldn't happen to be Shine, would you?"

Against better judgement, Shine answers honestly, "Yes. Why?"

The leader smiles. "All right, boys. Arrest them."

Shine sighs in exasperation. "Really? This again?"

Julia storms up to Shine and shoves him hard. She glares at him as she yells, "Damnit, Shine! What is it with you?"

Shine quizzically seeks, "Me? What did I do?"

"You were born! As soon as I join up with you, everyone wants to arrest me. You're cursed!"

"That's not my fault! I don't even know what I did."

"I told you! You were born!"

"Hey! I didn't force you to come with me!"

"If I knew I'd be arrested every five seconds, I wouldn't have!"

One of the horsemen looks over at the others. "Are they really ignoring us?" They all hop off their steeds and draw weapons.

"Pipe down!" the leader bellows, "You're coming along with us."

Marduk tries to play peacemaker, "Excuse me, sirs? On what charge are we being arrested on?" He is just as successful as the previous go around.

"How the hell should I know?" the leader responds. "We're just good employees following our employer's instructions."

"You mean…" begins Wendy.

Shine finishes, "Bounty hunters. Shit."

Marduk hasn't given up on diplomacy. "How can you arrest us when you don't even know what the charges are? That's madness."

"We're not paid to ask questions. Let's wrap this up, boys."

The heroes aren't about to go down without a fight. They begin to draw their weapons but stop as two more mounted hunters approach from either side.

"I don't think so," one of them sneers. Surrounded on three sides with weapons still undrawn, fighting is almost surely a suicide mission. They decide to go peacefully, but their captors knock them out one by one anyway.

Shine groggily wakes with a splitting headache. As his vision unblurs, he takes a look around. It's a similar predicament as at Verde's place. This time they are all in one giant cell, all weapons and armor stripped as expected. Shine is down to a thin undershirt and his pants. Julia is worse off, half naked with a black cutoff top and matching shorts. Shine grabs the back of his head in pain as he slowly stands up. It seems he was the last one to regain consciousness. He looks at Julia who stares daggers but says nothing. "Déjà vu," he mutters to himself. The party members who did not have the pleasure of being locked up the first time look confused about the situation. How many times does this guy get arrested? It's even weirder for Artemis seeing as she first met him in a dungeon.

She cautiously inquires, "Um… Does this sort of thing happen to you a lot, Shine?"

Though she knows the answer, Wendy can't help but to ask, "This isn't the first time you've been arrested?"

Shine sighs and casts his eyes down. "No."

"Twice in under two weeks," comments Ed. "Not a good ratio."

Wendy is even more concerned now. "Oh, I see…" is all she can manage before trailing off. She leans in close to Artemis and whispers, "*Pssst.* Hey, Artemis?"

"Yes?"

"Just how well do you know these people?"

"Not well. I met them the same night I met you."

"Do you think they might be hardened criminals or cold-blooded killers?"

"You know I can hear you, right?" Shine interjects.

Wendy's fair skin turns bright red. "Oops, sorry," she murmurs shyly. "You're not going to run us through or anything, are you?"

Ed steps between the ladies and Shine. Puffing out his chest, he declares, "Worry not, ladies. If 'e tries to lay a finger on ya, I'll defend ya to the death."

Wendy rolls her eyes. "I think I'd rather take my chances with Shine."

Ed grins and replies, "That's okay. Artemis here is the one I'm meant ta be with. Can't ya just feel the chemistry 'tween us?

Artemis blushes and turns her eyes away, "No… Not really…"

Ed persists, "C'mon now, darlin'. Don't be shy now. I know yer lips are achin' for my embrace."

Already in a foul mood, Julia doesn't want to deal Ed's antics. "Haven't I told you to knock it off with that crap?"

"Yer just jealous ya can't have me." He sticks his tongue out at Julia as an exclamation point.

Julia fires back, "Like I'd ever hook up with a shrimp like you!"

"Like I'd ever hook up with a baboon like you!"

Julia is boiling with rage. "What did you say?!"

An out of sight bounty hunter yells, "Pipe down in there!" His command goes unheeded. Ed turns back to Artemis.

"Sorry 'bout that. Now, where were we, darlin'?"

Wendy is annoyed but somewhat impressed by the thief's advances. "He's a persistent one, huh?"

Julia is on her last nerve. "Knock it off, or I'll knock you *out!*"

Ignoring Julia, Ed continues, "C'mon now, sweetie. I don't bite or nuthin'."

That was it, the final straw. "That's it, pipsqueak!" Julia bellows. "Time to die!" She storms over to Ed and punches him on the top of his head.

"Owww!" he cries. "Why are you so mean?"

"Why are you so stupid!?" She punches him in the head again. Ed runs. Julia gives chase. "Get back here, runt!"

They run around their friends in a frantic circle. They complete two full laps and show no signs of slowing. "Don't make this harder on yourself!" screams Julia.

"Help!"

The guard yells again, "I'm warning you! Shut the fuck up!"

Two more laps completed. Ed narrowly escapes a lunging grab. That makes Julia even angrier. "I'll catch you sooner or later!"

"*Heeeelllllp!* She's gonna kill me!"

The guard has lost his patience. "That's it! Time to bust some heads!" He storms down the corridor to the cell and witnesses the shenanigans firsthand. He draws his sword and smacks it against the bars a few times while screaming at them to stop to no avail. Swearing under his breath, he unlocks the cell door, opens it, and steps inside. "Stop messin' around immediately, or I'm gonna have to hurt you!" The chase continues. It's as if he doesn't exist.

"You'll tire out sooner or later!" yells Julia.

"That's fine as long as it's after you!"

The guard issues one final warning, "I'm going to count to three, and if you two don't stop, I'll beat you to a bloody pulp!" As he begins his slow, threatening countdown, a gruff-looking guy in the corner casually stands up and moseys over to the hunter from behind. As the countdown reaches one, the man knocks out the guard. Ed and Julia stop in their tracks. The entire party's gaze is now fixed on their cellmate.

"Umm..." Shine starts. "Okay, I guess that solves that problem. Have you been there the whole time?"

Wendy looks over at Shine. "You didn't see him there?"

"I think we all saw him," informs Marduk.

Just as Shine begins to feel embarrassed, Ed drives in one final nail, "Yer not too observant are ya, Shine?"

Eager to change the subject, Shine turns back to the man, "So, anyway, thanks, stranger. Who are you exactly?"

"None of your damn business," the man curtly replies.

"My, isn't he cheerful?" comments Wendy.

Shine continues to probe, "If you're in here, you must have had a bounty put on your head."

That gets a slightly better response, "Something like that. I'm getting out of here. Just stay the hell out of my way." He turns his back and begins to walk out of the cell.

Flabbergasted by this stranger's flippant attitude, Shine presses, "Whoa, hold on a minute. This place must be crawling with bounty hunters. How do you plan on escaping?"

The man turns back around. "Easy. I'm going to kill 'em all."

"Scary!" blurts Artemis.

Despite the arrogant, crass demeanor, Shine figures everyone's chances of escape are higher if they all work together. "How about we help each other escape?"

"Piss off."

Itching for a fight, Julia takes step forward and goads, "Are you in a bad mood, or are you always an asshole?"

The man barely glances at her before answering, "What was that, wench?"

"Did I stutter?"

Sensing things are about to escalate, Shine intervenes, "Easy, Julia. Starting a fist fight behind enemy lines isn't a very good escape plan."

Turning his attention back to the man, "Look, whoever you are, you seem pretty strong. We may not look like it, but we're pretty strong, too. Odds are we're going to have to fight our way out of here, so why don't we join forces for the time being? Afterwards, you can go be an asshole wherever you want. Deal?"

The man looks Shine up and down. He can sense the young warrior's resolve and respects his confidence, not to mention the promise of getting to hurt people. "One condition," he flatly replies.

"What?"

"I get the first shot at those damned bounty hunters."

"Deal. Can you at least tell us your name?"

"Duncan." The party tries to introduce themselves, but Duncan doesn't care to hear it. Normally, he'd take command and lead the charge, killing anyone who tried to stop them with extreme prejudice, but he's curious to see what these people will do. He can tell the scrawny, blonde guy is the leader and wants to see how he handles himself.

"Do you have a plan, Shine?" Marduk asks.

"Not really. Like before, we need to find our gear and weapons. Then, I guess we try to find an exit."

That's good enough for Ed, who joyfully exclaims, "Ha! A most masterful plan! Let's do it!" It isn't hard for our heroes to find their way out of the room. There's a door on the other side of a short hallway. Sunlight is beaming in from some thin windows near the ceiling. Clearly the door leads outside, but where are they? Marduk has a guess. Judging from where they were confronted, this is most likely Fort Perdition. It's an old, fairly large military fort in the northern part of Elysian Fields. The fort hasn't been used since the Elysian-Gizian War, the last major military conflict that ended eighty-five years ago. The old, somewhat rotted wood leads the party to believe the wizard is correct. It would make sense bandits or bounty hunters would use it as a base of operations.

Before heading out, the group searches the room for their stuff. It isn't hard to find. The hunters just tossed it all in a pile in a corner. Duncan's gear is there, too. He looks like a soldier. He has a full set of heavy, black armor sans the helmet and a large square shield. It isn't too dissimilar to the armor Pious's men wear. He also has a steel longsword that looks like it has seen some use. The party is curious to know just who Duncan is but refrain from asking. Getting an open answer is unlikely anyway. Once everyone is ready, the party heads out the door.

Fortunately for the heroes, the fort is large, and the crew of hunters isn't. There's only few to avoid while sneaking behind the old wooden buildings. Moving through without detection is easy. One hunter gets caught taking a piss and winds up unconscious in the bush he was relieving himself on. The heroes find the gate. It's shut tight. Two massive wooden doors are locked in place by a wooden crossbar. The crossbar is too high up to just walk over and lift. There is a pulley system to raise it up and away from the doors. Thick ropes lead up into a tower where there must be a crank. It looks like it'd take considerable time to open the gate, and they'd be exposed while doing so. Who knows exactly how many bounty hunters are in this place? The party decides to try and find another way out. They circle around the edge of the fort wall. It's old, so maybe there's a hole or a gap to escape through.

Edging around the back part of the fort, they find an open area with some worn training dummies. A couple hunters are messing around, playfully swinging their swords at them. The party manages to get the drop and knock them out. While doing so, other voices are heard. Several more hostiles are coming. Julia and Duncan each swing one of the unconscious hunters onto their backs, and the party books it out of there. There's a warehouse they can duck into and stash the bodies. It's dark inside. There aren't any windows. The only light comes from small cracks and spaces in the wood. Ed sniffs the air. Something smells really familiar. His eyes light up as he recognizes the scent. Gunpowder!

Barely able to contain his excitement, he suggests they blow their way out. His childish wonder is contagious. The party can't resist the urge to blow something up. It will take a decent amount of powder to create a hole large enough to quickly exit through. An explosion is going to instantly draw attention, so they need to be ready to run. They find an almost full barrel of gunpowder, and Julia carries it out of the warehouse. After creating a hole near the bottom, she lugs it over to the fort wall creating a trail of powder. She places the barrel on the ground next to the wall. There should be plenty to make a large hole. She returns to the group who are at the back of a building a safe distance away.

Wendy insists on doing the honors of lighting the trail. She carefully applies just enough Fire magic to start the fun. Shortly after, a massive explosion rings out nearly knocking everyone backwards. There's a huge hole! It's large enough that everybody can run out without having to duck or maneuver. As they sprint out towards freedom, everyone suddenly stops dead as a strong pull of chi nearly floors the party.

The heroes turn to see the source of the powerful, ominous presence. It belongs to the leader of the hunters, Drake. It's clear from a cursory glance he's no stranger to combat. His toned body is an intricate mural of scars and tattoos. A sheathed rapier is fastened to his belt. His arms are crossed sternly, yet he's grinning. How long has he been there? Drake is flanked by the remaining hunters, four on each side in a V formation.

Swordsmen make up the nearest four all dressed in various types of chainmail and leather armor. One of the horsemen is among them. His mage and archer compatriots must be elsewhere. Mages make up the furthest four combatants. Their robes are all different colors that match the orbs on their respective staves. It seems they are elemental mages, magic users who focus on a single type of magic. Marduk realizes this and hastily warns his comrades. He doesn't have time to explain much, but he can tell by their robes their respective elements. It's the classic four: Earth, Fire, Wind, and Water. They even have matching tattoo designs under their right eyes. They must have trained together, perhaps in a guild. The entire crew of hunters looks confidant and well organized. This isn't going to be easy.

Drake speaks to the heroes in an almost playful tone, "Where do you think you're going?"

Ed states the obvious, "Oops. Busted."

"Looks like it," Shine nods.

Drake's smile disappears, replaced by an intense demeanor. "You wretches have sure caused us a lot of trouble. I really don't want to deliver damaged goods to our employer, so how 'bout you be good little prisoners and head back to the cell?"

Shine smugly replies, "How about a counteroffer? We leave through this hole, you don't follow us, and we pretend this never happened."

Drake calmly surmises, "I suppose one broken jaw would be acceptable."

His words don't match his actions as he steps back and signals the hunters to attack. If our heroes aren't careful, a broken jaw will be the least of their worries. It would seem Drake doesn't want to bother dirtying his hands. That should probably be deeply concerning to our heroes, but there's no time to think about it as the eight bounty hunters begin their attack. The swordsmen quickly advance while the mages use various buffs. The Earth mage bolsters the sword fighters' defense by making their skin rock hard. The Fire and Wind mages bolster the four mages' magical attack power and resistance respectively. The Water user begins gathering energy for an offensive spell.

Marduk knows a buff spell or two of his own. He uses Wind magic to augment everyone's speed. Artemis takes aim at the Water mage. She wants to take her out before that spell is cast. A Piercing Shot to the face should do it. One of the swordsmen sees the archer prep her attack. He was going to engage Ed but switches priority. Big mistake turning his attention away from the thief. Using the extra speed boost from Marduk, he closes quickly in a perfect position to flank. His enemy just barely gets his shield in place to block. They begin to duel, with Ed deploying his typical strike and evade strategy.

Shine and Julia square off against two of the other melee fighters. Shine makes good use of his bronze shield, blocking a strike, then landing one of his own. However, the defense spell protecting his foe renders the cut superficial. The final swordsman tries to get around Duncan to take out Marduk. She manages to do so but only momentarily. Concentrating energy into his fist, Duncan cocks his arm back. He throws a punch at nobody. When he does, a ball of energy explodes forth, screaming at his target, striking her square in the back. Shine catches the attack out of the corner of his eye. It was some impressive chi. Hold on… Energy radiated outward as Duncan gathered it. He's a mage?!

Stunned by the blow, there's nothing the female fighter can do to prevent Marduk from delivering a ferocious blow of his own. The bottom of his staff smashes his foe right under her chin. It rocks her, despite having rock-hard skin. Marduk takes a couple steps back and uses his Sleep spell. That put her down. As he watches his foe's eyes close and body begin to slump, his eyes widen in horror. She is impaled by Duncan's sword! She was down. There was no need to kill her. Without batting an eye, Duncan pulls his sword from the corpse and moves to the next target.

Meanwhile, Artemis fires her arrow at the Water mage. The Air mage creates a wall of wind in front of his comrade. It's not enough to stop the shot, but the arrow is slowed enough to be dodged. The Water mage strikes back at Artemis. A scalding hot geyser spirals at her. There's no time to evade. She shuts her eyes tight and braces for impact.

She feels a strange sensation wash over immediately followed by a crushing blow. The geyser sends her flying backwards. It hurt like hell, but strangely, she wasn't burnt by the water. The force alone should have shattered her ribcage, yet she is relatively unharmed. She notices Duncan checking on her and realizes he had cast a spell at the last moment to raise her elemental resistance. That was the last thing anyone expected. The gruff loner went out of his way to protect her? He almost pays dearly for it as the Fire mage launches a massive Fireball at him. Duncan manages to block the brunt of it with his shield.

The Wind mage creates a low, sweeping current to trip Ed. The thief spills onto the dirt. The swordsman he's fighting sees a chance and goes for the finishing blow. Seeing her comrade in danger, Julia manages to shove her opponent away. If anyone is going to kill that pipsqueak, it's going to be her! Focusing chi into her axe, she slams the blade into the ground. A shockwave cracks the earth and zigzags towards Ed's attacker. It's not nearly as impressive as Conway's move, but it gets the job done. The swordsman flies into the air away from Ed.

Now the thief has a chance to end it. Narrowly avoiding a sharp blast of air from the enemy mage, Ed closes and thrusts a dagger at the fallen swordsman. His foe manages to block with his round shield, but Ed is savvy. Knowing only a powerful thrust could break through that rocky skin, he baited his foe. He sacrificed power for mobility. He wanted the attack to be stopped. Like a dancer, he elegantly pivots and spins around the shield to attack with the second dagger. There's nothing his foe can do. Now he thrusts full force, deeply penetrating his foe's side. The blade pierces a kidney, ensuring his demise.

Julia's assist allowed Ed to win his battle but left her exposed. Her adversary thrusts his blade. She cannot block or dodge. An arrow pierces the swordsman's neck. His eyes roll back in agony as ice begins to wrap around his throat and bottom half of his face. His attack wasn't stopped completely. Julia winces as the sword pierces her leather armor and through the skin. It only goes a couple inches deep. If not for that Ice Arrow, she'd probably be dead right now. Unable to breathe, their foe collapses onto the ground desperately clutching his throat. It will just be a matter of moments before he suffocates.

Only one swordsman remains, still dueling with Shine. Shine has improved quite a bit, and his shield has been a huge help. He's landed several blows, but that damned defense spell ensured they were just scratches. Meanwhile, the four enemy mages still pose a huge threat. They all look like they are about to use powerful attack spells. If they all attack at once, the resulting effect would be devastating. While everyone else was fighting, Wendy was quietly gathering mana.

She hasn't had much practice with this one, and the mages' magical defense has been boosted making her even more nervous. She's ready now. The sapphire atop her staff has lost all its luster. It is dark purple now, almost black. She points the staff at her targets. The four elemental mages are standing in a loose cluster. A dark purple cloud of miasma forms all around them. The color drains from their faces. Fatigue instantly sets in as the poison takes its toll. One of them doubles over and vomits. Then another. Whatever spells they were casting have been broken. The Fire mage desperately tries to cast another but catches an arrow between the eyes.

Shine and Duncan move in on the other three while Ed and Julia take on the final swordsman. Marduk uses some Wind magic to blow the miasma away. The rest of the group stay back, ready to give support if needed. It isn't. Barely able to move let alone defend themselves, the mages meet a quick demise by Shine and Duncan's blades. The last fighter is easily overwhelmed. Enduring Julia's fierce attacks leaves him open for Ed to deal the killing strike. The thief easily lands a killing blow thanks to his heightened awareness.

It's not over yet. Drake still remains. He doesn't seem too upset that his crew has been wiped out. Now he doesn't have to split bounty with anyone. Smiling at that notion, he casually begins calisthenics. The air grows heavy. This chi is even more intense than Conway's. A feeling of dread grips the heroes as they regroup to take on this final threat. Drake turns to them. He looks to be sizing them up, but his loose body language shows he still doesn't take them seriously. "Well now," he slowly, confidently begins, "I suppose since I don't have to split the reward now, I can just kill you all. Dead bounties are so much easier to handle, don't you agree?" He isn't in any rush.

The party begins to talk strategy before Duncan cuts them off. "Why the hell are we standing here talking?" He takes a couple steps in Drake's direction. "I'm going to beat you so brutally, your own parents won't recognize you."

Drake has a surprising response, "You picked the wrong people to side with, Duncan. They're worth a pretty penny. Tell ya what. If you turn the other way, I'll forget all about that little bar fight you started with my men."

Duncan's reply is much less surprising, "Piss off."

Drake sighs and says, "This is why I hate tryin' to be nice. I suppose if I tell Pious you were helpin' them, he might give me a bit extra."

Shine is so stunned he has to take a step back. "Pious? Shit, how'd he catch on to us?"

Drake realizes he just gave away some important intel but doesn't seem to care. He nonchalantly says, "Whoops. Cat's outta the bag. I guess I should kill you all before I let anything else slip."

Duncan impatiently declares, "Screw this. I'll take you out myself." He marches towards Drake.

"Whoa. Hold on a sec, Duncan," warns Shine.

"C'mon!" yells Duncan before rushing in. Drake casually draws his rapier. Wind chi swirls around it. Duncan slashes. Drake effortlessly avoids and smacks Duncan away with his free hand. The motion looked almost innocuous, but it sends Duncan, heavy armor and all, flying off to the side. He hits the ground going at least forty miles per hour. He savagely bounces and rolls across the fort. He's a hundred feet away from Drake when he finally stops. His back slams against one of the buildings. All his comrades can do is look on in terror. Somehow, he is still conscious. His arms shake violently as he tries to push himself up. He collapses in a heap. He is still alive but isn't getting up anytime soon.

"One down," Drake smirks. Artemis wants to run over to her fallen friend to heal him, but Drake is finally ready to fight. The air grows even heavier as he draws out more chi. Wind whips around his blade in a miniature cyclone. The heroes try to make the first move. Marduk uses Wind magic to increase their speed once more. He struggles to catch his breath after. Even simple spells can be very draining when cast on so many people at once. Artemis takes aim while the melee attackers charge in, hoping the added speed will overwhelm their opponent. Wendy fires Dark Ball. She doesn't think it will do much damage, but maybe it will distract him enough for someone to get in a good shot. Drake slashes the air in front of him. A massive blast of wind bursts from his blade. No, rather, a multitude of razor-sharp gusts do from a powerful skill known as Burstfire.

Wendy's attack is shredded apart. The melee attackers cannot completely dodge. They all collect decent cuts. Ed's right leg got caught, as did Shine's sword arm and Julia's side. The air cut through her leather and even Shine's chainmail like it wasn't even there. The support crew are far enough away to evade except for Wendy. Her spell left her open. She cries in pain and is barely able to keep hold of her staff as her shoulder is deeply lacerated. Artemis fires Piercing Shot before rushing over to aid the witch.

Drake sidesteps the arrow as if it was moving in slow motion. Then he zigzags towards his foes with lightning speed. His target is Julia. She's the slowest melee fighter, so he feels he can get in a quick strike and take her out. Julia focuses chi throughout her legs and torso for balance. Even with her increased mobility and reflexes, she can barely block with her axe. Drake follows up with another blistering slash then another. He keeps up the pressure. Julia isn't going to be able to block them all. Ed tries to strike Drake from the side. Drake swats him away without a glance or any interruption to his flourish.

Shine realizes he's going to have to use chi if he hopes to survive. His skills are extremely limited in that department, but he thinks he can pull off pretty good one. He closes his eyes and focuses on the rage he feels for all Pious has done. The tyranny. His father's death. The bounty. His chi begins to grow hot with the flames of rage. Channeling the wild energy into Rashida, it begins glowing as if responding to its wielder's will. Flames ignite.

Drake sidesteps Marduk's Fireball before continuing his assault on Julia. One of his slashes slices her left arm deep just above the elbow. Before he can follow up, Shine attacks. Marduk's speed spell allows him to close quickly. He swiftly slashes as hard as he can. Drake sees the attack out of the corner of one eye. Both eyes widen in surprise at its ferocity. A fiery, metal clash sizzles throughout the fort. He is forced to block and fall back. Shine presses. Julia is in too much pain to pursue. The wound she suffered is significant.

Artemis finishes healing Wendy and shouts at Julia. The warrior waves her off. She can manage with her injuries, and Artemis's chi would be better saved for offense. Wendy and Marduk synchronize to cast a powerful combo. Wendy prepares Deluge, and Marduk stands by with Shock ready to go. Ed uses chi for even more speed. Coupled with the magic, he's now as fast as Drake.

Shine has the bounty hunter's attention. Rashida's flaming attacks are forcing him to defend. Ed screams towards their foe with blistering pace. Drake's back is completely open. At the last moment, he leaps and contorts is body in an impossible fashion, evading the thief's lunge. Ed has to veer sharply to avoid impaling his ally. He tumbles to the ground. Not only does Drake land cleanly from his acrobatics, he is able hop away from an Ice Arrow aimed at his feet.

The mages attack! The electrified torrent is on target. Drake uses Burstfire again. It's ferocious enough to even slice the powerful combo apart. Not only that, Julia was caught in the scope, taking another deep laceration, this time to her leg. Artemis shoves Marduk out of harm's way, but her leg gets cut, too. Wendy was extremely lucky. A gust grazes her cheek as it goes by. A few inches to the right and that would have been it for her. Julia waves Artemis off again, but she'll have no part. The warrior's injuries are taking their toll.

Artemis doesn't have enough chi to completely heal her but should be able to stop the bleeding from a couple of the more severe wounds. Shine tried to land a blow on Drake as he used Burstfire, but the bastard is just too agile. He blocked and parried the attack. Shine is starting to fade. Rashida's flames are being fueled by his chi. The longer it is ablaze the more it saps his strength. For the moment, he can match up evenly with his opponent, but that won't be the case for long. Everyone is gassed. They need a trump card.

Ed thinks he has one. Hopes would be more accurate. He's only attempted to use this chi skill once, and it failed spectacularly. Julia mocked him for days. It is an interesting skill to say the least. The user lets chi gently flow from their body, radiating outward. Their body glows slightly as its bathed in the energy. That energy is used to bend the light around the user, creating an optical illusion, making them invisible. The last time Ed tried it, he put out too much chi and ended up glowing like a firefly. It took a half hour for the effect to wear off.

This time, he performs perfectly. His body is concealed by his own chi. That's just the first part. Now he needs to move in and attack while keeping the flow of chi consistent. It doesn't use much energy, so most people won't be able to sense it; however, Drake is no ordinary guy. There's a good chance he will detect Ed is stalking. Hopefully, the sly thief can get a critical strike before the bounty hunter can react. He is soon afforded a perfect opportunity.

As Shine gets pushed back by Drake's flourishes, Julia bull rushes. Artemis hadn't finished healing yet, but she doesn't give a damn. Marduk's speed spell has worn off, so she uses her own chi to aid her swing speed. She attacks with a furious flourish, an impressive feat with such a large weapon. Now Shine and Julia are able to coordinate attacks. Drake is skilled enough to handle both of them, but his hands are full.

Marduk cautiously approaches. He has an old trick up his sleeve, but he has to get much closer to his enemy than he'd prefer. Once close enough, the wizard creates a blinding flash of light. It not only catches Drake but Shine and Julia as well. It's dicey, but it will leave Drake open. Their foe intelligently leaps backwards. He's too skilled to let a lucky random swing be the end of him.

Wendy has just enough mana left to fire a final Dark Ball. Drake senses it but, still blinded, is unable to pinpoint it in time. It hits square in the chest. Fearing a follow up attack, he tries to leap away again but finds himself stuck. A perfectly placed Ice Arrow froze his feet. His vision is starting to return as he violently swirls chi around his legs to shatter the ice. He draws his rapier back and refocuses energy into the blade in order to fire off another Burstfire.

Before it's ready, he senses a presence behind him. Before he can react, a dagger drives deep into his back. He arches in pain, looking back to witness the shrewd thief fading into view. The knife went in deep, severing the spinal cord. Drake falls backward as Ed pulls the dagger out. Blood gushes from the wound. Drake is flat on his back, paralyzed. He tries to speak, but no words come out. Shine rushes over to try to question him for naught. Drake's body relaxes as life leaves him. Damnit. He might have been able to give them information on Pious.

The party is battered and exhausted but victorious. Artemis makes her way over to Duncan, who is still face down in the dirt. She gently shakes him. "Hey? Are you still alive?"

She hears a muffled reply, "Fuck off."

She sighs with relief and yells over to the rest of the group, "He's fine!" Artemis apologizes to Duncan. She doesn't have enough chi left to heal him. She does remember she still has one more vitality potion. It's not much, but it allows Duncan to get to his feet. He won't be much use if they get into another fight, but at least he can walk. Artemis assumes his grunt as he walks away means "thank you."

They regroup with the others. Ed is checking the bounty hunters' bodies for loot. They don't have much on them in the way of coin, but their weapons can be sold for a decent price. It's a lot to carry, so the party settles on a few of the pieces in the best condition, including Drake's rapier.

Once the looting is concluded, Marduk advises, "We should vacate the area in case there's more bounty hunters."

Shine concurs, "I agree." He speaks to Duncan, "It's been fun, Duncan. Not really. Try not to get into any more fights with bounty hunters."

As the party begins to head out from the exit they created, Duncan has just one word for them, "Wait." Everybody turns around and peers curiously at the dark knight. "I want to travel with you." Yet another surprise today.

The party isn't sure how to respond. Shine is skeptical. "I wasn't expecting that. Why?"

"Drake said King Pious put a bounty out on you. You must've done something to piss him off."

"Not yet," Shine explains, "but we're planning to. I don't know how, but Pious must have caught wind."

"That bastard has eyes and ears everywhere. What's your beef with him?"

"The short answer is he's a power-hungry tyrant that needs to be stopped."

"Yeah? And how do you plan to do that?"

"We're going to kill him."

"Hahahaha! You're a cocky bunch! Do you even have a clue how powerful he is? Sure, Drake is pretty tough by normal standards, but he's nothing compared to the bar King Pious has set. I'd take him out myself if he wasn't so damn strong."

Shine is unimpeded. "We're prepared for the worst. That's why I'm seeking allies to help fight. Why are you after Pious?"

"I have my reasons."

Shine shrugs and replies, "Good enough. An enemy of Pious is an ally to us. I'm not sure having you travel with us is a good idea, though. You don't seem to play well with others."

"Seems to me you need all the help you can get. If King Pious is onto you, this won't be the last time someone comes after you."

"Well, at least you're up front about things. There's not a hint of pretension with you is there?"

"Nope."

"Hmm... I'll tell you what. If everyone else is okay with it, you can join. How 'bout it, guys?"

The rest of the group has some apprehension towards this crude, mysterious black-armored mage, but he makes a strong point. They will need strong people in their corner, and he's nothing if not strong. He also helped Artemis when she was in peril. After a brief discussion amongst themselves, no one has any objections. The party introduces themselves. This time Duncan listens. Ed whistles at Duncan and tosses him something. It's Drake's rapier.

The thief explains, "Your sword looks kinda weathered. I betcha you'll get some good use outta this." Duncan agrees. He hangs on to his old sword as well. It's worn, but he'll still be able to get some decent coin for it. The party finally exits Fort Perdition. Caddis is only a day and a half's walk. The sun is just beginning to set. It should be no later than midday the day after next when they arrive. On the way, the party asks Duncan about himself, but he doesn't tell them anything. ♕

CHAPTER 10
Ghost Pirates?

It's around noon when our heroes step foot inside Caddis. The scent of salt is wafting in the breeze. A gull squawks as it soars overhead towards the ocean. Ed takes a deep breath, "Ahh... This is my kinda place." It is a large, picturesque, prosperous city thanks to having trade routes both by land and sea. Lorde Verde is actually the one who negotiated the maritime routes and owned the first merchant ships that embarked from port. Taxes are high like in most places, but the city thrives, nonetheless.

Now inside its tranquil limits and far away from Fort Perdition, our heroes finally feel like they can relax. The lighthouse isn't hard to find. It can be seen reaching above the far northwest outskirts sitting atop a rocky peninsula. They hope to find Tempora Mine's shipment there. Before that, everyone could use a bite to eat. Ed is more excited about the ale. Being a port city means Caddis has some imported brews.

The party enters the pub just in time to see a curious sight. Two men are standing in front of the bar having a heated discussion. That's common for a place this. What makes this particular argument interesting is how they are dressed. One is a stocky, muscular man with a thick black beard. He is wearing a blue bandana and has both a cutlass and pistol holstered on a large leather belt. A sailor? No, he looks like a pirate. His nose is red, cheeks are flushed. Clearly, he's had a few.

The other man is short, maybe a couple inches taller than Ed. He is dressed in a black hood and robes but not like a mage's. They are tight fitting, conforming with his body. The hood is masked, making only his eyes visible. There is a sword sheathed on his back. Shine has read about ninjas in stories, but he never thought they were real. Julia has seen ninjas before when they when they when they pilgrimaged to Cid a few years back. Ed saw a pirate once when he was young but never a ninja. Marduk has seen both in his many years on Terra. Everyone else is in the same boat as Shine. The heroes arrived just in time to catch a free show.

The pirate yells at the ninja in a booming voice, "What did you call me?"

The ninja fires back, "Did I stutter?"

"Take it back, pajama boy!" Most of the other patrons ignore them. This is a typical afternoon for the regulars. The heroes venture forth to get a closer look. Everyone has their own reasons for being intrigued.

The ninja taunts, "Who's gonna make me?"

"I'm gonna knock you out!"

"You and what army?"

"My fists are the only army I need!"

"Ha! Typical pirate relying on brute strength. You wouldn't land a single hit on me."

"All I need is one good punch to knock a pajama-wearing sissy like you out cold!"

"You pirates have no honor. Ninjutsu is the true path of a warrior!"

"Yeah, sneakin' around 'n' attackin' people from behind is real honorable. We pirates face our enemies head on! We're far superior warriors!"

"Ninjutsu!"

"Piracy!"

"NINJUTSU!"

"PIRACY!"

Fists fly. Duncan and Julia each fight the urge to join. Artemis shields her eyes with a hand only to find herself peeking. The pirate is unimpressed with his opponent's strength. "Is that the best ya got? Take this!" He throws a haymaker. The ninja could easily avoid it but doesn't. He bears the brunt, standing toe to toe and throwing one of his own. It's a good, old-fashioned bar brawl. A dainty blonde waitress boldly tries to break up the scuffle.

"That's enough you two!" she demands.

More fists fly. The ninja knows he cannot win a straight up fist fight against such a powerful opponent. Losing his cool, he reaches back for his katana. "I shall slice you to pieces!"

"Try it, little man!"

Before the fight gets out of hand, the waitress fearlessly steps between the drunkards. She clobbers the pirate in the face, then the ninja. That gets them to stop. "You two need to leave right now!" They're more afraid of her death stare than each other and back down.

The ninja sneers at his enemy, "See what you caused, brute?"

"Me? You lit—"

The waitress cuts him off, "Hey! Get out of here!"

The pirate grumbles and concedes, "Fine then. This isn't over, pajama boy." He walks out of the bar. The ninja soon follows. Feeling embarrassed at the scene he caused, he apologizes, "Please forgive me," before exiting.

The waitress shakes her head is angst, "Damn riff raff..."

"Well, that was interestin'," Ed remarks.

The waitress notices Duncan amongst the new customers. She stares sharply at him. "Don't you be causing any more trouble, ya hear?" It would seem this is where that bar fight Drake mentioned took place. Or maybe Duncan just gets into fights everywhere. With the festivities concluded, the party plops down at a table in the middle of the pub. Julia sighs with relief as she can finally put the heavy backpack down. The same waitress, Molly, serves them. As the party eats, and Ed downs imported ale like he's going to the gallows, they overhear something alluring at an adjacent table.

Ed's ears prick as he hears someone utter his favorite word, "treasure." Full of liquid courage, he has no issue investigating. He hops off the stool and walks over to the neighboring party of four.

"Treasure?" he loudly utters in a slurred voice. Marduk covers his face with his hand in embarrassment. The other party continues their discussion, ignoring the soused loudmouth. Ed slams his fist on the table. "Who's got treasure?" he demands.

"No one," one of them gruffly replies. Three of the men stand up. "There's no way in Hades we're going in there. Not for what you're offerin'. We're out." He and his crew take their leave. The man still at the table buries his head in his hands in exasperation.

"Damnit," he mutters. He is a scrawny-looking fellow with short brown hair and thick glasses. He's wearing an expensive-looking vest complete with a red bowtie and equally well-tailored pants. "Now who's going to help me?"

Ed casually hops onto a stool next to him. He pats his new friend on the back a couple times and proclaims, "Now, now there. If it's treasure ya seek ta find, I'm yer guy!"

The man removes his head from his hands and looks inquisitively at Ed. Some random drunk is the last person he'd want to ask for help, but he doesn't see any other options, so he may as well try. Pushing his glasses up with a finger, he inquires, "So what, you're some sort of treasure hunter?"

Ed gestures for a handshake and replies, "Yup. Sure am. What kinda treasure are ya seekin'?"

The man doesn't shake Ed's hand. He halfheartedly makes his pitch, "In the northwestern part of Elysian Fields there is a cavern, Hulda Cave. It is there where the fabled pirate Captain Barrett is said to have died."

Ed is literally shaking with excitement. He whoops with joy. Intrigued by Ed's sudden elation, the rest of the party walks over. "*The* Captain Barrett?" Ed gushes.

Ed's passion has caught the man's eye. He shakes Ed's hand and introduces himself, "Willard Smith. Dr. Willard Smith. Ed, was it?" Ed introduces the doctor to the rest of the party. Willard continues his story, "As I was saying, the cave is said to be Barrett's final resting place. He and his men drew the ire of the previous ruler, King Magnus II. They were attacking and raiding merchant ships with great success until one unfortunate day. They got greedy, or perhaps overzealous, and decided to raid a ship belonging to the royal navy. They were barely successful, narrowly escaping on their ship as a flotilla came in to aid. The pirates had been a thorn in the king's side for years.

"Magnus II was irate when he received word of the attack. Luckily for him, his fleet was able to track the pirates to Hulda Cave. It was believed that was their hideout. He created a blockade with his navy and sent a contingent of soldiers into the cave. A fierce battle ensued. The pirates fought valiantly but, in the end, were no match for the military's might. All the pirates are thought to have been slaughtered including the captain. However, some say he and a few men made it to safety. Barrett was taken into a hidden room where they stashed the most valuable loot. He was mortally wounded. There was nothing his men could do except give him proper send off, leaving him to die with the treasure."

Ed is salivating. "And you're lookin' for people to find that room and Barrett's treasure."

"Precisely."

Marduk inquires, "What compensation are you offering for our services?"

"If the tomb does exist, you can have whatever treasure you find."

"Wait," Wendy cautiously treads. "So, what if it doesn't exist?"

"Then you get nothing." That caveat makes the offer far less tempting.

Julia has a question of her own, "Why don't you explore the cave yourself?"

Dr. Smith hesitates before answering, "Well... You see..." he hesitates. It's apparent there's a huge catch.

"Spit it out," Duncan grunts.

Dr. Smith collects himself, "Right, shortly after I began researching into this, another rumor popped up. Some tomb raiders tried their hand at finding the treasure, but... only one of them came back. She swears the cave is haunted, and her crew was wiped out by the angry spirits of the fallen pirates. I don't know what exactly happened in that cave, but it drove her to madness. She sealed the entrance and now spends her time rambling about the end of days."

The entire thing sounds like a wild goose chase. A dangerous one at that. The party has better things to do anyway. They are quick to decline, but Ed begs and pleads with his comrades to take the job. He has been fascinated by pirates since he was a child, and now he has an opportunity to find the tomb of the most infamous pirate in Terra's history, not to mention get a boat load of treasure. The thief's excitement is infectious. They come to an agreement. First, they'll head to the lighthouse and make sure the shipment gets to the mine; then they can explore Hulda Cave. Dr. Smith gives them directions to his home to report what their findings. He assures the heroes he has no interest in the treasure. This venture is strictly for historical purposes for him.

It's a pretty good walk to the lighthouse from the pub. It is dusk as they get close. A bright light is beaming out from the tower to guide ships sailing in the night. Caddis Lighthouse is a special one. It no longer uses flame. Its caretakers, the Stubblebottoms, discovered a method of creating a brighter, more efficient light. They use mana.

Atop the lighthouse is a large glass orb. This orb is enchanted to store sunlight. At night or when it's foggy, that light is channeled and focused through a lens to create the beam. The process is automatic, the workings of an advanced enchantment which reacts to how much sunlight is present. Usually payment for such a skilled service is a hefty one, but the Stubblebottom's have a nephew who's a proficient mage who did it for almost nothing.

Our heroes are standing in front of a large, wooden door. The wood is quite warped. They knock several times, but no one answers. It is unlocked, so they venture inside to find the Stubblebottoms. Hopefully, the foreman, Matthew, was wrong, and they're alive and well. Someone must be home as there are lit candles on the walls. "Hello?" Marduk calls.

A woman's voice faintly travels from upstairs, "Coming, coming." An elderly woman gingerly makes her way down the spiral stairs. This must be Mrs. Stubblebottom. Her husband isn't far behind. Eventually, they make it downstairs, and the misses speaks to their guests, "Now, who is knocking at this hour?"

Shine explains they're checking on the shipment of lantern helmets for Tempora Mine. It turns out the order is just about filled, but there's a small snag. Rats. Confused, Artemis confirms, "Rats?"

"Yep," casually replies Mr. Stubblebottom. "Big ones."

Julia asks, "How do a few rats stop you from making helmets?"

"The order is in the basement, but it's infested with 'em now. Boy, they made an awful mess down there. It's best I show you." It's a ridiculous scenario, but the heroes have no choice but to play along.

Mr. Stubblebottom walks over to nearby table to get a candle. Placing his finger through the metal loop, he feebly lifts the candleholder and leads the party into the basement. The stairs end at a corridor. He points down it and says, "The shipment and the rats are down there. If we could just get rid of those buggers, we can get the shipment out."

Julia grumbles impatiently. "I guess we're playing exterminator." When they reach the end of the hall, there is a large storage room. Papers and various debris are scattered all over. A fallen cabinet blocks the entrance. Shine asks Duncan to lift it. He refuses, so Julia does it. As soon as it's lifted, a pair of rats scurry across the floor. They looked normal sized. Once inside the room, they spot a large hole in the wall on the other side. It looks like a rat hole, but it's way too big. Or is it?

A massive rodent lumbers out. It's the size of rottweiler! It hisses at the intruders. Two more emerge from the hole. They're big, too, but only half the size of the other. "Gross!" exclaims Wendy. "I hate rats."

"Well, let us get to it," asserts Marduk. "Once those big ones are gone, the rest will scurry." He decides to do the honors. The rats continue to hiss but don't engage, making them easy targets. He launches Fire Flurry in a wide spread. There's no way they can dodge and are belted by the fireballs. Luckily, the walls and floor are made of stone, so he doesn't burn the place down. A nearby box catches fire.

Somehow the rodents survived. They charge the party. The largest vermin lunges at Duncan who holds it off with his tower shield. Shine does the same with his. Julia blocks by holding her axe tightly in both hands. Her foe's jaws snap at her before it gives up and scoots past heading straight at Wendy. An arrow to the back slows it to a crawl before a Dark Ball finishes it off.

Meanwhile, Ed provides Shine an assist, attempting to flank, but the rat springs backwards in nick of time to avoid his blade. Duncan shoves his rodent back and belts it with Fastball. The force of the spell sends the giant critter crashing into the wall. The flames from the box spread onto some scattered papers. Wendy puts out the fire with a little Water magic before it grows any larger. Julia and Duncan charge the largest rat while Ed and Shine go after the other. The thief doesn't need to do anything, as Wind Burst stuns it long enough for Shine to land a killing thrust.

Duncan leads with his shield, moving at an angle that forces the rat toward Julia's axe. It hisses once more in defiance before lunging at her. Blood sprays all the way up the ceiling as her axe crashes down upon it midflight. There's a loud thud as it hits the stone floor. As expected, a few onlooking regular-sized vermin scurry out through the oversized rat hole. In the center of the room, there's a couple large boxes full of helmets. The heroes carry them upstairs to the Stubblebottoms.

Vermin defeated, shipment secure, the Stubblebottoms can complete the order. They grab some supplies from the basement and complete the last few battery-powered lanterns before screwing them to the helmets. They make one extra for the heroes as compensation. Artemis carefully wraps it in cloth to protect the glass lens and places it in the backpack. The party heads back into Caddis for another stay at the inn. While paying for the rooms, they notice funds are once again becoming scarce. Duncan barters his old sword for lodging.

Hopefully, this treasure really exists. They could really use the coin. In the morning, the loot acquired from the bounty hunters is sold off. There's still those sapphire earrings, too. After some haggling, funds are bolstered for the time being. Now they're ready to set out for Hulda

Cave. Whilst walking along the main road, a donkey-powered cart carrying two large, sealed crates rolls by. That must be the Stubblebottoms' shipment. The couple promised they would have their courier inform Matthew of the party's help. With passage through Tempora Tunnel secured, it's off to the cave. It isn't too far away. The heroes arrive midafternoon.

A giant moss-covered rock formation stands before the party. Crashing waves can be heard in the not too far distance. There is a stiff, salty breeze today occasionally misting the air with oceanic droplets. The rock formation and the cave system it contains extends to the coast. Supposedly, there's a hidden cove inside connecting to the ocean. That's where the pirates would dock their ship. It's a perfect hiding place. No wonder they were able to escape detection for so long.

Large boulders block the entrance. That's right, Dr. Smith did mention some crazy chick sealed the cave. That might be a problem. Wendy may have the solution. She notices some familiar-looking stones scattered amongst the rocky outcrops. Upon further inspection, she realizes it's flint. She gathers some of the larger pieces and coyly shows her friends. "What do you have there?" wonders Marduk.

Wendy grins widely and replies, "It's flint. I'm gonna make a bomb." Everybody wonders how the witch plans to do that. They don't have to wait long to see. She eagerly removes some gray ore from her robe pocket. Has she been carrying rocks around this entire time? They have a slightly red luster. Before anyone can ask, she explains, "It's magnesium. It's been enchanted with a little Fire magic, which is why it shines red. It doesn't take much to ignite it, especially enchanted like this. With the right combination of materials and magic applied, it can create a huge explosion." She piles the ore amongst the flint next to the obstructing boulders and advises everyone to stay "*waaay*" back.

Her friends watch in anticipation as she closes her eyes and concentrates. A gentle aura pulses from her body. The pile of ore glows red. At first, it's just a slight glimmer but quickly becomes brilliant. Moments after, KABOOM! It feels like the entire planet is trembling. The party has to turn and shield themselves from the heat and debris. When the dust clears, the result is impressive.

Wendy turns to her friends, who are gaping in amazement, and cheerfully declares, "Ta da!" However, no one can make out what she's saying. Wendy neglected to mention how loud it was going to be. Everyone's ears are ringing something fierce. Always appreciative of impressive displays of magic, Marduk feverously applauds. Wendy reveals she is working on crafting a smaller, contained version. A firebomb to use in battle. Unfortunately, that was all of her magnesium, so she'll need to procure more to make that a reality. She makes sure to pocket some flint before the party enters Hulda Cave. Most of the boulders have been reduced to pebbles.

Artemis shivers. It is noticeably chillier inside. Ed offers to warm her up with a full body rub. Julia slaps his hand away before it touches Artemis. Now Ed shivers as he rubs his hand. There's a strong, cool breeze blowing from deep within the system. Small droplets of water echo as they drip from stalactites and splash into shallow puddles on the floor. The first few chambers contain some interesting rock formations for those interested in that sort of thing but nothing exciting for the adventurers. It is dim yet brighter than expected. So far there's no signs the caverns have ever been inhabited. As the heroes make their way through a winding passage, they see wooden planks nailed to the walls. It's clear somebody was using the next room.

The cave walls have wooden reinforcements built in here and there. Most are badly damaged, if not reduced to piles of splintered wood. There are worn looking tables and chairs scattered about. Most of those are badly damaged, too, and cobwebs are covering just about everything. It is obvious a battle took place. That's a good sign. Now comes the tricky part, finding the hidden treasure, assuming it truly exists. There are arrows stuck in some of the walls and debris. Rusty swords and rotted wood shields are scattered about.

There are some skeletons strewn about near the equipment. The tattered garbs they are adorned with signals they were pirates. There're no signs of casualties on the military's side. This was a one-sided battle, possibly an ambush. Across the room, a wooden wall was built with a door. Not much remains of it. The door nearly falls off the hinges as our heroes head through. They quickly duck for cover as a cloud of bats pours from the passage. Their cries bounce about the chamber.

Continuing down another winding path, the party enters a room similar to the last with one important addition. There are several treasure chests. Everyone's excitement fast turns to disappointment upon discovering them to be open and bare. Either the military reclaimed the loot or thieves got here first. This room splits off into three paths. Only one, the widest path, has a doorway built in. The door is intact, but much of the wooden wall is destroyed. It would seem the attackers simply went around this doorway. This is likely the correct direction; however, that part of the cave suffered a collapse.

Peering behind the wall through a broken section, Ed notices a clear space. It's far too narrow to get through, but it's near the door. Maybe there's more room behind it. The door is locked. Duncan prepares to smash through, but to his disappointment, he doesn't need to. Ed, in his never-ending search for loot, finds a key attached to a belt on one of the pirate's skeletons. He gleefully plucks it and makes his way to the door.

As he walks away, the pile of bones begins to shake. Then it wobbles about, slowly rising to a stand. With his friends all pointing and shouting, the thief spins around to see a living skeleton slowly clambering towards him. "No fuckin' way!" he gasps, backpedaling away. Everyone is too shocked to move. Things like this happen in fables, not real life. Duncan quickly regains his resolve and acts. Concentrating mana into his fist, he fires his Fastball at the animated bones. The force of the blow explodes it into pieces. The skull bounces off the floor and lands near the party. They all jump back as it continues to move about, pushing itself along using its lower jaw, desperately inching closer to gnaw an ankle. Grimacing with disgust, Julia crushes the skull under her boot.

Freaked out by the living dead, our heroes quickly unlock the door. Ed was right! There's enough space to get through. Yet another winding passage leads into a large chamber, the biggest one so far. Broken crates and empty chests are scattered all over the place. There're quite a few bone piles. The party anxiously makes their way past them, fearing one will come to life as they search the room. Even after so much time has passed, it remains a chaotic scene. Not a single object looks to have survived. Even the cavern walls have scars. This must have been where most of the fighting occurred. Again, it looks like a one-sided affair in favor of the military, but there are some pieces of military armor amongst the wreckage.

It would also seem this is where the pirates were keeping their loot, but now the room is barren of anything valuable. There are no other passages. A dead end. The party doubles back to explore the other pathways. The first one they try leads to what appears to be what was sleeping quarters. It is a dead end, too. As they try the final passage, another skeleton is ambling down it. This one is holding a rusty cutlass. It has its back to the party. It turns around just in time to get obliterated by Fast Ball.

The heroes hear water ahead. Soon they arrive in the cove. There's a cracked, worn dock. The pirate ship is tied to it. The ship is horribly damaged. A tattered jolly roger flag is on full display attached to a cracked, tilted mast. The hull sustained major damage. The pirates must have escaped the naval battle by the skin of their teeth. This thing looks like it could sink at any moment. Like the other rooms, this one is devoid of anything of worth.

The pirates made their final stand here. It isn't as chaotic as the previous battle site, but there are still human remains everywhere. A few of them are walking around. Fresher remains are present. The stench of decaying flesh is nearly too much to bear. Julia notices one of the skeletons has dried blood on its clothes and cutlass. The corpses must be the unfortunate tomb raiders.

The heroes swiftly smash the creepy skeletons. As disturbing and intimidating they appear to be, they are slow and fragile. If one can keep their composure, the skeletons are simple enough to deal with. Ed wants to explore the ship for loot, but it's too dangerous. Even Duncan grumbles rejection. Like a petulant child, Ed throws a tantrum. Julia has to drag him off the pier. "Quit whining," Duncan gruffly orders the pouting thief. No treasure here either, but hope is not lost.

There is another path leading deeper into the cave. Shine and friends arrive in an empty chamber the size of the average person's living room. Much of the floor is spotted by shallow pools of water. Nothing manmade lies within. This room was unused. It's the only room that hasn't been explored. Ed cannot hide his dejection. The rumors were false. Captain Barret probably died with his men in the cove.

After some hemming and hawing to work through their state of denial, the party begins to depart. Before exiting, Marduk senses a strange presence. The other mages now sense it, too. A dark, magical aura is filling the room. Soon everybody feels it. Shine's jaw drops as a trio of ethereal beings fade into view. They circle the heroes a couple times before gathering in a row near the back wall. Shine shouldn't be so surprised considering they just saw walking skeletons, but for Theon's sake, there's actual, factual ghosts!

The specters begin wailing. No one is sure if it's a warning or just what ghosts do. It's the former. One of them zaps Julia with a bolt of lightning staggering her back a couple steps. She is eternally happy she decided to go with leather armor. Most of the shock was insulated, but it still hurt like hell. It seems ghosts know how to use magic. That raises all sorts of questions the adventurers don't have time to ponder. Shine slashes Rashida at the attacker. Unsurprisingly, it has no effect. How do you kill air? This is the mages' time to shine!

The melee fighters take a back seat and let the mana users do the dirty work. Duncan draws his rapier aiming to try out a new spell. Ed had told him how Drake used chi to create razor sharp winds. Maybe he can use magic the same way. Wind mana swirls around the blade. Duncan swings it straight on. A green, crescent-shaped burst of energy slices through the air and through a ghost. It does the trick. The ethereal being is cut in two. The halves slowly drift away from each other before completely dissipating. The others are impressed, but Duncan looks disappointed. Killing ghosts isn't as fun as killing people. Can you even really kill a ghost?

Seeing Duncan's success, Marduk uses his own Wind magic to take out another. Wendy doesn't want to be outdone. She doesn't know any Wind-based spells, but she has an idea. After hopping away from a lightning bolt, she attacks. The sapphire on her staff glows as she points it at the final specter. A freezing blast of wind rushes through it. The ghost freezes, becoming solid. It drops like a rock onto the floor and shatters. Marduk is again impressed at Wendy's talents. Duncan is, too, but acts like it wasn't shit.

Threat eliminated, the heroes now have time to process what they just encountered. First skeletons and now ghosts. The longer they journey, the stranger the occurrences they come across. An eerie ambience seems to hang in the air everywhere they travel. No one can shake this strange, foreboding sensation. For now, they must refocus on their current task.

Ed refuses to believe there's nothing to be found here. The party humors him as he adamantly begins examining the cave walls. As he crosses the halfway point of the back wall, he exclaims, "Eureka!" He feels a slight breeze coming from the other side of a crack in the wall. He wipes away some dirt and cobwebs. It's not a crack! Nature doesn't make perfectly straight lines. There must be a hidden door. If there's a hidden door, there must be a hidden switch.

He works his way back to his left, carefully feeling out every millimeter of the wall. He might have missed something before. He grins at his comrades as he finds what he's seeking. He pushes a small section of stone with his hand. A switch! The room shakes gently as the wall slides open. The thief cheers and leaps about the room in celebration. Something great lies ahead. He's sure of it.

The heroes make their way down the path. Before long, Artemis spots a broken arrow on the ground. The tip of the rusted iron head has dried blood on it. Someone pulled it out of somebody, possibly themselves, as they moved through here. The story said Captain Barrett had been mortally wounded in the battle. Could this arrow be the one that pierced him? As the passage opens up into another room, Ed runs ahead unable to contain his excitement. As the others catch up, they find him staring at something in the center of the room.

There's a skeleton lying atop a stone slab. Its arms are folded across its chest in an X. It's Captain Barrett! It has to be! There isn't much else in the room, but several unopened metal chests line one of the walls. Ed is shaking with excitement. This must be where the pirates kept their most precious treasure. Ed begins rapidly rambling how awesome this find is and how great Barret was in what is basically a gigantic run-on sentence. The rest of the members don't quite share Ed's adulation. Mostly, they're just creeped out and want to get the hell out of there as quickly as possible.

Before they can examine the chests, the adventurers are gripped by a dark, ominous presence. It is like it was with the ghosts only much, much stronger. They are not alone. Paralyzing fear takes hold as a dark cloud begins to manifest over Barrett's remains. The cloud swirls while slowly imploding. Soon it takes the shape of a sphere, and soon after that, a ghastly wraith takes form. Purple wisps encircle a patch of pure darkness resembling a hooded figure. There are no legs. Its body and arms are enveloped in a swirling dark cloud making it appear to be draped in an oversized robe.

The ominous entity is twice the size of a person. It lets out a piercing screech as two fiery red eyes ignite. They smolder like hot coals from Hades. It extends one of its jet-black arms outward to its side. Our heroes gets a good glimpse at the long, spindly claws it has for fingertips. Another dark cloud manifests around its outstretched hand. A massive scythe forms. The curved blade is six feet long. The wraith doesn't wait long to use it. Letting out another screech, it flies towards the intruders, widely swinging its sickle.

Everybody hits the ground, narrowly avoiding decapitation. The wraith circles around to make another sweep. As the heroes dive out of the way, Artemis manages to fire an arrow into its side. It doesn't do much damage, but it made contact. All weapons should be effective. Duncan tries to hit it with Fast Ball as it circles, but the specter is too quick. Seeing its enemy is now well positioned, it stops charging and hovers about. Artemis fires an arrow, but this time it passes right through. The wraith becomes invisible. Where did it go? That dark aura is still present. It must be trying for a sneak attack, but from where?

The heroes cautiously take defensive stances, slowly rotating to avoid being blindsided. The effort is for naught. The wraith materializes behind Julia. The massive scythe swings downward. Julia tries to evade but can't. She screams in pain as the blade slices deep into her back. It's a nasty gash. She can barely stand. The wraith fades again as Artemis rushes towards her comrade and eases her to the ground. Shine, Ed, and Duncan surround the healer as she attends to Julia. Marduk and Wendy begin gathering magic. When the specter appears again, they will be ready with powerful spells.

The wraith reappears. This time it is high off the ground, almost to the ceiling. It is too high and too far for anybody sans the mages to have range. As Marduk and Wendy square up to cast their spells, the wraith stretches out its free arm towards them. A wispy, dark red ball of energy manifests, then quickly disappears. The mages' knees buckle. Their spells break, and the mana evaporates away. It is all they can do to remain upright as they struggle to regain breath. It feels like all the energy has been sucked right out of their bodies. The wraith zooms towards them ready to finish things with that terrifying scythe. Shine and Duncan rush over. They are able to get in front of their allies and guard with their shields. A loud metal crash echoes through the room as they just barely able to fend off the killing strike.

Meanwhile, Ed tries to fight fire with fire. Using his Conceal skill, he sneaks around the room for an ambush of his own. Julia makes it back to her feet. She and Artemis rejoin the battle. Julia's wound isn't completely healed, but it will do for now. The wraith hovered backwards after its last attack failed. Duncan and Marduk nod at one another. Wind was highly effective against the ghosts. Maybe that will be the case here. Air spells are cast. The enemy counters. Again it stretches its free arm out. This time it uses a Wind spell of its own. A ferocious gale spirals at the heroes. Everyone caught in the blast is sent flying backwards, slamming into the cave wall.

Ed is the only one left standing. He managed to slink around the enemy. The wraith screeches in pain as the sly thief drives a dagger into its back. He tries strike with the other one, but it passes through harmlessly as the specter fades once more. Everyone else is still on the ground. Ed is all alone. He frantically runs and leaps about attempting to avoid the imminent ambush.

When the wraith reappears, it is a good ten feet from him. It casts Entropy, the spell that it used against Marduk and Wendy. Ed tries to dodge, but how do you evade an invisible spell? He collapses to the ground, desperately trying to catch his breath. Entropy is a fearsome spell. At this rate, everybody will be too drained to defend themselves.

Artemis has a countermove. She calls it Refreshing Wind. She sacrifices her own chi in order to restore her allies'. As she pushes chi out to each of her sides, anyone caught in the flow will have some of their stamina and chi restored. Ed is too far away, so he is on his own for the moment, but the rest of the party feels exhilarated. Artemis has to lean up against the wall. Restoring several people at once is an exhausting feat. It will take her a few minutes to recover. The rest charge their foe before it can attack Ed again. Outnumbered, the wraith floats backwards and disappears. No way the heroes are going to allow another sneak attack.

Marduk and Duncan begin firing off their air spells, and Wendy uses Chilling Wind. The spells aren't particularly strong. The idea is to fill the chamber with as much offensive magic as possible to catch the unseen enemy as it hovers around. One of the witch's spells connects! The wraith's shoulder becomes visible as it freezes. As its body rematerializes, Marduk connects with Shock followed up by Duncan's Fast Ball. Shine and Julia move it to attack, but the enemy darts away. It thinks it can take out Shine and Julia by casting Entropy and striking with its scythe before anyone can aid them. Duncan boosts his friends' magical resistance using a basic yet effective buff spell simply known as Magic Resist. Entropy's effect is minimal. The accompanying scythe slash is easily blocked. Sensing a counterstrike, the wraith blows its foes backwards with a less powerful, quickly gathered Whirlwind to create separation.

It tries to fade away, but Wendy connects with another Chilling Wind. Ed has made it back to his feet. He joins Julia and Shine in the charge. He's lost a couple steps but can still fight. The wraith frantically slashes its sickle about to keep the attackers at bay. Its reach is problematic. Normally, Ed would be able to dodge and get in close, but he just doesn't have the speed right now.

However, the melee fighters are backing it into a corner. The mages are slowly approaching, ready to prevent it from fading. Shine focuses chi into Rashida to use Radiant Sword for some additional power. Out of desperation, the Wraith lets out a piercing shriek that drops everyone to their knees. It zips to the center of the room and uses Whirlwind to blow the mages back. It scans for the easiest target. Ed is in bad shape. He looks like he's about to faint.

The wraith moves in to kill the downed thief. Shine and Julia move to protect him. Julia's axe clashes with the sickle, but the Wraith has superior leverage. It sends her skidding backwards. She falls backwards hard onto the ground. Now Shine is the only one standing between Ed and certain death. Artemis has ambled her way closer. She'd used more chi than she realized. She is in a perfect position to strike from behind but cannot focus her eyes and isn't sure if she even has enough chi to use an attack skill. She does have one final trick, another support skill.

She uses the last bit of her chi on Shine. His eyes grow wide as a surge of energy explodes from within. What a rush! He feels like he could cleave a mountain in two! Rashida's flames erupt into a blistering inferno. The Wraith slashes. Shine blocks with his sword and overpowers his foe, throwing it off balance. It barely blocks the next slash and the one after. Its guard has been broken! The Wraith tries to fade away as Shine has an open shot. The blaze scorches the specter even as it becomes ethereal. With one massive upward diagonal slash, Shine slashes it in twain. Horrifying cries emit from the entity. Its lanky arms thrash.

As the Wraith flails about in death throes, something strange happens. A bright white light explodes from the gash. It grows larger and brighter as the shadowy figure dissolves. The light arcs outward into a curved beam. It travels to the center of the room and halts in front of Captain Barrett's remains. The light begins to take form.

The heroes watch in amazement as another ethereal figure appears. This time it is a man. His body looks to be made of pure light. As the party cautiously gathers and approaches, the man raises a hand to his head. He grunts. "Ouch. What the hell happened?" Could this man really be the same being as that vicious Wraith?

Wendy seems to think so. She speaks to him, "Wow, you're a lot less scary looking now."

Bewildered, the man looks at her and gruffly grills, "What are you talking about?" He looks about the room. In a panicked voice he demands, "Who are you people? Where are my men?"

Marduk answers with a question, "Captain Barrett, I presume?"

"I am. What the hell is going on here?"

Shine informs, "We're a bit confused, too. You don't remember fighting us just now?"

"I-I don't know. It feels like a just woke up from a dream."

Shine continues, "I hate to be the bearer of bad news, but your dream is about to become a nightmare. I'm pretty sure you're dead."

"Dead?" Barrett scoffs. "Me? Impossible! I have twenty—No! Thirty good years left in me!"

Wendy flatly asks, "Why are you transparent then?"

Barrett is confused again. "What the devil are you talking about?"

"Take a look at yourself." Shine points.

Confusion turns into horror as Barrett examines his body. "I-I can see through my hands… Why am I glowing? What the hell…? What did you wretches do to me?!"

"Whoa, take it easy," Shine pleads. "We didn't do anything." He defers to Ed seeing as he seems to be knowledgeable on the subject. "Ed, do you remember when Captain Barrett was killed?"

"'Course I do!" Ed beams. Before answering, he cannot help but to gush to Barrett about how honored he is to meet the infamous pirate. After a smack on the head from Julia, he answers the question, "Sixteen oh two. Yep, sixteen oh two, I'm sure of it."

Shine replies, "Fifty-one years ago, huh?"

Ed addresses the Captain. "Ya hear that, cap'n? It's the year sixteen fifty-three. Ya been dead for o'er fifty years. Yer bones are layin' behind you."

Barrett isn't convinced. "Do you really think I'm dumb enough to fall for that? Just who are you people? And where the hell are my men?"

Marduk tries to get the Captain to recall, "Focus your mind and try to remember, Captain. You and your men were hiding in this cavern. The king's soldiers managed to track you down, and a fierce battle ensued. According to the legend, most of your men were slain, and you were fatally wounded. The ones who escaped must have laid you to rest here. Think back, Captain. Do you remember that battle?"

After a long pause, memories of the past flood into Captain Barrett's mind. It feels like a white-hot light sparked inside his head. The intensity causes him to cry out in pain. He stumbles back as memories continue their rapid influx. Once he is able to compose himself, he speaks, "Yes, I remember now. We were greatly outnumbered, but we managed to put up one hell of a fight. In the end, there were simply too many enemies. We retreated to the cove and made our last stand. I can't believe those dogs managed to find us. You say that was over fifty years ago?"

"Yes," answers Shine. "We were exploring this cave when we found your tomb. I guess a few survivors laid you to rest here. You appeared out of nowhere and attacked us."

"I attacked you? I can remember a battle that happened fifty years ago like it was yesterday, so why is my memory of you so hazy…?"

Marduk has a theory. "You didn't seem quite like yourself. You were veiled in a dark energy. It was like you were possessed by something."

"Yes, I have this strange sensation that I've been battling such a force for a long time. Could it be King Magnus's doing?"

Marduk explains, "I'm afraid he's no longer ruling Elysia. Magnus the Second died about twenty years ago. His son, Pious, is now king."

"Pious? I have never heard his name before, yet it feels like I've known him all my life. Tell me. What is the state of affairs in Elysia?"

"It's not good," Shine laments. "Pious began his reign as a kind, noble ruler. Seemingly overnight, he had a change of heart and became a tyrant. Relations with other nations are disintegrating, our rights are being taken one by one, and taxes are so high, many people can't afford food."

Barrett seems strangely unsurprised. "I can still feel a lingering presence. It feels… evil. I have a feeling in the pit of my stomach that something terrible is about to happen." He pauses and looks at Shine. "At the same time, I feel a powerful force coming from you."

Shine points at himself in surprise. "Really? Me?"

Duncan flippantly responds, "Yeah, really? *Him*?"

Captain Barrett continues, "It's almost like a great power is trying to burst forth from within you."

"Sounds painful," Ed jabs.

Barret declares, "It almost feels like we were meant to meet. You all saved my soul from eternal darkness and unrest. There's nothing I can possibly do to repay that, so this will have to suffice. I shall give you the knowledge of my secret technique."

Ed lights up with glee. "I 'member readin' 'bout that! No one knows for sure what it is. Some say it was some devastatin' attack you used ta sink ships. Others say ya create some sorta diversion to escape."

"Hahahaha!" Barrett laughs. "It's nice to know people are still telling stories about me. No, it's nothing grandiose. Actually, it's so simple, it's ingenious. I call it Disperse. It channels the user's chi into a small whirlwind that rapidly sucks in air and anything else caught in the pull, then violently explodes outwards. It's surprisingly powerful, enough to punch a hole through a ship's hull. It can also be used to toss shit around. It'll make a room look like a tornado ripped through. Hahaha! My men and I made some incredible escapes using that trick! I'm sure you'll find it useful."

Ed is grinning from ear to ear. "Ha! Nobody's ever gonna believe this happened in a million years. So, who gets ta learn yer lil' trick?"

Barrett points at Shine, "You there. What's your name?"

"It's Shine."

"Hahaha! How fitting! The one with the brightest aura is actually named Shine! That is just too perfect. Now I'm certain I'm destined to pass this on to you."

"What do I need to do?"

"Just stand still and close your eyes. Clear your mind." As Shine does so, Captain Barrett begins to glow brighter. Wind whips around the room in a giant circle. It rapidly shrinks as it is drawn into Shine's body until it is gone completely. Shine grunts in pain. It isn't as intense as Barret's memories flooding back, but the surge of information is still a lot to take. Shine's eyes are shut tight as he endures. In an instant, the surge is gone. Shine opens his eyes. He shakes his head a few times.

"Did it work?" inquires Marduk. "Do you feel any different?"

Shine isn't sure how to put it, "It's... it's hard to describe... Physically, I don't feel any different, but mentally—it feels like I just had an epiphany. Like I just realized some deep inner truth."

Ed quips, "Heavy. So, that's a yes?"

"Yeah."

Barrett laughs. "Hahaha! That was be easier than I thought it would be. You must have a knack for focusing chi." A look of relief washes over him. "It looks like my soul is no longer bound to this plane. I'm curious to see what my fate shall be. Will I see the gates of Eden, or the fires of Hades? Goodbye, travelers. Use that technique well. I'm sure it will aid you on your journey."

Shine smiles and offers farewell, "Goodbye, Barrett. You're certainly an interesting character. Try not to cause too much trouble wherever you end up."

"No promises." Barrett grins. Our heroes solemnly watch Captain Barrett's soul fade away, afterlife bound.

"Well, that was interesting," Wendy comments.

Ed excitedly agrees, "I can't believe I got to meet an infamous pirate, a dead one at that! He even gave us a new trick. I am kinda bummed 'e chose Shine instead of me."

Marduk acknowledges, "He must feel Shine has much potential. Shine has grown quite strong in a very short time. He even sliced that Wraith in two with a single swing."

Shine begins to blush. "I can't take all the credit for that. It was weakened thanks to you guys, and Artemis boosted my power. That was one hell of a technique by the way."

Artemis looks confused. "Me? Oh, no, I didn't do anything like that. All I did is make your own chi flow more freely."

Shine is shocked. "You mean…? That power was my own?" In that moment, despite all the strange happenings, the foreboding feeling that seems to be everywhere they go, Shine feels the future is bright. If he can learn to use chi to his full potential, who knows how strong he'll become?

Before leaving, there is one more small matter to attend to. The party forces the metal chests open. Ed is actually drooling over what wonders hide within. They don't contain the super rare, precious artifacts they were expecting, but there's plenty of gems and gold coins. That's good enough for the thief as well as his friends. Everyone fills up their pockets and backpack as much as they can. With this loot, they can afford better equipment and still have coin to spare. Things seems to get more perilous the more our heroes journey. They will need to be well equipped to endure. ♛

CHAPTER 11
Hope Springs Eternal, Hopefully

For now, it's back to Caddis for some much-needed rest. The plan is simple. They will report what happened to Dr. Willard Smith, then use some of their newfound wealth for equipment and items. From there, it's on to Tempora Tunnel and, finally, Giza. They'll figure out the next steps once they arrive.

Dr. Smith is shocked and enlightened by the heroes' tale of what transpired in Hulda Cave. Ed does most of the talking, raving and ranting like a madman. The doctor is still wary about venturing into the caverns, but he feels much of the danger has been eliminated. He is going to contact a few colleagues and put an expedition together to examine the site and learn more about Captain Barrett's final days.

Artemis purchases a new outfit. Her garments have seen better days. She buys some new leather shoes and a two-piece set of linen clothes, a tunic and pants. Both are forest green, a fond reminder of Verde's Woods. Its wonderfully lightweight, allowing her to move and react quickly in battle. It doesn't provide much physical protection but is rather good at resisting magic. She also trades up her iron-tipped arrows for some steel ones. Those should add some extra oomph to her shots. She could use a new bow but cannot bear to part with the one she has. It is the best one she's crafted thus far.

Julia is in need of new armor as well seeing as there's now a huge gash in the back. She's irritated with how short-lived its usefulness was. Steel plate may have been able to protect her from the Wraith's scythe. Despite this, she wants to stick with leather. She's been having nightmares about being boiled alive whilst dressed in full plate. She finds a higher quality leather set at the armor shop. It's made of ox hide, so it's a bit tougher than the cowhide garbs she has now. It even has steel studs for a little extra protection. She decides to also purchase an iron helmet. The heavy thing will slow her down somewhat but also help ensure her head doesn't get split open.

Duncan and Shine are satisfied with their current sets. The other two mages go shopping together at the magic shop. Marduk upgrades his staff. This new one is made of high-quality maple. It has a finely crafted quartz orb that helps magnify defense magic. He also purchases some new robes. They are wool, like the ones he has now, grey color included, but have been enchanted to slightly boost physical and elemental resistance. It will come in handy both in combat and harsh weather.

Wendy is happy with her staff but also gets some new robes. Wool is far too itchy, so she opts for silk. She cannot help but to stay with black. The dark silk has a beautiful sheen. Silk intrinsically reflects magic. It cannot bounce a spell back at an enemy, but it will naturally repel some of the attack. She also picks up some jade earrings with silver fishhooks. Jade is popular with mages who focus on the healing arts. It can ease one's mental state, which is important performing critical aid. Jade also slightly boosts magical potency. Wendy mainly bought them for the latter. Well, and because they look really, *really* cute.

Marduk and Wendy also buy magic tomes. These are spell books mages use to study and learn new spells. Most tomes are also enchanted with properties similar to the spells they contain. Marduk wants to focus on learning more defensive magic. His tome, *Shield*, increases physical defense and boosts vitality. He isn't a young adventurer anymore. This journey will be long and arduous, and he wants to make sure his body can keep up.

Wendy wants to focus on bolstering her attack power. Her tome, *Assault*, contains some powerful spells and increases the user's magical potency. The enchantment helps create more violent reactions, thus making it dangerous for healers but ideal for battlemages. Her philosophy is enemies can't attack you if they're already dead. In other words, the best defense is a strong offense.

Ed decided he needed a fashion makeover. Their recent adventures inspired him to adopt a more pirate-y look. Everyone thinks he looks ridiculous, but he couldn't care less. He purchased a horizontal-stripped blue and white shirt, a red bandana, a single gold loop earring, a thick leather belt, black cotton pants, and black steel toe boots. A full makeover. Aside from the boots, his attire doesn't have any combat utility, but he can't care less about that, too. At least it's lightweight.

He considered getting a pistol, but the only ones for sale are single-shot muskets. Reloading after every shot doesn't mesh well with his combat style. He'd rather dance about with his daggers. Revolvers are a rarity for civilians. They were fairly scarce to begin with, then military acquired contacts with the manufacturers, most of which are exclusive. Officers have standard issue sidearms though they still vary somewhat due to the different vendors.

It is becoming an expensive day, but the loot the heroes collected in Hulda Cave plus what remained from Fort Perdition more than covers it. There's still more to procure. They pick up some extra food and gear. Artemis stops by the apothecary to pick up some vitality and mana potions. She gets three of each plus some medicinal herbs in case someone gets sick or poisoned. You can never be too careful. Wendy manages to find some magnesium for sale. It isn't much, but she has enough to make a couple smaller versions of the bomb she used to open the cave. Even after that final stop, the party won't have to worry about funds for a little while.

The next day, they set out for Tempora by way of Salem. Once back in the somber village, Artemis has a request. She wants to challenge Conway again. Once they cross the Aker mountains, there's no telling when she'll be back this way. Everyone has gotten stronger after their failure, plus they have Duncan now. Shine doesn't want to spend any more time dealing with things outside their main objective, but he just can't say no to her puppy dog eyes. They're confident they can win this time and head for the Cave of Lost Souls to even the score.

Conway is surprised and mildly annoyed by their return. The Outcasts stare in awe at the outsiders' audacity. Conway has a fairly good idea why they're back. As the party approaches, walking with purpose, Conway takes hold of his obscene hammer and rises from his throne. He sternly addresses his hopeful opponents, "Back to try your luck again, eh?"

"That's right," Shine confidently replies.

Before anymore pleasantries can be exchanged, Julia breaks rank and marches forward, staring dead into Conway's eyes. "I got this. He's mine," she states matter-of-factly. The pain of the previous loss is still fresh within her. She feels like she has something to prove.

Marduk questions, "Are you certain, Julia? Conway is quite strong. I believe we'd stand a better chance fighting as a unit."

Duncan is chomping at the bit. "I dunno who this guy is to you, but something about him makes me really want to punch him in the face."

Julia doesn't even glance back at her friends. Her gaze affixed to Conway; she quietly, coolly replies, "This guy is an expert at fighting against groups of attackers. We have a better chance fighting one-on-one. I can beat him. I know I can."

Conway's face softens just a bit. Julia's bravery is impressive, but his confidence is unwavered. "You think you can best me one-on-one, girl? So be it." He pauses before issuing a warning, "But this is it. This your last chance. When I beat you, never show your faces here again. If you do, I will kill you."

Her friends don't feel this is the best course of action, especially with the added stipulation, but they know there's no reasoning with her. If they interfere, Julia will never forgive them, so everyone reluctantly falls back and places faith in the young warrior from Cid. Julia draws her axe from her back and flings the backpack behind her. She even removes her new helmet to aid her speed. Conway is a fast one. Mobility trumps protection. Conway steps out to face his adversary. The two combatants are statuesque, staring daggers into each other's eyes. A crowd of Outcasts has slowly gathered to witness the showdown. The warriors stand for what seems to be an eternity. Conway doesn't seem be in any hurry, so Julia makes the first move.

She charges head on. Unlike last time, she channels chi into her axe. She slashes quicker than Conway was expecting, but he still blocks with relative ease. Julia continues with several more slashes, but each blow is matched. Spotting an opening, Conway counterattacks, thrusting his hammer forward with one hand as if it were a spear. Julia twists her body to evade but is unable to counter. She will need to get in close to stand a chance. It won't be easy. Conway is just as fast, if not faster.

Julia charges in for another flurry. This time she takes a little power out of her attacks. When Conway counters, she'll be able to evade and get in close. Her opponent is wise. He senses what Julia is plotting and leaps back out of her range. Planting is foot hard in the ground, he springs forward, swinging is hammer wide. Julia backpedals to safety. Conway keeps coming with a spinning flourish. Julia blocks then evades. She gets in close!

Wait, why is Conway smiling? As she was dodging, he drew his hammer in close to his body. He suckered her in. Julia flies backwards as the top of the hammer is slammed into her chest. Out of pure instinct she redirects chi into her legs. When they touch ground, she slides backwards but is able to maintain balance.

Conway springs forward again. Even with his lanky arms and the hammer's reach, his opponent is out of range for a melee strike. Instead, he drives the hammerhead into the cave floor, sending a shockwave screaming at the warrior. Julia responds in kind. The cavern shakes violently as the shockwaves collide and cancel each other out. The warriors smile at one another. This battle is proving to be good sport for Conway. It's been a long time since either man or beast gave him a good fight. The combatants square off again, slowly circling each other.

Julia feels playing defense and countering is her best shot at victory. Conway can't help but grin as she gestures for him to attack. He is happy to oblige. He serpentines towards her, bobbing and weaving to throw his foe off. Julia stands perfectly still, keeping her eyes on Conway's waist. His center of gravity will tell her where the attack is coming from. He fakes a move to the left before darting forward and striking with a backhanded swing.

Julia easily blocks it as well as the follow up. She uses her strength to push Conway back and go on the offensive. Her opponent doesn't try to block. He evades her slashes with ease and hits her with an unexpected move, a spinning back kick. His long, twig-like leg doesn't look menacing, but it packs quite a punch. He catches Julia flush in the temple, which does nightmares for her equilibrium. It's a wonder she's even conscious. Maybe losing the helmet was a bad idea. Conway chains his kick with a fearsome upward swing of his hammer. The head smashes into his foe's chest and sends Julia flying away. She hits the cave floor with a loud thud.

Thinking his opponent is finished, Conway relaxes, but it isn't over yet. Not while she's still breathing. Julia desperately struggles to get to her feet. Her arms quiver like jelly as she tries to push herself off the ground. Against his better judgment, Conway doesn't advance to finish the fight. He wants to see if she can actually make it her feet. Eventually she does, albeit barely. Her legs are shaking. Her knees could buckle at any moment. Blood is splattered on her chin. She must have coughed it up. Conway is reluctant to continue. One more blow and she might die. He tries to get her to concede, "It's over. You've lost. Stop while you're still breathing."

Julia grimaces as she smiles. She wipes the blood from her face. "As if. You're the one who's going down." Bold words, but she knows she is in trouble. Her arms and legs feel like they're made of sand. She has no idea how she's going to be able to charge him or block the next attack. There's no choice. It's risky, but she has to do it. The warrior lets out a mighty scream as she unleashes all the chi left in her body at once. Such a technique will sharply increase the user's abilities, assuming the strain doesn't destroy their body. After that, the raging inferno of energy will burn out quickly. The fight must be ended fast, or she will be too drained to stand let alone fight.

Conway lets out more chi, too. His opponent is going to be deadly in that powered up state, but all he has to do is evade until his adversary burns out. Julia lets out an animalistic roar as the last bit of chi flows out. It's a strange mix of extreme pleasure and pain as her body desperately tries to handle the strain. She launches forward with incredible force. Her friends could have sworn there was a sonic boom. Her axe might as well be a dagger as she slashes with blistering quickness. It's faster than Conway anticipated. He is just barely able to block and is in danger of being thrown off balance. He leaps backwards and prepares to dodge her follow up attacks. He's able to evade the first couple but struggles to keep up with his adversary's speed. He is forced to defend and manages to push off to create some distance. He backpedals a few steps. Julia catches him off guard.

Conway drops to the ground as Julia flings her axe his chest. It was spinning with such velocity, he would have been cleaved in half if it had connected. Julia charges. She's even faster without her weapon. She closes on Conway before he can fully get back to his feet and clocks him with a brutal uppercut. As he reels back, she connects with a thrust. Conway slides back, barely able to keep his feet under him. Julia presses. Conway frantically thrusts his hammer. Julia sidesteps and grabs hold of the handle. She screams as she pulls the hammer closer and Conway along with it. She belts him with another punch. Conway flies backwards. Now Julia has the hammer!

Conway tumbles on the ground and comes to a crashing halt against the cave wall. Julia lets out one final scream as she leaps into the air.

Driving the hammer into the ground, she sends Shockwave streaking at her foe. There's nothing he can do. Conway cries out as his body is racked with pain. Julia lands and doubles over, unable to catch her breath. That last move completely drained her. Her legs are trembling badly, but she remains standing. Conway is down. Now he's the one struggling to get up. He can't. A gasp of air escapes as he collapses.

Conway just lies there, barely conscious. He's still lucid enough to realize what had transpired. He has lost. Everyone, heroes and Outcasts alike, stare in stunned silence. Julia drops the hammer as she falls to one knee. Her friends rush over. Artemis gives her a vitality potion. Julia gulps it down, and her breathing soon returns to normal. She gets back to her feet and makes her way over to Conway. He can barely even turn his head to look up as she extends a hand out. He smiles despite being in agonizing pain.

Julia pulls Conway up. Artemis gives him a potion, too. After downing it, he beckons for Julia to follow as he slowly ambles to his throne. He lets out a huge sigh of relief as he sits. Julia and friends gather. Conway takes a few moments to collect his thoughts before addressing the heroes. "Well, I'll be damned. You beat me, girl. You've gotten so much stronger in such little time. I'm impressed." Julia is beaming.

Duncan mutters under his breath, "I could have taken him."

Julia's expression turns back to business. "So, we can explore the caverns now, right?"

"Of course, of course. That was the deal."

Artemis squeals with joy and squeezes Julia as hard as she can. "Oh, thank you, Julia! Thank you! Thank you! Thank you!"

Julia's face turns red as Artemis nuzzles her cheek against her bicep. "Um… You're welcome," she shyly replies. The rest of the party congratulates her. Everyone except Duncan. He just stands there with his arms folded, convinced he could have easily won. Julia spots Conway's hammer on the ground. She lifts it and returns it to him. As she extends, Conway declines.

She looks at him in surprise as he says, "You keep it." Before she can question, Conway explains, "That hammer has served me well in my years here. It's perfect for squishing the giant bugs and other critters that inhabit the deeper regions of the cave. You've shown you're strong enough to wield it. I'm sure it will serve you well."

Julia isn't sure what to say. "Are you sure?" she asks.

"Absolutely. Think of it as a token of respect."

"C'mon, don't look a gift hammer in the mouth," prods Ed. Julia thanks Conway and accepts his gift.

The hammer is a truly impressive piece of craftsmanship. Its head is made of solid iron, making it incredibly heavy but incredibly powerful. Very few people are strong enough to hold such a hefty weapon, let alone wield it effectively in battle. It is a devastating weapon for those who can. The handle is made of carved ironoak bark. Ironoak trees were named after their toughness. The bark is quite hard, like iron, hence the name. This wood is petrified, making it closer to steel on the Mohs scale with half the weight. It's sturdy enough to withstand that giant iron head being swung around without snapping in two. Marduk concludes a mithril blade must have been used to carve it. Julia leaves her axe with Conway. She would feel bad leaving him weaponless.

The heroes walk to the gate leading to the rest of the caverns. Julia asks her friends to kill any hostile critters for her. Even after drinking that potion, it will be a while before she fully regains her strength. The guard nervously opens the gate for them. They may have earned Conway's trust and respect, but the rest of the Outcasts are still wary of the outsiders. As the party proceeds, it quickly becomes apparent that the first chamber is not the only one that is occupied. In the next room, there are mushroom farms and tents scattered about. Some areas have dirt floors. The water dripping from the ceiling provides the water for the crops. Buckets are positioned under some of the stalactites to collect the precious resource. The railway splits in two, leading to different chambers.

The party is directed to which way leads to the lower levels. All they have to do is follow the tracks straight for a while until they find an elevator. Before long, it becomes necessary to light a couple torches. The further they walk, the darker it gets, and there aren't any more of the Outcast's torches lighting the way. A few Outcasts shuffle about in the dark. Their eyes glimmers like cats'. They must have adapted somewhat to the dim surroundings. The caverns are much larger than anyone thought. After a half hour of walking through winding paths and various chambers, the tracks eventually lead to the elevator. Luckily, it's still in operation.

The Outcasts don't venture to the lower levels. Ever since the mines were abandoned, creatures reclaimed the caves. The party steels themselves. Who knows what dangers lie below? The elevator makes a loud hum as it begins to descend. The ride is bumpy due to lack of maintenance. The surroundings grow darker the lower the lift goes. Soon it's pitch black. There's a loud metal clank as the elevator arrives at its destination. Even the torches don't do much to illuminate the massive chamber the heroes find themselves in. Marduk has an idea.

He focuses mana into his staff's quartz orb, creating a magic light. It shines much brighter than the torches or the lantern helmet, but it will slowly drain his energy to use it. Those mana potions will come in handy as the party ventures deeper. Rails wind down various paths. There are some abandoned carts and equipment scattered about. There is one more level beneath them. If this spring really does exist, that's likely where it will be. The deepest, gloomiest regions have scarcely been explored. First, they need to locate another elevator.

The tracks narrow down the possibilities, but there's no guarantee any particular path won't lead to a dead end. It could take days of exploring to find the correct route. No one's sure what time it is, but it has to be getting late. This would be a good spot to set up camp. There are a few half logs in the backpack for just such an occasion. It won't be much, but a little added magic will prolong the fire long enough to get some rest. Wendy uses some of her flint to get the fire going. The party munches on a simple meal of apples and bread before getting some sleep.

They sleep in shifts a few hours at a time in case something tries to eat them. As the fire dies, the final sleepers awake. Marduk recreates his magic light. As it illuminates the room, the heroes find themselves surrounded by various creatures. They must have slowly gathered as everyone rested. The vicious menagerie looks eager to devour their prey. There are several large spiders, black salamanders, and seer worms.

Seer worms get their name not only from being able to navigate in pitch blackness but because of their ability to sense magical auras. They can easily pinpoint a mage's location just by the faint aura radiating from them. They crave magical energy and can drain it from their prey. Their main source of sustenance comes from beetles that populate the caverns. Mana is everywhere, and these insects channel it to signal one another in the darkness. However, the seer worms can also sense it, and use it to pinpoint tasty magic morsels.

Using a spell known as Drain, they use small amount of their own mana to ensnare others' and absorb it. Humans rarely come into contact these worms, but when they do, it doesn't usually go well for the humans. Even non-mages have latent magical energy in their bodies, as do all living things. Many researchers believe mana is the energy of life itself. In any case, the latent mana makes a hearty meal for the seer worms. Their victims, on the other hand, tend to pass out. They don't always wake back up.

There're a dozen hostile looking creatures in all. Great, more aggressive beasts. On the upside, if salamanders are present, there must be water nearby. There's no good escape route. No choice but to fight. Marduk is well aware of the seer worms' capabilities. He advises the mages focus on the other critters while the worms are dealt with by the others.

The spiders hiss as they slowly approach. The salamanders aren't far behind, flicking the air with their forked tongues. No time to waste! Everyone springs into action eager to end things quickly. Artemis fires an arrow at one of the worms. It effortlessly bobs out of harm's way. The worms begin their advance. They slither like snakes, using the back half of their bodies to push forward. Their front halves are raised mimicking a cobra readying to strike. They're probing for magic auras.

Duncan focuses his mana to increase his physical strength and launches Fast Ball at one of the spiders. It connects but does little damage. The other four spiders charge the party. They are belted by Marduk's fireballs. They're rocked but keep coming. Conway wasn't kidding. These are some tough critters.

Wendy tries out one her firebombs. She hurls it at the salamanders. After a brilliant explosion, it seems to have done some decent damage, but all the reptiles are still standing. Duncan draws his sword and charges the spiders. Ed and Shine take on the worms. There's only three, so it be should easy enough to handle them. Julia gets the attention of the four salamanders. She doesn't intend to fight them all alone. She just needs to get their attention so Artemis and the mages can flank.

Shine and Ed are met with an unwelcome surprise. Seer worms are one of the few of Terra's creatures that can use magic. The heroes are paralyzed as electricity resonates from all three worms, engulfing them in a massive wave. They like to immobilize more formidable prey to make it easier to use Drain. Seeing her friends in danger, Artemis dives and rolls forward. As she comes out of her roll, she fires three arrows at once. All three connect with a different worm. It does enough to stun them for a moment, and she immediately uses her healing chi to help her friends. She is just in time.

The worms launch themselves at their prey, spinning their bodies like drills. Shine gets his shield in front to block. Ed crosses his daggers to defend. Artemis evades her attacker. The trio smiles at each other as they counter in unison. Artemis lets out an unexpected warrior yell as she bashes one with her bow not once but twice. She then drives an arrow like a dagger into its front end. The worm flails about before falling down dead.

While Artemis is savagely slaying, Ed unleashes an impressive leaping corkscrew attack, slicing his worm into pieces. Shine simply slices his in two with Rashida. It doesn't seem dead quite yet, so he seals the deal with a thrust through its front tip. Shine and Ed turn back to gawk at the archer. The smushed, stabbed worm lies lifeless at her feet. She smiles sheepishly as they wonder who this girl is and what she did with Artemis.

Meanwhile, Duncan goes to town on the spiders. He uses his tall shield to wall off attackers as he slices four of one of the spider's legs off. He quickly moves and evades a bite from another. Four of the spiders go after him. One peels off and charges at Marduk. The wizard tries to hit it with Shock, but the arachnid avoids. Marduk screams as pain as its fangs dig into his arm. Wendy blasts it away with Deluge. The bite immediately swells like a balloon and turns purple. He's in a great deal of pain but not out of the fight. His *Shield* tome is doing its job strengthening his constitution.

Duncan exterminates three of the spiders with frightening efficiency. Another lunges at him but is stopped cold by Wendy's Chilling Wind. Duncan easily finishes it off with Razor Wind, cleaving the vulnerable target in two. Marduk uses Shock on one of the salamanders now surrounding Julia. A second Razor Wind finishes off the final spider before it can attack again.

Julia smiles as she gets to try out her new toy. She uses Shockwave. This time the added weight of her new hammer supercharges it. It explodes the ground in all directions just like Conway did in the first fight. All of her opponents are stunned. Artemis runs over to Marduk. She uses some of her medicinal herbs plus some healing chi to dispel the poison and heal the wound.

Shine and Ed rush to Julia's side to deal with the salamanders. Julia smashes two of their heads while they're still dazed while her friends slice the other two apart. The heroes can't help but be impressed with their performance as they stand strong amongst a pile of dead critters.

The battle was deftly handled. With each fight, they grow more in sync. Somehow everybody's unique skills sets seem to mesh together well. Marduk consumes a mana potion to ensure he can continue lighting the way unencumbered.

After a few hours, the party is disappointed to find themselves at a dead end. The rails led to an empty chamber. Too many wrong turns could be an exhausting endeavor. They backtrack double time as hisses pierce the shadows. Best to conserve strength and only fight when absolutely necessary. They get back to the point the tracks split with little trouble. On the way, a very large bat messed around and was impaled by Piercing Shot. They passed several shallow pools of slimy water. That must be where the salamanders like to soak. No way this stinky stuff is the fabled spring.

After a couple more hours of walking, the second elevator is found. Wendy shivers as they take it down. It's chilly this far underground. The rail tracks end here. Looks like this chamber is the furthest Salem's miners ventured before giving up. There's evidence a fair amount of excavating was attempted. A single abandoned cart sits at the end of the tracks. Fortunately, the path ahead is straightforward. Most of the tunnels are too small to even crawl through. Artemis just hopes the spring isn't hidden behind one of them. They've come too far to leave empty handed. She is sure they'll find the spring. They have to.

The path begins to narrow. It looks like the there's enough room to squeeze through the crevice to the next chamber, but thick cobwebs block the way ahead. The tight passage is a few feet long. Just about every inch is covered in sticky silk. At least there aren't any spiders around. Ed tries to cut the webs with a dagger and immediately regrets it. The webs are ridiculously sticky, and there are so many, the blade gets stuck. "Ew! Ew! *Eeeeeewwww!*" he wails, frantically trying to jiggle his knife free. Eventually, it comes loose. Ed frowns at the sight of the webs coating his beautiful blade.

Marduk consumes the second of the mana potions. "Shall I burn them?" he asks of the webs.

"No," replies Shine. "Let me try."

This is the perfect opportunity to try out the skill Captain Barrett bestowed to him, Disperse. He closes his eyes and focuses. Strangely, it feels like he's used this skill a thousand times. It feels second nature. A small cyclone forms in the center of the webs. It begins to rotate with surprising velocity. The vortex rips the webs from the wall, pulling them near its center. Thrusting out his palm, Shine explodes the cyclone outward. The webs go flying through the opening out of the way. It's an impressive technique indeed. No wonder Barrett loved it so much.

With the path cleared, the heroes make their way into the next room. It is a massive chamber. Marduk lifts his staff as high as he can, but the light does not reveal the ceiling. The darkness seems to stretch for eternity. The party wanders out somewhere in the middle of the room. Massive stalagmites line the floor. Each one is taller than Julia; some even outreach the magic light. Thick pillars of stone act as natural support beams.

A cluster of stalagmites form a small room within the enormous chamber. Cobwebs block the way in. Like the last ones, they are suspiciously devoid of spiders. Shine uses Disperse again, and the heroes head into the room within the room. Perhaps this where the spring is. Artemis's emotions flux between trepidation and hope. This area is larger than expected. After several minutes of walking, the other side still cannot be seen. The room is barren. Nothing seems to be here. Scuffling sounds echo around them. A hiss stabs the darkness. It is clear they are not alone.

They finally reach back wall, but it's a dead end. No spring here. There's no choice but to backtrack. Wasn't that where that hiss came from? It's hard to pinpoint. Sound bounces off the stone surfaces, scattering it. Another hiss echoes. This one sounded like it came from above. The cave ceiling is much lower in this area. Its dark shadow is just barely visible in the light. There are cobwebs up there, too, bunched in the middle of a group of stalactites. Marduk's eyes widen in fear as he slowly steps forward, staff held high. Those aren't just cobwebs. "A nest!" he exclaims.

Everyone scrambles towards the exit, but it is too late. A gigantic, spindly shadow descends in front of them, blocking the way out. Eight incredibly long legs slowly extend to the edge of darkness. A massive queen spider slowly approaches the ground. It is far larger than anyone had ever seen or could even comprehend existing. It is twelve feet tall. Its eight sickly yellow, charcoal pupiled eyes are the size of soccer balls. Its curved fangs are as long as Ed's daggers and just as sharp. The silk strand it is descending on is so thick it makes a loud snap as the queen breaks free and lands with a low thud. Its body is so massive, there's no way around it.

As if that wasn't bad enough, more hisses ring out. Several more spiders about the same size as the ones the heroes previously encountered lower themselves around their queen. Several more drop to the heroes' sides and the rear. The party is completely surrounded. The queen growls in unnatural fashion. As if they'd been issued a command, her subjects slowly begin to close. There's no time to strategize.

The queen will be tough enough to deal with by herself. Being surrounded like the is a recipe for death. Everybody has the same notion. The best plan of action is to quickly take out the arachnids in the rear and fall back. They may end up being backed against a wall, but at least they can prevent being outflanked. The enemy will be forced to attack straight on.

Marduk turns up the light's intensity to blind the frontal foes. That should buy a little time. Everybody with a melee weapon rushes the spiders to the rear. Artemis partially freezes one with Ice Arrow. It breaks its legs free easily enough but not quickly enough. Using chi to increase his speed, Ed is able to score a fatal thrust before it can react. Wendy slows another down with an icy wind. Shine ignites Rashida and finishes it off. Julia bashes another's head in with Conway's hammer. Conway was right about how well it squishes things. Duncan scores a few hits on his foe while dipping away from a hocked wad of venom. An arrow stuns it long enough to allow for the finishing blow. There's only two more in the back to dispatch until they're clear! Ed takes both out with ruthless efficiently.

The party falls back just in time. The enemies blocking the exit begin to attack. Marduk casts a defensive spell making everyone more resistant to physical attacks. Wendy uses a spell of her own to increase her own destructive power. Julia stuns the approaching enemies with Shockwave. The smaller spiders are stunned, but the queen is unfazed. Marduk quickly launches Fire Flurry. He didn't have much time to aim. A couple hit their mark, including crashing upon the queen, but she just keeps coming. Artemis impales a stunned critter with Piercing Shot. Wendy hits another with Dark Ball. It is rocked but still kicking. Duncan finishes it with Razor Wind.

He uses it again on the fast approaching queen. He targets a leg hoping to cut it off and slow her down. It might as well be a gentle breeze. She's now within striking distance! Marduk's spell left him open. Julia shoves him out of the way as the queen slashes downward with one of her front legs. Julia avoids a fatal blow, but her lower leg is cut deeply. Wendy connects with Dark Ball to zero effect. The queen tries to finish off Julia, but Shine blocks her leg with Rashida. The burning blade sears her. The queen squeals and recoils. It felt that one!

One of the smaller spiders has a good shot at Shine. Ed slips between them and delivers a fatal blow, but not before getting bitten on the arm. Grimacing in pain, he immediately hobbles back towards Artemis for assistance. The queen stares menacingly at the heroes. Shine could swear it was actually scheming a plan, but that's impossible, right? Whatever the case may be, she tries to take everybody out at once.

Darkness swallows the magic light as a cloud of black mana materializes in front of the queen. It's casting a spell! Her subjects creep back out of the line of fire. After a piercing hiss, the wave of Dark magic flies towards our heroes. Thinking quickly, Duncan casts Magic Resist. All anyone can do is brace as darkness consumes them. The protective spell does its job. Everyone is rocked by the attack, but no one is seriously hurt.

As Artemis is healing Ed, she spies something terrifying. More spiders are descending around them! She quickly finishes administering aid. A spider is just a couple feet away. It lunges at Ed. He narrowly escapes. A second spider arcs its hindquarters above its body and spews out a web. It wraps around the thief's legs causing him to fall. The web has him pinned to the ground. Artemis wants to help, but she has to deal with the creature coming after her.

At the front of the frenzy, a spider rushes Duncan and lunges. He shrugs off a blow from a front leg, and Shine slashes its abdomen apart. Both are sent flying back as one of the queen's legs swats them away. Another arachnid closes on Marduk. He's running low on mana and cannot cast a spell in time anyway. It lunges, fangs extended. Still hobbled, Julia smashes it out of the air. It makes a sickening sound as it collides with the ground. Green blood and various entrails explode everywhere. Marduk slowly removes some guts from his face, which is contorted in disgust. Julia is doused in blood. It should gross her out but, instead, just pisses her off.

Artemis nimbly leaps away from her foe's attempt to ensnare her in spider silk. She takes out one of its eyes with an arrow. Ed is helpless as the other one scurries towards him. Wendy sends it flying into a wall with Deluge. The combination of the *Assault* tome plus the buff spell is really giving her spells some punch. The spider isn't dead, but it lands upside down. It frantically wiggles and kicks the air. It will take some time for it to right itself.

Artemis narrowly evades her adversary's leg slash. She feels a sharp gust of wind rush by her. Marduk's Wind Burst blasts half the critter's legs off. It topples over. It desperately tries to use the remaining half to try to crawl towards Artemis. Bad idea. She bashes it with her bow until it stops moving. While she's berserking on it, Wendy runs over to Ed. She uses some low intensity Ice magic to freeze the webs. Ed's legs go numb in the process, but he's freed when the witch smashes the frozen webs apart with her staff. The thief springs up and makes short work of the spider who is struggling to flip off of its back.

That takes care of the last of the smaller spiders, or at least, the heroes hope so. Now to deal with Queenie. Shine and Duncan roll out of the way as she tries to follow up on her previous attack. She spits a wad of venom at Duncan. He blocks with his shield, but the poison immediately begins eating away at it forcing him to toss it to the ground. Ed dashes up to the front line. He avoids a ball of poison and gets in close. He starts hacking at one of the queen's front legs, but it's like chopping down an ironoak tree. He is forced to fall back as she flails the endangered limb at him before much damage can be done. She charges the party. Wendy slows it momentarily with Deluge. That gives Marduk enough time to blind her once more.

The queen squeals and bucks in pain. Julia, Shine, and Ed try to charge, but she quickly scurries backwards. Still blinded, she begins casting her Dark Wave again. There's no need to aim with a spell with such a wide area of effect. Artemis thinks up a strategy to take the arachnid down. She explodes one of those ginormous eyes with Piercing Shot. It bursts like a putrid balloon. The queen loses focus as she cries out. The spell is broken. The four melee fighters charge, two on each side with a plan of their own.

Shine and Duncan try a combo attack. Shine slashes with his blazing sword as Duncan fires off his Razor Wind. The wind fuels the fire causing it to explode outward. The force is enough to blow the queen's leg off. Wendy assists on the other leg, freezing it with her Chilling Wind. Ed and Julia begin to work it. Before they can maim her, the queen let's out a high frequency shriek. Its high pitch is barely audible yet excruciating. The heroes clutch their ears and fall to their knees. It feels like someone drove a knife straight into their eardrums and is slowly twisting it.

The queen leaps backwards and fires a thick silk strand into the air. It raises itself ten feet in the air. It gathers Dark magic, only this time she condenses it into small Dark Balls. There's a dozen of them maybe more spread about in front of her. The heroes are just barely shaking off the sonic attack as she unleashes them. Artemis and Ed's ears are bleeding. All they can hear is a high-pitched whine as the Dark Balls launch forth. Everyone is knocked back as they're buffeted by a ball. This version of her spell has a lot more stopping power. Even with Duncan's protection spell, everybody finds themselves in a great deal of pain.

They have to suck it up and start moving to evade whatever is coming next. The queen spews more balls of venom all about. Marduk is unable to get clear. Duncan's Razor Wind slices the glob in two. The halves fall to either side of the wizard. Everyone else manages to evade harm albeit barely. This is going to be a problem. The queen is up out of melee range and free to rain down attack after attack. Artemis knows what she must do.

The brave archer is barely able to catch her breath as it is, but she charges forward. Once close enough, she uses the last of her chi to fire an Ice Arrow at the silk strand. It hits dead on! She immediately follows up with a second arrow. Its steel tip shatters the strand, and the queen crashes to the ground. The impact stuns her, but only briefly. Our heroes only have a few moments to strike her while she's exposed.

Everyone is fatigued, but they need to find it within themselves to launch their final attacks. Rashida's flame is more like a smolder now. Marduk connects with Shock, popping another of Queenie's eyes. Wendy nods at Duncan. Her spells aren't well suited for this type of foe, so she casts Focus to power up Duncan's magic instead. In turn, the dark knight launches a massive Razor Wind. It almost completely drains his energy, but the powerful crescent wind slashes apart two more of the queen's eyes and gives her a nasty gash. She screeches, squeals, and thrashes about as half of her eyes have been destroyed.

Ed rushes in. He nimbly climbs one of the queen's long legs like a monkey and hops into her back. He begins rapidly stabbing her back with his daggers. Her hide is too thick for them to do too much damage, but that's okay. It's merely a diversion. As the massive beast bronco bucks to remove the thief riding it, Shine is ready to follow up. Wind chi swirls around the queen's remaining front leg. Artemis lands a couple more arrows into its body as all of that is going on.

There are too many attacks for her to respond to. Disperse blows the leg off! With both front limbs removed, the queen falls fangs first to the ground. Julia is waiting to deliver the final blow. With a mighty warrior's cry, she leaps into the air. She focuses the last of her chi into her hammer and smashes it down as hard as she can atop of the queen's exposed head. Her remaining eyes bulge out from the force. Blood splashes up from the impact point after a sickly smushing sound. Julia steps back to admire at her handiwork. Ed front flips off its back to his friends. Both of Shine's hands are on his knees. That last move took everything he had left.

The queen begins thrashing wildly, squealing in pain. The party is in awe that she's still alive after taking such a hit. They're not sure they have enough stamina left to finish the battle. They won't have to. Something's different. The queen's cries are louder and more frequent than before. It continues haphazardly thrashing about. It eventually rises onto its six remaining legs. It tries to charge the party but is too disoriented and veers off course. Smashing through a stalagmite, she rampages out from the enclosure with frantic speed. Soon she fades into the shadows. Not long after, the heroes hear a final squeal, followed by a horrendous crash, then followed by a low rumble. Silence. Is she finally dead?

Our heroes slowly gather themselves. They amble their way through the pitch-black room in the direction the queen ran off in. Marduk barely has enough mana to light the way. Eventually, they reach a wall and follow it. Ed takes a step forward and immediately halts as his foot meets nothing except air. After some brief investigating, it is deduced that the queen fell through a weak spot in cave floor, creating a massive hole. It's deep enough to where the light doesn't touch the bottom or reveal any of the queen's massive body. The wall curves sharply here. She must have run into the corner of the chamber.

As the heroes move by the pit along the wall, Julia realizes something. This part of the wall isn't as slick. It's rough. Marduk shines the light about. It's a boulder. There are several. Ed scrambles atop one. The wizard hands over the staff, and moments later, Ed cackles with glee. The queen knocked out a section of the wall! There looks to be another chamber behind the rocks.

The party manages to find a route through the rock and rubble without too much difficulty. There is a faint glow in the distance.

Daylight? It can't be. They're far too deep underground. Marduk takes a deep, relieved breath as he stops shining his staff. Artemis's anticipation reaches its zenith. She sprints ahead of her comrades overtaken with hope what she's seeking is at the end of the tunnel. Her allies hear a joyous squeal and run after her.

They're greeted by the sight of magnificent fluorescent crystals in all sorts of shades of blue, purple, and pink in all sorts of various formations scattered all around a small chamber's floors, walls, and ceiling. In the center, a shallow bowl naturally formed in the cave floor. Artemis is standing at the lip staring downward. She's literally shaking with joy. As her friends approach, they see the source of her jubilation. Clear water fills the bowl, beautifully shimmering with the crystals' reflections. This must be it, the hidden spring.

Artemis silently kneels down and cups her hands. She draws the water to her mouth. It is chillingly cool. It instantly refreshes her. More notably, she feels rush of energy as her chi returns. Quickly standing, she exclaims with joy, "We found it! We found the spring! Quick, everyone drink! It will restore your energy!"

Her friends follow suit. One by one, they feel their strength return. The cut on Julia's leg disappears. It's as if the battle with that frightful queen spider never happened. They all cheer and share congratulations. Even Duncan is swept up in the moment. As the excitement subsides, Marduk asks Artemis, "This certainly seems to be what you were seeking. How exactly do you plan to use it to help King Vanajit?"

"Well…" she begins. "I… I never really thought it through that far. Maybe I can get him to drink it or splash it on him like holy water. Anything that will bring him back to his senses."

"We should just beat him up until he does what we say," Duncan callously suggests.

Julia scowls at him. "You know, there's more ways to solve a problem than beating things up."

Ed laughs. "That's sayin' sumthin' comin' from you!"

Artemis takes the backpack from Julia and removes a vial. Once she finishes filling it with the spring water, she speaks, "I'm sure we'll figure something out." She pauses to wipe a tear from her eye. "Thank you. Thank you all. I would have never found this place without you."

Wendy smiles warmly and replies, "We're happy to help. If this stuff works, we'll be doing some good. Elysia is in desperate need of that now."

Shine has a more measured response, "I don't want to get your hopes up. We still have no idea if it will have any effect on Vanajit."

Ed is more optimistic. "All I know is I feel fuckin' fantastic after drinkin' it. If it won't do the trick, nuthin' will."

Shine shrugs and concedes, "I guess there's only one way to find out. Looks like we're heading back to Verde's Woods."

"Thank you all!" Artemis happily chirps.

"Maybe I'll get to kill something there," Duncan comments. Everyone assumes that means he's willing to help.

Ed takes a long look around, admiring the scenery. He whistles and revels, "This place sure is pretty. Who woulda thought a place like this could exist in all this darkness?"

Julia jabs, "That almost sounded poetic, Ed. You're not getting soft on us?"

He grins and smugly replies, "Never! I'm a cold-blooded killer."

As the everyone else talked and joked, something had caught Wendy's eye. There's more than just crystals strewn about. There seems to be some type of ore or minerals embedded in many of the rock formations. She's fixated on one such formation. She begins collecting some yellow-tinged material. Her friends notice her rapidly gathering it and come to see what she's up to. Whatever it is, it smells like rotten eggs. It must be corrosive, as she's wrapped her hands in cloth and is placing the rocks into a silk pouch. "What are you collecting there?" probes Marduk.

"Hydrogen sulfide."

"Sulfur? What do you plan to make with that?"

Wendy giggles malevolently before simply stating, "You'll see."

Everyone is a little bit scared of whatever the young witch is scheming. Good thing she's on their side. Whatever she's going to make, their enemies are surely in peril. Once she has gathered enough sulfur, the heroes begin the long walk back to the surface. If not for the spring's restorative properties, they may not have made it, as several small hordes of monsters attack during the journey back. All the hostile creatures are dispatched with relative ease. Fighting as one is becoming second nature.

Once back on the surface level, they report to Conway to share the good news. Conway instantly recognizes the look of accomplishment on everyone's faces as our heroes approach the throne. He grins and says, "Aren't we looking smug today? You found something down there, didn't you?"

Shine grins back, "A couple somethings. There was a gigantic queen spider down there. It had built quite the nest. She's been slain. Maybe you'll have a few less monster attacks now."

"Excellent!" exclaims Conway. "And what of the spring? Did you find what you were seeking?"

Shine proudly replies, "I didn't think we'd find anything, but it actually exists. It was hidden behind a cave wall."

"Oh? Is that so? Are the rumors true then? Does it have any special properties?"

"The jury is still out on that. It looks ordinary, but the room we found it in was covered with crystals. At worst, it should be some very potent mineral water. It did restore our strength when we drank it, so that's a good sign. We're on our way to test it on King Vanajit."

"Vanajit? The Fairy King? I don't understand."

Artemis fields that one, "Recently, the fairies have been attacking anyone who enters the woods. Lorde Verde was forced to close the road through them. I've spoken with Vanajit before. He's always very light-hearted and jovial. Now he won't even speak to me. I think some form of curse has befallen him."

"If that's the case, it will be quite the test. Let me know if it works."

Shine nods. "Of course." With the spring water acquired, the next stop is Verde's Woods. Shine still doesn't want to take any more time away from their objective, but with all he's witnessed since leaving Hanover, there may well be some dark force at play. If there's even a minute chance they can help the Fairy King, he cannot say no. They will rest up at Salem's inn and go back to the forest tomorrow. ♛

CHAPTER 12
The Fairy King

Morning approaches sooner than anyone would prefer. Our heroes slowly rise from slumber. Everyone takes a long time getting ready. Their trials are wearing them down. Artemis managed to get a head start. She's too nervous to lie in bed. She's running low on arrows, so she heads out to restock with the others groggily stagger around the inn.

The appreciative archery shop owner's discount still applies. Unfortunately, he didn't have any steel-tipped arrows in stock, so it's back to iron for now. She also crafted a couple more vitality potions using some local plants. The others are ready by the time she returns, and the party sets out for Verde's Woods. Artemis wasn't the only busy bee. Yesterday, Wendy spent much of her leisure time concocting something with the sulfur from the Cave of Lost Souls. She is being quite secretive about her work. It must be something diabolical.

It is just after noon when they reenter the woods. They have to climb back over the fallen tree. At least this time nothing attacks. The path leading to the Fairy King isn't far. Artemis points it out. It's right off the main road, obscured by thick vines. No wonder nobody noticed it the first time. They could hack and chop through, but Shine isn't about to pass up another chance to show off Disperse. If you got it, flaunt it! Barrett's trick easily clears the way. The path leads to a large meadow.

That is Vanajit's castle. It is a castle in name only. Fairies don't need to build houses. They simply sleep in the trees. There is a small fairy-sized forge to make weapons along with looms and crafting tables. Everything is out in the open. When it rains, they use large leaves to protect their equipment and shelter in small huts. King Vanajit sits on a throne made of rock and woven vines near the northern edge of the field. A beautiful stone fountain rests in the middle. Spigots sculpted in the shapes of fairies and mythical beasts gently spit water in the eight cardinal points. Thick vines block the entrance. One more display of Disperse, and the heroes step foot onto royal ground.

Fairies flutter about, carefully eyeing the intruders. Word spread of the travelers that slayed their kin. They are too afraid to make a move, fearing the same fate. The throne is bare. The Fairy King is nowhere to be found. The heroes try to ask the fairies where their king is, but they just fly away in fear. As they seek a fairy willing to spill the beans, Marduk senses a dark presence. It feels just like in Hulda Cave right before Captain Barrett appeared. Soon, everyone can feel it. Using that sensation like a compass, the heroes are led to the fountain. The darkness is strongest here. What could that mean?

Before there's any discussion, Artemis removes the vial of spring water from her pocket. There's no rational thought in her actions that follow. Some deep instinct compels her. Before anyone can stop her, she removes the cork from the vial and pours the water in the fountain. "What the fuck did you do that for?" demands Julia.

"Does this mean we can go now?" grumbles Duncan.

Artemis doesn't respond. Her gaze is fixed on the center of the fountain. She calmly speaks in a whisper, "Just wait." Her friends do just that, but nothing happens. After almost a minute, they've seen enough.

"You wasted it," Shine accuses. As those words jump his lips, the water in the fountain begins to churn.

It soon intensifies to a rapid swirl. The dark force grows ever stronger. A black cloud manifests above the center of the fountain. It's just like it was with Barrett. A shadowy figure bursts forth, zigzagging around the meadow. The fairies are even more fearful of this ominous entity than the humans. They flee the meadow in panic. Perhaps, this has always been the true source of their fear. The shadowy wisp slows and comes to a stop, hovering above Vanajit's throne. It begins to take shape, and in moments, a pointy-eared humanoid floats before the adventurers.

Shine is reminded of vampire fables. This visage is the size of an average person, not a fairy. It is clad in a black silken shirt with long, baggy sleeves and skin-tight black silk pants. Its long hair is even blacker than its clothing. Its mouth is warped into a permanent, sinister grin. Two fangs protrude, glistening in the sun. Its four wings are long and rainbow colored. Their shape resembles that of a dragonfly's only pointed at the tips. Its pointy ears are the only fairy-like aesthetic. Despite all this, Artemis instantly recognizes him.

"Vanajit..." she utters. He looks nothing like a fairy, but Barrett looked nothing like a human when they first encountered him either. This could very well be the Fairy King. The heroes prepare for battle. The melee fighters form the front line whilst Artemis, Marduk, and Wendy head to the rear for support. Duncan takes a flanking position between the lines. His unique skillset allows him to flex between assault and support.

"Who dares enter my palace?" the king demands.

Artemis takes a step forward. "Um... It's me, Artemis. I've come to ask why you have turned your back on humanity."

"You mean the humans who constantly wage war and kill their own kind? The ones that callously chop down my trees? The ones that exiled you? No, humanity turned its back on *me*."

Ed tries to be voice of reason, "Don't ya think that's a bit harsh? Damning everyone for the actions of a few?"

Artemis pleads, "The Vanajit I know was never that cynical. What happened to you?"

Marduk warns his friends, "There is an incredibly dark energy coming from him. It feels just like when we fought Captain Barrett. He is dangerous."

Shine has the same notion as the wizard. "It looks like Vanajit is possessed, too. I think the spring water made him mad more than anything."

"What are you rambling about?" demands Vanajit. "This forest is now off limits to humans. Leave before I force you to."

Shines sighs and bemoans, "Why does everyone always want to do things the hard way?" Duncan smiles as he cracks his knuckles, eager to take on this new foe.

Artemis boldly addresses the king, "I don't want to fight you, but if that's the only way to knock some sense into you, I'm ready to go all out."

Vanajit cackles maniacally. "You weaklings think you stand a chance against me? Come then! Meet your demise!"

In a blink of an eye, Vanajit disappears. Shine's eyes bulge as the king's hand wraps around his throat. How did he cover that distance so quickly? Shine's eyes roll back in his head. It's not from lack of oxygen. It feels like his very life force is being drained. Julia takes a wild swing, but their foe zips backward to a safe distance.

Shine doubles over desperately trying to catch his breath. "What the hell was that?" he gasps. This enemy is indeed dangerous. That speed even concerns Duncan, although he'd never admit it. Artemis is the only one unfazed. Nothing is going to break her resolve. As Vanajit speeds backwards, she stares daggers into him as she lets an arrow loose. Vanajit easily lists away from it, but the attack got his attention.

Artemis steps forward. Without a modicum of hesitation, she declares to the king, "I don't know what happened to you, but I'm going to stop you no matter what." Her uncharacteristic display of valor inspires her comrades. Duncan immediately increases their magical resistance. Whatever that thing used on Shine, it was magic based. Marduk boosts their speed. Wendy increases all the mages' attack power. Vanajit disappears again. This time his target is Julia. His beady red eyes widen as she grabs his arm before he can reach her throat.

"I don't think so," she says coldly.

Vanajit breaks free and escapes before anyone can attack. His body begins to glow. What spell could this dark entity be casting? Best not wait to find out. The archer and mages quickly attack. Vanajit is forced to break the spell to evade. He begins rapidly circling the party until he is just a blur. Moving with incredible speed, he blinks in and out of sight at various points.

The heroes know a direct attack is coming, but from where? They don't have to wait long to find out. Vanajit appears near Ed in a perfect flanking position. The nimble thief spots the ambush at the last second and dodges. Only a single finger makes contact, yet Ed's body stiffens like he was just struck by lightning. His body immediately slumps and turns pale. He's been poisoned! Artemis runs to his aid with the last of the herbs. Crap. Should've restocked those before coming here.

Vanajit flickers about. The mages try to hit him with spells, but they're basically shooting blind. This time the king tries to use that deathly touch on Wendy. Out of pure instinct, she's able to use her tome as a shield. Marduk swats at their foe with his staff but misses. Vanajit falls back. Everyone else is too far away to strike despite their speed boost. Vanajit's attack did grant Artemis time to heal the thief. She removed the poison. At least, she thought she did. He still looks fatigued. Before she can figure out what is happening, Duncan shouts the answer, "It's a curse!"

That's not good. Curses are essentially the magical equivalent of poisoning. Dark mana slowly drains the victim's life force until they die. It's said that the afflicted suffers great misfortune whilst under a curse. There are all sorts of tales of warriors' weapons or armor suddenly breaking, horses dropping dead, leaving the victim stranded, among many others. There are only two known ways to lift a curse: a priest or mage well-versed in Holy magic removes it, or the victim drinks holy water. Our heroes don't have either. There is a priest in Salem. Maybe if they flee now, Ed can be saved.

As if sensing the heroes' intent, massive vines grow over the exit. Undoubtably, it was Vanajit's doing in order to cut off any chance of escape. Artemis gives Ed a vitality potion. It restores him back to fighting form, but the curse still afflicts him. Curses do tend to drain energy slower than poison, so he should be able to fight for a while without feeling the effects. Artemis gives him the last two vitality potions just in case. Hopefully, the bit about bad luck is just a myth.

Vanajit finishes darting about and attacks with his Corrupting Touch. He goes after Shine again, but he blocks with his shield. In that moment, the young man realizes something. The enemy isn't wielding a weapon. That puts him at a severe reach disadvantage. If not for his speed, Vanajit would be open to attack. Anticipating his foe will dash backwards again, Shine gives chase. Even with Marduk's speed spell, he isn't as fast, but Vanajit isn't expecting it. There's a small window between when he slows and when he can dash again. That's all Shine needs.

As Vanajit decelerates, Shine thrusts his sword. The Fairy King slips away but is cut on the arm cut by Rashida. Just a bit faster and that would've been his chest. Artemis tries to follow up with an arrow, but their enemy catches it out of midair and tosses it aside. Duncan connects squarely upon the king's chest with Fast Ball. Or so he thinks. It was an after image! Vanajit is back to zipping about.

Our heroes cannot afford to be touched again. Anyone afflicted with a curse might not survive long enough to find aid. Ed uses his chi to boost his speed, intending to intercept Vanajit. The mages make the most of Wendy's magic buff. They try to hit the speedy foe but, this time, use wide range attacks. Marduk launches Fire Flurry, Wendy expands the scope of Chilling Wind, and Duncan uses an advanced variation of Razor Wind to send a quintet of crescents flying. Everybody chose a different direction to cast giving the team a better chance of success. Their strategy works! One of the dark knight's wind blasts hits it mark.

Vanajit is stunned. Artemis fires an arrow. It's in line to strike right between the eyes, but the Fairy King effortlessly catches it. The archer swears Vanajit is sneering at her despite his frozen face. She sneers back as ice begins to spread across his hand and arm. It spreads down to his forearm, but the Fairy King seems unfazed. Ed charges forward before their foe can evade. He's got a clear shot! The thief springs into the air with daggers drawn. He slashes them both downward but hits nothing. As he lands, he turns to see the king hovering in place. *I missed?* he thinks to himself. Vanajit looks over to him and winks before vanishing. Maybe that bit about misfortune was true. Ed rarely misses vital organs let alone completely whiffing.

The Fairy King's arm is still frozen, making him easier to spot. It also seems to be slowing him down some. Shine decides now is as good a time as any to try out a new skill. He focuses chi into Rashida but not to ignite it. He does his best to predict when his target is more or less in front of him. After carefully picking his spot, he swings Rashida wide. As he does, chi bursts forth from its tip creating a blade of pure energy. It is five times as long now. The energy doesn't curve as he swings. One would think it was part of the metal blade itself.

Vanajit is belted by the attack. Shine's chi isn't strong enough to cut through him. Instead, it smacks the king to the ground. Shine and Duncan charge with their swords. Ed tries to follow but is too winded. He drinks the second potion to stave off the curse. One left. Julia figures her weapon is too slow for a direct attack even if she channels her chi. She takes careful aim Shockwave to not hit her own teammates. It reaches Vanajit before her allies and before he can rise off the ground, allowing Shine and Duncan to drive their blades deep into his chest and end the fight.

Not so much as a whimper escapes Vanajit as he's hit by not one but two critical strikes. Something isn't right. Shine and Duncan quickly pull their swords from the king's body. Dark purple, almost black blood sprays from the wound. They are blown back by a blast of Dark energy. The ice around Vanajit's arm breaks away. He's clearly sustained a lot of damage, but his body isn't responding naturally. All bets are off. Our heroes are just going to have keep hitting him until he goes down. Their foe isn't eager to give them that chance.

The Fairy King glows. Everyone knows a spell is coming. This time, Vanajit doesn't give them a chance to break it. He begins zipping around while continuing to gather energy. The amount of stamina and control it must take to use both abilities at once must be staggering. Marduk yells for everyone to move as orange magic glyphs form around their feet. As the party dives clear, massive pillars of flame burst forth.

Ed tries to leap away but loses his balance before leaving his feet. He can't fully clear it, and half his body is engulfed in flames. He screams in agony and begins writhing on the ground. If not for Duncan's Magic Resist spell, he'd surely be dead. Artemis rushes over to heal him. It's going to take her rest of her chi to heal an injury this severe. Even when she does, that damned curse is still sapping the life from him.

The powerful spell leaves the Fairy King exposed, but no one is in position to counter. Marduk tries his lightning spell while still halfway on the ground, but Vanajit drifts away. It would have been a glancing blow at best anyway. Vanajit glows once more. This time he remains still. That's a good sign that he's getting tired, too. Duncan is the only one who manages to get up and in position for an attack. His Fast Ball connects, but it's not enough to break the spell.

Julia bull rushes their foe. She hopes to outrun the spell and be in position to strike while he's open. Artemis is still on her knees healing Ed. Neither of them are going to be able to escape as the circles appear under them. Shine dives out of the way of his. As he's falling, out of pure instinct, he uses Chi Sweep to extend Rashida's blade. He smacks his friends out of harm's way. The archer and thief are sent rolling along the ground just barely avoiding the inferno. They'll be sore from that jolt tomorrow, but it's better than being extra crispy.

As Shine protects his allies, Julia makes her charge. Her eyes widen in surprise as the circle forms just in front of her instead of under. Not only can the spell target multiple people, it can lead moving targets, further confirming how skilled and powerful this enemy mage is. Julia leaps forward and to the side as the pillar of flame erupts. She winces in pain as it grazes her. She's burnt rather good but no more than a bad sunburn. She won't allow it to stop her. She continues her charge.

Expecting a frontal attack, Vanajit tries to dodge to the right but can't move quickly enough after casting. Julia had no intention of going for a direct attack. She knew he'd try to dodge it. The warrior springs forward to Vanajit's left flank. As she sails past him, she swings her massive hammer with a ferocious double backhanded attack. The hammerhead pummels Vanajit flush in the back. He flies forward. A line drive! As his body hits the dirt, he bounces several times and lands... right by Julia's friends!

Shine is the closest. Vanajit is down on all fours struggling to rise. Shine screams as he drives Rashida downward with both hands. It pierces Vanajit's skull. Against any other opponent, it would have gone straight through, out his chin, and into the earth. That doesn't happen, but it goes in deep. There's no way it didn't slice well into Vanajit's brain. As Rashida is pulled out, blood sputters and spews from the top of the Fairy King's skull like a backed-up faucet. Shine takes a couple steps back expecting their foe to drop dead. The king levitates into the air, still horizontal to the ground, blood still spouting. He floats upward and rights himself. Exasperated, Shine shouts, "You have gotta be kiddin' me!"

The dark blood stops flowing. The Fairy King hovers unmoving for several seconds. Then, a white light begins to shine from his head wound. The light shoots forth. A blinding flash fills the meadow. Everyone shields their eyes. As the light fades, Vanajit's body starts shaking violently. A black cloud engulfs him as his body flies forward, stopping above the center of the fountain. After the cloud slowly dissipates, a fairy adorned with a golden crown floats there. He clutches his head in his hand. His posture is identical to Barrett's when he was defeated. "What the—?" the king utters. "What happened? My head..."

Artemis breathes a deep sigh of relief. Vanajit seems to have been freed from the dark forces controlling him. She smiles warmly and says, "You weren't yourself, so we knocked some sense into you."

The king's ears prick as he hears the voice of an old friend. Lifting his head, he gazes at the heroes. Still foggy, he speaks, "Oh, it's you, Artemis? I feel like I just awoke from a terrible nightmare. What happened?"

Artemis does her best to explain, "Well... the short version is you suddenly became very angry with humans and ordered the fairies to attack anyone who entered the forest."

"You mean to tell me I wasn't dreaming?"

"That's correct," confirms Marduk. "You weren't aware of what you were doing?"

"I was aware, but I wasn't in control. It was like being trapped in a dream that I couldn't wake up from. I saw my subjects savagely attacking people. I yelled, screamed, and begged for them to stop, but it was as if they couldn't hear me. I swear I heard someone laughing maniacally while it was happening. It was torturous."

Shine feels like he's speaking to Barrett all over again. The eerie similarities cause feelings of dread to grip his soul. "That's really creepy. It looks like you're back to normal now. That dark energy is gone."

Vanajit nods. "It was strange. First, I was enveloped in darkness, but I could see a light shining in the distance before everything went dark again. Then, I felt a warm glow. Everything went dark, but this time, I awoke in control, and you were all standing before me."

Shine thinks to himself, *Maybe that spring water did more than I thought.*

Vanajit continues, "It would appear I am indebted to you."

Shine motions his head towards Artemis. "Artemis is the one you should thank. We wouldn't have come here if it wasn't for her."

Artemis begins to blush. Her eyes cast down. "Gosh, you don't need to reward me or anything. I'm just happy you're better."

Vanajit chuckles and replies, "I see you're as humble as ever. There is something I want to do for you. You come here often to pick herbs. Are you skilled at crafting potions?"

"No, I just know a couple basic ones. Mostly, I use the herbs for incense or cooking."

"Well then, how about I help you become a full-fledged herbalist?"

The archer's eyes light up. "That would be great! I'm sure we'll need lots of potions during our travels."

"Then it shall be so! Close your eyes. I shall impart my knowledge upon you."

"...O-okay."

There's a distinct feeling of déjà vu as a faint light envelopes Artemis. Information rapidly flows into her. Visions of herbs she never seen before along with their properties flash before her eyes. The visions cease. The glow fades. Artemis blinks her eyes a few times. Her sight and mind soon clear. She feels like fifty years' worth of herbalism and potion crafting knowledge just entered her brain. She gazes up at the Fairy King and thanks him. Even though she saved him from a fate worse than death, she feels indebted, and the king isn't finished just yet, "There is one last gift I wish to give you."

Extending her palms forward she begs, "Oh no, I couldn't possibly…"

"I could," Ed chimes.

While everyone was talking, a few fairies cautiously reentered the meadow. Seeing their king restored to his kind, noble self, they rushed to tell the others of the grand news. They are all now gathering around their king. Vanajit beckons for one of them to come forth and whispers in its ear. The fairy snaps into attention and flutters to the throne. There's a chest behind it. The fairy opens it and brings the contents to Vanajit. It's a small fairy bow. Vanajit closes his eyes and the bow glows pink. The heroes watch in amazement as it grows into a human-sized weapon. Artemis recognizes it instantly. He can't be giving *that* away. She can barely speak, "…I-is that…?"

As the bow floats through the air towards the archer, Vanajit answers, "That's right. My most prized bow, the Sultan Bow." It's a beautiful recurve bow crafted from maple wood. There are gold plates affixed near the center providing some defensive capability. There is also a sight to improve accuracy. The string is made of enchanted spider silk. It is incredibly hard to break, and simply touching it makes one feel a sense of calm and focus.

With such a finely crafted bow, she can land a fatal strike on an enemy from over two hundred and fifty yards away, almost five hundred with her Piercing Shot! She knows she's supposed to say thank you but is completely fixated by the bow's beauty. Vanajit smiles and says, "You're welcome. Oh, and feel free to pick some herbs before you go. They should provide excellent ingredients for you to try out your new skills."

Ed admires the Sultan Bow. "That is one fine lookin' bow. Too bad I ain't any good with 'em. I'm sure Artemis here will put—" The thief grimaces and falls to a knee. Shit, the curse! Everyone was so preoccupied they forgot all about it.

Vanajit dreads what's wrong. "This man has been cursed… Was this my doing?"

Ed smiles through his teeth and looks up at the king. In a pained voice he replies, "Don't worry 'bout it. Wasn't yer fault…" He collapses face down.

"Ed!" Wendy shouts in concern. "We have to get him to town."

Vanajit puts their worry at ease. "I can heal him. Allow me." He closes his eyes and begins casting a spell. He uses Holy magic to lift the curse.

Ed slowly stirs and makes his way to his feet.

Shine pats him on the back. "You had us worried there."

Ed places his hand on the back of his head and laughs, "Naw, ain't no curse gonna take me down. Well, least not when there's a mage 'round to fix me." His friends can't help but to burst out laughing. Even Duncan chuckles a bit but pretends he's coughing when he sees Julia looking at him. Artemis thanks the Fairy King several more times. Shine nearly has to drag her away. Before they go, she picks some herbs as the sun sets.

"Whatcha gonna make with these?" asks Wendy.

Artemis shrugs. "I'm not sure. So much knowledge filled my mind at once. It's a lot to sort through. I have a few ideas, but I haven't decided yet."

Wendy looks down and kicks the dirt. "I wish someone would give me a ton of chemistry knowledge…" After herb picking, the heroes head back to Salem. It's dark when they arrive. The moon has almost fully risen. The innkeeper seems irked to see them yet again. Despite what Wendy and her friends did for the village, the witch is still somehow guilty in many of their eyes. The innkeeper is one of those people. She thought the witch was gone for good. Her wish will soon be granted. Our heroes can finally head through Tempora Tunnel and past the Aker Mountains to Giza. It will likely be a long time before any of them set foot in western Elysia again. ♛

CHAPTER 13
Fallen Empire

A full night's rest provides little respite for our fatigued heroes. All the constant hiking and fighting is taking its toll. However, lingering any longer isn't an option. They want to reach Giza as soon as possible. All this backtracking has them feeling like they're behind schedule despite never really having a timetable. There is one final stop. They are compelled to make one last detour back to the Cave of Lost Souls. Shine promised Conway they'd report back on how things went with King Vanajit and respects him too much to break his word.

Conway wasn't expecting his unlikely allies back so soon, or at all really. He rises to greet the party. Without missing a beat, he asks, "So, how did things go with the Fairy King?"

Artemis chirps, "Turns out I was right! He looked completely different than last I saw him. He attacked us, but none of his subjects did. They seemed afraid. All ended well after we knocked some sense into Vany."

"Interesting. So, was he actually cursed?"

Shine answers, "Yeah. It seems to be becoming a common occurrence lately. We'd already dealt with a cursed man before this, and he was already dead."

"I see. It would seem this plight isn't just limited to Salem. I grow wary of what's over the horizon."

Marduk nods in agreement. "Yes, I fear some great evil is fast approaching."

"I'm glad you found the spring. Perhaps it will help off stave off this plight. I neglected to ask you where exactly you found it. That spring's power may be worth risking venturing down there."

Artemis replies, "The spring is on the lowest level of the caverns. It's connected to a gigantic room covered in spider webs. Their queen is dead, so it should be safe. From the elevator, head straight and go down the tunnel to the right. If you follow the south wall for a long while, you'll eventually find the room."

Conway smiles and affirms, "I'll have to send a team down there. Thank you for the info. You are truly good people. I'm glad Artemis found her way to you. You have done our people a great service. Perhaps I was too quick in condemning all of humanity."

"Don't mention it," Julia politely dismisses. "I'm just happy we could help."

With the final loose end tied, it's finally back to the mission. The detour was more than worth it. Conway's faith in mankind has been restored, and that feeling will resonate with his people. As happy an ending as it was, the heroes still cannot shake that ever-present foreboding feeling. Elysia is in desperate need of hope. Removing the tyrannical King Pious will do just that. The sooner he is gone, the sooner Elysia can heal and grow once more.

Our heroes set out for Tempora Tunnel. This time, they are careful to watch out for bounty hunters. If they get captured a third time, Julia may literally kill Shine. A little too much caution is exercised. A poor quartet of ragged travelers nearly has an intimate encounter with Julia's hammer because she thought the group was eyeballing hers. Aside from the near unprovoked bashing, the trip is peaceful. No fierce battles with cursed beings or any combat whatsoever. The heroes' bodies aren't able to keep pace with their wills. Their tempo is noticeably slower than normal, but it helps them recover. They will be well rested and ready to face the dangers of Khamsin Desert.

Before long, they arrive at the entrance to the mine and head in. This time, the shelves are well stocked with fresh metal helmets. Good, the delivery made it. Julia removes the lantern helmet the Stubblebottoms awarded from the backpack. She volunteers Shine to wear it. After all, he is the leader, so he should be the one to lead them through the darkness, right? He feels silly wearing it, but oddly enough, it kind of pairs well with his copper chainmail. The foreman, Matthew, spots them coming helmet and all. He smiles and nods in approval of Shine's new look. "They gave you a little gift, eh?"

"Yep," Shine casually replies.

"I'm still not one hundred percent comfortable letting you folks down there, but how can I say no after you helped us? The courier mentioned you when he dropped off the shipment. A deal is a deal. I should warn you, the desert has grown dangerous lately. Sandstorms have been tearing through it something terrible."

"Isn't that normal for a desert?" Wendy asks.

"Not like this. They've never been this frequent, and they seem to be getting stronger every day. If you see one coming, don't be stupid. Get yourself to shelter."

Ed crosses his heart. "We promise."

"Go ahead then. Just try to stay out of the workers' way."

Matthew steps aside and lets the heroes into the elevator. Soon after, they are in the mines. It's not quite as dark as the Cave of Lost Souls, but it would be difficult to navigate without a light. Marduk is happy he doesn't have to use magic this time. He was more drained last time than he let on.

Tempora Tunnel is an engineering marvel. Giza had been mining their side of the range for decades, even before the Great War. After Elysia conquered most of their territory and expanded to the west side of the range, they, too, began mining the Aker mountains. The plan to connect the respective mines via tunnel came about fifty years ago. It took nearly a dozen years to complete even with the joint effort. Before then, most of the mines were built in natural cave systems. The tunnel was dug, blasted, and chiseled from either side until the workers from the two nations eventually met in the middle, an incredible sixty miles.

The tunnel isn't particularly wide. There's just enough space for two sets of rails allowing carts to be moved faster and easier. With a quick route to transport ore and precious stones across the vast range, trade was greatly bolstered upon completion. It's a full day's walk from one mine entrance to the other without pausing. It takes most people two or more to complete the trip. By the time Shine and company reach Giza's exit, it will be sunrise the next day. It is quite the walk, but the heroes decide not to stop. Noxious gases can waft through at any time, and no one likes the idea of going to sleep and never waking up.

It's still early when the party finally reaches the Gizian mines. The workers haven't even made it down yet. As the shaft elevator ascends, wind can be heard whistling from above. As the elevator nears the surface the whistle grows into a roar. They are in a room just like the one in Tempora, half wooden, half mountain. The wind is blowing like crazy outside. Julia and Duncan force the door open revealing a magnificent but troubling sight. A sandstorm is whipping through the area just like Matthew warned. They let the door blow shut. "Damn, that's one helluva storm!" Ed exclaims.

Marduk believes it is best to heed Matthew's advice, "Perhaps it would be wise to wait out the storm." Shine is itching to get to Giza. The nearer he gets to Leed's Castle, the more anxious he becomes. Giza is only five miles to the east.

He insists they press on, "Screw that! Giza is just down the road. We can make it." The party is split about what to do. Marduk readdresses the danger. Wendy takes Shine's side.

Artemis comments, "Umm... this sounds like a bad idea."

Julia adds, "Yeah."

Duncan is defiant as usual. "I ain't scared of a little sand."

"I second that," Ed agrees.

The vote is four to three in favor of braving the storm. Julia and Duncan force the door back open. The sandstorm is nasty. Everyone does their best to shield their eyes. Luckily, the wind is coming from the north, so sand isn't flying right in their faces. Each step forward is a laborious effort. As everyone trudges along, the storm seems to grow stronger. "Whew! This is brutal," Shine notes. His words are just barely audible.

"Don't be such a pansy," Duncan taunts. No one is quite sure how far they've actually walked, but they must be at least halfway there.

Wendy is gradually falling behind. She murmurs, "Shit... This is really tiring. I don't know how much longer I can go on."

"We're almost there," Shine encourages. "Just hold on a little longer."

Several strenuous steps later, Ed remarks, "I feel like I'm gonna blow away..."

Shine is worried about Wendy. Her voice sounded weak. "How are you holding up, Wendy?" There's no response as they manage a few more steps. The roaring wind must have drowned her out. "Wendy?" Still no answer. Now he's panicking. He stops and begins to search for her. The rest of her friends follow suit. Ed spies her. She's face down in the sand.

"Shit!" he yells. "She's down! Duncan, help me carry 'er!"

Duncan springs into action. "Right!" He lifts the witch from the sand and tosses her over his shoulder. As the party presses forward, he grunts and says, "I think she gained twenty pounds in sand."

Shine tries his best to inspirit his allies, "Tell me about it! We're almost there. Ready? Let's hurry!"

Ed only makes it ten more steps before stopping. He's completely wiped out. "Looks like this is far as I go..." The thief collapses. Before anybody can get to him, Marduk falls. Julia drops the backpack and her hammer to try to pick Ed up. Shine tries to help Marduk. Neither are successful.

Shine utters, "I think this was a mistake," before falling. The world around him grows dark.

He groggily wakes to find himself lying on a thin cot on a stone floor. It does little to pad the cold, hard ground. He is covered in a tattered tan blanket speckled with stains. Torches glow brightly all around. He throws the blanket off and sits up. All his allies are there, too. He breathes a sigh of relief as he realizes someone must have rescued them. Julia smiles and walks over to him. She speaks to him in an uncharacteristically sweet voice, "You're finally awake. How do you feel?"

"Fine, I guess." Julia punches him in the head. "Ow! What the hell?"

"What did the foreman tell us, moron? If we see a sandstorm, don't be stupid, and take cover, but *nooo*, you just had to try and march us through it."

Shine sheepishly replies, "Yeah, that wasn't one of my better decisions. At least everyone is here. Who saved us?"

Julia shrugs, "No idea."

Shine stands and surveys their surroundings. The building is made entirely of stone. There are high ceilings supported by marble columns and baroque buttresses. Elegant stained-glass windows adorn the walls. Some are patterns of solid colors; others have images. Theon and several of his saints tower over him. It would seem they are in a church. The immediate area has been converted into a shelter. Cots line the auxiliary altar; peoples' possessions are scattered about.

No one else is there. Everyone is gathered in the main altar. The priest is wrapping up what sounds like a rousing sermon. His booming voice echoes off the stone walls. Everybody has the same idea, and one after another, they head through the transept and into the main altar.

A large stained-glass window accentuates the back wall. It is an image of Theon creating the sun. Large torches flicker on either side of the altar framed by massive statues of crosses. Some are carved from marble while others were formed from copper. The priest is standing in the center telling his flock to remain vigilant in these trying times and to never let their faith waiver. "Faith is not only the source of our strength but Theon's as well," his voice booms. "Remain strong and faithful, for it is the faithful who give Theon his power. We must remain vigilant, and He will answer our prayers."

With the sermon concluded, the patrons begin shuffling away. A disheveled woman in baggy robes and scraggly gray hair pushes past Shine muttering about the end of days. A few people leave the church, but most make their way back to the shelter. A red-headed man wanders over to the party. He is dressed in white robes. A silver Theon cross hangs from his neck. Another priest?

The red headed man smiles gently and welcomes the guests, "Hello there. I see your all up and about. Thank Theon. You gave us quite a scare."

Duncan grumbles. "A priest, huh? I don't like priests." The man is unaffected.

Julia asks him, "Do you know who saved us? We owe them a huge thank you."

The man points at himself. "That was me. The name's Hermes. It's a pleasure to meet you all."

The party exchanges pleasantries, except for Duncan, who remains silent. Shine has to introduce him. Hermes continues, "I spotted you on the outskirts of town and rushed to find aid. I was praised to find enough brave, willing souls to carry you all here. As you can see, we're using the auxiliary altar as a shelter. Most of the townspeople's homes are completely buried in sand. It is a most frightening time."

Marduk eyes the magic staff harnessed across the priest's back. It is made of copper with a ruby orb adorning the top. Just beneath it, the staff has a pair of angel wings protruding from the sides. Hermes must be a mage. That's not surprising. Many priests practice Holy magic to heal the sick and injured. His white robes are a stark contrast to the other priest's dark brown attire.

"You are not from around here are you, Hermes?" Marduk prospects.

"No, I am a traveling priest. I hail from the island of Oria. We are a bit different than most sects of Theonism. In order to be ordained, we must travel the world for five years learning about the various peoples and cultures of the world and give aid to those we find in need."

"Ah, so you're a priest in training," Wendy concludes.

"Yes, in two years' time I will be able to return home and regale my people of my travels. Then I will officially be a man of the cloth."

Wendy inquires, "So, what brings ya here, Mr. Almost Priest?"

"The Gizian people have always deeply interested me. Before the war, the Gizians practiced a different religion, Firianism. They were forced to convert in the terms of surrender. I have a theory that their god, Fira, is actually one of Theon's saints. I believe the two religions are actually one and the same."

"I'm bored." Duncan grunts.

As rude as it was, Shine agrees. They have a mission to get back to, and this guy can probably ramble on for days. Shine is skeptical that there's any higher power. Hanover practices Theonism (as does every town), but the village isn't what you'd call devout. There's no grand cathedral like Giza. They just have a small wooden chapel. People would attend Mass on Sunday, but it was more out of tradition than seeking enlightenment. Recent events have caused the young man to reassess his views, but there's more pertinent things to worry about. He decides to end the conversation before Hermes tells them the entire history of Giza. "Well it was nice to meet you, Hermes, but we need to be going now."

"Oh, no worries. I actually need to be going as well. I have an audience with the pharaoh. I believe I have discovered the source of these accursed sandstorms." Just like that, Shine's interest is rekindled, but Hermes quickly takes his leave before anyone can probe further. The party decides to take a look around town. Hopefully, there's a diner or pub that hasn't been completely buried. Nearly dying really builds up one's appetite.

A few members of the group are curious to see what Giza is like. Like Cid, Giza is a sovereign nation, despite being smack dab in the center of Elysia. It used to be a vast empire. It expanded all the way to both the northern and southern coasts, as far east as the Great Woods and all the way to the northwestern coast. Caddis went by the name of Berenice and was a burgeoning village before being captured. Like most military conflicts, the Elysian-Gizian War, or simply Great War, started over a land dispute. Fast forward thirty-six years to when the Elysian army had nearly achieved total victory. Giza was the last remaining city. Even the capitol, Thonis, fell. Elysia knew their military was stretched too thinly to occupy the capitol for long. This and wanting to encourage surrender led to the decision by King Magnus I to raze the city.

The pharaoh at the time ended up being mortally wounded by King Magnus during the battle for Thonis and died soon after. With their leader gone, the Gizians reluctantly decided to negotiate terms of surrender. The harsh desert would make an invasion treacherous and likely cost many lives, so Elysia was willing to turn to diplomacy. Elysia was already over expanded from their conquests, so they allowed the Giza to remain its own nation. However, the conditions mandated Giza is not allowed to have a military and must convert to Theonism. King Magnus wanted to erase as much of their culture as possible to lessen the chances of an uprising. Beaten down and leaderless, Giza had no choice but to agree.

Giza managed to prosper after the war, but now it is in a dire state. It is more sand than city. At this rate, it will be completely retaken by the desert. The atmosphere is dismal. The citizens are in poor spirits. All of those sermons about faith and vigilance aren't working. A popular pub is one of the few places still open. It is jam packed inside. Many townsfolk are drinking their troubles away. The party manages to find an open table in the far corner. When an exhausted, overworked waitress finally makes her way to them, they order food and ale before proceeding to figure out their next plan of action.

There are two routes to Leed's castle from here. To the southeast, there's a road running between two plateaus that leads out of the desert. From there, it will take about a week to get the castle, which is to the northeast. The second route is more treacherous. They'd have to travel northeast through the bulk of the desert and then across Roraima Plateau. Once across, it would only be a two-day march to the castle. Option one is the more sensible choice. If they get caught in a sandstorm in the middle of the desert, no one will save them this time. There's a far less chance of that occurring on the southern route.

As they finish their meal, Shine's eyes pop out of his head when he sees the tab. This place is charging triple the norm. The owner is using the storms to gouge people! The heroes are irate. Shine demands to speak with the owner. A horseshoe-haired man with a bulbous nose walks over. He tries to wriggle a convincing explanation of the exorbitant pricing. He doesn't get very far. Duncan promptly grabs him by the collar and lifts him into the air. The dark knight persuades the owner to tear up the bill and promise to lower his prices. Before leaving, Ed announces to the patrons that the owner is buying everybody a round. That raises the people's spirits a bit. The party exits amongst rousing cheers.

As our heroes reach the southern exit, a man yells to them in the distance, "I wouldn't go that way if I were you!"

Shine shouts back, "Yeah? Why's that?"

"Road's out. Rockslide."

Julia throws her arms in the air in frustration, "Oh, for fuck sake!" Guess it's though the desert. The party will move as quickly as they can and hope a storm doesn't whip up. As they walk through the center of the city, Artemis stops and stares longingly up the grand staircase leading to the palace.

"What is it?" Julia asks.

"… That priest, Hermes. He said he found the source of the sandstorms. It sounded almost like he had some idea on how to stop them."

"That's ridiculous," snipes Duncan. "What's he going to do, pray them away? You can't stop a sandstorm."

Artemis continues to gaze at the palace. "Maybe so, but… what if there was…"

Shine's shoulders slump. His head droops down. Halfheartedly, he asks, "You want to try and help, don't you?"

Artemis spins around and stares at Shine with her puppy dog eyes, "*Pleeeaaase?*" Why can't he ever say no to that? He begrudgingly agrees to find Hermes at the palace to appease her.

There's about two hundred marble steps between them and the main doors. Statues of past pharaohs and other important figures line either side of the staircase. Large sections are buried in sand, but there's a winding path to the top. Once inside the palace, finding Hermes will be easy enough. He's most likely in the throne room with the pharaoh.

The guards are like road signs leading the heroes forward. Up the main hall, up the stairs, and down another hall. Two large, regal-looking doors with red velvet padding are open ahead. They can hear two voices. The discussion sounds heated. The guards refuse to let the heroes in the room and pull the doors shut. The debate within is loud enough to still make out.

Hermes pleads, "Pharaoh Khafra, please hear me out."

"Hmph! I shall not entertain your ridiculous theories!"

Hermes persists, "These sandstorms aren't just mere coincidence. There has to be an underlying cause."

"Nonsense! Giza has always had to deal with the harsh desert. We've endured countless storms, and we shall continue to endure."

"They have never been this severe. The city is almost completely buried, and the storms show no signs of calming. Are you going to wait until the entire city is lost to the desert before you listen?"

"These storms are indeed severe, but they are just storms. There's no divine curse. Talk of such things will only lead to unnecessary panic."

"People are already panicking. People are trapped inside their homes and separated from their families. The situation has become a crisis. If nothing is done, I fear the worst."

"Oh? What would you have me do? Pray to Theon to make the sandstorms go away?" Duncan snickers at the suggestion.

Hermes pauses and takes a deep breath. He is prepared for what is about to cross his lips, but he didn't want to pinch this particular nerve if it could be avoided. There's no choice. Once steeled, he's ready to drop a bombshell. He stares Pharaoh Khafra square in the eyes and states, "In this case, I think praying to Fira may be more appropriate."

The pharaoh glares. If looks could kill. "Watch your tongue, boy!" he demands. "That name is not to be spoken here!"

"It would seem I've touched a nerve. I have extensively studied your people's history and past religion. At the risk of sounding arrogant, I may know more about Firianism than you, Pharaoh."

Pharaoh Khafra is aghast by the mention of Fira. The heroes try to make sense of his harsh reaction. Hermes mentioned the name before, but no one really understands what's happening. The heroes continue listening hoping all with be explained. The pharaoh regains his composure and indifferently dismisses, "That is just an old fairy tale to me."

"Oh? Is what why your crown is adorned with Fira's gem?"

Shine looks to his friends. "Does anyone know what they're talking about?"

"I'm completely lost." Julia groans.

The pharaoh continues, "That is none of your concern. The same goes for the affairs of our city, priest. If you have no other business to discuss, I must ask you to take your leave."

"All I ask is you allow me to explore Wosret's tomb. If I'm right, I may be able to stop the storms."

"You're asking me to let you, an outsider, enter our most sacred grounds? Out of the question!"

"I'm fully aware of the gravity of my request. The tomb seems to be at the epicenter of the storms. If I can find a way to lift the curse, I can st—"

"Enough!" Pharaoh Khafra booms. "I already told you I shall not entertain any theories regarding evil spirits and curses!"

"The fate of Giza rests on it! Please, Pharaoh!"

"I have heard enough! Guards! Escort this man from my castle!" The palace guards move to surround Hermes.

"Ooo... That pharaoh guy sounds pissed," Ed remarks.

The priest's words resonated with Wendy. "Hmm... What the priest was describing... Doesn't it sound a lot like the events we've been experiencing?"

"You have a point there," Shine concurs.

Artemis asks, "Do you think there's something to this 'curse'?"

Shine answers, "It's hard to say. It might be a good idea to try to help that priest out."

Duncan cracks his knuckles. "Does that mean I get to beat up the guards?"

"Ugh..." Julia disapprovingly grunts. "It's always violence with you. Not everything can be solved with brute force."

Marduk agrees, "Yes, becoming an enemy of the state likely won't be an appropriate solution."

"Let's see if we can sway this guy," affirms Shine.

The heroes storm into the room. The guards at the door yell for them to stop, but there's nothing they can do except give chase. Hermes is surrounded on three sides. Pharaoh Khafra stares at the interlopers in disbelief as his throne room is intruded upon. "More outsiders? You all have some nerve barging in here unannounced!"

Marduk once again plays diplomat, "I apologize for the intrusion. We couldn't help overhearing your conversation just now. We may be able to provide some insight on your situation."

The pharaoh shakes his head in vexation, "Lovely... More people to try and convince me of some divine curse. Be gone!"

The wizard continues, "Not necessarily, Pharaoh. Our group here has been traveling together for a while now. In those travels, we have encountered many strange events. Events that are seemingly impossible. Two of our group hail from a small village where, in a decade's time, a pristine lake transformed into a swamp, and the neighboring cave once filled with minerals seemed to decay. On top of that, some villagers became horribly deformed. We also passed through a forest whose normally docile inhabitants began attacking travelers. After battling their king, he himself claimed to be possessed by some dark force. There was also a pirate who was slain in battle over fifty years ago whose spirit once again roamed Terra. He, too, claimed he'd been possessed by some dark force. Now, we find a city ravaged by sandstorms. I don't know exactly what's happening to our world, but if this priest has a theory, it would be wise to test it."

The pharaoh is unmoved by the grand speech. "That is a very entertaining story, but it proves nothing."

"Perhaps not, but given the current state of affairs, wouldn't you agree it would be wise to explore all possible solutions?"

"Not when it involves wild stories of curses and entering our sacred ground."

"Wow, this guy is really stubborn," Shine remarks.

The pharaoh glares at Shine. "This *guy* is the Pharaoh of Giza, and you shall address me as such, boy. If all you people have to offer is more talk of curses, my answer is no."

Hermes makes one final plea, "Please listen to reason. I cannot speak for these travelers, but I bear you nor this city any ill will. I, too, have witnessed many disturbing events on my travels. As a priest of Theon, I am compelled to help those in need. This man's story confirms what I already know deep within my soul. The world is drastically changing. I fear something terrible is about to happen."

The pharaoh is exhausted by the debate. "...And that boy calls me stubborn. The fact of the matter is these storms are Giza's problem, and we shall handle it ourselves. I cannot allow you to step foot on our holy ground on a hunch."

Despair grips the young priest. "I wish there was some way to make you see what I see..." An idea flashes. He turns to Marduk. "You there. Old man?"

"It's Marduk."

"Sorry. Marduk, you said earlier you encountered a possessed spirit, right?"

"The spirit of Captain Barrett, yes."

"That may just be what is happening here." Hermes pauses to collect his thoughts before addressing the evermore agitated pharaoh again, "Pharaoh Khafra, Wosret was mortally wounded in battle, was he not?"

The pharaoh drums the armrest of his throne with his fingers. He is just about out of patience. "Yes. What of it?" he asks half bored and half stern.

"As you walk towards the tomb, the sand slopes sharply downward no matter which direction you approach from and then curves back up to the base of the tomb. It's like something is bursting forth from the tomb itself, pushing the sands outward. If it's possible for a spirit to reenter a body, perhaps Wosret has returned. The rage he must feel failing to protect his people. His empire falling. Perhaps the storms are a manifestation of his rage."

"You expect me to believe a long dead pharaoh somehow came back to life and is whipping up sandstorms because he is mad? That makes absolutely zero sense."

Shine answers before Hermes can, "You don't have to believe it. Just let us check it out. We may not look like it, but we've got some experience in this sort of thing."

The pharaoh's mouth drops in disbelief. How many times does he have to tell these people? "You expect me to let—"

Shine interjects, "Yeah, yeah. Sacred ground. Got it."

A shocked guard mutters aloud, "I can't believe he just interrupted the pharaoh. He's going to get himself beheaded."

Before the pharaoh can compose himself, Shine pushes, "Look, Pharaoh. Like my friend here said, we've seen far too many strange things in far too little time. I'm not the type to believe in spirits or curses either. Then one literally stared me right in the face. Something strange is happening, and seemingly all of Elysia is affected. You yourself have a city that's half buried in sand. All we ask is that you let us help this priest investigate. Best case, we find a way to stop the storms. Worst case, we eliminate one possible cause. Is your *sacred ground* so important that you'd risk the lives of your citizens?"

There's a long pause as the pharaoh weighs those words. The guard from before can't seem to keep his mouth shut. "Yep, he's so beheaded," he blurts.

The pharaoh resonates with Shine's confidence and resolve. He cannot place it, but there's something different about this one. After an eternity stretching few moments, Pharaoh Khafra delivers his answer, "It has been a very long time since anyone spoke to me so sharply. You claim Giza is not the only area experiencing strange events?"

Shine nods. "It seems like something weird is happening everywhere we go."

The pharaoh stops again to ponder. "Hmmm..."

Sensing the magnate is teetering, Hermes moves to close the deal, "How about it, Pharaoh? Will you allow us to explore the tomb?"

More silence. The heroes anxiously wait. Finally, they have their answer, "Two conditions."

That's a yes! Hermes quickly agrees, "Of course."

"You report directly to me regardless of if you find anything. Show those resting there their proper respect. Don't touch anything unless you absolutely have to."

The priest looks composed, but internally, he is jumping for joy. He remains formal. "Agreed. Thank you, Pharaoh."

The pharaoh snorts and turns his head away. He isn't fully comfortable with what he'd agreed to, but if there's even a slim chance this can save his city, he'll indulge the adventurers. He shoos them away with his hand and bluntly says, "I suggest you leave before I change my mind."

With a new comrade in their ranks, the heroes exit the throne room posthaste. As they make their way out of the castle, Hermes expresses his gratitude, "You guys showed up in a nick of time. Theon must want me to explore the tomb."

"I don't know about all that," replies Shine, "but we overheard your conversation and just couldn't stand by. Strange things are happening, and if they are all somehow connected, maybe this tomb will provide us with a clue." He's glad he let Artemis guilt him into finding Hermes. As important slaying Pious and avenging his father is, the young man cannot help feeling there may be a higher calling, something even greater than ridding Terra of this tyrant.

The priest's smile is glued on tight. "If we can just get these dreadful sandstorms to stop, I'll be happy. Have you all been traveling together long?"

"Yes and no," Shine answers. "Our group has been slowly expanding as we go. It seems like an eternity since I started, but it's only been a couple months."

"I see. Where are you headed?"

Shine contemplates telling Hermes of their quest but decides against it. He has met very few priests, but none of them looked like they'd be any use on a battlefield. Better not chance getting stuck with dead weight. "No offense, but what we're doing isn't something you just tell someone you barely know even if they are a priest."

"Fair enough."

"What makes you so certain the tomb is connected to the storms?"

"I won't know for sure until we investigate, but it seems to be their epicenter. The architects used magic to help protect the tomb. When magic is involved, anything is possible."

"If we're heading there, we should do it quickly before another storm whips up."

"Agreed. A word of caution: Wosret's Tomb is full of traps to keep grave robbers out. We will need to tread carefully."

The gravity of the situation seems to have evaded Ed. "I get to go grave robbin'!" Half the party begins to correct him but just sigh and shake their heads instead.

By the time the heroes reach the tomb, night has fallen. Countless stars fill the cloudless desert sky. A coyote howls in the distance. A nearly full moon bathes them in its light. The ruins of Thonis are a silhouette in the distance. Some of the taller pillars and buildings that weren't completely destroyed poke up at the night sky. It's cold out. The temperature dropped sharply once the sun rested. Everyone can see their breath. There is an eerie feeling in the air, and they aren't even inside the tomb yet.

The strange atmosphere makes this endeavor even creepier. Ed is still in high spirits, more excited to loot and plunder than deal with an alleged curse. Hermes is the most apprehensive. Encroaching on a peoples' sacred ground doesn't sit well with him, and if there actually is a curse, he has no idea how to handle it. Lifting curses is one practice he isn't too keen on. He can handle simple ones, but something powerful and elaborate enough to spawn massive storms is out of his wheelhouse. He must have been sick during *"divine curse"* day. Everyone else feels varying levels of trepidation. Except maybe for Duncan, who seems as cool and calm as always, but who knows with that guy?

Before long, the heroes find themselves staring down a dark corridor at the mouth of the tomb. The moonlight is swallowed by darkness. It's pitch black inside, so torch time! The corridor is narrow. Old, worn braziers line the wall, glowing in the torchlight. Good. They can light braziers as they go to avoid getting lost. Shine and Hermes do the honors of being the torchbearers. There's a gentle roar as the braziers ignite.

The corridor is bare sans a few cobwebs. Hieroglyphs are carved on either side through much of it. Everyone assumes it's a warning about trespassers being forever cursed or something. Too late to worry about that. Before long, there's a T-Intersection. Left or right? Coin flip. It's tails. The party heads right. A narrow corridor splits off to the right soon after. There's a stone door straight ahead. Lighting the path as they go, the heroes walk to the door. It's locked. Things are off to a great start… Duncan wants to use his fists as a key. Hermes protects the door-in-distress from its would-be destroyer. They promised Pharaoh Khafra they wouldn't tear the place up.

Maybe the other way will be fruitful. It leads to medium-sized room without a pesky door getting in the way. Painted marble pillars line either side of the entrance. The paint is mostly faded, but they seem to depict Gizians worshipping a deity. A large sandstone block conspicuously rests near the middle of the room. Was it left over from construction? Some small snakes slither out of the torchlight into the shadows. The room is empty, sans the conspicuous stone block. All the treasure, bodily organs, and whatever else must have been entombed deeper inside. There's a door on the other side of the room, but it's locked, too. Duncan's fists clench. "Don't even think about it," Hermes warns.

Wendy sees something opposite the door. There's a large, metal switch rising up from the floor. It is large enough for a person to easily stand on it. The witch does just that. Her ninety-pound body isn't enough weight to depress it. Julia pushes her aside and bashes it with her hammer. That worked! A metallic click rings through the room followed by light rumbling and grinding. The locked door descended through the floor!

Julia smiles with satisfaction as she lifts her hammer. As she does, the switch pops back out, and the door shoots back upward, sealing the way once more. To keep the door open, someone will have to stay behind. Or will they? That giant stone block the middle of the room suddenly makes tons more sense. Julia volunteers Duncan to help her push it into place. He's the second strongest and needs to work off some door-related frustration. Five very long minutes later, the block settles on the switch, and the door is open again.

There's a short corridor leading to another door. Small vases line the walls. Age is taking its toll on the tomb. There's some shattered vases and rubble where part of the wall collapsed. A huge snake is coiled on top of the debris. It raises its head and hisses. There's no room to go around, and it doesn't look to be moving anytime soon. There's only enough space to approach two-by-two.

Shine and Duncan slowly encroach. Shine wields Rashida in one hand, and the torch in his other. The snake wastes little time lunging at him. It gets skewered on his sword. Snake kabob. He pushes the serpent off Rashida as Duncan glares at him. What was he supposed to do, get bit just so Duncan could be the one to squish it? Everybody keeps moving.

This door is unlocked. This room is narrow, too, but wider than the last. After some brief exploration and fire lighting, the entirety of the space is visible. It's more like a corridor stretching east and west. The party entered from the east side. There's another metal switch but no giant block. There's another ordinary looking door across the room at the western end. The door in the middle, however, is much larger and more ornate. Ancient symbols are carved all over it. Hermes brings a torch close. The cyphers are written in Giza's ancient language of the same name. They're pretty worn, but it seems to speak of ancient keys.

There are four cylindrical-shaped metal objects aligned into a row near the center protruding outward. They seem to be some sort of locking mechanisms. Magic ones, to be precise. If the door requires keys, these are where they must go. Whatever lies past here must be important. Duncan is fed up with all the locked doors. This time no one is going to stop him from busting his way through. He concentrates mana into his fist and punches the door as hard as he can. The door flashes brilliant gold as a magical barrier repels the blow and sends Duncan flying back into a wall. He curses under his breath and prepares to attack again. Everyone gang tackles him and holds him down until his anger subsides. They try the other door. It is locked as well. Julia and Ed groan in unison as Artemis harrumphs. They're not having much luck thus far.

Backtracking, the heroes go back towards the tomb exit. They proceed down the corridor to the left of where they came in. It is the same as the other; a narrow corridor splitting off and ending in stone door. The heroes take the split. The room ahead has seen better days. Much of it has crumbled. The remnants of a giant block can be seen under some rubble from the collapsed ceiling.

There's a small, metal chest sitting on a wooden table. Ed gleefully picks the lock. He frowns to see nothing but a small brass key inside. He nearly tosses it aside, but Wendy grabs it. It must unlock something. The switch to open the door seems to be intact, but they won't need to worry about that. The door is badly damaged. So badly no one minds if Duncan finishes it off. The hall leads back to the large, ornate door. The tomb was built with some symmetry it seems. No sense in going that way. Not one of the previous locked doors had keyholes.

The heroes head through the last unexplored door. This one is unlocked! The room has a few statues lining the walls and arranged around the middle the of the room. There are tables full of trinkets and, of course, spiderwebs. Hermes slaps Ed's hand as he tries to paw some emeralds. The thief is surprised there's anything to loot at all. It wouldn't have been difficult for robbers to venture this far. The Gizians must deeply cherish the tomb as holy ground.

The party is led to a long hallway. As they walk down, a swarm of scarabs bubbles up from the sand like a backed-up drain sending the party running. They quickly head through a door on their right and soon reach a rope ladder. The floor of the room it's in has mostly crumbled away. There's more or less just a cracked, winding stone bridge leading to it. The heroes cautiously make their way across and up the ladder. Wendy gulps loudly as the causeway cracks a little more as they cross. The floor manages to hold.

The ladder leads to the center of the room above. Moonlight shines in from a hole in the ceiling, illuminating most of it for the heroes. Four granite statues of demons are aligned in the cardinal directions surrounding the hole. Four bronze statues of fire dragons are perched in the corners fiercely glaring into the center of the room. There's a doorway to the left, but a four-foot-wide row of giant metal spikes block the way. There's a fair amount of rust on them, but surely, they are still plenty sharp. Each one is two feet long. The skeleton of a huge snake is near them. It must have triggered a floor trap. Clearing the spikes will be dangerous.

Before anyone can try, loud hisses fill the room. A quartet of large scorpions with stingers at the ready emerge from the shadows cast by the demonic statues. The room isn't exceptionally big. Avoiding those deadly tails will be tricky. The scorpions eagerly click while snapping their claws. It has been ages since they'd had such a feast. Marduk blasts one with Fireball. His eyes widen in surprise as it has no effect. Another scorpion begins to glow and then breathes fire at the heroes. The energy isn't chi. They can use magic?

There isn't time to worry about that now. The heroes need to act fast. Shine blocks the flames with his shield. The other three scorpions begin their approach. Wendy hits one with Deluge while Artemis uses Ice Arrow on another. The one hit by water is shoved back and hits the wall hard. It has trouble shaking off the blow. The other squeals as its body is frozen almost completely. Water and ice seem to work quite well against these arachnids. The final approaching critter stabs with its tail despite being out of range for a direct attack. To everyone's surprise, a needle-like burst of purple chi shoots forward from its stinger. Marduk is nearly hit square in the chest. Luckily, Julia was there to shield him with her hammerhead.

The firebreather casts another spell. This time it's Earth magic. A violent tremor abruptly shifts the floor where the heroes are standing. A couple fall over, and the rest are kept at bay. The frozen scorpion shatters free of its icy prison, and the one Wendy nailed has also recovered. All four move in quickly and strike with that purple chi attack sending everyone ducking and diving for cover. An arachnid moves into range for a direct sting on Ed. The thief is swift enough to attack first, but the enemy catches his dagger with its claw. Before it can sting, Marduk slices its tail off with Wind Burst.

Duncan finishes it with a slash of his rapier and flows into Razor Wind on the next closest critter. It shows surprising agility, leaping away at the last moment. The other two are now both standing side by side. They both prepare to breathe fire. As their mouths open, two arrows fly down their throats. Weird, sickly gargles leak out as they die. Three down, one to go. Wendy hits it with a toned-down Deluge. She displays expert control, dimming the attack enough to not send it flying while still being forceful enough to stun. The scorpion is staggered, allowing Julia to easily smash it a strong hammer bash.

Everyone collects themselves after the strange battle. Nobody expected to be dealing with magic scorpions. Animals and insects using chi is a rare enough occurrence. Magic is almost unheard of. Seldom few such as fairies and dragons have been officially documented casting spells though there's plenty of folk tales circulating about many others.

Stranger still, those metal spikes recoiled into the floor as soon as the last scorpion was slain. Were they one of the tomb's traps? What kind of magic could pull off such a feat? Maybe they'll discover some ancient secrets here. Marduk is excited by the possibility. The priest is more interested in learning more of Giza's history. Speaking of him, Shine couldn't help noticing Hermes didn't do a thing in battle. That's disappointing. The priest is no good in a fight after all.

The door leads to a room the same size as the previous. There's a plain stone coffin in the center. It must belong to someone close to Pharaoh Wosret, maybe a family member or advisor. Canopic jars with the deceased's organs and various treasures are scattered about on tables and on the floor. The Gizian people used to have a tradition where they removed some of the deceased's organs and placed them in canopic jars so the departed will have them in the afterlife.

It's an old Firian ritual. This pyramid was nearing completion at the conclusion of the Great War, and the Gizians were allowed to bury their fallen leader within making it the final Firian ritual that would ever be performed, a somber, sullen moment in history. The wizard and priest murmur excitedly upon laying eyes on the crypt. Ed is busy scanning for loot to pluck without anybody noticing. Artemis is creeped out. Wendy is tempted to open the sarcophagus to see the mummy inside.

A wooden shelf with a small chest is located on the other side of the room. It is the same kind as the one the key was inside. It's almost as if the mummy was symbolically placed to guard it. Something feels fishy. Sensing there may be a traps, Julia flings her hammer ahead to the ground in front of them. A section of the floor sinks, and a volley of arrows fire across the room. There could be more, so everyone stays back and let the thief do his thing. He nimbly navigates his way across, moving too quickly and too lightly for any hidden switches to depress. The chest contains another brass key. Progress!

Now it is back to that long hallway with the beetles. It is scarab free at moment. The party makes haste to the other side before that changes. This door is locked. Unlike the others, it has a keyhole. A brass key fits perfectly in the lock. After the door is unlocked, the key briefly shimmers silver before crumbling into nothing. Even they are magic. The party is now in another long hallway. This one also has a door to the right and one at the end. The heroes decide to go straight. This door is locked, too. Another keyhole. Click! Their last key crumbles to dust. Everyone hopes not to see another locked door in the next chamber.

This room is curious. One of those sandstone blocks is near the door, which means there must be a switch. The room is a maze of stone hallways and pillars, plus portions of the floor collapsed for added difficulty. Duncan nearly falls down a hole but pretends he didn't. Everybody spreads out to search the room, lighting braziers as they go. The switch is found in the northwest corner of the room almost directly opposite the door they entered. The pathway leading from block to switch is tricky. Before doing anything, everyone fans out to find a viable route.

Once the path is negotiated, Julia and Duncan begin the laborious task of moving the block as their friends guide them to not get the block stuck or, worse, plummeting down a hole. An excruciating half hour later, they finally succeed in activating the switch, but nothing happens. All that time and energy spent was for naught. Hermes remains optimistic. "Hmm… I bet this switch unlocked part of that large door," he ventures.

"It better have done something," Julia pants. "Pushing that thing was no picnic." Artemis pulls out a vitality potion and gives it to the laborers. The herbs from Vanajit's royal garden allowed the budding herbalist to create a more potent version. Half a vial each nearly restores Julia and Duncan's energy fully.

The other ingress is unlocked. They are led down another hall and up another ladder. The room upstairs is tiny and bare containing only an unlocked door. The next room is more interesting. There's a door on the other side. It's magically locked. No key needed, which is good because they're out of those. Two dusty, gold-backed mirrors conspicuously sit here. There is a hole in the south wall. The party can see moonlight shimmering down into what appears to be another room. Everyone is intrigued by the new development.

Marduk deduces it's a classic light puzzle like in the adventure novels he read as a youth. Reflecting the moonlight should trigger something. A small crystal is protruding from the wall by the locked door. Guiding the moonlight into it likely is the key. There must be a way into the south room. There's no reason to doubt the wise wizard, so nobody objects. The heroes backtrack towards the aperture they passed earlier downstairs in the hallway before the giant room where they had to push that obnoxiously large sandstone block through a miniature maze.

Once there, the party finds a small room filled with hieroglyphs and containing all sorts of treasure scattered atop tables and counters. There's also some more canopic jars, but no sarcophagus. Ed is much more interested in the treasure than the creepy organs. This time Hermes is unable to prevent the thief from nabbing some gold coins. As soon as he does, a section of the ceiling opens, and a coil of snakes drops down. Ed manages to avoid them, but he's done touching treasure for at least five minutes. The snakes aren't hostile. They seem more confused as to what just happened. They aimlessly slither about and flick the air uncaring about the humans.

No one is ready for what the next room holds. There are two doors on the north and south sides. The floor is grated all around the edges of the room. They appear to be spike traps. Everyone is relieved it wasn't triggered when they entered. There is a large, square-shaped granite pedestal in the center of the room with wooden torches at the corners. In the center of the pedestal is a sarcophagus. Those organs from before must belong to whomever is inside. Strange, usually organs are kept in the same room.

This sarcophagus is more elaborate than the first one, but there's no way it is Wosret's. It must be somebody close, though, perhaps a family member. The door behind the heroes slams shut, and they hear a loud click. It just locked. Immediately after, the spike traps release, blocking any attempt to smash a blocked exit down and run. The four torches light simultaneously. Something very bad is about to happen.

The sarcophagus lid slowly slides open. A linen-wrapped arm reaches out over the side. A mummy slowly stands and turns towards the heroes. Forgetting she's in the presence of a priest, Julia blurts, "Holy fucking fuck! Is that fucking mummy?" It is indeed a fucking mummy, and like most things our heroes encounter, it wants to kill them.

Wendy can't help but to ask, "What do you think it wants?"

"Maybe it's just lookin' for its mummy," Ed jokes.

Julia groans and exasperates, "Really, Ed?" as she readies her weapon.

Never missing an opportunity to hit something, Duncan breaks rank and charges in. He scores a direct hit with a slash of his rapier. Their foe is unaffected. Not a single strand of linen was cut let alone its body. It slowly swats at Duncan. He could easily dodge it but wants to strike again. Such a slow attack won't harm him. Or not.

Duncan is sent twisting backward like a ragdoll and crashes into the other three mages. He rubs his cheek as he stares in angry surprise at the mummy. Shine tosses the torch aside. Julia slings the backpack away. They, along with Ed, charge in. They all land perfect strikes, but again the mummy is unaffected. They're wise to avoid its sluggish counterattack. Artemis fires Piercing Shot at its chest. The force of the blow sends the mummy flying back, but there's still no visible damage.

The heroes strategize as their enemy lethargically rises. The plan is simple. Hit it with an all-out assault. Some form of attack must be effective. Chi? Magic? Elemental? Only one way to find out. Before anybody is ready, the mummy lets out an eerie wail and sends Dark magic pulsing at them. Duncan casts Magic Resist but cannot apply it to everyone. Hermes, Ed, Shine, and Julia are sent crashing into the wall. The others managed to brace themselves thanks to the spell. Ed springs up and charges. Wendy uses Deluge as Artemis fires an arrow. Sand and dust explode outward from the mummy before the attacks connect. An awed Ed stops dead. It disappeared!

As fast as it vanished, it reappears in another cloud of dust. It's right behind Ed! He tries to dodge, but the mummy grabs his wrist. Ed torques himself away, but immediately feels fatigued. He knows this feeling all too well. He's been cursed again. This time he's certainly a goner so far away from aid. The mummy vanishes again. The priest springs into action. He runs to aid the thief, placing his hand on Ed's chest. A warm white glow emanates from the priest as he gathers Holy magic. Ed instantly feels like himself again. The curse has been lifted! That's a handy trick. The Holy spell is simply called Uncurse. Hermes can handle basic curses with it.

The mummy returns. It is now on the other side of the room. It lets out another cry and sends Dark Pulse at the heroes. The torches are knocked over but remain lit. Everyone is able to get out of the spell's radius. Hermes charges forward, leaping over a torch. He stands between the sarcophagus and the mummy wielding the torch in one hand, and his angel winged staff in the other. There is no direct path to him if he needs aid.

The mummy takes a long, slow step towards the brave—maybe stupid—priest. Hermes raises his staff and yells, "Begone!" A blinding white light fills the room. Unlike Marduk's Flash spell, this light is highly energized with Holy magic. Engulfed in the brilliant light, the mummy writhes and wails in pain as if it had been lit aflame. It's not enough for it to be gone, but their enemy is stunned, allowing everybody to rally.

Time to go all out! Artemis uses Refreshing Wind on the melee fighters, supercharging her friends. Wendy powers up the mage corps and then uses Chilling Wind. Small patches of ice bespeckle their foe. Its back arches backward as it's hit by Razor Wind. Marduk uses a variation of Shock, causing lighting to strike down from directly above the target. Rashida's flame burns brightly as Shine slashes. Ed follows up with a flourish. Julia completes the chain, swinging her hammer like a baseball bat.

The mummy crashes into the wall leaving a respectable impact crater. It slumps down onto the spikes but is somehow still standing. Finally, it collapses face first. Its body begins to dissolve away. The spikes in the floor recoil. There's a click signifying the door is unlocked once more. The mummy's duty must have been guarding the tomb. Wendy and Artemis down half a potion each to restore their magic and chi, respectively. Khafra is never going to believe what they just witnessed. Everyone is becoming true believers of curses.

The heroes travel through the south doorway and enter a small room. There's a large blue-painted chest on the other side. After carefully inspecting for traps, they walk to it. Hermes's eyes grow wide at what it contains. He gently lifts out a beautiful staff. It is made of polished bronze. Torchlight elegantly flickers in its reflection. A figurine forged of gold connects the staff to a ruby that is cut to resemble flames. The figure is of Fira, the god Gizians used to worship before their religion was outlawed. Hermes can only manage a whisper, "The Staff of Fira."

Its original owner was none other than the late Pharaoh Wosret. Legend says it can harness the flames of Fira himself. Hermes has never practiced Fire magic, but upon touching the staff, he feels a strange power grow within. His eyes shift to a look of understanding. He smiles as he gazes at the beautiful artifact. He's got a new favorite staff.

"Aww... How come ya get to loot treasure, but not me?" Ed whines.

Julia snipes, "Because bad things happen when you touch things."

Hermes remarks about his new weapon, "This staff was wielded by Wosret himself. It is of extreme historical and archaeological importance. Much can be learned by studying it."

"So, you plan to donate it to science?" Marduk asks.

"Yes, of course... after I'm finished using it."

Ed flatly accuses, "Yer gonna keep it forever, aren't ya?" Hermes quickly changes the subject, suggesting they get a move on.

Onto the northern passage. There's a ladder ahead which leads them to the room where the moonlight is shining down. A mirror identical to the others rests along a wall. The party moves it under the moonlight and focuses the light through the hole. Nothing happens. Some more adjustments are necessary. They return to the two-mirrored room. The mirrors are bolted into the floor but can be rotated. After some light dusting and turning, they hear a high-pitched chime as the moonlight is perfectly reflected into the crystal next to the sealed passage. There's loud grinding as the door descends down into the floor until it is completely gone from view. In the next room, there's another chest with a small key, and a ladder leading down.

It doesn't take long to find the key's home. Once down the ladder, another locked ingress is at the end of a corridor. The key crumbles like the others after being used. There are two doors and another ladder in the next room. They go vertical, and there's two paths to choose from here. Make that one. The southern area suffered a collapse, and the path is totally buried in rubble. One of the top corners of a door can just barely be made out among the debris. The clear path leads them to a room filled with more gold-backed mirrors. It's a good thing the moon is out tonight. They arrange the mirrors with relative ease and move through the open door and on to the next challenge.

This chamber has a metal switch but no block. Metal bars create a barrier on the north wall. A small chest is behind them. It's the same type all the keys have been inside. They'll have to find a way in. There is a stone doorway leading in, but it's one of those magic ones. After some brief discussion, it is deemed finding a block might not be necessary. Julia and Duncan sure hope so. Pushing those heavy things is no picnic. The party has a clever idea.

Ed stands next to the sealed door as Julia's hammer smashes the switch. Ed heads in before it can reset, grabs the key, and one more hammer swing lets him out. Hermes notices a square-shaped hole in the ceiling. There's probably a block up above, but they outsmarted the room. There's a second door in this room. It leads to a small chamber with a ladder leading up. There's also a door to the south. The heroes choose the door and find themselves in a large room with a stone block. The area is too large for torches alone to fully illuminate it.

Marduk does his magic flashlight thing to wash the darkness away. There's no switch in sight, but there are many pits in the floor. They are only a few feet deep; however, if the block were to fall into one, getting it out would be quite arduous. There's a wide door on the south side of the room. It looks to be wide enough to squeeze the block through. Marduk dims his light and they head over. It has a keyhole lock, and they're out of keys. Duncan tries to bust it down but is repelled backwards by magic like the last time. Some people just never learn. More careful navigation will be required to get the block into its home. First, they need another key.

The party returns to the ladder, hopeful it will lead them to another key. In the above chamber, there are doors posted in each of the cardinal directions. East most likely leads above the room they tricked, so they skip it. South is first. As the heroes enter the room, metal bars shoot up from the floor in front of the door, blocking the way back. The room is fairly large. About half of it is cast in shadow. Clicks and hisses ring out. Marduk turns his light back on to see what beasts they need to deal with.

An assortment of giant snakes and scorpions are slithering and skittering across the room. Hermes and Shine toss the torches towards the center so Marduk can save his magic for combat. The space is lit well enough to see any incoming hostiles before they can get within striking distance. The critters are felled with relative ease. The heroes are becoming proficient exterminators. The metal bars recede. Unconvinced the chamber was nothing more than a trap, the heroes split up to search the area. Shine and Hermes each light the way as everyone fans out. A small chest is discovered in the corner of the room. There's a key inside.

Now to the west room. It is another barren area sans another metal chest. Expecting traps, Ed goes to work. He nimbly evades wall-fired arrows, floor-sprung spears, and some falling snakes on his way to the chest. The party exits with one more brass key in their possession. One of them is for the north door. They head through.

Someone created a mini labyrinth here. It is simple enough to navigate. Shine slides his hand across one of the walls as he leads the way eventually reaching the middle. There is a sandstone plinth dead center. There is a small metal switch on it. They presume it's for one of the locks on the large, ornate door back by the tomb entrance. After double checking the east door to confirm suspicions of an unneeded sandstone block and make sure they don't miss anything vital like keys, they head back to the block room with the shallow pits.

This time, Shine, Hermes, and Ed are tasked with maneuvering the block. Julia takes a torch and walks ahead to unlock the door. When it's opened, there is a large square hole in the floor a few feet away in a narrow corridor. With some careful pushing and pulling, the sandstone block inches closer to the passage and eventually down the hole. It falls for a while before anyone hears a crash. It must have fallen all the way back down to the first floor. The last room of this section of the tomb has been searched, so the heroes head back down the ladder. They head back through the second-floor rooms to the other ladder leading back to the first floor.

Soon they are back in the three-doored room. One way leads back the way they came. There are two more paths to choose from: west or south. West wins the coin toss. An L-shaped hallway leads to an octagonal chamber. Most of it is covered in sand but is otherwise empty. It's by far the largest room yet. There's no way nothing is here. Maybe something is buried in the sand.

The stone floor leads into the center, ending in a peninsula. There's a few braziers lining one edge of the pass plus one in the middle of the far edge. They are larger than any in the rest of the pyramid. After those are ignited, there is enough light to barely make out the edges of the room. Something is reflecting back. More braziers are hanging from the walls. Nothing else seems to be here. Maybe it's another puzzle. Lighting all the braziers may trigger something.

Shine and Hermes step off the stone path to get to work. The instant the duo steps foot onto the sand, a terrible tremor rocks the room. The sand in front of the party bulges upward. A massive wyrm bursts forth! "Gross," Wendy disgusts. It is a slimy, ugly thing. The wyrm is at least thirty feet long and six feet thick.

It wraps its body in a loose coil. Its head towers ten feet above the adventurers. It has no eyes, just a massive vacuum-like mouth, yet it feels like it's leering at them. Slimy drool leaks from the giant orifice. It is a dangerous beast. Giant wyrms are extremely rare, which is good because a single one is capable of taking out an entire platoon of soldiers. Records from Giza's former military can attest to that. Did someone put this thing here as a trap? Metal bars rise to block the exit. Yup. It's a trap. The torches and backpack are ditched.

The party pairs up into twos and spreads out across the room. The melee fighters, Duncan included, take frontal positions while Artemis and the mages stand behind. Before anyone can make a move, the sands begin swirling violently around the room in a vicious cyclone. Is this wyrm the cause of the sandstorms? The sands rip and tear at the heroes. Everyone winces and tries to shield their eyes. It may not be nearly as large as the storm they unwisely tried walking through, but it is much windier. Tiny cuts are accumulating everywhere there is exposed flesh. It's painful, but they're just going to have to suck it up and endure. The faster the wyrm dies, the faster the storm will subside.

It doesn't waste any time with a follow up spell, creating a powerful earthquake. Even as spread out as our heroes are, half of them are slammed to the ground. Julia and Ed charge in while Marduk and Duncan attack with Shock and Fastball. The wyrm's size makes it an easy target but also a tough one to damage. Julia's hammer bounces off its thick hide sending her backpedaling several steps. Ed slashes furiously with his daggers, but they cannot pierce that concrete skin. Neither spell has an effect either.

The wyrm slings its tail with frightening speed sending Julia and Ed flying. Hermes climbs to his feet and uses Theon's Light. It doesn't do much; however, the massive wyrm trembles just a bit. Artemis uses Piercing Shot. The power of the skill penetrates its hide. Against a normal foe it would be a significant wound, but it is just scratch to something this big. It barely even reacts to the hit. Everyone is slammed down by another tremor.

The swirling storm isn't letting up. If the wyrm doesn't kill them, the tempest will. Tiny lacerations are multiplying at an alarming pace. Shine has an idea, but there's little time to strategize. This enemy can cast powerful spells almost instantly. All Shine can do is yell for Artemis to power him up with Surge like against Barrett. As she does, he yells, "Duncan, Marduk! Wind!" and hopes they see what he's planning. The rest aren't quite sure, but it's obvious they need to buy Shine a little time.

Hermes uses Theon's Light while still halfway on the ground. Wendy aims a Deluge at the beast's head while Julia and Ed attack directly. The latter two are sent flying back from another brutal tail whip. A painful penance, but it gave Shine enough time to execute his plan. He focuses his chi and uses Disperse. Surge allows for much more energy to be channeled into the technique.

Marduk and Duncan instantly recognize what to do and cast their Wind spells at Shine's cyclone. The wind generated is more intense than even what their foe created. Everyone struggles just to hold their position. A massive boom shakes the room as Disperse cancels out the sandstorm. That's one obstacle cleared. The priest yells for everyone to close ranks.

The party obeys and pays for it, suffering from another quake. Everyone falls. Hermes springs to his feet. His body begins to glow white with Holy magic. He casts a healing spell. A warm light bathes himself and his allies. Everyone is instantly rejuvenated. Most of those nasty little cuts close. It is an impressive display of magic, but a costly one. Despite its increased potency, it takes a full mana potion for him to replenish his mana.

The battle is more or less reset. Duncan boosts everyone's elemental resistance in case the enemy creates another storm. It should help them keep their balance against the tremors, too. This adversary is too large for everyone to attack random spots. They will need to focus on a specific area if they hope to damage it.

The wyrm doesn't let them formulate a plan. Its massive mouth opens wide. The four sections curl apart and spread until its head looks like a disgusting, rancid flower. A foul stench fills the chamber. It hacks up a giant ball of slime. The slime careens towards the party and drenches Marduk. Not only is it really gross, the sticky substance makes it hard to move. The wyrm rears its head back. It lunges forward slithering at the vulnerable wizard to gobble him whole. Duncan grabs his ally and dashes away, barely avoiding being swallowed.

The beast looks like it is going to crash into a wall from its own momentum, but at the last moment, it curves sharply and coils. It begins rearing back for another charge. It is met with a Piercing Shot to its open mouth. Its head shoots upward and back, slamming against the wall. That looked like it hurt! The party tries to close, but the leviathan recovers quickly and keeps everyone at bay with a wide sweep of its tail. It generates another sandstorm. The heroes' skin naturally toughens in response thanks to Duncan's spell. The sharp sands will eventually erode the spell away, but they'll be fine for now. Another shockwave shakes the room. This time everybody remains upright. The wyrm isn't finished yet. It hocks up a volley of slime balls. Everyone manages to get clear. The salvo leaves it exposed.

Time to go on the offensive! Ed uses Conceal. He's going to try and get in close to try and actually do some damage. Hermes's first instinct is to use Theon's Light again, but he pauses. He swears he can hear the staff of Fira whispering to him. It wants him to unleash its power. He closes his eyes and begins to focus his magic. Wendy and Artemis try a combo attack to create an opening for Shine and Julia to strike directly. Wendy widens the scope of Deluge, dousing a good section of their foe's body. Artemis follows up with Ice Arrow. The beast writhes as much of its body freezes over. It didn't like that very much.

Shine and Julia charge. The wyrm tries to swipe them away with a swift tail strike, but the duo evades and keep coming. Julia strikes first baseball swinging her hammer as hard as she can into a frozen section.

Shine's fire sword slashes immediately after followed up with a stabbing thrust. Green blood spews from the wound. The wyrm's mouth opens wide to try to eat Shine, but when it does, a blistering Fireball nails it. Duncan used Fastball to give Marduk's Fire spell some added oomph, so much so it broke the sound barrier. The top half of the leviathan writhes in agony. It slams its tail into the sand repeatedly from the pain.

Ed is able to get in close. When he becomes visible, he's just inches from his target. He focuses chi into a single dagger and drives it with as much strength as he can muster. It penetrates deep, almost down to the hilt. He starts running along the wyrm's side, tearing a long laceration. Blood gushes out. As gruesome as it appears, even that wound is relatively minor for a creature of this size.

The wyrm charges, knocking the three fighters away. It isn't concerned with eating them this time. It just wants to create some distance. Everyone else gets out of its path as it charges forward. Coiling on the other side of the room, it wastes no time in casting Tremor. This time, most of the heroes fall. Duncan's spell has hit its limit. Everyone is too widespread to recast it on everyone.

The dark knight is the only melee fighter remotely near the enemy. He charges ahead, but even he isn't crazy enough to try and take the creature one-on-one. He just hopes to get its attention so the ranged fighters can attack and for the others can get back into position. He stops about ten feet away and fires another Fastball. It has almost no effect but gets the wyrm to focus on him. It spews more slime, this time in a wide spray. Duncan blocks most of it with his shield. However, the bulwark cannot stop the wyrm's tail from sending him soaring. The shield took the brunt preventing any serious injuries, but now he's way out of position.

Wendy uses Miasma. The purple poison swirls around the beast's head. It tries to shake of the noxious fumes to no avail. The cloud dissipates quickly as the sandstorm swirls it around and blows it away. However, the wyrm is afflicted. The poison isn't nearly enough to fell their foe, but it will slowly sap its strength.

The wyrm tries a new trick. It burrows under the sand. The sand is deep enough to completely hide it. The heroes know what's coming. The question is where. They smartly spread out as much as possible so their enemy can only hit one person. Ed and Julia focus chi to increase their speed. Shine and Duncan ready their shields. Everyone else nervously braces and begins slowly circling with no good way to protect themselves. Seconds feel like hours as everyone awaits the strike.

The sand under Julia bulges. She tries to run but cannot completely avoid the enormous annelid as it bursts forth. She is sent sailing. That move was only part one. As the wyrm descends, it whips its body around. It's ridiculous length nearly encompasses the radius of the room. Luckily, it isn't in the center or everyone would have been walloped. Part of its tail scrapes along the far wall as it revolves.

Julia is still in flight from the previous attack when the tail buffets her. She slams into the wall hard enough to cause significant cracks. Artemis sees her friend's body crumple and immediately runs over. Other than her, Hermes was the only one out the tail's range. The sandstorm's effects are wearing everyone down. They are getting cut up pretty bad. Things won't end well if the battle goes on much longer.

Hermes is finally ready to take his shot. Filled with ancient knowledge, he unleashes an arcane spell. The air grows hot. Heat shimmer hot. Massive pillars of flame burst upward from the ground, engulfing most of the wyrm's body. The flames burn so brightly, those looking on have to shield their eyes. Smoke billows from the victim's skin. A putrid stench like a carcass decaying in the desert sun fills the room. The wyrm collapses but is still wriggling.

Somehow, it still has some fight left, but it will take a while to get back up. Its giant mouth is agape. The sections are quickly curling and opening as it tries to regain breath. More importantly, its most vulnerable spot is now wide open! No one with a melee weapon is close enough to capitalize. They can barely get up after suffering that last attack, and Artemis is busy healing Julia. Hermes is completely drained.

Marduk, Wendy, and Duncan manage to get their feet and hobble together. They are breathing hard, too. They have to cover their mouths to not inhale the sand still whipping about. The wyrm's head begins to twitch and shake. It will recover soon. Wendy boosts their magical attack power, and the trio prepare to use the last of their mana for one final strike. Wendy launches a massive Dark Ball twice its normal size. It buffets the wyrm in the mouth. Duncan and Marduk use the Fastball and Fireball combo from earlier. Wendy's added buff doubles the fireball's size, too. As it screeches towards their target, the powered-up Fastball expands the flame even more.

A massive, searing orb as big as the wyrm's head blazes with supersonic speed. A massive explosion booms outward nearly knocking the mages down. The wyrm's body shoots vertically, seizes, and stiffens in a perfectly straight line as if it were just struck with a massive electric shock. Its tail mashes against the wall. Thick, black smoke billows from its mouth as its head crashes back down to the sand. Slime pools from its agape mouth as the smoke thins. The storm subsides. The leviathan has been slain!

It was a brutal fight that left everyone battered and fatigued. They gather in the center of the room. The mages down the last two mana potions. A good portion of their energy is restored. Everyone shares the last of the vitality potions. There were two left, and it's enough to restore most of their stamina. Everybody will need to be careful from here on out and conserve stamina and magic.

Something strange happens before they exit. A tiny area of sand begins to swirl about on the ground inches from the deceased wyrm. A steel key rises up out of the sand. The back is fashioned to resemble a demon skull. Two large teeth protrude from the front. Surely, it will be needed at some point. If their experience in the tomb has taught them anything so far, it is that magic keys are useful.

The heroes make their way back through the L corridor to the previous room and through the final unexplored door. At this point, they just want to hurry and finish the expedition. The jury is still out regarding if the wyrm was in fact the one causing the storms. The ominous-looking steel key makes everyone feel there is still more to do, nonetheless. Hopefully, whatever remains will be uneventful. The less trouble encountered, the better. The final door takes them down a long hallway ending with an unlocked door.

The next area is a strange one. They are on a narrow path raised six feet above the ground. The edges of the path are crisp. Someone designed it this way. The mystery to why is solved quickly as a section of stone depresses under their feet. Another trap! The room shakes as three sections in ceiling grind open. Sand pours downward. The heroes quickly and carefully navigate the pathway as the room rapidly fills. They reach the opposite door just as the sand reaches their feet.

After a L-shaped hall, the party can go left or right down another corridor. They choose left and find another sandstone block. The accompanying switch is further ahead where this route dead ends. Julia and Duncan move the block into place. A faint grinding can be heard in the distance. It definitely opened something. Back to the right. There's an open passage leading to the next room where the door must have been.

In the next room, there's a switch behind a stone pillar. Nothing obvious happens when it is pulled. It must be part of the locking mechanism on the fancy door. That makes three, meaning there should be just one left. The doorway out appears to be locked, but there's no keyhole. It automatically slides up into the ceiling as they approach. As soon as everyone is through, it slams back down. They've come full circle. This is the first hallway from where they entered the tomb. The braziers they lit flicker gently. Hermes remembers there was a switch they passed. Surely the block from the third floor is in place now.

The heroes make their way back to the chamber with the quadruple-locked door. Three of the mechanical locks have regressed into the stone. The sandstone block is sitting just a couple feet away from the switch. Once in place, the final lock is opened. The ornate door begins to glow. The room shudders violently as it slowly rises up into the ceiling. There's a long staircase leading down.

Fear, excitement, and anticipation grip the adventurers. This path must lead to Wosret's final resting place. Upon descending the steps, they find themselves staring at a massive, extravagant door. Beautifully painted gold plates depicting the fire god Fira and his worshippers are welded onto the thick iron. There is a large keyhole. Shine uses the demon head key. It's a perfect fit! A loud metal click rings out, and the party pushes the heavy door open.

This must be it, Wosret's Tomb. The chamber is enormous. Much if it is buried in sand. Thick stone pillars jut upwards to the ceiling. Each one has large hieroglyphs carved in them. The heroes can put the torches away. Beams of sunlight extend from the heavens. Morning already. Near the center of the room rests a magnificent sarcophagus. The lid is off, propped up on the side. That's probably not good.

As the adventurers approach, they hear an unnerving wail. A mummy wanders out from behind one of the pillars near the back of the chamber. It is wearing a ragged gold and blue nemes. That must be Pharaoh Wosret. Upon seeing the intruders, Wosret immediately begins walking towards them. He's not like the last one. He easily strides with sureness of a man in his prime, not a decrepit corpse. Our heroes steel themselves for one last battle. They take their normal positions. Out of potions, they cannot afford to allow this to go on for long.

Ed uses Conceal to try and get around Wosret, who responds by launching a fireball from an outstretched arm. The thief drops down, narrowly dodging. Stealth is out. Wendy powers up her magic with

Focus and prepares Deluge. Duncan fires Fastball. Wosret doesn't dodge. Instead, he effortlessly smacks the magic away and counters with another fireball. Duncan blocks with his shield, but the Pharaoh immediately follows up with another attack, sending a tremor streaking at the dark knight, knocking him down. Julia charges head on with Shine and Ed in flanking positions. Wosret sidesteps Deluge and leaps backwards to avoid Marduk and Artemis' attacks.

The charging fighters don't pursue. The enemy is too far back, and they'll be out their support's range. Everyone slowly closes in making their way around the sarcophagus. If they can keep pushing their foe back, he'll be surrounded. Wosret doesn't let that happen. He sprints with incredible speed along the back wall to get to a more open area. Ed has a shot at him as he passes. His dagger lands a blow, but like the mummy before, it seems to have zero effect. The heroes won't have any idea how much damage they're actually doing. No choice but to attack until the enemy drops.

Wosret swiftly circles around the party before settling on a position near the middle of the crypt. As he's doing that, Duncan signals for everyone to close rank. He casts Elemental Shield. He's had enough of being floored by Earth attacks. With a sweep of the hand, the risen pharaoh sends a broad arcing wave of Earth chi at the cluster. Being hit by Earth chi like this is akin to having a stone slab smash into you. The wave is knee high. A direct hit can potentially break legs, even with their buff. The mages and archer quickly move back out of range.

Shine and Duncan drop to their knees and place their shields in front to stave off the attack. Julia and Ed use their chi to leap over the wave and counterattack. Julia sends a tremor of her own. Their adversary easily avoids it, but Ed is able to close. He manages to score with a flurry of slashes and springs back to safety as the mummy tries to touch him. No way he's going to be cursed a third time. Artemis launches a Piercing Shot from clear across the room with pinpoint accuracy thanks to Vanajit's bow.

The pharaoh wasn't expecting such a strong attack from such distance but manages to only take a glancing blow to the shoulder. Shine and Julia close in from the front while Ed circles around to flank from the rear. Wosret is stunned by Theon's Light. Marduk launches Fire Flurry while Wendy uses a widely scoped Chilling Wind. Those spread-out spells aren't meant to cause damage. Rather, the idea is to prevent him from evading their fast closing allies. That doesn't stop

Wosret from trying. He quickly darts to his left and nimbly evades the fireballs. Artemis uses Triple Shot. One hits the mark but doesn't slow the pharaoh, who looks like he'll be able to dodge the melee attackers.

Duncan runs in and with a flick of his wrist, launches Razor Wind from his rapier. It crashes into the pharaoh and seems to slice straight through, but there's no cut. It does stop him in his tracks. He is smacked by Shine's Chi Sweep, which knocks him closer to Ed and Julia. Ed capitalizes by leaping into the air and driving both daggers into their foe's back. He ducks and rolls as Wosret swipes.

Now it's Julia who takes flight, Julia driving her hammer down at the mummy's head. Wosret pivots and braces for the blow, crossing his arms in a X above his head. He takes the heavy iron hammerhead full force. He's barely even moved back. A strong burst of Wind chi explodes outward as he breaks guard. Julia careens away. Ed tries to sweep the legs with his blades. No effect. Wosret grabs Ed and flings him away like a ragdoll.

Shine rushes in, Rashida burning bright. Wosret's body begins to glow. A massive swell of chi nearly drives Shine to the ground. The gravity around the pharaoh feels like it tripled. A massive wave of pure energy blasts outward sending Shine, Ed, and Julia flying across the room. Duncan is caught in it, too. Without missing a beat, the pharaoh raises his arm above his head. A red magic circle materializes on his palm. A salvo of fireballs rocket into the air.

There's one for each hero, and they seem to be locked on to boot. They quickly arc downward before beelining at their targets. Duncan blocks with his shield. Ed just barely manages to roll out of the way while Shine partially blocks from the ground with his aegis. Julia takes a direct hit, but her leather armor does a good job dispersing the heat. Artemis dodges hers as does Hermes. Marduk tries to cancel his out with his own Fireball but is caught in the resulting blast. Wendy takes a direct hit. She immediately drops to a knee, wincing in pain. Hermes runs over to heal her.

Another magic circle forms as Wosret prepares a second barrage. His casting hand freezes as its hit by Ice Arrow. Duncan belts him in the chest with Fastball and charges in. Seeing the priest busy healing, Wosret maneuvers around the dark knight and rushes Hermes and Wendy. He swats an arrow away as he closes quickly. Hermes tries to stun him with Theon's Light and shoves Wendy out of the way. It almost works. A thrust kick sends the priest sailing. Fortunately for him, it didn't have as much power thanks to his spell. Wosret manages to lay a finger on the witch, which is all he needs. Wendy immediately begins feeling fatigued. Even breathing is a burden. So, this is what being cursed feels like.

Fearing a direct attack, she quickly backpedals away. Her legs feel like jelly, but she is able to get far enough away that she's comfortable trying her new toy. She reaches into her robe pocket and flings a vial at Wosret. A pinch of Fire magic ignites it. A foul-smelling green liquid explodes all over their foe. An acid bomb! She used some magnesium and the sulfur from the Cave of Lost Souls to create a truly insidious weapon. Wosret doesn't writhe in agony, but his head drops slightly and his shoulders slump, which is telling enough for this unnatural foe. He seems to be stopped at least momentarily.

Hermes rises. Once back up, instead of running over to lift the curse, he pulls out a vial of his own and tosses it to Wendy. It looks like ordinary water but has a slight aura of Holy energy. After a fumbling catch, Wendy downs the holy water as she turns and sprints away from their adversary. The water does the trick. She immediately feels better. Wosret tries to catch her from behind with a fireball, but the fire reacts to the acid and backfires. Arm now ablaze, he gives chase. Shine, Julia, and Ed pursue, but they're too far away. Duncan manages to intercept, leading with his shield. It bashes the mummy and pushes him back a little.

Wendy is free to get to a safe distance. Wosret grabs Duncan's arm, but the thick plate armor prevents him from being afflicted. Seeing the pharaoh's fireball backfire, Marduk fires one of his own expecting the acid to cause the same volatile reaction. Duncan breaks free just in time and falls backward to the floor to avoid his ally's spell. It explodes on contact, engulfing their enemy in flames. Even that doesn't visibly bother him, but it surely did a lot of damage.

Hermes decides to try his luck. Fire magic is the ticket right now, and he has an incredibly powerful spell at his disposal. Duncan sees the priest back off and gather mana. The flame-carved ruby on his staff glows. Duncan takes a defensive position with his shield and places himself between the priest and mummy.

Wosret senses enemies closing from behind as an arrow hits his chest. Chi surges out from his body as he tries to blast them away with a wave of energy. The heroes are ready for it this time. They are still pushed back from its power but manage to brace themselves and avoid any significant damage. Wosret doesn't seem happy. Wendy is free from his curse and he moves in to attack her again, swiftly serpentining across the room. The witch's first instinct is to slow him down with Chilling Wind, but she doesn't want to extinguish the flames. The mummy's speed makes it difficult for anyone to get a bead on him as he winds towards their friend.

The witch has a plan, but her enemy will have to get closer than she'd like. The sapphire on her staff glows dark as she channels magic into it. Wosret lunges, arm outstretched. Feeling the heat of the flames, Wendy lets him have it. A trio of consecutive Dark Balls smash into their foe. It was draining spell to use, but its stopping power is impressive. Wosret stumbles backwards and lands flat on his back. He probably won't stay down long, so Artemis connects with Ice Arrow to freeze him to the ground. It smothers most of the flames but allows Wendy to retreat.

Wosret shatters the ice and pops back up. His enemies are closing from behind again. They're too close to blast away, so he turns to face them. Shine attacks first with Radiant Sword. Wosret catches the blade with one hand and flings Shine away, but his arm is reignited. Ed follows up with a low slash to the legs as he glides by, narrowly avoiding being grabbed. A bolt of lightning strikes the pharaoh from above as Julia swings straight at his chest. The nimble mummy evades the hammerhead and knocks Julia away with a spinning kick.

Hermes yells for everyone to get clear. Shine and Ed hastily fall back, and Julia rolls away. The priest unleashes Flames of Fira. The allies nearest the target feel a rush of intense heat as the area erupts. Wosret tries to use his speed to dodge, but the spell's radius is too wide. He's completely engulfed in flames.

As the fearsome flames subside, the heroes watch in uneasy anticipation. Was that enough? Thick smoke rises up from the pharaoh's body. He is no longer aflame, but his brownish wraps are now black. His body shudders violently, but he does not fall. He lets out a wicked cry. His posture resembles a wolfman howling at the moon. His body glows an intense red, but this time, no attack comes. The heroes recognize this technique. Wosret just emptied all his reserves just like Julia did against Conway. They brace themselves, waiting to see what the fiend has in mind.

The attack comes fast. Wosret's speed has doubled. He's almost too fast to track. Marduk is the first victim of the blitzkrieg. The enemy flashes in front of him. The wizard looks down in horror to see a charred palm on his chest. It feels like all the life has been sucked out of him. He's been cursed! Wosret throws a punch for good measure. The elderly wizard hits the ground hard and is barely conscious. His magic tome is likely the only reason why.

Artemis is the next target. She is able to block with her bow at the last second to avoid the deadly touch but is kicked hard and slams back into a wall. Wosret bolts towards Duncan. The dark knight's shield protects him only for a few moments as the speed and force of their foe pushes him back. With a mighty punch to the shield, Duncan is sent tumbling backwards. The mummy charges Shine next, who tries to knock him away with Chi Sweep. Wosret easily leaps over it and keeps coming.

Seeing her friends in peril (and to not be outdone), Julia unleashes all of her chi as she uses the skill she'd aptly named Berserk. Shine tries to block Wosret with his shield, but the pharaoh grabs him by the throat with and throws him. Now Shine is cursed, too. Hermes wants to attack, but he's low on mana. He doesn't have any more holy water either, so he'll need the remainder of his mana to lift curses. Ed avoids the mummy's Corrupting Touch but is kicked hard. Wosret turns to face Julia. The brave warrior is charging head on, glowing with energy. She swings her hammer with lightning velocity. Wosret blocks. The two begin exchanging blows, going toe to toe in an all-out brawl. Wosret knees her in the gut, stunning her. He has her in perfect position to use Corrupting Touch.

He freezes in his tracks as Wendy uses the last of her mana to hit him with a boosted Chilling Wind. Julia's hammerhead glows brightly as she focuses all her chi into it. She swings it upward, a devastating iron uppercut. Wosret shoots at least twenty feet in the air, nearly touching the tomb's high ceiling. Marduk tries to hit him as he falls with Vertical Shock but is off the mark. The pharaoh hits the ground so hard, he bounces upward several feet. He uses the bounce to right himself and land on his feet with cat-like agility.

Julia is closest but is too tired to follow up. Berserk drained her to the point she nearly lost consciousness. Her hammer is the only thing holding her up as she uses the handle for support. Wincing in pain, Ed throws one of his daggers at the enemy's back. It not only scores a hit but pierces through! Whatever magic has been shielding Wosret has been exhausted. Ed throws his second knife, but Wosret sidesteps.

Seeing their foe vulnerable, Shine chucks his shield. It contacts Wosret's shoulder hard, and Shine uses the last of his chi for one last flourish with Radiant Sword. Meanwhile, Hermes made his way to Marduk. He lifts the curse and heals the wizard just enough so he can stand. The last bit of mana will need to go to Wendy and Shine's curses.

Stunned by the shield, Wosret cannot block Shine's ensuing upward diagonal slash. Shine chains together three good hits before his opponent manages to block and push him away. Shine prepares to attack again, but Rashida's flames die! He's out of energy. The curse sapped his remaining strength. Wosret lunges, arm reaching for the young man's throat.

Shine just barely manages to pull Rashida close to stop the attack, but now his enemy has a firm grip on his sword. Shine's eyes widen in fear as the mummy begins pulling the Rashida away. If he succeeds, Shine will be helpless against the next attack. With a sharp yank, Wosret forces Rashida from its master, and it is flung to the dirt. He rears his other arm back to thrust at the hero. Tiny points of Wind chi create claws. Shine's eyes shut tight. Wosret strikes. His outstretched arm stops just inches away as a Piercing Shot explodes into his head.

Artemis was well over two hundred yards away, but that didn't stop her from scoring a direct hit. Breathing heavily, she immediately drops down to her knees. Wosret staggers backwards raising a hand to his head. His body is quivering, but he's still standing. A final Fastball from Duncan knocks him down. He flails there for a few moments like a turtle on its back. His body ceases to glow. His arms and legs go limp and fall, leaving him sprawled on the tomb floor. His body begins glowing once more, only this time he's enveloped in black magical energy. The mana implodes towards his midsection before exploding outward. The heroes feel a sharp rush of Dark wind, then nothing.

The air is still. That had to be it, right? The battle must be over. Unlike their previous encounters, Wosret doesn't assume a different form or come to his senses. His body slowly turns into dust and dissipates. The heroes stand in stunned silence. The magical aura once emanating from the pyramid fades with the pharaoh while Hermes uses the last of his mana to lift the last curses.

"What happened?" Artemis ponders.

"I dunno," replies Shine. "This was different than the last times."

Hermes is new to seeing possessed beings and inquires, "This wasn't like the other times you spoke of?"

"No," explains Marduk in a pained voice. "Captain Barrett and King Vanajit both regained their true forms, and their minds were freed. Being deceased, Barrett's soul then found its way to the afterlife."

"Hmm…" Hermes muses. "I've heard tales of people's spirits being unable to move on. Sometimes they have unresolved issues on this plain and remain as ghosts or spirits. Pharaoh Wosret was a fierce opponent in battle and deeply loved his nation and its people. It's not hard to imagine his soul was unable to find peace."

"But then why the sandstorms?" asks Wendy. "Why would he nearly bury the city he loved?"

Shine takes a stab, "Maybe whatever afflicted Barret and the Fairy King also afflicted him. He may not have been in control of his actions. He's also been dead an awfully long time. Maybe his soul immediately crossed to the afterlife."

"I thought ya didn't believe in that sorta thing," Ed jabs.

Shine unemotionally answers, "With everything we've seen, it'd be stupid to rule anything out."

"Maybe…" Wendy half agrees.

"Who cares?" Duncan bluntly asserts. "The mummy is dead. That should stop the storms. That's all that matters."

Ed smiles. "Crass as always, Duncan. Yer right though. Mission accomplished. Now let's get the hell outta here. I think I can sleep a week." Nobody argues. They barely have enough strength to make the trek back. Better not waste any time. The room is brightly lit from the sunlight pouring in. It's going to be hot when they leave.

The heroes slowly amble back to Giza. They're dead tired and drenched in sweat as they enter the city limits. Fortunately, the bathhouse was one of the few buildings that wasn't buried. After a little smooth talking and palm greasing, Ed convinces the owner not only to reserve the entire place for a few hours but to also wash their clothes, something they desperately need to do. Duncan's armor smells like something died in it, and everyone else's isn't much better. The deal was an admirable, masterful display of business acumen. One that was nearly erased when Ed was caught trying to sneak over to the women's side.

After a much-needed soak, our heroes return to the palace. They are quickly granted an audience with Pharaoh Khafra. He remains stoic but is eager to know of their findings. "Do you have any news?" he calmly asks.

"I'll say," Shine begins. "You might not believe it, but here goes. Hermes was right. The sandstorms were coming from the tomb. The entire place was bathed in a magical aura. When we defeated Wosret, it faded away."

Khafra's expression remains stern. "You expect me to believe Wosret's remains were walking around the tomb?"

Shine vividly recalls how stubborn the pharaoh was during their first conversation. He is in no mood for debate. "Believe it. Don't believe it. I really don't care," he replies flatly. "We defeated him and put his spirit to rest. That ended the storms."

"That is a very far-fetched story."

Hermes rejoinders, "We have nothing to gain from lying to you."

"Really?" countercharges the pharaoh, eyeing Hermes's new staff. "I recognize that staff. It belonged to Wosret. Didn't I tell you not to touch anything?"

Hermes begins to blush. "W-well..." he stammers.

Ed is quick to cover. "Such an important historical artifact shouldn't just be sittin' a dusty ol' tomb. We thought you might wanna display it in the palace or a museum or somethin' for yer people to admire and learn from."

Khafra is skeptical but intrigued. "Hmm... You strangers are certainly an interesting bunch. If the tomb was cursed, what do you think it means?"

Shine shrugs. "I really wish we knew. Like we told you before, a lot of strange things have been happening, but we've yet to find a connection."

"In any case, you were willing to help us in our time of need. Such an act cannot go unrewarded."

"We didn't do it for a reward."

"I did," Ed quickly corrects.

The pharaoh busts out laughing. "Hahaha! Not an ounce of shyness! I like that. Come with me to the treasury. There you'll get to choose your reward." The heroes follow Pharaoh Khafra down to the basement.

Once in the treasury, they have a choice between three items. The first is an elaborate sword with a golden hilt and orange-tinted blade carved to resemble flames. It is said to contain the element of Fire within it. They already have fiery weapons covered. The second is a gold ring adorned with a large sunstone sandwiched between two smaller sapphires. Khafra is wearing one just like it. It is a ring normally only bestowed to pharaohs. It has the properties to ward off poison, increase one's luck and vitality, and even bring out leadership qualities in the wearer. The third item is a beautiful gold and bronze shield emblazoned with the Gizian crest, a hawk soaring beneath the sun against a blue field. Shine and Duncan are satisfied with their shields.

They are about to settle on the ring when, surprisingly, the priest says he wants the shield. His abilities are much more suited for healing, and his most powerful attack spell takes a while to cast. He'd prefer to maximize his physical defense so he doesn't get sniped by an arrow or in case a melee attacker manages to get close. It's uncommon but not unheard of for mages to opt for shields instead of tomes. After all, Duncan has heavy armor *and* a shield. Ed is a little disappointed he doesn't get to wear the shiny ring, but there's no argument. Khafra allows Hermes to hold onto the Staff of Fira. He has a feeling deep within his soul the staff is better off in the heroes' hands than anywhere else.

After the final goodbyes, the party is ready to get back to their mission. Sandstorms or not, the desert is a harsh place to walk through. They'll rest for today and set out early, northeast bound. Roraima Plateau will get them within a couple days march to Leed's Castle. Before long, they'll finally be able to pay King Pious an unfriendly visit. Shine is growing more anxious the closer they journey. He can nearly taste vengeance on his tongue. He's been reluctant to tell the others Pious slayed his father. At first, he was worried no one would follow him. A noble cause revenge is not. The longer he delays, the harder telling them becomes. Maybe he'll say something after Pious is dead. Or maybe he never will.

Hermes goes off to pawn his old staff while Artemis stocks up on arrows and gathers some more ingredients to make potions. In addition to the leftovers from the Fairy King's garden, she's able to make two vitality and mana potions of decent quality plus a new one that can boost physical defense. Ed is growing tired of his pirate look (or, more accurately, the weird looks he keeps getting) and acquires some light brown linen garbs. He keeps his boots and dons a new tunic, pants, and a white shemagh which will come in handy in the desert. He resembles a Gizian assassin from the Great War. Funds are starting to dwindle. They may end up needing to take a job or two to ensure their war chest doesn't become barren. ♛

CHAPTER 14
Tales from Jiju

After a not-so-fun walk through the desert, our heroes are happy to see green grass again. They've arrived at the hilly plains of northern Khamsin. East will take them through the plateau, while west leads back to the destroyed Hasina Bridge. They pass a massive gravesite on the way to the next town, Jiju. The small village is one of the oldest in all of Terra. It used to be much larger until a plague wiped out most of its citizens. Today, Jiju is a peaceful place to stop. The adventurers can use a rest before embarking across Roraima Plateau. Maybe they'll find a way to earn a little extra coin, too, but it's not likely in such a sleepy town. There isn't much to do; however, there's one point of interest Julia would like to visit during their stay.

Like her hometown of Cid, Jiju has a long tradition of martial arts. There is an ancient temple, Tao Monastery, where people from all over Terra and Jijuans alike train to become warrior monks. The final trial involves completing some task in a shrine atop the plateau, but not much is known of what it entails. The Jijuans favor hand to hand combat and only use weapons when absolutely necessary. Lately, that has been to drive out wild beasts encroaching on their territory.

The most dangerous of all are dragons. Dragons used to be fairly common many, many years ago, but the more man expands, the scarcer they become. Now dragons can only be found in remote, isolated regions. They try to avoid humans as much as possible, probably because humans usually try to kill them. Food must be becoming scarce for them to venture close to people.

The monastery is the first stop on the list. Julia is eager to spar with the warriors there to measure her progress. It isn't hard to find. Despite only being two stories high, it's the tallest building in the village, situated in the center of the north end of town atop a hill. The building is beautiful. Its features are made of dark, stained wood framework, walls painted white, and long, narrow red vertical shingles on the rooftops. There is a golden spire resting at the apex. Each floor has its own roof with a curved, wavy pitch resembling a flower. Two large mahogany doors with large brass knockers in the shape of dragon's heads signal the entrance.

The main hallway is wide and leads all the way back to the master's audience hall. The walls on either side open up, revealing two sizable wooden sparring rings. Two pupils are sparring in one while what is assumed to be a trainer looks on. Heading straight to the audience hall, the heroes stumble upon a meeting. As they wait so Julia can meet the master, something much more urgent is about to sidetrack them once more.

An elderly man, Master Zhan, sits on a large wooden chair. You wouldn't call it a throne, but it still gives the impression whoever is in it should be listened to. Master Zhan is bald but has an extremely long white beard that reaches his calves. He is dressed in gold and blue robes. A gold charm dangles from his neck. Standing opposite is a young man with purple eyes and brown hair matching his brown robes. "What's going on?" Wendy wonders.

Shine replies, "It looks like we wandered into another meeting."

Master Zhan addresses his pupil, "You have greatly improved your skills, Ken."

The pupil respectfully bows and responds, "Thank you, Master. I feel that I am finally ready to start the final trial."

The master strokes his ludicrously long beard. "Hmm…"

Ken is quick to plead his case. "I am far stronger than I was when I first came here. I know I can pass the trial."

"You are indeed strong, among the top of the class. However, you still struggle when it comes to focusing your chi. At your current level, you would not be able to complete the trial."

Ken doesn't like that answer. He glares at his master and boldly states, "I've been training here for over a year! If I'm not ready now, then when?"

"Be patient, Ken. Most pupils need to train for far longer just to reach the level you are at now. Your impatience is your greatest weakness. It prevents you from calming your mind and focusing your energy. Perhaps in another year you shall be ready." Ken's fists clench in frustration.

Before he can reply, the large mahogany doors burst open. A pupil runs in screaming bloody murder. "Master Zhan! Master Zhan!"

Sensing something is amiss, Master Zhan rises from his seat. Shine and company move aside to let the young man through as does Ken. The master speaks with much concern, "What is it, Jian?" What's wrong?"

Jian can hardly talk from all the running and panicking, "It's horrible...! Ruo—The shrine—He... He..."

"Calm yourself!" the master booms. "What happened to Ruo?"

As the master speaks, two more pupils enter the monastery. They are carrying something. It is a wooden gurney. A bloody sheet is covering something or, more likely, someone. They slowly carry the gurney to the others. Master Zhan's demeanor immediately turns sullen. "He was killed during the trial? How did this happen?"

"He was late in returning, so I went to the shrine," Jian explains. "He was collapsed outside the entrance covered in blood. I rushed over to him. He was still conscious but barely. He managed to utter just one word before he died, 'dragons.'" Trainers and pupils are beginning to gather around to see what the commotion is.

Master Zhan is aghast. "Dragons inside the shrine? This is terrible. Truly terrible."

"Why would dragons invade our shrine?" worries Jian.

"That's none of our concern. Our response is the same regardless. We must form a plan of attack and prepare a party to clear the infestation."

Ken is immensely unsatisfied with that answer. He and Ruo were close, practically brothers. "Those bastards killed Ruo, and you want to sit here and talk? I can handle them myself. Ruo shall be avenged!" Master Zhan pleads for his bullheaded pupil to stop, to no avail. Ken sprints away to exact vengeance.

Master Zhan raises a hand to bury his face. He shakes his head and sighs. "Such an impetuous man... I hope he doesn't get himself killed."

Moments after Ken stormed out, a young woman in a floral dress entered the monastery. She is frantically looking around. "Ruo? Ruo?" As she approaches the audience hall, she spots the bloody sheet covering a body. "Oh no..."

Jian's eyes cast down. "Mei Liu…"

Tears begin rolling down the poor girl's face as Master Zhan expresses his sympathy, "I'm sorry, Mei Liu. Words cannot express my sympathy for you."

Mei Liu slowly looks around the room. Her mind is struggling to process this sudden tragic turn of events. Eventually, she speaks, "This can't be true. He can't be dead! He can't be!"

Master Zhan does his best to explain what happened, "Dragons invaded Ranakpur Shrine while Ruo was taking his final trial. I'm so sorry, Mei Liu. I truly am."

Fresh tears roll down. "I knew his training would lead to something terrible! Now he's gone! What am I supposed to do?" Mei Liu runs out of the monastery. The heroes overhear one of the onlookers comment she and Ruo were engaged. Even Duncan has a heavy heart. Who wouldn't?

Jian shakes off his sorrow the best he can. There's nothing they can do for Ruo. Grieving will have to wait. There's an immediate threat that must be dealt with. "Master, what about Ken? We can't let him go in there alone."

Master Zhan remains pragmatic even in these most dire circumstances. "Dragons are fearsome enemies. Rushing in will only lead to more death. Unfortunately, we are ill-prepared to face such a threat."

"Are you really suggesting we just abandon him?"

"Not quite." The master eyes the odd-looking traveling troupe. "You there!"

Shine looks at him quizzically and answers, "Us?"

"You witnessed everything that has happened, so you're fully aware of the situation, yes?"

Shine sighs before replying, "I have a feeling where this is going." He pauses for a few seconds before continuing, "Yes, we understand the situation."

"I know you owe us nothing, but you are clearly battle hardened and well-equipped. That man who stormed out of here will surely get himself killed. Would you aid us in our time of need, travelers?"

Ed is excited by the notion. "Hell, I'll do it just to see a dragon up close."

Duncan concurs, "I've always wanted to fight a dragon. I'm in."

Unlike them, Wendy actually cares about the life at stake. "We really can't just stand by and let someone die, right?"

Shine nods in agreement. "That's right. We'd be happy to help. Just point us where to go." Their eagerness to help makes Master Zhan smile.

"I am glad to see there are still such selfless people out there. Ranakpur Shrine is a bit east of here. Simply cross the bridge to the south and head northeast along the path through the mountains. Your destination will be easy to spot."

So much for a leisurely tour. Trouble seems to follow our heroes wherever they go. On the plus side, they get to explore an ancient shrine and fight dragons. Few people can claim they've ever seen one, let alone take it on. They will need to tread carefully, however. Dragons have been on Terra long before humans, and they haven't survived this long due to luck.

They are omnivorous but prefer flesh and are apex predators. Their tough scales and sharp, curved claws and teeth allow them to take down any prey they encounter. By the time they are adolescents, they grow wings but can only flutter short distances until adulthood, which takes hundreds of years. The most frightening detail has nothing to do with their physical abilities. Dragons are highly intelligent. Many researchers claim if dragons had opposable thumbs, they'd be the dominant species on Terra. They are one of few beasts that have the mental capacity to use magic. It is unknown if, like humans, they must be born with the ability or if is a consistent trait.

Ranakpur Shrine isn't far. The heroes arrive within a few hours. It is still midday as they gaze upon the shrine. It is a three-story tall rectangular building made from stone mined from the local mountains. It is a weathered, innocuous-looking building far from a tourist attraction. Its sole purpose is to put the pupils of Tao Monastery's skills to the ultimate test to see if they are worthy of monkhood. The interior is large, filled with giant open spaces. One can easily get lost if you don't know where you're going, which no one embarking on the trial does. Normally, access is forbidden to anyone who hasn't passed the trial or is currently taking it.

The heroes enter the shrine to find themselves in one of those vast, sprawling rooms. Pillars of granite adorn the room, sprawled all along the walls and floor in no apparent pattern. They are ornately carved to look like thorny vines are wrapping around. Several are damaged or completely collapsed. The floor is full of cracks and broken stones. There is a strange energy in the air that's hard to place. It feels like chi but not like anyone has ever experienced before.

Not much searching is necessary in finding Ken. He is standing in the northeast side of the massive room, and he is not alone. He is surrounded on three sides by three dragons. The party cannot help but to pause to admire the magnificent beasts. They're each about twelve feet long and easily over five hundred pounds. Long, brown, steeply arched wings signify they are adolescents. The scales on their heads are light green, almost yellow. The scales grow progressively darker going down the body ending in a purple tail tip. Five orange-tinted horns adorn their heads. Even from a distance, everyone can clearly see the rows of razor teeth and menacing claws, three frontal and one back on each leg. One good swipe can separate limbs with ease.

Our heroes can admire them some more after they're dead. Right now, the priority is stopping Ken from getting himself killed. They have no idea what level of skill he possess, but if dragons are as fierce as everyone says, he has no chance taking out three by himself. The dragons roar menacingly. "C'mon, you bastards!" Ken challenges.

Ed is still admiring the lizards. "So, that's what a dragon looks like. Neat!"

Julia is more concerned about the man about to get eaten. "We should probably help him."

Shine nods. "Yep. Same plan as always. Kill things."

"It's scary how often violence solves our problems," notes Wendy as they rush to Ken's side.

He doesn't look happy to see the rescue party, but there's no time to talk about it. The dragons begin their assault. Shine, Artemis, and Marduk take the one on the left. Julia, Wendy, and Ed take the one on the right. Duncan and Hermes join Ken in the middle. The area is spacious, so there's plenty of room for each group to operate without bumping into each other or catching friendly fire.

The left dragon inhales. A strange odor nobody can quite place wafts through the battlefield. Shine readies his shield. He and his teammates ready themselves for fire breath. All dragons breathe fire, right? That's not what exits the beast's mouth. A strange, light purple cloud billows out. No one is sure what it is, nor do they want to find out. Shine protects with his buckler while Artemis and Marduk step back and fan out in opposite directions.

The dragon rushes Shine, who is still in a defensive posture. He is barely able to keep his shield from flying out of his hand as the enemy slashes with its front claws, deeply gouging the aegis. The archer and wizard attack in tandem to stop Shine's guard from being broken. The lizard swats the arrow away with its tail but is struck by the lightning spell. Shine slashes as the dragon hops back. He scores a hit but only manages a scratch.

The beast is cunning enough to recognize when it's being flanked and begins running to its left. The old man should be the easiest target. It wants to circle around to his side and attack. Marduk pivots to face his enemy and retreats as Shine moves up to intercept. Artemis shifts position to get a better angle. As Shine and Marduk's paths are crossing, the squad feels a rush of chi as the beast's claws begin to glow purple. It leaps through the air with incredible speed, aiming to take out the wizard before he escapes out of range.

Artemis hits it in the chest midflight with Piercing Shot. Even that barely penetrates its scaly armor. She tries to follow up with a second shot, but the dragon smacks it away with another tail swipe. It then immediately begins running back to its right trying to outmaneuver its opponents. Shine tried to rush in after the archer's attack and is now out of position. The dragon has a good line on his friends. Marduk tries to slow it down with Wind Burst. The beast cancels it out with its own wind with nothing more than a wing flutter.

Artemis tries to connect with Ice Arrow, but the monster evades and keeps coming. It leaps at her, glowing claws outstretched. She barely manages to roll away. Instead of going after her, the dragon quickly spins and charges the wizard. He's not nearly as nimble, and the enemy knows it. As it raises its leg to slash, Marduk uses his Sleep spell out of desperation. The dragon's leg drops. Its head droops. It tries to shake off the spell. Soon, it overpowers Marduk's mana and snaps back into focus.

The momentary slowdown allowed Shine to get between them. His sword is ablaze. He figures the dragon will go for the easier target in Artemis instead of attacking him head on. He's right and is able to run alongside the beast as it makes its move. Seeing the cut off, the dragon leaps upwards and back. Shine tries to pursue but gives up the futile effort. A few strong wing flaps propel the dragon a safe distance away. Mana radiates as it glows green. The aura is strong, on par with advanced mages.

Julia's team is faring a bit better. Her size and raw power are proving troublesome for their opponent allowing Ed to freely flank and Wendy to cast from a safe distance. Using Poison, the witch manages to slow the beast down a bit. Ed's daggers aren't doing much damage to those iron-like scales, but the cuts are beginning to multiply as Julia presses. The dragon finally manages to shove her away with its horns and subsequently smacks Ed away with its tail. Like its ally, this beast aims to take out the most physically frail of the group. It beelines for Wendy. Unfortunately for it, she had time to buff her magic and prepare a fierce Chilling Wind. The frozen blast slows the beast sufficiently enough for her to fall back. Ed leaps onto its back and drives his daggers down as hard as he can. It rears and bucks, but the daggers are stuck in there good. Ed is holding onto them for dear life.

Julia sees a chance to flank and get in a clean shot. Sensing her approach, the dragon stops worrying about the little man riding it and spins to face the warrior. Before she can get in range, she catches a blast of Dragon Breath, the purple smoke Shine's group had witnessed. The cloud stops Julia dead. It is a strange, painful sensation to say the least. It's as if a viper's venom had been weaponized into a deadly cloud. Sharp, shooting electric pain courses through her body, and she immediately goes numb. She can barely get her arms and legs to operate.

The dragon lunges forward, jaws agape, tilting its head to rip out the paralyzed warrior's throat. Still atop the beast, Ed can only look on in despair. Wendy puts everything she has into Deluge. The force of the surging water pushes the dragon's head away. Its jaws catch only air. However, its body crashes into Julia, and they both spill onto the floor. Julia has gone almost completely limp from Dragon Breath. The dragon is slow to get up. The crash shouldn't have done much damage. Wendy's Poison seems to finally be taking effect.

Still mounted, Ed manages to pull his daggers free. His enemy knows a fatal blow is coming but cannot shake him off. Ed catwalks on its back for a few steps before throwing himself down, daggers extended. The blades pierce the beast's neck. It roars in pain. Ed pulls his daggers out. He remains ready in case another blow must be struck. Wendy drags Julia a safe distance from its jaws just in time to rescue her from a surely fatal bite. That chomp was the last gasp. The dragon grows still.

Meanwhile, the dragon Shine's team is facing unleashes its magic. A giant, wide tornado stretching all the way to the shrine's ceiling roars towards them. All anybody can do is brace for impact. The cyclone flings the threesome like ragdolls. Artemis gets the worst of it. Her body slams into a stone pillar so hard, it breaks in two. Several of her ribs are broken. She won't be getting up anytime soon. The dragon goes for Marduk, who is struggling to get to his feet. Wincing in pain, Shine leaps up and knocks it away with Chi Sweep. The force of the blow stuns the dragon for a few moments allowing Shine to stagger his way between it and his friend. He doesn't know how much longer he can last against such a powerful opponent.

Duncan is frustrated by his teammate. Ken insists on fighting the thing head on despite wearing nothing but wool robes and only equipped with brass knuckles. The dark knight's thick armor and shield is much better suited for a head on approach, but the young pupil is relentless in his strikes. His punches don't seem to be doing much more than pissing the lizard off whilst preventing Hermes from using his magic without hitting him. Duncan finally has had enough and knocks the brawler away with his shield. It was a good thing, too, as the dragon would have bitten the pupil's arm off if not forcibly moved. It tries to bite Duncan, who shoves his tower shield between the snapping jaws. He leaves it there, then grabs Ken by the waist as he goes in for another flurry of punches.

"What the hell, man?" Ken exclaims as Duncan carries him away from his enemy. Now Hermes is finally free to attack. He doesn't hold back, releasing Flames of Fira and engulfing their foe. Its scales protect it enough to quickly shake off the spell, but damage was clearly done. Duncan's shield is red hot. The edges melted a little bit. The dragon manages to free it from its jaws, and the heavy aegis clatters to the floor as Ken shoves Duncan away. "Stay outta my way!" he screams before charging in again.

With his opponent stunned, he has time to gather chi for a more powerful attack. As he launches into the air, electricity explodes from his fist. He delivers an electric punch right between the eyes. The dragon's head snaps back. That punch caused some harm! As the beast shakes its head, Ken displays some impressive agility. He front flips and corkscrews his body in midair. He lands straddling the beast's long neck.

Duncan pauses, wondering what in Hades this guy is doing. The fighter wraps his arms around the beast's bottom jaw. He forces the dragon's head up with all his might. He cannot raise it much but enough that Duncan sees his plan. The softer scales on its neck are exposed. Duncan attacks, thrusting his rapier. Blood gushes as he yanks it out of their foe's neck. He barely avoids a final claw slash before the dragon collapses. Duncan lifts his piping hot shield. Good thing he's wearing gauntlets. He and Ken go to aid Shine's team while Hermes tends to Julia. Ed joins the combat, too, but Wendy has to sit out. She is completely drained.

The last dragon is surrounded. It knows not of these new enemies' strengths or abilities. It pivots around and keeps the new challengers at bay with a wide spray of Dragon Breath. It rushes Shine and swipes with Dragon Claw. Shine blocks with his shield, but the force of the attack sends it and him flying. The dragon moves in for the killing blow, but Marduk uses Flash to stun it. Shine barely gets back to his feet. He has no idea how he'll be able to dodge or counter another attack. Though blinded, the dragon senses weakness and runs at the blurry figure in front of it.

Shine feels a rush of wind blow past him. Artemis managed to fire off Piercing Shot from a prone position on the ground. It explodes into the beast's front left leg, crippling it. Ed flanks from the rear and begins slashing at its right rear leg. The dragon tries to smack him away with a tail swipe but can't. Ken has firm grip of its rear. He gets flung away shortly after but not before Ed exploits the softer area at the back of the knee, lacerating the leg deeply. Duncan takes out the other rear leg with a close-range Razor Wind.

The beast is far from dead, but with only one good limb, there isn't much it can do. It frantically whips its tail and snaps its jaws about. Ken rolls out of the tail's range and begins pummeling the dragon's ribs. Ed follows suit on the other side, furiously slashing away. Marduk blinds it once more, allowing Shine to get around those deadly jaws and repeatedly thrust Rashida into the side of its neck. Finally, it dies.

Julia and Wendy join the others while Hermes mends Artemis's ribs. Ken stands face to face with Duncan and glares into his eyes. He's still fuming about being shoved aside and carried away like a helpless child. He looks at the strangers around him looking ready to them on. "I didn't ask for your help, strangers," he states gruffly.

Duncan fires back, "Yeah, you were doing a great job getting tossed around before that."

Shine scolds him, "Duncan! Why are you always so combative?" He apologizes to the pupil, "Sorry. Your name is Ken, right?"

"What's it to you?" Ken sternly grills.

Shine shrugs nonchalantly. "Honestly, nothing, but Master Zhan asked us to come find you."

"Damn that old man! Dragging outsiders into our affairs. What's he thinking?"

"He was trying not to let you run off and get yourself killed, jerk," Wendy rebuts.

"I can handle this on my own." Ken breaks eye contact with the group. He looks like he's about venture in solo.

Duncan, being Duncan, glibly asks, "Like that Ruo guy did?"

That struck a nerve! Ken's eyes flare. He storms up to Duncan, getting right in his face. "What the hell did you just say!? How dare you? How dare you speak his name!"

Julia rolls her eyes. "Wow, Duncan. Shine just told you two seconds ago *not* to be combative."

"I actually agree with him on this one," Shine replies, shocking his friends.

As he's speaking, Hermes and Artemis rejoin the party. Hermes and Wendy share a mana potion as Shine continues, "These dragons are really powerful. It'd be tough to kill one all by yourself, let alone a group of them."

Ken crosses his arms and looks away. "Pffft..."

"You know I'm right," Shine presses. "If you go tearing through here half-cocked, you'll be ripped to shreds."

"So, what are you here for? You wanna take me back to the monastery? Let those bastards get away with killing Ruo?"

"Well... that was the plan," Shine mischievously replies. "However, since we're already here and all..."

Julia covers her head with her hand. What is this guy getting them into now? "Really, Shine? You just can't help causing trouble, can you?"

Shine's tone returns to it's normal matter-of-fact state. "We're better equipped for dealing with dragons. I don't have anything against martial arts, but blades, armor, and magic will be far more effective."

Ken is still wary of these weird outsiders. "You owe our people nothing. What are you hoping to gain from this? Money? Influence?"

Ed perkily replies, "I just really wanna explore deez ruins. I bet there's some cool artifact's 'n' treasure just waitin' to be discovered."

"I'm also curious to see what secrets lie in here," Marduk remarks.

"I just want to kill some dragons," Duncan flatly adds.

"I want to do all of the above," Shine affirms.

Ken looks at the outsiders in stunned silence. His jaw actually drops a bit. "That's your motivation? Exploring and fighting just for the sake of exploring and fighting?"

"Heh heh! Ya, I guess so," Ed beams. "We've been doin' so much of it lately, I guess it just kinda became second nature."

Ken cannot believe what he's hearing. "You strangers are... strange."

Hermes can empathize. His new allies joined him on nothing but a whim and a desire to help those in need. "This isn't an ordinary group, that is for certain, but their motives are pure," he says assuringly.

"You want to avenge your friend, right?" asks Shine. "How about you join up with us for a bit? I'm sure we'll be able to clear these dragons out of here."

Ken remains skeptical, "You understand if I'm apprehensive to join a group I don't know."

"Fair enough," Wendy replies before reassuring him in the most ominous way possible, "Keep in mind, if we really wanted to harm you, we could have easily done so already." An evil expression crosses her face. "That or just left you to the dragons." Creepy, yes, but she makes a strong point.

After thinking it over for a few seconds, Ken responds, "Fair enough. All right, I'll join you for now. Be forewarned, if I sense even the slightest hint of betrayal, I'll fight you to my last breath."

"Hahaha! You got guts, kid!" Duncan exclaims while awkwardly slapping Ken on the back. "This might be fun!"

Artemis looks at Ken in amazement. "Wow, you got Duncan to express joy. Amazing..."

Shine interprets for a perplexed Ken, "I think that's their way of saying 'welcome.' Anyway, I'm Shine. This is Julia, Ed, Marduk, Artemis, Wendy, Duncan, and Hermes." He points at each one as he says their name.

Ken seems to have been put at ease. "Nice to meet you. As you already know, I'm Ken. Sorry about earlier. I let my emotions get the better of me. We don't get many travelers around here."

Marduk smiles. "Don't mention it. Shall we continue on?"

"Damn right!" Ken exclaims.

Before long, the explorers find the first trial of Ranakpur Shrine. Heading north, they spot a fire-breathing statue blocking the way forward. The stand is made of granite. A winged dragon carved from jade is spewing fire from its mouth like a flamethrower. There is an empty hole where its eye should be. The fire doesn't seem to be fueled by magic. Chi can also be used to enchant objects, and the slightly heavier air around the statue seems to confirm that's the case. The flames feel unnaturally hot. Duncan wants to run through anyway, but Ken insists against it. The shrine was built to test wits and force pupils to focus their chi, not use it to barge through with brute force. There must be a more subtle means of passing through.

The party turns back to explore the rest of the room. A massive diamond-shaped stone pillar is centered, taking up a good two thirds of the room. They head to around to the other side. The south wall of the room opens up. There's a rope ladder leading down. The adventurers find themselves in a long dirt-floored room dotted with large rocks. There's a shallow cliff on the west side about ten feet deep revealing a lower section. There are some narrow stone steps leading down to it. On the east side, there's a gated door blocking the way forward through a hall leading north. Not far from it is a granite block not too dissimilar than the ones in Wosret's tomb though it's about half the size.

Ken is new to this, but the others are all too familiar with this scenario. There must be a switch somewhere. It is found on the bottom level. Navigating the block through the field of stones will be cumbersome. Ken insists on being the one to push the granite block seeing this is supposed to be his trial after all. He isn't weak by any stretch of the imagination, yet he cannot get the cube to budge. Duncan belly laughs and pushes the student aside. He is no more successful. "What the fuck?" he angrily questions the air.

Ken has an inkling what is going on. He stands before the stone, closes his eyes, and concentrates. Sticking out an open palm, he pushes his chi outward like an extension of himself. The block glides forward a couple feet. Brute strength will do nothing to move it. One must properly control their chi to manipulate it. Too little and it won't move. Too much will send the block flying.

Ken again demands to be the one to navigate it. Master Zhan wasn't kidding about him not being good at focusing chi. It is a painful, grating exercise to watch him clumsily try to maneuver the block through the stone field. Eventually, he gets it to the switch. The metallic sound of the sliding metal can be heard elsewhere. The path forward is clear.

Onward through the hall. It leads them to a small room connecting at the corner. Dragon statues adorn the other three. The Jijuans sure seem to hold the beasts in high regard. In the center of the back wall is a small pedestal. A crimson ruby orb rests atop it. As the heroes enter, a cloud of bats swarm from the ceiling. They look to be ordinary fruit bats. Normally they're docile towards people but not these. This must be their nest.

They swoop down to attack. Everyone hits ground. The bats circle around for another dive. Artemis notches an arrow, but she doesn't need to fire. Hermes's Theon's Light stuns the cloud midflight. They flutter gently to the floor. From there, it is child's play. Wendy seems upset after. "What's the matter?" Ed asks. "Did ya get blood on ya?"

Wendy frowns and sullenly says, "I like bats."

Orb in hand, the party heads back to fiery jade statue. As expected, the orb is a perfect fit, and the flames die out. After rounding a corner, there are several paths to choose from, but one is blocked by metal bars. They head south back towards the entrance. This path inclines upward, and they find themselves on a dirt floor on a level overlooking the vast entrance room. There is a curious sight to behold, too.

Not far away, maybe thirty feet, an adolescent dragon and adult lioness are staring each other down. Both being highly territorial predators, neither wants to back down. The unlikely pair of apexes slowly circle each other. At some point they shoot glances at the humans encroaching on their negotiations. The circling stops. The dragon nods in the heroes' direction, and soon they both begin walking towards them.

"D-d-did those fuckers just conspire 'gainst us?" Ed sputters.

"It's an animal thing," states Duncan, seemingly understanding.

It doesn't make much sense, but it's happening, and they have to deal with it. There's space to split off into two groups though everyone will still be bunched a bit tight. The lioness charges ahead. She is lit up by Fireball. Unlike the dragon, it doesn't have thick scales to absorb heat. Only some super extraordinary feline would be able to stand up to such a blow. This is one of those.

The fireball stuns her only momentarily, and she doesn't seem to mind that her fur is on fire as she resumes her charge. "You gotta be kitten me!" jokes Ed as she barrels down on him.

"I hate you so much right now," Julia grumbles. She swats the lioness away from her diminutive companion with her hammer. The beast looks like it's going to land flat on its back but uses cat-like (go figure) agility to turn upright. She lands softy on all fours just in time to catch an arrow between the eyes. That did it.

Her would-be ally wasn't even close to in sync. The dragon casually strolled into position while the lion attacked. It wasn't nearly close enough to make a move when its furry friend died. Like the lizards earlier, this one isn't stupid. The humans displayed dangerous mettle and have a severe numbers advantage. Fluttering its wings, the dragon floats in reverse. As it does, its body begins to glow green. Everyone knows what that means.

Luckily, there's a little cover this time, and the adventurers duck behind some large rocks that are scattered here and there. The heavy winds are rendered useless. The heroes move out, but as they do, another dragon lumbers around the corner behind the other. One would think by its body language it just stumbled upon the battle, but in fact, it heard the ruckus and headed over. It casts Cyclone, too, forcing everyone back to cover.

This may prove problematic. It's going to be hard to get close. A change in strategy is needed. Marduk and Duncan lead the attack. Both have strong Wind-based abilities. They can counter and hopefully cancel out Cyclone, freeing the others to get into range. Both dragons start to glow. A dual spell! This is going to be tough.

Wendy boosts the front line's magic. It sounds like someone fired a cannon as the beasts' combined attack twists its way forward. Marduk and Duncan take the brunt with their own Wind magic. Both are sent flying. Marduk is nearly blown off the ledge down to the hard stone floor of the entrance room. They couldn't stop the spell completely, but the winds were slowed enough to where their allies can close before the spell can be cast again.

Both dragons spew Dragon Breath, forcing the melee fighters to slow before running straight into it. The breath wasn't a defensive move. Rather, it was to allow the dragons to be the aggressors. The lizards charge through purple cloud and lunge at the nearest foes with glowing claws. Their targets manage to sidestep. Next, they aim to go for the support crew, but the numbers are against them. Hermes casts Theon's Light, stunning the beasts. Wendy hits one with Deluge, and Artemis halts the other with back to back Ice Arrows. This allows the melee warriors to close and attack. Duncan and Marduk follow up on the other supporters' attacks. There's too much too quick for the dragons to handle, and they fall shorty after.

Rounding the next corner, the party is above the west side of the entrance room. This area is almost as big as the level below it. It's dotted with rocks and several dragon statues. The carcass of what looks to be an elk lies near the center. Near it is a small cluster of baby dragons. The dragons must be wanting to build a nest here. Even the babies are extremely dangerous to an ordinary person, and a swarm of them can even best seasoned veterans.

The half dozen dragonlings aren't enough to pose a threat to a group so large. The wee critters are easily disposed of. Ken manages to kill one with a single punch to the head. Not to be outdone, Duncan slays one with Fastball. He smirks at Ken. He says nothing, but the message is clear, *Ha! I punched one from a distance and killed it! Beat that!*

Continuing on through a passage to the southwest, a couple more baby drags meet their demise. The party is led north, and after slaying a lone adolescent dragon, they come to a rope ladder. There's a pressure plate on the floor like the first switch. Up the ladder is the block. It is quite a distance away. Ken tries to show off by pushing it all the way off the ledge with one burst of chi, but it stops just short causing Duncan to snicker like a schoolkid. One last little push and the block falls down into place, but nothing seems to happen. Doubling back, they see the fruit of Ken's labor. A section of wall juts out on the east wall. A dangling rope that hadn't been there before leads to the floor above.

There's another room with dragon statues, followed by a corridor, followed by a room full of granite pillars. As ornately crafted as the objects in the shrine are, seeing them over and over causes them to lose their luster fairly quickly. Luckily, there was another lone dragon in the pillared room to keep things interesting. A passage to the south leads them around a corner to a set of stairs. The paths are long and uneventful, allowing the heroes some time for their chi and mana to recover. Once up the stairs, they soon find themselves at a fork. Right or straight?

They go right and eventually come to much more interesting room. There is a large pit in the middle that looks to be manmade. There is a way to navigate to the other side using pathways leading along the walls. There's an orb on the other side of the pit. This one is green, probably made of jade. Walking around isn't a simple task. Metal spikes are periodically shooting out of the floor on either side. They're laid out symmetrically as is the room.

The first couple traps are easy enough. The first is just a single row; the second is two rows. The third is more cumbersome. A long strip of spikes blocks the way. They are stabbing and receding in waves. Running across as soon as the nearest ones disappear should allow one to cross safely. Shine goes first and clears it easily enough. There is another row of spikes making an L around a corner. Each set rises and falls through the floor in unison. Turning that corner before the spikes extend will be tough. Shine bolts through as soon as the spikes descend. The corner slows him more than he thinks, and he ends up needing to dive forward to avoid becoming shish kabob.

The orb is just ahead, but there's a problem. There's a large hole in the floor in front of its pedestal, making it out of reach. Behind Shine is a tall granite block about ten feet high. Ken demands he be the one to move it when Shine yells the situation to his companions. Not this time, Ken. It will be much easier and much less dangerous to let Shine do it. He's not great at focusing chi either and takes special care not to knock the block over as he slides it along the floor. It's an ugly sight watching the block sputter about. It nearly topples a couple times but eventually falls in the hole. It fits perfectly, completing the path. Shine pockets the jade orb and cautiously makes his way back to his friends.

The other path leads to an even more interesting room. It shaped like a fat plus sign. The floor tiles are distinctly different from any others in the shrine. Boulders are scattered all over the floor. They look to have been arranged a certain way on purpose, but no one can conclude the rhyme or reason. A set of metals bars gate off the corridor on the other side. Two of the tiles, one on each side with an opening, are depressed much like the switches they've become so familiar with. The nearest one is the only tile they can step on, but nothing seems to happen when they do. Things become odd after that. Shine steps forward onto the next tile. A faint chiming sound rings out from nowhere as the gray tile mysteriously turns yellow. The same thing happens when he steps forward to the next. Julia follows him. As soon as she touches that first yellow tile, both of them immediately return gray.

It is a weird occurrence, but the reason must be related to opening the gates. Even weirder, the puzzle seems to be fueled by magic despite being inside a shrine that was created to test one's chi. Perhaps that is to prevent anyone from "hacking" the puzzle to change the tiles at will. It is a test of intelligence. After scouting the room and doing a little experimenting, Marduk believes he has the answer. "I see…" he muses while stroking his beard.

"Have you figured it out, Marduk?" asks Artemis.

"Yes, I believe so. Every time we step on a gray tile, it turns yellow, provided we've stepped on that first depressed one. The instant a yellow tile is stepped on, all the yellow tiles turn gray once more. I believe the objective is to step on each and every tile in the room without touching any of them twice. The boulders must have been arranged to force the testee to plan ahead and plot a course between both depressed tiles while stepping on every tile once and only once."

Ed scratches his head. "Sounds complicated. Good luck with that."

"How is this supposed to test chi?" Wendy inquires.

Ken explains, "Like magic, chi requires a person to be able to focus and clear their mind. Navigating this room requires the same. One false step results in failure."

Like all the trials, Ken wants to complete this one on his own, but everyone else volunteers Marduk. He quickly figured out the key to solving the puzzle, so he's their best chance of success. The old wizard normally walks slowly. His typical speed is that of a professional sprinter compared to his speed now as he carefully plans each move. It takes a while, but amazingly enough, he manages to step on every tile just once in one go and end on the depressed one next to the gate. The tiles pulsate several times and return to their normal gray color as the metal bars recede into the floor.

The roar of flames can be heard up ahead. The jade gem finds its home in another jade dragon statue, and a pair of babies meet their demise the next room. Stone steps lead back down to the second floor. Another teenager goes down as the adventurers are led around a corner and down another flight. Not long after, they're in a small room with a sapphire orb. Now they just need to find where to stick it. There aren't any more unexplored areas in this section of the shrine, so it's back to the huge room where the dragons wanted to make a nest.

As they turn the corner to head back to the third floor, keen-eyed Ed spots something. There is a shallow corridor to their left that clearly dead ends. There is a collapsed pillar, and there's something underneath it covered by dust and rubble. A subtle glint caught the thief's gaze. Upon inspection, it is just what he had hoped for, a treasure chest! He drags the green-painted box of joy out from under the rubble. Ken is wary to open it. If that pillar hadn't collapsed, the chest would have been just sitting in the open. He's certain it's a trap, a lesson in self-discipline to not steal from the shrine.

As eager as Ed is, he's no fool. He thoroughly inspects it for traps before picking the lock. No traps, but the contents are disappointing. All that's inside is a tiny vial of vitality potion. Makes sense. The shrine is huge and pushing those blocks with chi is draining. It would be hard for a single person, even if they've trained hard to have enough stamina to get all the way through. Ken is happy to down the potion. Odds are he'll have to use chi again to clear a puzzle, not to mention the added trial of slaying dragons.

Eventually our heroes make it back to the would-be nest room. A single adolescent dragon made its way there. It is distraught at the sight of the slain children and attacks in a frenzy. It is dispatched quickly, so blinded by rage, it left itself wide open. Julia landed the final bow with Conway's hammer. "Whew! How many of these things do you think are left?" she wonders.

Ken answers, "Dragons aren't known for gathering in huge numbers. Their ranks must be getting thin by now."

"I hope so," comments Wendy. "All this walking and killing is tiring. I just want to get to the end so we can leave."

There was a path they didn't try earlier in this room on the northwest corner. After leaping over a six-foot-wide collapse in the floor, the next test awaits. Most of the floor has collapsed, but that may have been on purpose. Most of the chasms are too deep to see the bottom, and too wide to leap over, but small square-shaped sections are much shallower. The gaps could be jumped over easily enough if not for the tall granite blocks inconveniently situated on the opposite sides. The goal is straightforward enough. Use chi to pull the blocks into the holes thus creating bridges. It is easier said than done. Simply pushing a block forward with chi is pretty easy. Pushing one's chi outward, essentially grabbing an object, and pulling it towards yourself is an entirely different animal, and by the looks of things, it must be done four times to get through the room.

Ken tries his best on the block directly in front of them. Julia has to use her chi as an anchor as Ken nearly pushes it away. The pupil closes his eyes and begins some deep breathing exercises to settle his nerves. Once calm, he slowly moves his arm forward. This time, instead of extending his palm, he points a single finger at the block. He visualizes his chi as a length of rope. He then swings his arm in a sidearm motion as if he were flinging a rope in a fashion that would wrap around the block. Finally, he quickly pulls his arm back hard, dragging his chi and the block with it towards him.

The block slides over the hole and teeters for a few seconds before falling in. The sharp angle prevents it from being flush with the floor but was maneuvered well enough to be easily climbed over. The next two blocks fall in similar fashion before he gets it perfect on the final hole. He needs to take a moment to catch his breath. Using chi so intricately is a painstaking, draining process both mentally and physically. After his breathing slows and an insult from Duncan, he's ready to continue.

Ahead lies a ledge overlooking a previously explored room, the one with a gated passage near the nest room. Another block is there. There's no visible switch. They must have missed it on the level below. Surely, it opens those gates. Artemis does the honors this time. Focusing chi is crucial for any warrior, but it is especially important when trying to pinpoint with a bow and arrow. She is a natural, effortlessly gliding the block off the ledge. The party carefully climbs down the rocky face, and the archer finishes the job. The switch is in an alcove around the corner. As expected, the metal gates open. Stairs lead back up to the second floor.

The above room reveals another fire-breathing statue, the sapphire orb's final resting place. The party is disappointed to find the path ahead blocked by metal gates. Two obstacles? Whatever is on the other side must be important. There seems to be an upper level behind them, but the wall is too smooth to assail. There's also a hallway leading east. They recall another passage just before the gated room they'd just accessed. Coin flip time! Backtrack or go east? Heads. Backtracking it is.

The path loops around and leads to a staircase. Its right under that upper level. A good-sized chunk of the back wall has collapsed exposing the outside. That must be how animals keep getting inside the shrine. A mountain ram runs past as they enter the room. It nearly bowls over Wendy, but at least it wasn't itching for a fight. There's a carcass in the room, too. The thick, curled horns identify it as another, less fortunate ram. A dragon must've gotten it.

The stairs lead exactly where they thought, and yet another switch and block lie before them. There are actually three levels with the block on top, the switch in the middle, and the lowest where the gates are. It is quite a ways for the block to reach its perch. Ken is far less enthusiastic about this one. Julia handles it. She's sloppier than Artemis but neater than Ken. They hear the satisfying metal slide as the gates open.

On the way back down, the party encounters the ram again. This time it's bolting from a dragon. They get the lizard's attention and use the element of surprise to quickly exterminate it. Before heading down the path that was just opened, Ed can't help but to explore the other way. He is still bummed about the crappy reward in the treasure chest and hopes to find another one with better loot. It turns out to be a good decision. Several more tests await them ahead.

The first is another room requiring every tile to be stepped on. This room is larger than the last. It takes Marduk a couple tries before completing it. Immediately after, the next room is filled with metal spikes shooting up from the floor. There are several rows, and they're all fairly long. It will be difficult for the slower members to make it across. Shine and Ken volunteer to venture ahead. After a bit of nervous sprinting, they pant with their hands on their knees on the other side of the room.

There is a conspicuous button on the wall. Ken thinks it's another trap, but Shine casually presses it anyway. The spikes recede and stop moving. The path is clear for everyone else. There isn't much else to see on the other side. The end of the hall is also the end of the path. Ken moves another granite block off a ledge onto a switch below. Closely arranged pillars form a wall blocking the corner from the rest of the room. The switch must have opened something, and that something most likely is on the unexplored path.

Looping around, the adventurers find themselves in the room with that last switch. As they enter, they walk over a recession in the floor between two thin metal plates. That must have been where the gate was. There's a maze of pillars. Ken throws his hands up in exasperation as they see more block pushing is required. This time it's more of a slab. There's a long, thin chunk of granite that they need to negotiate to create a bridge over a wide pit. The pupil chugs one of the two vitality potions and gets to work. He clumsily drags the slab around pillar after pillar before finally dropping it across the pit.

On the other side of the pit, there are stairs leading up to the third floor. Ken is salivating. He can sense he's close to the end of the trial. It's been a while since any dragon encounters, too. Maybe they cleared them all out. If not, the rest of the monastery's warriors can sweep the shrine after. There's a long, wide corridor with more pillars evenly spaced along the walls. It leads to a large room. In this large room is an exceptionally large dragon. The adolescents from earlier are minuscule compared to this great beast. Shine looks upon it with horror and amazement. It's as big as his house! Marduk gasps. "A grand dragon!"

"Legendary," Ed gawks. His comment couldn't be more apt.

Dragons live for hundreds, sometimes over a thousand years. It takes roughly five hundred of those years to become fully grown, though it's hard to pinpoint seeing they far outlive humans. Rubble is scattered all about. The dragon had smashed its way in from the roof. The last rays of the setting sun beam down. As the party enters, the beast shows off its glorious, thirty-five-foot wingspan. Its bone structure is similar to a bear's. It normally walks on all fours but can stand and walk on hind legs for a bit. Its front legs are better described as arms. They are longer and thinner than the hind legs, perfect for swiping those four ridiculously long, curved claws on each end. They look like they can shred steel like it was tinfoil.

Wisps of smoke waft from its nostrils as it gazes on the fiends that have slain its kin. The smell of brimstone fills the air. This one is a fire breather, no doubt about it. Its massive, long tail slowly wags on the ground. Its wings shudder as it stretches. Even that subtle motion sends a strong gust of wind at our heroes. The air feels heavy. Heavier it grows as the grand dragon gazes upon its enemies. The energy radiating from it makes even standing difficult. Large granite pillars encircle the leviathan. They shudder under the magnitude of its aura.

The mages stay as far back as they can. Duncan removes his armor as the chi users slowly, warily creep forward. Duncan realizes even his thick armor is useless against such a beast. Maximizing mobility is his best shot at survival. Survival. That's all the heroes can hope for against such a fearsome opponent. He keeps his shield. It should be able to protect against the dragon's fire, or at least one claw slash. The chi users have to release about a third of their energy just to be able to move normally. They will have to stick and move as their support peppers it with attacks. Artemis stands halfway between the warriors and mages. It a good distance to fire effectively from, and she can toss potions to either row. The pillars will provide the heroes some cover.

The grand dragon lets out an ear-splitting roar. Everyone from Artemis inward drops to their knees in pain. The beast immediately casts a spell. As its body glows green, the front lines take cover behind the pillars. Duncan and Hermes get down as low as they can on a knee with shields planted in front. Wendy and Marduk lie flat on the ground behind. The mages should have enough protection from this distance to avoid damage.

The room dims as an ominous cloud forms in front of the dragon. It expands to fill most of the room and begins to rotate. There's an eye. It's a hurricane! The cloud explodes outward filling the room with fierce winds and torrential rain. The room floods instantly. Luckily, most of the water rushes down the hall. The mages avoid any real damage but nearly get swept away by the current. The pillars barely withstood the gale. One didn't. Ed had to leap away, as the top half of his nearly crumbled atop his head. Exposed, he was blown backwards and had to drive his daggers into the floor to anchor himself. Even with that effort, he slid another foot back.

Ed quickly springs up to rejoin the front line. The mages move in. The grand dragon goes after Julia. Its claws turn purple as it focuses chi for a Dragon Slash. Smartly, Julia assumes the pillar will be shredded and runs. She turns and pushes off of it for extra acceleration before sprinting. The dragon's first slice annihilates the pillar, and the second narrowly misses Julia.

Artemis scores a Piercing Shot to the chest, but their foe is unfazed. It gives chase to Julia. The dragon isn't particularly fast, but it doesn't need to be. Quickly spinning its massive body, that lengthy tail whips around. Its range nearly takes out Shine and Ed as is destroys the nearby pillars. Julia turns and blocks with her hammer. It absorbs the brunt, but she still is sent soaring backwards.

The mages attack in unison. There's no point in conserving energy. Only incredibly powerful spells are going to affect a creature this mighty. Marduk and Wendy combine with an electrified Deluge. Duncan charges forward and swings his sword upward to aim Razor Wind at the monster's chest. Hermes unleashes Flames of Fira. The spell is right on target. Even its wide scope barely contains the beast in its flames. It stops the dragon's charge. It's hard to tell if the other spells did anything at all. Artemis quickly tosses the final mana potion to Duncan, who shares it with the other mages.

The front line goes on the offensive. They try to employ a strategy that has proved effective: target the hind legs to immobilize the enemy. Julia can't get around its huge frame and instead gets dangerously close to smash the dragon in the torso. Shine takes one leg. Ken and Ed take the other. Rashida burns bright, and Ed's daggers have a healthy glow. Ken focuses his chi to boost his attack power and strikes with electrified punches. They furiously hack and slash at the redwoods but only manage minimal damage before earning the dragon's ire.

It knows exactly what they're up to and isn't having any of it. It turns towards Shine and slashes. As it shifts, Ken and Ed have to backflip to avoid being buffeted by the tail. Shine blocks with his shield. It is shredded like paper. He quickly backpedals away. Ed and Ken repeat their attack. Artemis tries to take out an eye with Piercing Shot. The beast moves its head just enough to miss the eye but is struck right just above its upper jaw. It didn't like that. The grand dragon pivots to the archer and lets out a blistering blaze sending her diving for cover.

The beast tends to the pesky humans slashing at its leg. Ed and Ken are able to nimbly avoid its claws. Shine sees a chance to resume his attack. The leg Ed and Ken were after is now in Julia's sights. The mages gear up for another attack. Hermes has to hold back. His spells would catch his allies. Marduk uses his Vertical Shock to strike the lizard's head while Wendy and Duncan try to weaken an arm with balls of magic. Julia puts all her chi into a hammer swing. The impact actually gets the beast to flinch, but its leg remains well intact.

It spins in a three sixty, swinging that lethal tail. Ed leaps clear and gets behind a pillar, as does Ken, but Shine and Julia get slammed. Shine is sent careening into a pillar. His adrenaline is so high, he barely feels the impact and quickly rolls behind it. Hermes moves up to heal Julia. He sees Artemis frantically point at the dragon. Julia is in the open, and the enemy aims to end her. Hermes uses Theon's Light. The flash is enough to stop it momentarily, and Artemis does some fast-paced healing. Now two people are exposed, and the dragon won't be stopped long. Marduk launches Fire Flurry. Wendy buffs with Focus and launches a consecutive trio of Dark Balls. Duncan moves up to cover Julia and Artemis. The archer heals on the move as they take cover to share the last vitality potion.

The grand dragon breathes fire at Duncan, who blocks with his shield. It's barely able to handle the heat. The melee fighters rush in. Julia attacks head on. She knows she won't be able to do much, but maybe she can distract the enemy so her friends can take out the legs. Artemis fires Ice Arrow at the right hind leg to soften it up. The mages prep another salvo. They are forced to abandon that plan. With enemies on all sides, the beast decides to cast Hurricane. The melee fighters are caught in mid charge and scramble to get to cover. The mages move back to their original position and brace like before.

Everyone manages to get clear, and no pillars collapse this time. However, now everybody is spread out. It's just what their foe wanted. It whips its tail around the room, taking out several pillars. Julia's and Artemis's were spared, but the others are forced out of hiding. Ken and Ed are near each other out in the open. The beast breathes fire at them. They divide in opposite directions to dodge.

The dragon rushes at Ken. The mages don't have time to cast. Artemis tries to freeze a foot with Ice Arrow to no avail. Julia uses Shockwave. She pours some extra chi into it. The shockwave splits into three rifts and collides with the dragon. It is slowed just enough for Ken to get up. He leaps backwards as the dragon slashes. The middle claw cuts his arm deep but nothing too dire. Any closer and his arm might be on the floor right now.

It doesn't feel like it, but the heroes have done some damage. That overwhelming chi is much less whelming now. Both hind legs are bleeding. The right one seems to have suffered the most damage. The mages get ready to use the same salvo as their first. The dragon isn't about to let that happen. It flaps its magnificent wings, blowing them backwards. They are once again separated from their allies. This time, the dragon decides to take out the magic users. It lumbers forward.

Artemis knows her arrows will do nothing in this predicament. Ken is the nearest ally, so she uses Surge on him as he sprints by. Slow ground speed is one of—maybe this creature's only weakness. The melee fighters close and resume attacking the hind legs. Marduk casts Blind to minimal effect. It does throw the beast's accuracy off, allowing Wendy to avoid being sliced in two. As the witch sidesteps, she flings her last sulfur bomb at the dragon. Ken and Ed move back as it explodes on its right hind leg. The beast roars in pain so loudly, everyone is stunned. The dragon knows its leg is in bad shape and scraps its plan to take out the mages.

Instead, it tries to take out Ed and Ken but, in doing so, positions the badly injured leg in the mages' sights. Julia and Shine are shoved to the ground as its tail smacks them in the back. They get up to resume attacking but stop and immediately back off as they see the priest is about to cast. The melee fighters just barely get clear as Flames of Fira engulf their foe. Like with Wosret, the acid ignites creating a secondary explosion of flame. Even those iron-hard scales cannot prevent the leg from catching fire. Marduk blasts Fireball. Dark and Fastball soon follow. The dragon roars. The leg buckles.

The beast tries to cast Hurricane to blow its enemies away. Ken and Ed resume their assault. The leg gives out! The dragon falls forward; the spell is broken. Its head is low to the ground, easily in striking range. Shine and Julia had begun making their way to the front having sensed the beast was about to fall. Piercing Shot takes out its right eye. A Vertical Shock to the skull stuns it.

Julia leaps into the air and slams her hammer down. The leviathan's head it too big for her to land a hit square on top but strikes its temple. Shine's swings his blazing blade into the dragon's partially open mouth. His aim is true, slicing right where the jaws come together, cutting it deep and busting the hinge. Ken and Ed try to join in on the fun, but the dragon manages to get back up. Even after all that, this beast isn't finished. Magic surges outward for another powerful cast. The aura is erratic. It must be becoming desperate.

Ken does something insane. He leaps onto the leviathan's snout as its head rises. It eyes him with its one good peeper. All those blows to the head left the beast disoriented and unable to shake him off. Ken's right fist sparkles and cracks with electricity. Artemis's little boost allows him to easily concentrate all his chi into his fist. He unleashes it with a powerful Thunder Punch between the dragon's eyes. There's a blinding yellow flash. Electricity explodes in all directions. Ken can feel the beast's skull break from the force. The dragon's head reels so far back, it nearly topples into its backside. Ken leaps off as it falls once more. This time its head crashes into the ground. It lets out a weak roar as it tries to rise. With a final growl, its eye shuts, and its body becomes still.

The dragon has been slain! Our heroes slowly gather around its head. They watch it cautiously, not entirely convinced it's dead. Ed pokes it with a dagger. Artemis closes the wound on Ken's arm. "Whew! That thing wasn't messing around!" declares Shine.

"They aren't called grand dragons for nothing," comments Ken. "One this size must be over seven hundred years old."

"That's almost as old as Marduk!" jabs Ed.

Marduk ignores him. Stroking his beard, he concurs with Ken, "Yes, I recall reading that an adult dragon continually grows in size and strength. It takes many decades for an adult to grow into a grand dragon. I have tangled with dragons before in my more exuberant years, but this is the first time I have ever encountered a grand dragon. They are truly magnificent."

"It must have been leading the others," Ken thinks. "They sort of act like a general in an army. Slaying it should cause any stragglers to scatter on their own. The monks will be able to handle any that remain."

Artemis smiles at Ken. "You must be relieved having avenged your friend."

Ken nods and forces a smile. This victory is bittersweet. "I'll rest a bit easier now. This appears to be the final chamber. There should be something in here proving the trial's completion."

The pupil finds what he's looking behind a pedestal at the back of the room. There is a charmed necklace on the floor next to the wall. The grand dragon's spells must have blown it there. Its two halves create a yin-yang pattern. One is green, made of jade, the other red, made of ruby. There is a hole in the middle bordered by a gold plate and filled with a white pearl. The charm is identical to Master Zhan's. Ken picks it up and shows his comrades. "This is an Elani Charm."

"Is it important?" asks Wendy.

"Very. It is an ancient charm almost as old as Jiju itself. There's several interpretations to what the three pieces represent. Master Zhan teaches us they represent body, mind, and soul. Green is mind, red is body, and white is soul. In a nutshell, body and mind are deeply intertwined. One cannot master one without the other, so they are represented in a yin yang. Whoever can master both will achieve great understanding and power, but there is an even more powerful source of energy locked within us all. Soul. The power of our very lifeforce, our essence. It is cut off from body and mind. We're not able to access its energy like the other two, but it is thought that through a great many years of training and mediation, one can achieve Enlightenment and tap into this source."

"Neat," comments Ed. "Anyone ever done it?"

"There's a legend that in the early days of man there was a sage named Zhuanxu who achieved Enlightenment. It is said he aided mankind when a scourge of demons tried to overrun the land."

"*Sooo…*" wades Wendy. "There's no proof anyone actually did it."

Ken's head drops. "…No…"

"Hmm…" Hermes wonders aloud. "There's a similar story in the Book of Theon. When human civilization was fledgling, King Malice rose from Hades to conquer the realm. The world was nearly destroyed in the war, but Theon and his saints, aided by man, managed to force Malice back to Hades. There was an unnamed man said to have been crucial to defeating the Demon King. He is known as the Hero of Light. I wonder if the two stories are really one and the same."

Shine shrugs. "Who knows? Stories like that are fun to tell around a campfire, but right now, we really need to get back to the monastery."

"Yes!" exclaims Ken. "Let's inform Master Zhan of the good news." The long walk back to the entrance of Ranakpur Shrine is (fortunately) uneventful.

Back at Tao Monastery, Master Zhan is pleased to see Ken alive and well. He stands and greets the rescuers, "Ah, you've returned with Ken safe and sound. Excellent."

Shine can't help but to smirk as he answers, "Not only that, we took care of your little dragon problem."

Master Zhan is taken aback. Literally, he has to take a step back. "Is that so? I told you earlier you needn't burden yourselves with that task."

"We thought we'd be better equipped to handle them. We slayed the alpha, but there's probably still a few hanging around for you. We're big on sharing."

"Hahaha! You are an entertaining bunch."

"There's one other thing, Master," Ken casually mentions. He shows Zhan the Elani Charm.

The Master's eyebrows rise. "Ah! So, not only did you help clear the dragons, but you completed the trial. Excellent! It seems I have misjudged you, Ken."

The pupil is humbled by his Master's praise. "I can't take all the credit. I wouldn't have been able to do it without these kind warriors."

"Even so, your skill and courage during this crisis has proven you worthy. I hereby declare your training to be complete!"

Ken's face turns bright red. Even with the trial completed, Master Zhan had been so adamant before that he wasn't ready. He never expected this outcome. He can barely speak, "Th– thank you, Master."

"Come forward, Ken. The time has come to teach you my ultimate technique. Relax your body and clear your mind." Our heroes have witnessed this scene twice before. Whatever is about to be imparted onto Ken will surely be grand. As the flash of light fades, Ken stares at his hands. He slowly speaks, "I-it feels like an immense amount of knowledge and power just surged into me."

Master Zhan strokes that ridiculous beard. "Precisely, I have imparted some of my knowledge unto you. That technique is called Grind. It can grind an opponent's chi into nothing and reduce boulders to dust."

Ed claps in approval. "Sounds handy. Color me jealous."

Ken is still staring at his hands. "Incredible! I can feel the power flowing through me. I'm sure it will serve me well."

"Congratulations, Ken," remarks Marduk. "So, what comes next for you?"

"Good question. I've been doing nothing but training for over a year. I don't know what to do with myself."

Master Zhan already has a plan. "I have some thoughts on that. Why don't you accompany these warriors on their journey?"

"Really? You don't want me to stay at the monastery, Master?"

"For whatever reason, these people seem to bring out the best in you. Traveling with them will serve you well. I have nothing more to teach you, but the world has endless knowledge waiting for you to discover."

Shine is overjoyed. He was planning to recruit Ken. This just sealed the deal. "No objections on this end," he beams. "We'd be glad to have you, Ken."

Ken grins. Master Zhan is right. There's something special about these people. He nods. "I can't say no to that. All right! I'll join up with you!"

Shine slaps him on the back. "Great! I'll fill you in on why we're traveling later."

Master Zhan turns his gaze to the heroes. "Now, as for you warriors, your aid shan't go unrewarded. I have something for you as well." They are reluctant to accept a reward, but with funds dwindling, they'd be fools not to. Zhan walks over to a chest behind his chair. He tosses Shine a burlap pouch filled with gold coins. "It isn't much considering all you've done. I wish there were something more I could do for you travelers. Your deeds shall always be remembered by the Jiju people." The heroes thank the Master. Ken says his final goodbyes. It takes a while. Many of the students and trainers gather to congratulate him. Strangely, Jian isn't among them.

Eventually, the party exits Tao Monastery. It was dark by the time they got back to the village. It's onto the inn for now. Everyone could use a long rest anyway. Tomorrow, they'll restock and set out. Once they're past Roraima Plateau, Leed's Castle will be within reach in just a couple days. For now, they relax. Shine tells Ken of their mission. He's all for it. Even this tiny, out-of-the-way village has felt the sting of high taxes. Soldiers sometimes come through either looking for dissenters or to strong arm army recruits from the monastery. During their stay, they usually make a terrible mess and help themselves to the village's women.

It's an uncomfortable subject Ken eagerly changes. He begins to tell his new friends tales of his training. Everyone begins exchanging stories of their past experiences. Even Duncan joins in telling of a glorious bar fight he once started. When it's Shine's turn, he realizes he doesn't really have any stories outside of this journey. He'd never realized how sheltered his life was in that sleepy town. He is tempted to tell the others about the night King Pious attacked and killed his father, but he still cannot bring himself to say it. Instead, he just sheepishly shrugs and says he had a boring life before meeting his companions.

In the morning, the heroes gather supplies. Julia heads back to Tao Monastery wanting to spar with some of the students. The apothecary is well stocked, to Artemis's delight. She restocks on potions and gathers a few herbs to craft more before picking up some more arrows. Both needing new shields, Shine and Duncan head to the weapons and armor shop. Shine tries to learn more about his mysterious ally, to no avail.

Inside, the blacksmith mutters to himself, "Why did I open a weapons shop in a village that fights with their hands?" His eyes light up as two patrons enter. He treats them like royalty. Not a winning sales strategy. Duncan plays hardball, negotiating a trade. He offers his gouged, gently melted shield for the smith to melt down and reforge in trade for a new steel tower shield. The owner smith caves. Shine casually mentions how they slayed dragons at the shrine and receives a nice discount. He buys a steel buckler.

Ken is lounging outside the inn when Jian approaches him. Ken assumes it's to offer congratulations, but his friend looks troubled. Jian nervously asks, "Hey, Ken? You haven't seen Mei Liu around, have you?"

"No, what's up?"

"I went by her house yesterday. She was obviously distraught but also acting strangely. She was just slowly pacing back and forth. She wasn't crying, just mumbling to herself. I tried talking to her, but it was like I didn't exist. I came back this morning, and she was gone. I'm worried about her."

"She took Ruo's death the hardest. Just give her some space."

"Yeah, it's just that… well, yesterday while she was mumbling to herself, the word *catacomb* came up a few times."

Ken jumps up in surprise. "The catacombs? Why the hell would she be talking about *that* place?"

"I don't know, but it's no place for a young girl. It's no place for the living at all."

Now Ken is worried, too. When the plague swept through Jiju all those years ago, an underground shelter was constructed. The villagers thought the air itself had become poisonous and hastily built a space to wait it out in some underground caverns. By the time the plague ran its course, about three quarters of the population had died. Bodies were piled up in the streets. Jijuans are a deeply spiritual people. They were afraid to bury the bodies in the graveyard, fearing the plague would taint and desecrate the remains of those resting. Burning the bodies wasn't permitted either, for there is always a chance the soul can linger inside the vessel even after the mortal coil is severed, and the ancient Jijuans believed souls could be destroyed.

Destroying a soul for any reason was considered a grievous sin. Therefore, the shelter became a catacomb. A place to lay the victims to rest without risking tainting sacred ground or accidently committing a terrible taboo. No one goes down there, and not just due to bad memories. For all anyone knows, the disease may have survived, and venturing in could cause the blight all over again. Who knows what other diseases have festered with the dead as well?

Ken rushes to gather his new friends. There's no time to track everyone down. If Mei Liu really went down there for only Theon knows why, there isn't a second to lose. Marduk, Wendy, and Hermes are still at the inn. Ed wandered off to pick up chicks. Good luck, there's only two single women in the entire village. The other party members are still away. Jian has the solemn duty of arranging Ruo's funeral. It will be in just a few all too short hours. Four will have to do. They rush to the catacombs at the northwest edge of town. Ken spots Duncan walking alone, sporting his new shield. Ken yells for him to come with. Duncan doesn't like being ordered around but senses there may be fighting, so he runs after them.

The entrance to the one-time shelter is a pair of large, rusted iron doors leading underground. Ken swings them open, and the party rushes inside. Torches have been lit. Someone is definitely down here. They spot Mei Liu standing up ahead. "Mei Liu!" calls Ken.

She slowly turns around. She looks anxious. "Y-yes?" is all she says.

"What the hell are you doing down here?" Ken demands.

She doesn't answer and instead says, "Ken? I heard you stormed off to the shrine as soon as you heard of Ruo's death. I'm glad you're safe. I heard what happened. Thank you for avenging him."

Duncan interjects, "Don't mention it. Glad to help. Now, why the hell are you down here?"

Mei Liu stands in silence, unable to even make eye contact. She finally tries to explain before being interrupted. A stranger hurries up from deeper inside. He stops suddenly, astonished at the gathering in front of him. "Hey! Who the hell are you?" he demands.

The party is equally surprised. "Huh? Who woulda thought a catacomb would be such a popular hangout?" Wendy quips.

The strange man seems worried. Overconfident, too. "Crap, the villagers might be on to us. That, or you people are in the wrong place at the wrong time. Either way, you're not getting out of here alive!" The fact he's sorely outnumbered doesn't seem to matter to him. He's either really strong or really stupid.

Hermes gently moves Mei Liu back. "Stand back, miss. We'll handle him." Their attacker is on the stupid side of the spectrum.

He recklessly charges, wildly swinging his cutlass. Wendy effortlessly stops him in his tracks with Dark Ball. They should probably question him, but Duncan runs his rapier through his throat, so that's not going to happen.

"That was fun," Wendy comments nonchalantly. "It looks like some thieves have made this their base."

"Creepy place to set up a base," notes Hermes.

Mei Liu peers longingly down the hallway. "I wonder… Could they… Oh no!" She is shaking with fear.

"What is it?" Ken asks with a concerned tone.

Mei Liu answers, sort of, "*Waking the Fallen*. This is not good. Not good at all!"

Now everyone is confused. "*Waking the Fallen*? What's that?" inquires Marduk.

Mei Liu explains, "It is a very old magic tome from a time when this village still practiced magic. A group of mages was studying necromancy."

"Necromancy?" Marduk probes. He knows exactly what it is but wants to see just how much this young lady knows.

Mei Liu continues, "It's an arcane magic used to summon demons and resurrect the dead. It was outlawed a long time ago, so I'm not surprised you've never heard of it."

Hermes has heard of necromancy, too. He is deeply concerned now. There's a hint of anger in his voice as he speaks, "The practice was banned by the church, and all books regarding it were ordered to be burned. Even I don't know much about it."

Wendy asks Mei Liu, "You think the thieves are after this magic book?"

She shakes her head. "I don't know. It may be a coincidence—I pray it's a coincidence, but if it isn't, everyone is in great danger." Wendy can't help but laugh. They have an uncanny ability to stumble into trouble. Duncan's solution to the problem is the same as always, violence. He grins as he cracks his knuckles.

Mei Liu curiously gazes at the outsiders. "Gosh, you people are so eager to help. Is everyone like this in other cultures?"

"Nah," replies Wendy. "I'd say we're the exception."

Marduk asks Mei Liu, "Do you know where this *Waking the Fallen* may be found?"

"No. It may have been destroyed a long time ago. If it survived, I'm sure it's well hidden."

"Okay, we'll have to look out for secret doorways and switches," Ken concludes. "Too bad Ed isn't here. This sort of thing is his wheelhouse. Stick close to me, Mei Liu. These thieves seem to be the attack first, ask questions later type."

The party begins exploring. There are many hallways in all directions. Many of the walls house shabby, wooden coffins. There are signs of the former shelter all over. Dusty, cobweb-covered tables, chairs, cabinets, barrels, crates, and other items are strewn about. There are even some old bookshelves. There are still a few surviving books. None of them are the tome in question. There's a locked wooden door down one hall. Maybe there's a key somewhere. If not, Duncan will be more than happy to break it down. They find a storage area and then some old, moldy cots where the sleeping quarters must have been. No sign of what they seek. No thieves either, but torches are lit throughout.

They find themselves in a food prep area. There's still some old food in some of the cupboards. What's left of it anyway. Shriveled black fruit and vegetables along with rock hard, mold-covered bread. The stench is nauseating. Somehow, it's even worse than the stench of the dead that permeates throughout the catacomb. The party is quick to exit the area, but before they go, Hermes sees something glinting on the floor. It's a key.

The heroes return to the locked door, and the key fits perfectly in the lock. More sleeping quarters turned mausoleum. A lone thief stands in the center. He coughs as he slowly staggers towards them. He is gravely injured. "The boss..." he gasps before collapsing.

Duncan is unhappy. "Damn, someone got to this one before me."

"He's in really bad shape," Wendy observes. "Hermes, can you heal him?"

The priest sullenly shakes his head. "I'm afraid not. The mortal coil binding his soul has been severed. He will be dead in moments."

Duncan tries to get some answers, "What happened? Who did this to you?"

The thief manages just one word before expiring, "...Zombies..."

Hermes frowns. "He's dead."

"How terrible…" mourns Mei Liu.

"Um… Did he say '*zombies*'?" Wendy nervously clarifies.

"That's what it sounded like," confirms Marduk.

Wendy turns even paler than usual. "That is seriously scary. I really don't want to deal with the walking dead."

"How's that even possible?" Ken wonders.

Mei Liu deduces, "*Waking the Fallen*. Someone must have found it."

"Cool, saves us the trouble of finding it," Duncan indifferently responds.

"It's not cool at all!" snaps Hermes. "Such magic is an affront to God! We must get that tome and destroy it!"

Duncan looks sideways at the priest. "What the hell got into you all of a sudden?"

Hermes angrily states, "Necromancy uses Dark magic to reanimate the dead and pull demons into this realm. Using such magic is extremely dangerous, and tantamount to spitting in Theon's face!"

Duncan is unmoved by Hermes's passion. "Well, when you put it that way, it sounds bad, but Dark magic can be just as good as Holy in the right hands." He sounds intrigued.

Wendy comments, "No offense, Duncan, but I seriously doubt your hands are the right hands."

"No one's hands are!" Hermes insists. "Dark magic is destruction incarnate. It can even tear the fabric between realms and throw the universe into a state of extreme flux. All existence could be extinguished."

Clearly, Hermes is in no mood for a philosophical debate. Duncan holds his palms out. "All right, all right. You win, preacher. If it means that much to you, we'll destroy it. I just think necromancy would be cool to learn. No need to get your robes ruffled."

Hermes crosses his arms and looks away, "Hmph. I hardly think the end of all existence is '*cool*.'

Marduk is eager to get back to the task at hand. "If you two are quite finished, we should not waste any more time."

"Marduk's right," Wendy agrees. "You two can argue about it later. Let's focus on our mission." Their argument left her uncomfortable. She clearly uses Dark magic. She worries Hermes secretly hates her because of it. Duncan and Hermes are ready to move on. Wendy comments with facetious glee, "We get to fight zombies now! Great…"

After rounding a corner, they can hear strange sounds up ahead. It sounds like a man cackling. Following the creepy laughter leads to what at first appears to be a makeshift library. There is a large summoning circle carved in the center. Ancient Jijuans must have practiced magic here. A hooded man stands in the center of the circle with his back to them. He is dressed in dark purple robes with gold trim. He is holding a staff made of ash wood. It has an onyx orb transfixed to the tip. Blood and dead bodies are scattered throughout the room. This mage must have killed them. The heroes stop to survey the situation.

"Who's that guy?" wonders Mei Liu.

"Probably the boss," Ken responds. "Only one way to find out."

Before anyone can take a step forward, the killer mage, back still turned, greets them, "Welcome!" He turns and eyes the troupe. "You folks don't look like villagers. The more the merrier, I say! Hahahahaha!

"What the hell is he going on about?" questions Duncan.

Ken interrogates the mage, "Are you the leader of this group of thieves?"

The robed man nods. "I was, yes."

"Was? What happened here?" Marduk demands.

The mage smiles from ear to ear. "I'm glad you asked," he excitedly responds. "Do you know what this room was built for?"

"It appears to be a summoning circle," answers Marduk. Everyone pieces it together. This is not simply a mage. He is a necromancer.

Mei Liu steps forward and accuses, "So, it is true after all. You there, thief! You found it, didn't you? You found *Waking the Fallen!*"

The necromancer cackles. "Hahaha! Is that what you call it? I like it! Its real name is far too long and complex. Wakingthefallenwakingthefallenwakingthefallenwakingthefallen! Yes, that sounds much better! Hahahahaha!"

Wendy observes the obvious, "This guy isn't all there, is he?"

Hermes is seething. "All this death. And for what, to use a forbidden art?" What happened down here? What did you do?" he grills.

The necromancer proudly proclaims, "I did exactly what this tome was meant to do. Raise the dead. An endless supply of soldiers who have no fear and feel no pain. Hahahahaha!"

The priest presses, "What happened to your crew?"

"I killed them. Rather, my undead army did."

It confirms what they already knew, but the necromancer's cheerful demeanor about it enrages Hermes. "You killed them!? Why would you do such a thing?"

"Why? Simple. Living soldiers don't always follow orders. Now they do exactly what I tell them to do."

Hermes takes a couple steps forward. He looks like he's about to attack. "How dare you," he seethes.

Even Duncan is concerned by the priest's uncharacteristically aggressive behavior. "Whoa. Easy there, preacher."

Hermes rants, "That magic is an affront to God! Not only that, you used it to slaughter your own people. You… You shall not be forgiven!" He closes his eyes and tries to calm himself. "Theon, forgive me if I take pleasure in killing this man." Everyone is worried about the priest, but he's right. This foe has several screws loose. Talking will accomplish nothing. Rabid dogs need to be put down.

Duncan draws his rapier. "See what you did, Mr. Thief? You got Hermes all upset. Now we have to kill you."

The necromancer is perplexed. "Why are you all so angry? This is a joyous day! Today you all get to join my undead army! There's just one small problem." His demeanor turns sinister. "You're still alive."

"Be careful," warns Mei Liu. "This man isn't some run-of-the-mill thief. He must be a highly skilled mage in order to use that tome."

Marduk is just as angry as Hermes, only more levelheaded. Still, tinges of anger can be heard in his normally calm tone, "It is clear to me that this man tricked a band of thieves into helping him find that tome. They were just pawns he discarded as soon as he met his objective. How devious."

Mei Liu pleads to the heroes, "There's no way a man like him can be allowed to have such powerful magic. Please, do whatever you must to stop him."

The necromancer cackles maniacally. "Allow me to introduce you to my minions!" He raises his arms in a V. The onyx orb glows as five holes tear open in a V around him. The undead slowly rise from the pits. Mei Liu steps back out of harm's way. The necromancer moves back, too. He is content to let his zombies do the fighting for him. The heroes step into the room. Duncan joins Ken up front. The dark knight will have to focus on swordplay. He and Ken are the only close-range fighters.

As expected, the zombies are slow. There's plenty of time to size them up before making a move. The zombies gravitate towards the two warriors up front. As one staggers within Duncan's range, he thrusts his sword into its chest. He expected it pass through the decayed flesh like a hot knife through butter. However, it meets with much more resistance than anticipated. It gets stuck halfway through the body. The dark knight tries to yank it out. Just before he does, the zombie leans forward.

A putrid, green cloud of gas belches out of the corpse's mouth. A foul stench fills the room. Duncan manages to pull his rapier free, but the gas nearly causes him to faint. Nausea swells up. His vision blurs. Luck, or maybe pure instinct, makes him stumble backwards. Hermes rushes to heal him. Who knows what vile toxins are inside these things? Wendy blasts the zombie to the ground with Deluge.

Ken takes one on. He punches it full force in the chest. His hand stings with pain. It was like punching a brick wall. The zombie barely budged. The Dark magic reanimating them is also strengthening their bodies. The monk put too much into his attack. He's in too close! He screams in pain as it chomps down on his forearm. He's not about to back down and belts his enemy with a vicious uppercut. It knocks the zombie up and onto its back. Feeling no pain, it immediately begins to rise. Ken wisely backs off some Hermes can heal his arm. The wound is turning black. Necrosis. Good thing there's a priest in the house. As said priest tends to his companions, Marduk and Wendy step up.

The zombies are bunched tightly as they creep forward. They are a perfect target for a couple of skilled mages. Chilling Wind freezes and halts the frontmost three. The other two walk into them yet keep trying to go straight. At least they're dumb. Marduk uses Wind Burst in a similar fashion Duncan employs sending a crescent-shaped wind at the horde. The front three are sliced in two. The wind came in at an angle. The left zombie is sliced at the waist, the center at the chest, and the right winds up decapitated. It falls over dead (re-dead?).

The other two frozen bodies survive the fall to the ground. They thaw and crawl forward. Severing their heads seems to be an effective way to drop them. Recovered from their ailments, Ken and Duncan move back to the front. They stomp the heads of the crawlers. Duncan slices another's head off. Ken puts some chi into his thrust, caving the final zombie's head in like a pumpkin. He winces from the odor emanating from his fist. He's going to need several long, very hot showers to get the stench of the dead off of him.

The necromancer doesn't seem too upset his minions were destroyed. More like mildly annoyed. He shrugs and says, "Well, you know what they say about making omelets." Before anyone can figure out what that's supposed to mean, he raises his arms again. A rush of Dark energy surges throughout the room. The dead thieves begin to stir. No wonder he was happy to sit back. He had reinforcements! There are eight new combatants. The reanimated thieves are basically puppets on strings, so they cannot move as quick as they would if they were alive; however, they are at least twice as fast their decayed predecessors. Their bodies were scattered all over the room and are now closing in on three sides.

The heroes close ranks. Marduk and Wendy prepare to cast. This time, the necromancer isn't sitting back. With a wave of his wand, Wendy and Marduk feel a strange sensation come over them. It feels like all the air has been sucked out of the room. Their spells break. The necromancer cast a binding spell! They look to Hermes for assistance, but there's nothing he can do. Bind is one affliction he cannot remove. They'll have to fight at close range. Undead thieves are closing in. Hermes stuns them with Theon's Light. The Holy energy is particularly effective. Ken and Duncan move to opposite sides of the formation. Everyone is forced to scatter as the necromancer sends a barrage of icicles slicing through the air.

Ken and Duncan are forced closer to the enemy. Two thieves apiece. They're forced to engage. The other four zombies swarm at the mages. They try to close ranks but are forced apart. This time a ball of ice formed between them and exploded into a razor sharp, frozen crystal. Marduk and Wendy each take a bandit while Hermes has to fight two of them. The zombies are fairly slow when it comes to attacking. Their sword swings are easily dodged even by the elderly wizard. However, the mages' staves have little effect. The zombies never flinch or so much as wince as they absorb hit after hit. All Marduk and Wendy can do is stick and move.

Hermes has better success. His metal staff is much more effective, and he has a shield. He blocks one zombie's lazy sword swing and bops the other one the head. Its skin sizzles as the ruby makes contact. The force of the blow is enough to fell it. He then smacks the other in the face with his aegis. It knocks his foe back, but it is not a fatal hit. The necromancer looses a wave of Dark energy at the priest who is unable to block. The wave sends him and his opponent crashing to the hard ground. The necromancer didn't care his minion was in the line of fire. At first guess, it is because of his callousness, but that's not the case. Dark magic has virtually no effect on a puppet corpse.

While the staffers do their best not to get bitten, Ken and Duncan hurry to finish off their quarry and get back to their allies. Duncan has an easy enough time. The zombies are far too sluggish. One of them swings and has its arm lopped off for the effort. Its head soon follows. Duncan pivots and sends a close-range Razor Wind at the other's throat. Two down. It's a bit tougher for Ken, who is only armed with brass knuckles. He avoids a sword slash and gets in close. A series of quick jabs followed by a strong thrust ends one zombie. As the other tries to flank, it is met with a brutal roundhouse kick to the jaw. Its head twists three quarters around. It falls to the ground never to rise again.

Duncan's magic caught the necromancer's eye, and he quickly binds the dark knight. He tries to do the same to Hermes, but the priest senses the subtle change in the air. There's a technique to stopping such a spell, a sort of mental lockdown. It is similar to meditation where the user blocks out all noise and distractions to create a mental barrier of mana. It's part a battle of wills and part a question of who has more mana. Hermes has the willpower to stave off the powerful enemy's spell, but bracing left him open to attack. As an undead thief's blade closes in on the priest's throat, Ken knocks the fiend away with a cross kick.

Hermes allows Ken to take on the zombie while hastily casting Theon's Light at the necromancer. The evil mage's skin burns from the Holy magic. Duncan helps Wendy and Marduk finish off their opponents as Ken punches the last one's head clean off. To be fair, its neck was already cut halfway through, but it still looked pretty cool. Hermes recasts Theon's Light before the necromancer can recover. He falls onto a knee in pain. The heroes approach swiftly. Not swiftly enough.

Their foe casts an insidious spell, ripping the life energy from the party and using it restore his constitution. Everyone is caught in the attack. The dark mage lets out a savage roar as energy floods into him. He immediately follows up with Dark Wave. Duncan and Ken take the brunt. They're knocked back into their allies. Hermes is the only one standing. He tries to cast a spell, but the necromancer is ready for it, and now the priest's magic is bound as well. It's an unfortunate situation being magic heavy against an opponent who can seal mana.

Ken jumps up and sprints towards the necromancer. With the undead out of the way, he can move in close and force their foe to defend. After a leaping sidestep to escape a missile-like burst of magic, the monk is in range. This foe is surprisingly spry, evading Ken's flurries of punches and kicks and blocking with his staff. Duncan joins in, moving on left flank. The necromancer isn't about to let them team up. As Duncan attacks in unison with his hard-punching friend, the dark mage knocks them both away with an impressive twirl of his staff. He immediately follows up with Dark Wave blowing them away.

With his comrades in peril, Marduk knows he must act. He isn't as nimble as he once was. Attacking head-on will leave him on the floor, too, assuming he can even get to the enemy before a decisive blow is struck. He closes his eyes and focuses his mind. Once bound, breaking the spell isn't an easy task. Decades worth of mental muscle memory aid him overcoming the obstacle in a nick of time. Their foe is building mana for a finishing move. Blind stuns him. Marduk looses Shock. The necromancer blocks and dissipates it with his staff. Seeing how their wizardly friend broke the binding spell, Wendy and Hermes attempt to do the same. Duncan ditches the magic route and goes after the enemy with sword and shield.

Ken manages to get to his feet and rushes in. This time, the evil mage can't stop the double team. He manages to block and evade but is being pushed back. Duncan catches him off guard with a clever move, a spinning lariat with the edge of his shield. The mage doubles over from the blow and catches an uppercut from Ken. They did some damage, but that energy the necromancer stole ensures he's still well in the fight. The uppercut knocks him in the air, but he is able to regain balance to land nimbly on his feet. As he descends, he casts Life Drain on the aggressors. Ken and Duncan drop to their knees. Most of their energy has been sucked by the vampiric spell.

As they fall, Marduk tries to connect with Wind Burst, but their foe uses Magic Missile to cancel it out. He wants to follow up with an Ice spell on the wizard, but Wendy is unbound. She strikes with Chilling Wind, and the necromancer is forced to use his Ice spell for defense instead of offense, creating a shield out of ice. Wendy is breathing heavily. This isn't good. The enemy can match them to a stalemate more often than not, and when they do deal damage, he steals their energy. The witch feels magic radiating from Hermes. He's free now, too. He wants to attack but tending to Ken and Duncan is more important. They've taken not one but two of those accursed Drain spells.

Wendy realizes the same. She does something unexpected. She charges the necromancer head on. Odds are she won't land a single hit, but if she can distract him for just a few seconds, it will give Hermes precious time to aid the others. The necromancer isn't expecting her to attempt close combat. Just before she took off, he recast Bind on her. The witch didn't bother trying to stop it and is now beelining at the dark mage.

As he readies himself to take the girl on, Marduk casts Shock, forcing him to dodge. It doesn't stop him from trying to take out Wendy with Magic Missile. She swats it away with her staff and keeps coming. She does her best to connect with her staff, but she's a novice at close quarters combat. Blocking and parrying her strikes is child's play. The necromancer smacks her across the face with the butt of his staff. Wendy shows true grit and keeps coming. She's doubled over by a whack to the gut, and the necromancer punts her away like a football. Ken catches her and semi-gently plops her on the ground as he runs in.

Hermes had enough time to do his healing thing. It left him out of mana, so he joins Ken and Duncan in the melee. So does Marduk. The necromancer wasn't expecting that. He's no fool. He knows who the most dangerous attackers are and must make defending their attacks a priority. Fists, swords, and staves fly in a furious flurry. Trying to take on four foes at once at this range is a bad idea. When Duncan tries to use his shield as weapon again, the dark mage hops backwards. He tries to blow everyone back with Dark Wave. The quick cast means less power. The heroes anticipate it and brace. They are pushed back but only inches. They go right back on the assault.

The necromancer uses his staff to block both Marduk and Duncan's attacks at once. As he does, Ken goes for a low kick just below the knee. It connects and staggers their foe momentarily. Hermes smashes his face with the staff of Fira. The necromancer's skin sizzles as the fiery ruby touches him. Duncan goes in for the kill, thrusting his rapier at their enemy's black heart. The evil mage cannot block, and the blade pierces him deep. It's a fatal wound, but he can survive it if he manages to drain someone.

As he tries to cast, Marduk smacks his staff away. No matter. It's just a conduit. The necromancer tries to cast again. Ken punches him square in the face with as much chi as he can muster as Duncan simultaneously rips out his sword. Blood sprays everywhere as the mage flies back into the wall. He crumples in a heap. Shortly after, he's completely on the ground. He looks up and smiles at his adversaries. Blood is running from his mouth. "Impressive… Looks like I'll be joining the dead…" The black tome falls from his hand as his body stills.

As terrible a person he was, Hermes cannot stop himself from grieving at the loss of a fellow human. Shaking his head, he solemnly states, "What a strange, terrible man."

Duncan is indifferent as always. "The world is a better place without men like him in it." With the danger over, Mei Liu walks over to the heroes.

"I had no idea something like this hidden under the village," Ken remarks of the magic circle. He turns to Mei Liu. "Speaking of which, Mei Liu, you never told us why you were down here."

She's unable to look him in the eyes or offer any reasonable explanation. "Well... Ummm... Uh..."

Ken already knows the answer, "You were looking for *Waking the Fallen*, weren't you?"

"Yeah..." is all she can utter.

Ken puts his arms around her and pulls her close. "Mei Liu, we all miss Ruo, but he's gone, and there's nothing you can do to change that."

Hermes concurs, "Yes, that is one of the world's absolute truths. The dead cannot be brought back to life."

Mei Liu looks up into Ken's eyes. "After seeing that crazed man, I understand just how terrifying necromancy is. Still, I want to at least be able to say goodbye."

"That may still be possible," Duncan presumes. "Hermes, is it true that a person's mortal coil can be reattached to a soul?"

Rage fills the priest's eyes at the suggestion. "Such magic shouldn't be pra—"

Duncan cuts him off, "I didn't ask you if it *should* be done. I asked if it was possible."

Hermes is silent for a long while before answering. "...Yes, if Ruo's soul is still lingering near his body, it can be reattached using Dark energy. The problem is, the darkness will corrupt the soul. Even the purest spirit will eventually turn into evil incarnate. Ruo's consciousness will be overtaken until there is nothing left but a twisted creature that exists solely to destroy."

"We don't need to bring his soul back for long," Duncan assures. "Just long enough for them to say goodbye."

Mei Liu leaves Ken's embrace and walks over to Duncan. Tears are welling up in her eyes. "You'd really do that for me?"

"Yeah, you'd really do that for her, Duncan?" Wendy asks in disbelief.

"You got a problem with that?" he snaps.

"Of course not. I'm just surprised to see you... care."

Hermes isn't persuaded. "You just want an excuse to practice necromancy, don't you?"

"This is about more than that."

"Why then? Why do you insist on using this blasphemous magic?"

"You've never lost anyone close to you, have you?"

Hermes isn't sure how to respond. That question caught him off guard. "...No... I suppose I've been very fortunate in that regard."

"Then you have no idea how she's feeling. All she wants is to say goodbye to a loved one. Are you really going to say no to that?"

The rest of party thinks they must have suffered severe concussions in the last battle and this is all a hallucination. Duncan is actually acting... human. Did he lose someone dear to him? Wendy believes so. "Aww... I'm sorry, Duncan. I had no idea you lost someone. That's why you're always so cold. Who was it?"

"None of your damn business."

Wendy blushes and sheepishly replies, "Then again..."

The dark knight's words have swayed Hermes. He still doesn't love the idea, but if it gives Mei Liu closure, so be it. He asks Duncan, "Necromancy is extremely difficult to control. Do you think you can do it?"

"I have some experience using Dark magic. I can control it for a bit."

That response doesn't instill confidence. Hermes replies, "I still don't approve of this, but if some good can be done, even with Dark magic, I cannot refuse." Wendy feels better. Hermes admitted Dark magic can be used for good. Maybe he doesn't hate her after all.

Marduk smiles and says, "Then it's settled. We'll try to bring Ruo back."

Mei Liu is overwhelmed with gratitude, "Oh thank you! Thank you! Thank you! Thank you!" Tears of joy are streaming down her face.

"Great," remarks Ken. "Can we get out of this creepy-ass place now?"

Duncan picks up *Waking the Fallen* from the floor. He also takes the necromancer's staff. It will allow him to focus and control Dark magic more easily. Eager to escape the stench of death and decay, the heroes double time it out of the catacombs. Mei Liu returns home. The party returns to the inn. It will be dark in a few hours. Ruo's body has already been buried. In his haste to find Mei Liu, Ken forgot all about the funeral. This will be his chance to say goodbye, too.

The rest of the party members are all back at the inn by the time they return. Ed struck out with the ladies. Julia had a blast sparring but lost the final match against one of the trainers. Everyone is shocked to hear the escapade they missed out on. Julia is relieved she did.

Zombies just sound too creepy to deal with. The party will meet Mei Liu at the graveyard after dark. No one should be there to witness their occult ritual.

Gathered around a fresh burial plot, the heroes and Mei Liu prepare to recall Ruo's soul. Mei Liu is fidgeting with anticipation. "I have to admit, I'm a little nervous," she confesses. "The magic we are using was banned for a reason."

Duncan maintains his cool demeanor, but this time it isn't out of cockiness. He's skeptical to whether this idea will work at all, "Before you get your hopes too high, let's see if this Ruo guy is even around. How about it, preacher?"

"There is definitely a spirit here," Hermes confirms. He forewarns, "I never met Ruo, so I have no idea if it's his soul or not."

"At least we know there's a chance," Shine encourages. "All right, let's do this."

"Um… What exactly are we supposed to do?" asks Artemis.

Duncan replies, "This book explains how to attune the magic and the necessary incantation."

"Have you ever done anything like this before, Duncan?" Wendy inquires.

"Never."

"My confidence is wavering," Marduk comments.

Hermes stares into Duncan's eyes. "I'm still opposed to this."

"Don't care."

The priest knows there's no stopping this. Everyone is too gung-ho to quit now, so he concedes, "Just be careful, Duncan."

Duncan retorts, "Careful isn't in my vocabulary. All right! Let's summon a spirit."

The dark knight readies his new onyx staff and thumbs through *Waking the Fallen*. After finding the page he needs, he begins speaking in an unrecognizable language even Marduk isn't familiar with. He finishes. Silence. There's no wind tonight. Not even crickets are chirping. The dead quiet accentuates the eerie atmosphere. After half a minute, Artemis asks, "Did it work?"

Ed points out, "Nuthin's happenin'. Ya musta missed somethin'."

Duncan glares at his impish ally. "You try reading this shit, little man." Suddenly, the sky flashes unnatural color. Everyone looks around confused.

Artemis warily asks, "Umm… Did everything just turn purple for a sec?"

A few seconds later, the sky flashes again. The ground shakes violently. A multitude of burial plots bulge. The limbs of the deceased burst from their resting places, slowly clawing their way back the world of mortals.

"Yeah... You definitely did something wrong," Shine glibly concludes.

Duncan simply shrugs. "Oops."

"I think this qualifies as more than 'oops,'" Shine returns.

Ken unenthusiastically states, "Time to kill more zombies... Or is it re-kill?"

Julia is thoroughly freaked. The undead are even scarier than she'd imagined. "I don't care what you call it!" she yells. "Just make them go away!"

At least a dozen zombies emerged. Most are just aimlessly milling around. The few nearest the party spot fresh meat and slowly stagger over. It doesn't take long to dispatch the dead. Reburying them all will take forever, however. After a quick sweep of the graveyard to ensure no stragglers are missed, the wannabe necromancers reconvene at Ruo's grave.

"That was really scary!" Mei Liu exclaims.

Julia is still shaking with fear. "I fucking hate zombies!"

Shine is still a little scared himself but retains his calm demeanor. "Sorry, Mei Liu. It looks like we weren't able to bring Ruo back.

Everyone expects tears, but to their surprise, Mei Liu smiles. "It's okay. You have already done more than enough to help."

Duncan is more concerned about the fact he failed. "Damnit, necromancy is a lot harder to control than I thought."

Ken also feels closure. "I would've liked to see Ruo one more time, too. Oh well, there's nothing left to be done. Let's head back."

As the party begins their exit, a nearby bush meekly murmurs, "Hel-Hello...?"

Everyone scrambles to locate the source. Did a villager witness that taboo spell? Mei Liu's eyes grow wide. "That voice..."

The bush tepidly asks, "Is it safe to come out?" Before anyone can answer, a man emerges from the shrubbery, yet the branches and leaves remain still as he moves. It's obvious he's ethereal.

Ken stares in disbelief. "Ruo?"

Mei Liu's eyes fill with tears, "Ruo? Is it really you?"

The ghost walks over to her and shyly replies, "Heh heh, yeah, it's me." He stops to get his bearings. "What's going on? I remember being badly injured. I blacked out, and when I woke, I was here surrounded by zombies."

Marduk realizes, "He doesn't seem to recall being slain."

Mei Liu had gone over all the things she wanted to say a million times over, but now, as she gazes upon her fiancé, words escape her. "Ruo…" is all she can manage.

Ruo tilts his head and frowns. "Hey, what's with the long face? Aren't you happy to see me?"

Tears burst from Mei Liu's eyes as she blurts, "When you went to the shrine, you were attacked, and… and…"

Relief washes over Ruo's face. He was certain she was on to something bad he did. He tries to console her, "I must've been in really bad shape if you're this upset. But, hey! It's okay now, darling! I feel fine now. Cheer up, wouldja?"

His words have the opposite effect. Rivers are streaming from his fiancé's eyes. Her voice cracks badly as she speaks, "No, Ruo, you're not. When you were attacked, you… you…" After a long pause, the most devastating word finally jumps lips, "…died."

Ruo is shocked, confused, and concerned for his love. He truly has no idea what happened to him. "Died? What are you talking about? I'm right here, Mei Liu."

Hermes somberly interjects, "I'm afraid it's true, young man."

Ruo looks around at his strange company. "Mei Liu, who are these people?"

Ken is the one to reply, "They are warriors who helped us defeat the dragons."

Another look of surprise overtakes Ruo. "Ken? You're here, too? This is all so—" Ruo screams in pain and falls to his knees. He's doubled over, clutching his head in his hands. "Gah! My head! Grrr…"

Mei Liu rushes over to him, crouching down to tend to her love. "Ruo, what's happening? What's wrong?"

Hermes knows the answer. It is exactly what he was fearful of. "It seems the Dark magic is indeed what pulled him back down to Terra. It is beginning to consume him. Ruo! Listen carefully, there's not much time to explain. You died from your injuries. We used necromancy to recall your soul so Mei Liu could say goodbye to you. The Dark magic is beginning to consume your soul. If we don't break the bond, your soul will be taken over, and you will become a demon."

A thousand thoughts and questions scramble through Ruo's mind. He looks up at Mei Liu. "Is that true, Mei Liu? Did I really die?"

Her tears have finally stopped. She sniffles and answers, "Yes, I just wanted the chance to say goodbye."

"I'm so sorry, Mei Liu. You must be devastated. I guess you were right about my training after all."

"Don't apologize. I know how important it was to you. I'm sure if it weren't for those damned dragons, you would have completed the trial."

"Heh heh, yeah, that was one hell of a difficulty curve." He pauses. His eyes cast down. "I don't know what to say. I'm not very good at this sorta thing."

Mei Liu scoffs and replies, "Tell me about it. When you proposed to me, you were stumbling on your words so badly, I thought you were having a seizure."

"Hahaha! I thought I was going to faint! My training was a breeze compared to that!" "I'm happy I got to see you one last time. Now I—" Pain racks Ruo. He doubles back over. "Gahhh! Damn!"

"Ruo?"

Hermes comes forward. He gently places his hand on Mei Liu's shoulder. "It's time, Mei Liu. If we keep him bound here any longer, nothing of the man you love will remain."

She nods. "I understand. Goodbye, Ruo. Continue your training in Eden. I expect you to be much stronger the next time we meet."

Ruo smiles through the pain. "It's a date. Goodbye, Mei Liu."

Hermes orders, "All right, sever the bond, Duncan." Ruo's ethereal body glows white. Dark energy flows out of him, down into the earth before disappearing completely. His body slowly fades away, his soul Eden bound.

Everyone was touched by the emotional farewell. "He's gone..." Artemis laments.

Mei Liu wipes her eyes as she rises to her feet. "Farewell, Ruo."

Ken walks over to her. "Are you all right?"

She turns to him and answers, "I'll be okay. I feel much better having gotten to say goodbye. I can't thank you all enough."

Shine smiles and says, "Glad we could help."

She asks, "Are you going to stay in Jiju long? We'd love the chance to show our appreciation."

Shine politely declines, "You have a lovely village, but we have a pressing matter to get back to."

"And I'm going with them," adds Ken.

"You're leaving, Ken?"

"Yep, Master Zhan thinks traveling with these warriors is the best thing for me now that my training is completed."

"Oh, so you managed to finish the trial? Ruo will be happy to know that. Well, I guess I get to say two goodbyes tonight."

"Take care of yourself, Mei Liu."

"You as well." She takes a final look at our heroes. "You guys better keep him safe!"

Duncan laughs and replies, "Don't worry. We won't let him get into too much trouble."

Mei Liu smiles back. "I'm holding you to that. These past few days have taken a lot out of me. If you'd all excuse me, I think I'm going to get some rest now."

"Of course. Farewell," Marduk replies.

As she makes her way out, the party takes a few moments to process everything that just transpired. "Do you think she'll be okay?" Artemis wonders.

Hermes is hopeful. "She'll mourn for a bit. After that, she'll move on. Having closure will greatly aid the healing process."

Wendy comments, "I'm surprised Duncan, of all people, was the one who wanted to help the most."

Everyone is caught off guard as Duncan finally opens up a bit, "Until I met you people, I only used my skills for personal gain. I have to admit, it felt good to use them for something selfless for a change."

"Aww… It sounds like you're turning over a new leaf, Duncan," Artemis affectionately expresses.

Duncan folds his arms in protest. "Don't get your hopes up."

Shine wants to get back to the quest at hand. "It's about time we moved on. It was nice helping her, but we have a king to slay."

Julia admits, "We're getting close to castle. I'm starting to feel anxious."

"I'm getting excited," comments Duncan.

It will be light in a few hours, and everyone is too wired to rest, so the heroes decide to head out to their next destination. Before long, our heroes are nearly to the other side of Roraima Plateau. It is daybreak. The road ahead forks. The southern route will lead them to Cid, but Marduk suggests they continue eastward. At the edge of the plateau, there's a popular tourist spot simply called Lookout Point. Much of the central plains can be seen from this point, including Leed's Castle.

Shine is excited. He's never seen the castle before. Gazing at it with his own eyes will surely strengthen his resolve. It isn't too far to the lookout. In just under an hour, the heroes arrive at the plateau's edge. To the southeast, there it is, Leed's Castle. It a clear day, yet the castle is barely visible. It is wrapped in a strange purple fog, omitting much of it from view.

"What's that strange fog?" Hermes queries.

"It doesn't look normal," Wendy remarks.

It's not Ken's first time seeing it. He explains, "We first noticed that fog a couple weeks ago. No one has traveled close enough to figure out what it is."

"Whatever it is, it probably isn't good," Shine muses.

Marduk agrees, "Yes, I am getting a sense of deep foreboding as I gaze upon it."

Shine remains steadfast, "If it is something bad, I'm sure we'll figure something out. We always do."

His tone was steely, but Shine's confidence is waning. Revenge is so close he can taste it, but a deep sense of dread threatens to overtake his resolve. His compatriots feel the same. That strange cloud is frightenedly ominous. Something in Terra seems terribly wrong, like some great tragedy is about to befall the world. Is the key to stopping it killing King Pious? ♛

Eric Heicher